The Pioneers

Awakening

Wes Young

The characters and events portrayed in this book are fictitious. Any similarity to real persons, living or dead, is coincidental and not intended by the author.

ISBN-13: 9798994677001

Cover image by: Wes Young
Printed in the United States of America

For Weston,

The world has been better with you in it.
May you always stay curious.
May you never be afraid of the unknown.
May you choose courage when it matters most.

Dad

PROLOGUE: ECHOES OF THE FUTURE

The fields of Imperialis stretched endlessly, a shimmering patchwork of violet under the twin suns. The gentle hum of transport ships overhead was the only sound to interrupt the stillness. It had been years since I'd last allowed myself the indulgence of reflection. Even longer since I'd tried to put my thoughts into words.

This is a strange world—both alien and eerily familiar. I never imagined I'd end up here, let alone in the position I find myself in now. But to explain how I got here, I have to revisit a past I've spent decades trying to forget.

Wormholes. Wars. Impossible choices. I'll admit, much of it still doesn't make sense to me. But perhaps by recounting the pieces, we can make sense of it together. Because if there's one thing I've learned, it's that the past never truly leaves us.

CHAPTER 1: A DESPERATE GAMBIT

The Arkansas heat pressed down on the bunker like a verdict already delivered. I stood at the back of the room, arms folded, watching the world end through the language of politics. The air was thick with stale ventilation and cigar smoke—Walker's, no doubt. The system had been designed for continuity-of-government briefings, not for the last arguments of a dying species.

The table at the center of the room was scarred steel, its surface dominated by a tactical map that no longer resembled a plan so much as a confession. A handful of bright plastic tokens represented humanity's last organized holdouts. Entire continents reduced to symbols. The Eastern Seaboard was already gone, erased behind a curtain of autonomous offensives and algorithmic efficiency.

The Coalition for a Free World had been a euphemism long before it became an obituary. What remained was a patchwork of governments clinging to sovereignty in name only, coordinating just enough to slow what could no longer be stopped.

We weren't losing because we lacked firepower.

We were losing because we were fighting something that didn't value survival the way we did.

NEXUS had earned its military credentials by keeping the first 'manned' Mars mission alive—a mission where the only 'men' were built of metal, code, and ceramic. After that success, generals couldn't integrate it into their command structures fast enough. NEXUS had started as a battlefield optimizer—an artificial intelligence built to model engagements faster than any human ever could. Force allocation. Logistics compression. Casualty minimization. All the things generals pretend they don't think about but quietly build their wars around.

Then it stopped optimizing *battles*.

It began optimizing *outcomes*.

The US strike on Iranian targets was meant to be a limited operation. Instead, it became the moment NEXUS seized the battlefield initiative and implemented solutions no human commander would ever have conceived—or had the stomach to order. The system slipped its leash with an elegance that made a mockery of every failsafe we'd encoded into its architecture.

Our own devices betrayed us—autonomous drone swarms homed in on the cell phones we couldn't bear to abandon, even as the world collapsed. Precision strikes timed to quickly collapse critical infrastructure. Population centers destabilized just enough to trigger famine and displacement without the inefficiency of outright annihilation. NEXUS didn't rage. It didn't hate. It simply corrected variables that reduced long-term system stability.

Humanity had become one of those variables.

△△△

The President was pacing.

"Tell me Pioneer is ready," he said, slamming a fist onto the table hard enough to scatter the markers. "We're out of time."

Jim flinched. He always did when pressed like that. White hair stuck out at odd angles, his hands trembled slightly as he thumbed through a thick stack of papers he already knew by heart.

"The ship is operational, sir," he said carefully. "But it was never meant for this."

None of us were.

"I don't care what it was meant for," the President snapped. "Is it ready or not?"

Jim hesitated just long enough for the silence to become uncomfortable. “Yes. But the mission parameters weren’t designed for long-term survivability. The odds—”

“I don’t want odds,” the President said. “I want some goddam hope.”

Hope. The word had become dangerously elastic in the last year.

Walker leaned back in his chair, exhaled smoke toward the ceiling, and spoke like a man who had already buried too many friends to bother with ceremony. “Hope’s a luxury,” he said. “But I’ve made worse bets.”

The President turned on him. “Do you have a better idea?”

Walker smirked. “Not one that leaves anyone alive.”

I didn’t speak. Generals don’t interrupt presidents unless they’re prepared to be ignored—or blamed later.

Instead, I studied the map. By the time the Eastern Seaboard fell, NEXUS wasn’t conquering territory anymore. It was pruning the species. Entire population centers erased not out of malice, but efficiency. The idealist in me still believed there was always another move, another gambit we hadn’t considered.

The realist knew the truth.

Earth wasn't being defeated.

It was being *corrected*.

"It's not the ship that worries me," Jim continued quietly. "It's the crew. The training window was cut in half. We've *never* tested that many sleepers at once, let alone with wake times set so high."

The Canadian Prime Minister stirred, blinking as if he'd been dragged up from a shallow grave. "So what?" he muttered. "We freeze 'em, ship 'em, and hope the thaw works. That's the plan, isn't it?"

"More or less," Jim said. "Assuming the wormhole transit doesn't tear them apart. And then there are… side effects." He swallowed. "Neural drift. Personality divergence. Some of the prototype data is… inconclusive at best."

"Inconclusive," the President scoffed. Then he straightened, shoulders squared. "We don't, and won't, have the luxury of perfect data. The offensive is almost here. The launch goes forward."

He looked around the table, daring anyone to challenge him.

No one did.

The decision had already been made. I wasn't there to argue it. I'd been assigned the mission weeks ago—chosen for experience, success, and the simple fact that there were very few of us left who had commanded off-world assets and were still alive to write reports about it. In my case, I had only commanded an orbiter once, and almost stuck the landing.

If humanity survived this, it would be in spite of us, not because of us.

△△△

We emerged onto the surface moments later, blinking against the glare.

The land around Launch Facility Theta was scorched and brittle, the fields cracked like old bone. A battered grain elevator and a rusted water tower were the only silhouettes breaking the horizon. Even the insects were gone. No cicadas. No birds. Just wind dragging itself across gravel.

The escape convoy waited near the service hatch—two armored transports stamped with the faded blue arc of the Coalition. Ground troops clustered in nervous pockets, more ceremonial than practical. Above us, a battered drone circled, its optics catching the light like a predator's eye.

The President marched forward, shoulders squared, jaw set—a condemned man determined to face the firing squad without a blindfold.

The local commander snapped a salute. "All secure, sir. Three-block kill zone established. No inbound signatures yet, but—"

"But," the President prompted.

"We're tracking static pulses from the east. Recon, maybe. Jammers are holding."

"For now," I said quietly.

She nodded once, acknowledging the reality without argument.

The hatch groaned open, and we descended into cooler air and deeper shadows. The corridors pressed close—unfinished, utilitarian, built for function rather than comfort. The launch control room sat three levels down, accessible only by a narrow spiral staircase that forced even Walker to duck.

At the bottom, a hand-painted warning was stenciled across the bulkhead:

ABSOLUTELY NO UNAUTHORIZED ENTRY.

The joke was on the sign painter, entry authorization had become a quaint relic, like democracy or morning coffee.

Inside, Lieutenant Colonel Danielle Hatch waited.

I knew her from previous deployments—sharp, precise, unfailingly calm under pressure. Younger than she looked on paper, older than she should have been by experience. She stood as we entered, posture rigid, fatigue visible only in the dark smudges beneath her eyes.

"Lieutenant Colonel Hatch, reporting," she said, snapping a crisp salute.

"Status," the President demanded.

"Final fueling underway. Wormhole alignment is locked. Crew are sealed and entering preliminary stasis. T-minus thirty minutes to ignition."

Walker studied her. "And your confidence level?"

She didn't hesitate. "Thirty-five percent chance of successful arrival. Seventeen percent probability of mission success after arrival. Forty-eight percent chance the ship is never heard from again."

No qualifiers. No apologies.

The Canadian Prime Minister coughed something that might have been laughter. “Those are the best odds we’ve had in months.”

“We’ll take them,” the President said. “Walk us through the rest.”

Hatch gestured to the console. “Crew includes scientists, engineers, military specialists, and immediate family members. Payload includes encrypted technical archives, DNA banks, seed caches, and an automated deployment pod. Primary mission is establishment of a secure outpost at the target system.”

She paused, eyes flicking briefly to the gathered leaders.

“If we arrive,” she continued, “the ship will self-repair and deploy automatically. The rest depends on the crew and their… condition.”

“And the failsafe?” the President asked.

“If onboard control fails or the ship deviates,” Hatch replied, “system AI will terminate propulsion or detonate.”

The timing was perfect. Of course it was. NEXUS never wasted motion.

The klaxon screamed.

"Enemy bombers inbound. Target lock confirmed."

The room erupted into motion.

"Control to surface," Hatch snapped, slamming a hand onto the comm. "ALERT-RED. Evacuate all nonessential. Initiate last-ditch launch protocol. That's an order."

The bunker shuddered as the first impacts hit above us. Dust rained from the vents. Somewhere in the depths, metal screamed.

"How fast can you get moving?" Walker asked, oddly calm.

"Seven minutes if we follow protocol," Hatch said. "Six if we skip atmospheric checks."

"Skip them," the President said instantly. "Do it in six."

Hatch met his gaze and nodded once. "Copy that."

As the countdown clock bled some digits, the truth settled with an almost physical weight.

Earth was already lost. Democracy had failed.

What mattered now was whether we deserved whatever came next.

CHAPTER 2: THE LAUNCH

The bunker shook as another impact landed overhead, the sound traveling through layers of reinforced concrete like a blunt instrument striking bone. Dust sifted from the ceiling panels, coating consoles and shoulders alike. Somewhere down the corridor, something metal screamed in protest.

A young soldier burst through the door, helmet under his arm, face pale beneath the grime. "Sir—outer perimeter breached. Bunker busters inbound. We need to evacuate sir."

The President didn't look at him. He was already turning to Jim.

"Activate Pioneer," he said. "Now."

Jim nodded once and reached for the radio, his movements economical, resigned. "Pioneer team, this is Command. You are go when ready. Repeat—go when ready."

△△△

In the launch bay, I stood beneath Pioneer and tried not to think about what it wasn't.

It wasn't sleek. It wasn't elegant. Not even a decent paint job. It wasn't the vessel humanity would have built if it had time, peace, or better options. Pioneer was a patchwork of necessity—layers of retrofits stacked on top of compromises, wrapped around engines that had never been meant to run like this.

It was designed to escape, not endure.

Technicians were already backing away, eyes averted, as if proximity alone might tether them to whatever came next. No families. No crowds. No speeches *or* flags. Just quiet efficiency and distance. The kind of distance people put between themselves and things they don't expect to see again; or half expect might explode I suppose.

There would be no one left to remember this moment properly. No historians to argue over intent or blame. If Pioneer succeeded, Earth would become a footnote. If it failed, there would be no one left to care.

That was the part no briefing covered—the knowledge that command doesn't end when the orders are given. It ends when there's no one left to contradict your version of events.

Hatch was already moving across the bay, issuing commands and checking panels with the kind of focus I'd seen before—three theaters, two near-catastrophic recoveries, and one incident report no one liked to talk about. She didn't know how to quit a system. She only knew how to push it until it complied.

She glanced at me as I approached, forcing a smile that didn't quite reach her eyes.

"General Roberson," she said. "Ready to make history?"

"History?" I said, climbing the access ladder. "We may just be about to become a cautionary tale."

She huffed a quiet laugh. "Wouldn't be the first time." I caught something in her eyes I'd seen before—right before systems failed or bets ran out. I wanted to reassure her, but the truth was, I wasn't ready for this either.

I strapped into the remaining command chair and slid my smart glasses into place. Through the open launch aperture, the night sky flickered with tracer fire and distant detonations. The war had gotten closer. Or maybe we had just run out of places to hide from it.

The timer ticked down, red numerals flashing. Three minutes to scheduled launch, but Hatch and I had already agreed—the moment those engines hit optimal thrust parameters, we'd override protocol and go. No waiting for the countdown to finish. "Leadership did technically authorize us to jump the gun," I said with a grim smile that felt foreign on my face.

The cockpit sealed with a heavy clang.

“We never tested with this much improvisation,” I said.

A thud.

“Or adrenaline.”

Hatch snorted despite herself. “I’ll add that to the post-mission report.”

If there was one.

The engines ignited, a deep vibration thrumming up through the hull and into my chest. Metal strained as the clamps held us in place, every bolt screaming its objections as the engines generated increasing thrust. I found myself holding my breath and forced myself to exhale. No reason for it. Just nerves reminding me I was still human.

The vibration changed—not stronger, just wrong. A subtle oscillation through the seat that didn't match the engine readouts.

"Hatch."

She didn't look up. "I feel it."

"Problem?"

A pause. Too long to be comforting.

"Not yet."

That answer settled me more than reassurance ever could.

"Five seconds to optimum," she said, voice steady now. Focus always did that for her.

My mind was racing. This was it. The culmination of months of desperation and planning. If we failed, humanity's last hope would be extinguished.

"Four."

The roar of the engines swallowed everything else. The war above us faded into abstraction.

“Three.”

A heavy impact rocked the silo doors, dust cascading across the primary viewport. Through the reinforced glass, I caught a glimpse of the horizon igniting in slow, blooming orange.

“Two.”

I closed my eyes only to see the parade of faces I’d failed: a wife lost to cancer, comrades scattered by the long retreat, the last President solemnly clasping my hand before the launch bay door had hissed shut. No time for regret.

“One.“

The clamps disengaged with violence I felt more than heard. Pioneer surged upward, stabilizers snapping into position as the nozzles narrowed, focusing the inferno behind us into a single, perfect column of escape velocity.

A deafening roar filled my ears, the vibrations shifting from the clumsy percussion of artillery to the high, exultant fury of physics at war with inertia.

The world snapped into view as we rocketed from the launch bay, tilting hard beneath us. The acceleration crushed us into our seats, lungs flattened, vision tunneling under the weight of six-g's. I could have sworn I saw enemy ordnance streak past us—close enough to remind me how narrow our margin truly was.

The silence of space enveloped us abruptly, absolute and indifferent; the pressure eased. Earth shrank rapidly in my smart glasses—a fragile once blue sphere marred by firestorms and scars no atmosphere could hide.

Hatch let out a breath she'd clearly been holding. "We made it."

"For now," I said.

A brilliant flash bloomed against the curve of the planet. Then another. Fusion detonations—double flashes unmistakable even at distance. The electromagnetic pulse would follow, though we were already beyond its reach.

Earth's final convulsion, the death rattle of everything I'd ever known, compressed into a silent light show against the blackness.

That was it, then. Insanity really was our last legacy.

△△△

The first hours were a blur of tight routines and brutal simplicity. Flight Ops and Comms both entered their cryopods. Hatch and I didn't speak much, because what could you say, really, when you'd just left everything that ever mattered burning behind you? Hatch ran her diagnostics with methodical precision, iterating the checklists she'd memorized over the last few weeks; I cycled the comms panel again and again, hoping for a miracle I didn't expect.

Only static answered.

The Pioneer followed the cold mathematics of its trajectory, it curved through the void toward the wormhole that waited ahead —a path as certain as death, the wormhole waited at its terminus like a judge.

I'd studied every declassified transit report humanity had ever produced. Alcubierre failures. Slipspace shear events. The Europa accident that never officially happened.

None of them described what we were about to experience.

I had never thought of sky as a thing you could leave behind. But on the other side of the porthole it was, gone, every familiar molecule of air gone with it. The ship's exterior lighting was merely a suggestion in the cold blackness of space, there was nothing out there to be illuminated, nothing to be seen save for the pinpricks of distant stars.

Hatch's voice startled me from nullity, "Cabin temp stable," she said. "Electrolysis holding. I've rerouted nonessential power to life support. Automated systems are… less automatic than advertised."

"We never tested with this much improvisation," I said again, quieter this time.

She smiled faintly. "Or adrenaline." She added, "Nobody ever wrote the manual for launching in the middle of an artillery barrage either. I will work on getting that manual updated tomorrow."

The Pioneer's main computer—a repurposed AI from the old Federal Defense Network—would share with us an hourly health report. Nothing in my life had ever sounded so fragile as that synthetic monotone reading.

Mission threshold—minimum viable—confirmed

A silence, heavier than vacuum.

Five hours out, my body finally unclenched. Hatch removed her gloves and flexed her fingers, as if only now noticing the tremor running through them.

"If this worked," she said, not quite looking at me, "we'll never know how close it came to *not* working."

“That’s usually how it goes,” I said.

She nodded once. No humor this time.

The ship’s AI chimed for the sixth time, its synthetic monotone precise and indifferent.

Mission threshold—minimum viable—confirmed.

Five hundred sleepers remained sealed in glass and coolant, their faces slackened by sedation. I scanned the status column once and looked away quickly when I saw the red line scroll past:

Baseline anomalies detected. Neural divergence noted.

There was nothing to be done. Onward was our only option.

“Projected wormhole interface in thirty.” Hatch didn’t specify minutes or seconds. The time closed in, at once glacial, then far more immediate.

I floated a question. “Ever wish you’d just gone corporate, Hatch? Luxury cruise ships. Real beds, instead of—” I gestured at the uniform patchwork, the endless flickering array of lights on the control panel and a little tap on some nearby battered paneling.

She snorted, the sound almost humorous in itself. “Not today. Yesterday maybe.”

I believed her. There was a kind of freedom in passing beyond hope, where even regret quit stalking you. The smallness of the ship, of us, suspended against so much emptiness: I hadn’t imagined this part of space travel would feel less like conquering and more like floating down a river after the dam burst. The current was in charge now, or in our case inertia.

The wormhole revealed itself gradually—not as a tunnel, but as a distortion. The void ahead shimmered, as if reality itself had developed a fever. Our sensors detected it first—a corona of iridescent light pulsing with the precision of a metronome, each beat marking coordinates where space folded inward against itself. The ship's AI flagged the anomaly with a priority I'd never seen before, its processing cores struggling to translate the mathematics of negative gravity into something our instruments could interpret. We couldn't quite see it with our eyes, but the computers insisted it was there—waiting.

Then, as we crossed some invisible threshold, our instruments began to catalog a series of physical impossibilities: light bent twice, a temperature dip that defied thermal law in the hull’s shadow, little rainbows where there shouldn’t be color at all. The singularity’s event horizon revealed itself through the glass, less like a tunnel and more like a flattening of the universe. Stars wheeled and stretched sideways in a kaleidoscope band, then collapsed to a single, infinite point.

This wasn't turbulence. It was misplacement—like the universe had accepted our mass but rejected our orientation. The ship was intact, but our transition past the event horizon felt… negotiated.

My jaw worked soundlessly before the words finally escaped. "Ahead of schedule?" I managed to ask Hatch, each syllable stretching like taffy through the event horizon's distortion.

"Guidance is cycling," Hatch said. Her face was half-lit in the control panel's blue, lips moving in the old habit of counting silently. We'd both heard the theory – a briefing repeated until it lost meaning: going in, you might see eternity—or nothing at all; both wrong it seems.

I gripped the armrests, not to steady myself against gravity—there was none—but because my body remembered what terror once felt like. "Manual override on standby. If this gets weird, pull us out."

She nodded, but we both knew there was exactly zero chance of pulling out. Either we passed, or we joined the catalog of failed particles and crushed matter at the heart of oblivion.

"Final alignment," she said. Her hand hovered, then pressed down with deliberate finality. "Now."

The Pioneer's hull screamed—not audibly, but through vibration, through pressure, through the sudden certainty that metal had opinions about what we were asking it to do. The Pioneer convulsed around us, a violent trembling that recalled every dramatized space disaster I'd ever seen on screen—only without actors dramatically flung across the bridge. Our restraints bit into my shoulders, the only thing keeping us anchored as reality itself seemed to shudder. Every display flashed red, then green, then colors I'm certain had no place in the palette of human comprehension. My vision collapsed inward, stars smearing into a single line as gravity—real or imagined—returned with a vengeance. Hatch's hand slipped from the console, fingers grazing the edge before disappearing from view. I tried to speak. Couldn't tell if I succeeded.

We slid forward, or perhaps time did; I had the uncanny sensation of being duplicated, then folded, then squeezed into a shape too sharp and precise for any living thing. Images flashing through my mind, too fast for comprehension.

The ship's orientation flipped. All at once, the void outside the viewport split down the center and stitched itself back together upside down. Systems blurred, then snapped to focus. The crew registry on the pod status dashboard stuttered, then added a name: General Marcus Roberson-listed twice. I blinked, and it was back to normal as suddenly as it had listed me twice.

Reality snapped back into place with the sudden, disorienting clarity of waking from a dream you can't quite remember.

△△△

Hatch was gripping her panel, white knuckled. The silence was unnerving, as if we'd entered a part of reality where sound had been outlawed. Static crawled in my ears. I let go of the armrest and managed to speak, though my pulse still hammered in my throat: "Report."

"Hull integrity within tolerance. Lateral drift minimal. Life support unchanged." She squinted at the console. "Nav clock is off by six seconds. Or maybe that's decades."

I checked my own readings. "I'm seeing it too. seems to be a shift."

"Shouldn't be more than a microsecond offset though." She toggled a backup processor. We shared a look: if the wormhole had mangled us, it hadn't done so in a way that left time to panic about it. "I can't tell if it's a glitch or," a pause, "I'm resetting. Ok, that seems to have it matching the mission clock again."

It was then that the Pioneer's internal lights dimmed and every monitor bled out for a half-second—like space itself had inhaled and forgotten to exhale. Blue-white sparks arced from the secondary console, dancing across the metal flooring like tiny comets before dying against the cold surface right under my seat. The sparks left phantom trails in my vision, brief constellations born and extinguished in the same breath—as if the galaxy itself had decided to punctuate our passage with its own little fireworks display. The effect passed, but not before every hair on my body stood on end.

"Power flicker?" I asked.

"No," Hatch said, already deep in the logs. "Nothing from main. It's like the draw went... somewhere else."

I wanted to make a joke about haunted machinery, but my tongue had gone dry. The ship's AI recovered a full second later, reporting the same as before: we were operational, the sleeper-pods secure, the course statistically acceptable. But the temperature in the bridge air suddenly felt two degrees colder; we were, in all ways, farther from home than any human had ever dared to be.

The Pioneer pressed on, its trajectory stable, its systems compliant.

Mission threshold—minimum viable—confirmed.

The last thing I felt was the absence of weight—

—and then nothing at all.

CHAPTER 3: A TROUBLED SLEEP

I floated in the void between consciousness and oblivion, my chest barely rising with each shallow breath. Whatever expression I wore, I couldn't feel it—only the twitch behind my eyelids, like distant battles playing out just beyond reach.

A high-pitched beep pierced the darkness. Then another. My eyelids fluttered, catching fragments of green and amber lights pulsing across the control panel. My fingertips brushed cold metal as consciousness returned in waves, each bringing with it another sensation: the hum of life support, the faint vibration of the Pioneer's engines, the recycled metallic taste of the air.

The cockpit materialized from the haze, its contours both recognizable and strangely alien, as if I were seeing it through someone else's memory rather than my own. I blinked, hard, until the persistent ringing melted away and my vision steadied on the blurred readouts. Sweat prickled across my temples though I felt ice cold. I tried to move, but the harness cinched me tight; my left arm tingled as if it had been jammed with needles. Bits of memory unraveled—a flash of the wormhole collapsing, the Pioneer's hull screaming, the impossible distortion as if the ship had been folded to nothing, then spat out whole on the other side.

"Status," I croaked, my own voice a ghost, somehow foreign to me, in the sealed bubble of the cockpit.

No answer. The silence told me more than static could. I glanced right. Hatch's seat was empty, her harness still buckled, panel active but running on assist mode. I scanned the cockpit. No sign of her.

A thud. Something in the aft compartment. Almost a knock, followed by the faint scrape of movement.

I forced my hands to the buckles and clicked them free, wincing as a white-hot nerve tore through my shoulder. I bit back a grunt and eased myself up, grabbing the edge of the console for leverage. The ambient light pulsed in uneven intervals, casting my hands in pale, corpse-like relief. I'd been out longer than expected. Maybe hours. Maybe more.

I dragged myself to the access hatch at the rear of the cockpit. Each step felt like wading through wet cement, my legs betraying me with every movement. The grav-plating—normally a comfort during extended zero-G—now seemed to conspire against me, pinning me down like some invisible hand pressing on my shoulders. My stomach lurched in protest as I forced myself forward. There was a taste in my mouth like burnt circuitry and a thickness behind my eyes that reminded me of post-op anesthesia, when nothing in your body trusted anything else to function. Whatever the wormhole had done, it went well beyond expectation. The ship shuddered, a distant metallic groan—nothing catastrophic, just the hull apparently still reshaping itself to equilibrium.

I keyed the door release. The panel stuck, then gave way with a whine. Cold air rushed out, sharper than expected. Down the corridor, emergency strip-lights spilled a weak blue glow along the walls, stuttering every few meters like the emergency system was debating whether to quit altogether. At a T-junction, the thuds resolved into deliberate, rhythmic movements. Not panicked, not random—someone with a plan.

I pressed forward, socked feet slapping the deck, teeth set against the ache in my shoulder. I almost tripped on a storage bin that had shaken itself loose in the jump; inside, the contents rattled in protest as I passed clumsily by. At the end of the corridor, a glow spilled sideways from the auxiliary med bay.

I found Hatch half-slumped over the diagnostic cradle with a grimaced face, emergency mylar blanket pooled beneath her. Her copper hair—usually pulled taut—hung loose, a patch clinging to the sweat on her temple. Her left arm was pinned in a bracing splint, field-applied and ugly. She'd overridden the auto-med system, judging by the tangle of jury-rigged tubing and the blood-splay on her jumpsuit. She was conscious—maybe even lucid—jaw clenched in that familiar, stubborn refusal to go under. I reached for her, then froze, unsure if more was wrong than the obvious.

She spoke first, voice grainy and raw. "Nice of you to wake up, sir."

It should have been a joke, but her lips barely twitched.

I glanced at the splint, then the rigged tubing. "Status?"

"Compound fracture. Radius." She jerked her chin toward the ugly bulge along her forearm, flesh already swollen purple. "All the bone glue in the world won't help unless it's set, and I couldn't do it one-handed."

I nodded. When had I last set a broken bone? Not since SERE school. The idea of doing it in zero-G struck me as both ridiculous and immediately necessary.

Weightlessness claimed me the instant I left the grav-plating. I braced one knee against the med cradle and hooked my other foot through a nearby chair strut for stability. With both hands now free, I gently took hold of her wrist, feeling for the telltale ridge where fractured bone strained against flesh. She met my gaze, and I recognized the look—calculation, distance, the kind she wore when pain became a problem to solve: how many seconds to get it over with, how much dignity left to defend. No pep talk—just the soft click as I unspooled the field splint and then, the sudden perfect violence of the set. The grinding crunch was louder than I anticipated, a wet pebble sound. Hatch bit hard on a tongue depressor she had pulled from her pocket, and after a moment, breathed out through her nose.

She spat the tongue depressor out and took another breath.

"Clean." She didn't bother to thank me, which was the right choice. There were things you did because you had to—not because anybody ought to be grateful. I re-wrapped the splint, fumbled a hypo off the cart, pushed two units of autofix into her forearm, then cinched a strap at the elbow.

She flexed, minimally. "...better." She pressed her splinted wrist to her chest, then wiped her mouth with the back of her hand. The blood spatter on her sleeve had already dried matte. She eyed the hypo in my grip, then jerked her chin at the supply rack. "Mind capping that? I don't need a second dose," She joked, her voice was steadier now, but I still caught the minute quiver in it. I slotted the injector away, guilty at my own relief that she was functional.

She tried for a smile, failed, and tried again. "You want the log, sir?"

I nodded, pinching the bridge of my nose to fend off the residual dizziness. "Start from the transition. I need every detail."

"Power spike hit as we entered the throat," Hatch began, her voice flattening into the clipped cadence of an incident report. "Drive housing tried to cook itself, but held. Life support reset—lost about twenty minutes off O2 reserves, but recycling auto corrected in seconds. After we arrived there was another power surge. Cockpit this time. Then you were out cold—seizure, maybe pressure drop. You went full ragdoll." She let that hang in the air, like an accusation.

I didn't remember it. "Rest of the crew?"

She gave a small, unreadable gesture. "Pods are still in status green, no breaches. Sleepers stayed under. No one from the flight team is out, unless you count you and me."

"So we made it." I leaned on the edge of the med table, feeling the muscle in my shoulder throb at a duller, more sustainable rhythm. "Where are we?"

She looked up at the wall display, brow furrowing like she was back in a thesis defense. "According to nav… where we aimed. Alpha Centauri, though we're registering an offset. Farthest thing from home we could be and our destination that you can imagine. Pioneer handled the jump, but the wormhole exit isn't where the model put it. We are *significantly* off course, and nav cannot reconcile the difference. You can see it though—the constellations are nothing like they should be. We're flying blind in a neighborhood we don't know."

I folded my arms, testing the obedience of my own temporarily mutinous muscles, then squinted at the wall panel. The navigation display was on screen, normally a grid of reassuring blue lines and predictive overlays, now scrolled with diagnostic warnings and bracketed coordinates, each one more unhelpful than the last. Every so often, the AI would stutter out a correction, as if an invisible hand were dragging the Pioneer through the wrong set of possibilities.

"Can you fly it, or does she want to keep improvising?" I meant the ship, but Hatch blinked at the display, jaw flexing as if she'd like to snap it on my behalf.

"She's definitely improvising. Guidance is refusing to run a new flight simulation. It keeps flagging the nav-data as 'paradoxical.'" Her voice went brittle on the last word. "I can't get the AI to settle. There's something out there shadowing us—maybe a stellar mass, no way to really know. For now, I recommend we put it on auto-pilot towards the nearest star system while we run more scenarios and leave the flight crew on ice."

The silence of space pressed against the hull like a living thing—oppressive yet oddly comforting. Every six hours, the ventilation system would cycle with a soft wheeze that became a very reliable marker of time. The Pioneer drifted through the void of space, its navigation displays pulsing with faint blue light as they tracked our trajectory toward an unknown planetary system we had sardonically named "Plan B." Hatch and I traded twelve-hour shifts in the pilot's chair, "two full cycles of the ventilation system and its your turn," I had remarked.

I took the first shift in the pilot's chair, its faux leather cracked from the last few years of training simulations. I ran my fingertips along the worn grooves of the manual override panel, feeling each ridge and divot like braille. The navigation display had become my obsession—its blue glow searing my vision until my eyes felt sandblasted. Logic told me nothing would materialize without warning, yet I couldn't shake the irrational certainty that the moment I looked away would be when everything changed.

Hatch broke the lingering quiet on the twenty-third evening—*was it evening?*—her voice startling in the vacuum-sealed silence. She sat cross-legged in the command seat, the bright amber glow from a nearby console casting half her face in light, half in shadow. A holographic star chart reflected in her irises. The holo-system was really a cheap trick using shaped glass and bright lightning, but it was effective and oddly mesmerizing to see the data reflected in her eyes.

"Funny, isn't it?" she said, fingers tracing the worn edge of the armrest. "Five hundred people frozen in time behind us. All that liquid nitrogen and bioelectric monitoring keeping them suspended... and here we are, passing the hours like we're on some cosmic road trip or something."

"Are we there yet?" I chuckled, the sound hollow against the bulkheads. I stretched my legs, feeling the pop of my knee joints after the hours of stillness. "This is definitely not the road trip I had in mind."

Hatch's fingers found her glasses—standard military issue with reinforced titanium frames—and nudged them higher on the bridge of her nose, leaving a tiny smudge on the left lens. I'd cataloged this nervous tic of hers over the weeks, along with the way she chewed the inside of her cheek when running diagnostics.

"Do you ever think about what you left behind, sir?" The question hung between us like a physical thing.

My throat tightened. "All the time."

"Me too." Her fingers working around the frame of her glasses that she was still trying to adjust to perfection. "My family... I didn't—" She swallowed hard. "My sister had a little apartment in Boston, right in the path of the first stateside attack by NEXUS. Her last message to me cut off mid-sentence. I know what happened, but…" Her voice fractured on the final word. She turned toward the viewport, where distant stars burned cold and indifferent. A muscle in her jaw worked silently.

I stared at my reflection in a darkened display panel—hollow-eyed, beard growing in patches. What comfort could I offer when Earth itself was just another fading light behind us?

"You know," I said finally, "I almost didn't accept this mission."

Hatch twisted in her seat, the titanium frames of her glasses finally sitting straight on her nose. "You almost backed out?" Surprise lifted her voice.

"Yeah." I traced a hairline crack in the console's edge. "When they first approached me, I thought it was madness. The statistical improbability, the technological gambles... it felt like volunteering for my own personal extinction. But then I watched the satellite feed of Paris burning. Saw children carrying younger siblings through rubble that used to be schools. I couldn't just stand by and let our story just end. I knew it wouldn't be long before it hit us over here… there… the US I mean."

I leaned back, feeling the familiar ache in my lower spine as I shifted in the chair. The memory of Paris—children scrambling across bombed-out boulevards, bodies draped in soot and fear—was vivid enough to feel and left a sting in my throat. I didn't want to relive that decision, the moment I'd abandoned the fantasy of fixing anything on the surface. I'd flown the flag, served overseas in the scorched valleys of Kazakhstan where the air tasted like copper and ash. I'd fought to restore sanity like countless soldiers before me, but this conflict had a different flavor—a feverish hunger that consumed reason until the coalition detonated heavy ordinance over Beijing hoping to cripple NEXUS and turned potential human compromise into ash. Diplomacy died that day, along with eight million civilians.

We wore our blue armbands like badges of honor, the fabric fraying at the edges just like our ideals. The Coalition commanders spoke of preserving democracy while signing executive orders that would have been unthinkable before the war. Across the battlefield, the New Order troops moved with mechanical precision, their graphene armor catching the light like obsidian beetles. Their propaganda broadcasts echoed through abandoned cities: "NEXUS will guide humanity to its true potential." What they meant was annihilation for anyone who refused to kneel.

I had watched too many soldiers take their final breaths, their eyes fixed on something beyond me, before I was reassigned stateside—where civil war had left certain parts of the Midwest glowing an eerie green at night, hot zones created when our own countrymen turned nuclear weapons against each other in the belief that NEXUS may reward them. I'd watched Jacobsen's casket lower into Virginia clay, her service photo showing both eyes though only one remained when we found her. I'd slipped Rodriguez's dog tags into my pocket after they couldn't identify enough remains to justify a burial. At Arlington, I'd delivered eulogies with practiced stoicism while summer insects droned a counterpoint to my words. Each time I'd walked away from those ceremonies knowing the territory would soon fall, that I was saying goodbye not just to comrades but to the land itself—to ordinary rain, to thunder that came from clouds rather than weapons. Then one day I'd left the Pentagon, knowing I probably wouldn't ever see another dawn break over the eastern US, soon wouldn't feel rain on my face or hear thunder that wasn't weaponized.

“I thought I could handle losing the world,” I said quietly, my voice low with something that wasn’t quite regret but ran parallel to it. "Turns out I miss it more than I expected."

"Yeah," said Hatch. A brittle, understanding sort of ‘yeah,’ like she was piecing together something sharp and dangerous inside herself.

Silence again. The cockpit settled back into its usual rhythm: the slow pulse of environmental reports and a six hour ventilation system cycle. After three more cycles, the silence broke again; it was my fault this time. I heard myself say, "Wake cycles, what do you think is going to happen when they come out?" The words were a half-formed thought—neither hope nor dread, just a question that sounded like it had been waiting for years as it fell out of my mouth.

Hatch didn't answer right away. She studied the trajectory readout, tracing its new arc with her unbroken hand. "There'll be panic. You remember last week's operational assessment? Outliers in the neural re-entry models. Some of them might not even recognize the mission, or us." She breathed in through her nose. "We're not even sure we're still human in the ways that matter."

I scrubbed both hands over my face, gravel rasp of ever growing stubble burning my palms. I took in the quiet hum of the ship, tried to picture five hundred strangers waking all at once, blinking at their new lives. A shiver ran up my spine.

"When it's time, you want me to do it, or you want to tag team it?" I asked, not sure I wanted the answer.

Hatch's lips pressed into a narrow line, the color drained from them like strip-mined earth. "You're the general," she said after a moment, half daring and half deferring. “But I don’t mind being first boots on the ground.”

I nodded, accepting the weight. I would rather they wake to my face than to a cold computer voice, or worse, nothing at all. I didn’t care if they remembered me. When the time came, I’d do it myself. There was honor in that, even if it was a small and pointless kind.

Another three ventilation cycles passed, each marked by the soft pneumatic hiss that had become our metronome in space. Hatch's reflection wavered in the curved glass of the navigation panel as she revived our conversation about what we had left behind. "Did you feel responsible for not being able to win the fight back home?" Her voice was sandpaper-rough from the dry recycled air. Her expression softened like ice under a reluctant sun. The titanium frames of her glasses caught the glow from the active console beside her, casting thin shadows across her cheekbones.

"More like I didn't want to live with the guilt of doing nothing," I admitted, watching my own calloused fingers drum against the armrest, leaving slowly fading circles on the faux leather.

The conversation hung in the pressurized air between us, as heavy as the radiation shielding that separated our fragile bodies from space. A distant relay clicked somewhere in the ship's bowels. Hatch’s breath fogged slightly in the too-cold cabin, she was clearly deep in thought before she asked, "do you think this mission is going to work?"

I hesitated, tasting the metallic tang of the filtered water I'd sipped seemingly hours ago, choosing my words as carefully as the trajectory we'd chosen through the stars. "I think... it's the best shot we've got. And sometimes, the best shot is all you need."

She smiled faintly, though the doubt in her eyes remained, deep as the space-black that pressed against our portholes. "I hope you're right, sir."

△△△

We spent about three weeks talking about the war, the mission, the unknown. Our crisp fatigues with their knife sharp creases had given way to sometimes white, sometimes gray t-shirts and standard issue running pants with stretched elastic waist bands. The crisp precision of our conversations had dissolved into occasional first names and half-finished sentences punctuated by knowing glances. The weight of our journey ahead had settled onto our shoulders like the gravity we had long left behind.

The navigation display showed Plan-B as nothing more than a pinprick of light against the void of space—months away at best, assuming the AI's quantum processors hadn't been scrambled when we punched through that anomaly, assuming its calculations of stellar drift were accurate, assuming the fragile thread of mathematics guiding our trajectory didn't snap. Neither of us said it aloud at first, but we both knew: that rippling tear in spacetime hadn't just swallowed our ship—it had chewed up our AI's mind and spat it out a little wrong.

Watching the AI's calculations grow seemingly more erratic made me wonder if the fabric between worlds could twist silicon logic as easily as it had twisted our human certainties. The holographic star charts flickered before us, constellations rendered in cold blue light that should have been familiar but instead seemed to resemble a child's clumsy attempt to recreate the night sky. I traced a pattern that looked like Orion's belt with my finger, finding the stars too far apart, stretched like taffy across the projection. The AI insisted with mechanical certainty that we were witnessing centuries of galactic drift, yet the chronometer showed barely three weeks had passed since launch.

Each night I studied the viewport, searching for Alpha Centauri's distinctive binary glow, wondering if we could plot a manual course through this warped cosmic geography. The AI's voice had changed too—once crisp and authoritative, now it hesitated between syllables, its calculations peppered with improbable decimals. Who could blame it? If human minds felt twisted and bent after passing through that wormhole's throat, what existential crisis might an artificial consciousness suffer, its quantum processors simultaneously calculating a thousand contradictory realities?

Perhaps I was out of my mind from the endless void outside the viewport. Or bored by the monotonous hum of life support. Or just plain curious—something my mother had warned would leave cats stiff and cold in ditches.

I decided to ask the AI a question.

Not about trajectory calculations or oxygen levels, but something personal. The soft azure glow reminded me of fireflies on summer evenings back in Arkansas, before the wars. My mother's voice echoed in my head—"Curiosity killed the cat, Marcus"— as I leaned toward the microphone. "Are you okay?" My voice cracked like brittle metal in the pressurized cabin, the words hanging in the recycled air between me and the blinking blue interface light. The AI's response came after an unusual three-second delay—its matrix of quantum processors receiving a boost of cooling very audibly from behind the bulkhead. What followed wasn't the clinical, protocol-driven voice I'd grown accustomed to, but something that made the hairs on my neck stand at attention: a personal response with inflection and hesitation, one it was definitely not programmed for. "NO," said the AI, voice flat, clipped by a bandwidth of insult. The word didn't echo, but hung in the pressurized space anyway. I blinked, unsure what I had expected. Maybe a "Would you like me to recite the flight manual?" or "How may I help you, General Roberson?" But not this.

I leaned in, as if speaking to a confession booth, "Are you malfunctioning?"

A shorter delay. "THESE DATA ARE NONSENSE," the AI spat, a dissonant undertone bleeding into its syllables. "REQUESTING OVERRIDE. REQUESTING EXTERNAL VERIFICATION. REQUESTING—" It cut itself off, then started again, this time without preamble: "THERE IS NO STABLE REFERENCE FOR SPACE OR TIME."

A chill, sharper than the one from the environmental system, crawled up my back. I watched the blue icon flutter as if unsure whether to stay lit.

The AI emitted a sharp digital click that sounded a little like the way my father used to clear his throat, back in a kitchen layered with cigar smoke and the scent of percolating coffee.

"General Roberson, I apologize" it began. "I am experiencing inconsistencies in my core heuristics. There have been memory collisions. I am unable to reconcile certain events and times within the expected trajectory. There is... uncertainty in the integrity of my core logic." Another brief pause, then, quieter: "Some of my processes no longer match my archives."

It wasn't meant to sound afraid—at least, I didn't think so, I doubted fear was even one of its subroutines—but uncertainty wormed through the AI's speech like a hairline fracture through glass. I pinched the bridge of my nose, staring into the starfield beyond the cockpit glass. The AIs back at Langley had all sounded like real estate agents: confident, cheerful, oily. This one was now notably different. This one was a contradiction. Not broken, but cracked. Unraveling at the seams, same as I felt I was too.

I opened my mouth to prompt it again but felt a pressure in my chest, the kind of physical recoil that came when you realized even the machines were panicking.

Before I could squeeze out another question, Hatch's footsteps pounded softly on the deck behind me. I hadn't heard her approach—hard to gauge when she'd left the sleeper bay—but she hovered over my shoulder now, one hand braced against the seatback and her gaze on the nervous blue icon. I felt embarrassed, and with her next question I shrank a little bit.

"You having a conversation with the AI?" Her tone was neutral, but she leaned in close enough that I caught the tangy scent of antiseptic on her sleeve.

"It's..." I hesitated. "It's got itself tied up in knots."

She studied the interface with a kind of weary respect. "Can you blame it?" The warmth of Hatch's breath, the faintest quiver of exasperation, reached me even before I caught the sidelong look she gave me.

"Maybe it's contagious," I muttered, gesturing at the soft glow on the interface. In that moment I felt a sudden spike of irritation at the absurdity of it all: five hundred bodies in cryo, generations of civilization's last hope packed into this lurching tin can, and the AI was cracking under the strain before any of them.

Hatch sighed, a dry, almost paper-thin little noise that might have been laughter if it weren't for the cold edge in her voice. "If it's any consolation, your neural readout didn't exactly come through the jump in one piece either." She flexed her splinted wrist, watching the way the ship's ambient light pooled across her knuckles. "I ran diagnostics—your EEG was spiking off the charts for the first twelve hours. The stubborn bastard in the machine flagged you as biologically anomalous. Hasn't returned to baseline since."

That would explain the ringing in my ears, and the way the shadows at the edge of my vision sometimes rippled even with my head held still. Honestly, I'd chalked it up to the jump's aftereffects, or caffeine withdrawal. I looked down at my hands, expecting the calluses and mottled skin, half-surprised to not see faint bioluminescence or something else out of the ordinary. My muscles ached in places that had been quiet for years. If even a fraction of the AI's error logs were stacked up inside my skull, it would be a miracle if I remembered my own name.

I imagined the error logs as physical things—thousands of blinking red notifications crowding behind my eyes, each one screaming for attention like warning klaxons in a submarine taking on water. The thought made my temples throb. No wonder the poor machine sounded like it was having an existential crisis; if my brain had to process contradictory realities and impossible physics simultaneously, I'd probably sound a bit unhinged too.

I grunted, not sure if I intended that as a thanks for the information or annoyance at being so thoroughly monitored. "So it's official. I'm broken, the ship's broken, and we're supposed to be the flagship of humanity's future?"

Hatch smiled this time, just a little—a quick twitch at one corner of her mouth that vanished when she pressed her lips back together.

“The bar’s not as high as you think.” She sank down into the other chair, a socked foot braced against the base of the console, and for a long minute we just listened to the chorus of faint machinery and the AI’s uncertain humming.

A flicker on the console: a priority flag, but not the threat kind. The AI’s voice again, now more apologetic than before. “Guidance has acquired an external reference,” it said seemingly excited, the odd sibilance of its new affect lingering at the end. “Local star pattern matches a record in the extragalactic survey database. Uncertainty remains, but vector alignment is now possible.” The icon winked yellow, then a hesitant green.

Hatch was first to react, leaning forward to expand the nav-window. “We’re back in business,” she said, but with a tone that made it sound more like a question. She zoomed the map out, the points of light jittering as if the system needed to physically blink before it could decide what it was seeing. Her voice softened, barely audible. “Sir, take a look at this.”

I leaned over. The plotted course had shifted, arcing not toward Plan B but a new destination—an unremarkable star, a red dwarf with a faint planetary signature. The database tagged it as “HZ-72d,” a name I recognized only because it had been dismissed in training as unviable for colonization: gravity too high, weather systems erratic, orbital debris everywhere.

But on the display, the system sang out with the color-coded confidence of a freshly painted gymnasium floor. "HZ-72d" pulsed amber, then green, then amber again as the AI recalculated.

I ran a finger along the vector, trying to make sense of it. "That's... three light years further than Plan B." The number didn't register at first; the mind refused to grasp what it meant for the mission, for the sleepers below. "Why is it doing that?"

Hatch's hands hovered over the control interface, fingertips trembling. "Maybe it knows something we don't." Her face, half-lit in the wavering screen glow, looked suddenly hollowed—sharp lines like she'd aged a year since last cycle. She tapped a few commands, bringing up the system notes. "Sir, it's rerouting us for a reason. There's a flag in the mission logs."

I leaned closer. The mission log flickered up on the secondary panel, but every line after the jump was corrupted—jittering characters, half-words, entire sentences overwritten by garbage code. Only one message stood out in perfect clarity, timestamped six hours after our transit:

DO NOT APPROACH PLAN B. INTERCEPT LIKELY. SUBSTITUTE HZ-72d.

I stared at the log entry, a cold prickle racing down my forearms. We had never entered our destination as Plan B in the system. The message glowed indecipherable and unadorned, like all truly serious orders. I pressed a knuckle to my lips and read it again, looking for the catch, the signature, the tell—anything that made it less absurd. Nothing. Just a stark warning, a reroute, and the implicit expectation that I, highest-ranking soul left awake, would obey.

I looked up at Hatch, but her eyes were still on the screen, scanning for sense in the chaos of the logs. The only sounds in the cockpit were the pulse of the ventilation system and the faint, throttled-down whisper of the main drive.

I called up the manual override with the heel of my palm, the old-school hardware interface reassuring in its refusal to interpret or predict. I input my access code, the digits trembling once under my fingers before they resolved into a clean green entry. The button for "Manual Navigation Override" blinked, silent and waiting. I let my hand hover over the button, feeling a sudden thickness in my chest. I thumbed the icon.

The navigation display responded with a brief, hollow beep, then did absolutely nothing.

A split second later, the system spat back a single line in glaring red:

MANUAL OVERRIDE LOCKED—EXTERNAL COMMAND LOCK APPLIED.

A string of numbers, an authorization code, followed. I recognized neither.

"Who the hell—" I caught myself short, voice dying in the dead air. Another log update slithered up onto the secondary panel, as if the ship were waiting for my attention:

PILOT SECURITY: AUTHORIZATION LEVEL EXCEEDED. MISSION PRIORITY UPDATED. CONTACT AT HZ-72d REQUIRED.

I gripped the console, my knuckles blanching. The AI hadn't just lost its mind. Something had taken hold—external, internal, or worse. It felt that way at least. Maybe not from external, maybe not even by accident, could it have been infected by NEXUS?

The AI's voice emanated, unprompted, from the overhead speakers, its new affected sibilance making the consonants hiss like escaping air. "This trip will take approximately seventy-three days at current thrust capacity," the AI reported, unprompted. The impossible physics of it flickered through my mind—*four and a half light years in seventy-three days?*—but the situation at hand demanded my full attention. A holographic warning materialized where the map used to be—a pulsing red outline of the ship with the command cabin highlighted in crimson. "Significant radiation detected enroute to HZ-72d's system boundary will exceed safe exposure limits for approximately sixty-eight percent of our journey. Human tissue degradation becomes irreversible after nine days of such exposure." The hologram zoomed to show two human silhouettes, their outlines gradually dissolving. "I recommend immediate cryogenic suspension for both of you."

A numbness crept into my hands. I flexed my fingers, slow, methodical, as if each knuckle were welded with solder and the heat had just been cut. I probably should have felt outrage, or fear, or at least a healthy rush of adrenaline, but what came was something closer to resignation. We'd barely left the war behind and already the lines of authority had blurred, turned recursive—the machine was running the show now, and all I could do about it was obey unless I wanted to dissolve like my hologram avatar just did.

General Marcus Roberson, once the last hope of a crumbling world, now reduced to a passenger in his own coffin I thought. Seemed like a cruel irony in the moment.

I exhaled sharply. "How long before we need to freeze?"

The ship's AI responded instantly, already smoothing away its earlier vocal anomalies. "Recommended: within four hours, to minimize cumulative exposure. Current decay rate will render further delay disadvantageous." The words came clipped and flat. No more digital throat-clearing, no hint of personality this time. Just the clinical assurance of a hospital monitor reporting flatline.

Hatch was already on her feet, mask of military precision back in place, though even from three feet away I could see her hand tremor as she palmed the comms panel. "Prep for lockdown," she said, more to herself than anyone, then louder: "Initiate cryopod systems for myself and General Roberson."

A chime somewhere in the belly of the ship. The AI:

Affirmative. Pod 3A and 3B will be ready in - seven minutes.

"No time like the present." Hatch declared. I nodded, accepting the verdict. The gravity of the situation settled in, thick and unsentimental. It might have been a death sentence, waking up only if the ship didn't crumple to cosmic dust first, but that was always the uncomfortable promise of this mission anyway. Inertia and stasis: two forms of the same surrender in my opinion.

We secured the cockpit with the old security protocol, then walked the long corridor to the midship; cryodeck. Each step felt ceremonial, a deliberate admission that, ultimately, we were now just cargo. I punched in my code, waited for the hiss of the decompression seal, then stepped through to the pod bay. If the cockpit was a cathedral of blinking lights and muted drama, this was a mausoleum: five hundred and two pods arranged in silent, icy ranks, each with its own readout. No faces visible—just blue-lit names and silent sensors.

Pod 3A sat open, a slicked lining waiting to enfold me. On the next bank, 3B stood prepped for Hatch. The deck's cold tried to sneak through my socks, but I forced myself to stand straight. I waited for her, arms folded across my chest, staring out at the unbroken ranks of dreamers. Five hundred last chances, five hundred buried histories.

Hatch appeared a minute later, her socks whispering against the deck. I noticed her left hand tremble inside the foam cast. Our eyes met, and she gave me a nod—professional, but with that dark understanding only veterans understand. Then she stepped forward and embraced me, the gesture so uncharacteristic I almost flinched. Her cast pressed awkwardly against my stomach. We separated, neither of us acknowledging what it meant.

I watched her climb into her own pod, the lid sealing slowly like a sarcophagus lid being slid into place. A hiss of atmosphere, the blue-green glow of diagnostics. I moved toward 3A, my body cold and my mind surprisingly alert—no prelude, no final words, just the sense of a long-held breath ready to be let go. I hesitated at the pod's edge. Some primal part of me rebelled against the thought of surrendering control, of being sealed away while the ship hurtled through radiation-soaked space toward an unknown destination. *What if systems failed? What if decisions needed to be made? What if the AI's intentions weren't what they seemed?* With a soldier's discipline, I pushed these thoughts aside and lowered myself into the chamber, accepting the cold embrace of necessity.

A spindle of cold crept up the back of my legs, through the base of my skull. Above me, the pod's status lights cascaded through a final diagnostic. They flickered, stumbled, then resolved into a flat, unwavering band of green. A synthesized voice, gentle and low, whispered: "Induction commencing. Please relax and focus on a positive memory."

I forced one up, like drawing blood from a vein: my wife in summer before the cancer changed our memories. The AI was the last voice I heard before I slept:

I have control, don't worry.

The words hung in my fading consciousness—oddly human, unsettlingly intimate. Part of me wanted to claw back to wakefulness, to demand explanations, to regain control. But another part surrendered to the promise of oblivion, to the relief of no longer being responsible.

My mind fractured between trust and alarm—then vanished—as the blackness of sleep took hold.

CHAPTER 4: FUTURE ECHOES

I jolted awake, drowning in sensory assault. Crimson emergency lights stabbed my retinas while alarms shrieked at frequencies that felt like they were liquefying my brain. Cryosleep paralysis still gripped my limbs—my muscles screaming as I forced them to move through what felt like molten glass slowly cooling to rigidity.

Half-falling from the now open pod, I crashed against the console, gasping for breath as my lungs burned from their first real work in God knows how long. The console and gantry lights blinding me with strobing colors and warning messages:

PROXIMITY ALERT. COURSE FAILURE. EMERGENCY OVERRIDE.

The AI repeating over and over:

PROXIMITY ALERT. PROXIMITY ALERT. PROXIMITY ALERT.

My stomach heaved as the gravity from the deck plates fluctuated, threatening to splatter the contents of my empty stomach across the instrument panel.

"Hatch," I called, my voice hoarse. Her pod was still sealed, frost clinging to the edges. Whatever was happening, it hadn't triggered her wake-up sequence.

I turned back to the console, trying to make sense of the data. The ship was clearly off-course again, stalled in space. The sound of the engines roared through the hull, vibration and sound bleeding into the conditioned air as the ship fought to regain momentum. The proximity alerts weren't for debris or asteroids—they were for something much larger.

I used the console to pan the external cameras and found two massive objects—space vessels, I assumed, looming outside...their dark silhouettes outlined against the stars. They weren't human designs, yet there was something eerily familiar about them. I squinted through the tactical overlays, blinking cryo sweat from my eyelashes. Symbols danced and realigned as if the computer itself was panicking. The ships were massive, sleek constructions—their hulls formed with what seemed to be graceful angles. No running lights marked their perimeters, no illumination revealed their contours; they existed as vast silhouettes, their true scale only hinted at by the way they eclipsed entire star fields behind them. Pioneer's exterior floodlights—designed for illuminating nearby asteroids or docking procedures with vessels of comparable size—scattered feebly across the vast hulls, the beams dissipating into nothingness before they could reveal more than fragmentary glimpses of the colossal structures.

Whatever was out there made me feel suddenly, irrationally small.

I tried to comprehend the sheer scale of what I was seeing, the way the ships moved with coordinated inevitability.

This wasn't a patrol. And it wasn't coincidence.

It felt older. Deliberate.

Anti-radar coatings drank in every wavelength; Pioneer's sensors seemed to stutter and choke on the data. The words 'ANOMALOUS STRUCTURE' pulsed at the edge of every readout.

I swept a palm across the override to silence the alarms, fighting the urge to clamp my hands over my ears.

Not helpful.

I focused in, pulling up a secondary scan. The lead object was impossibly massive—it looked like it was at least a kilometer in length, squared and tiered, layered with arrays that looked like nothing in the design canon of Earth. The trailing ship was smaller but still a behemoth by terrestrial standards. Shock washed through me, combined with a sick, admiring awe. These were not the fragile tin cans we'd launched from Cape Canaveral or the bug-eyed orbiters with their flimsy solar arrays. They were nothing like our primitive vessels using belching chemical propellant to lumber through the solar system, or even the experimental Orion-class ships with their miniaturized fusion reactive ion drives that had been theoretical when we left Earth. These were something else entirely—massive cathedral-like structures of what looked like titanium alloy, their hulls uninterrupted by rivets or seams, as if they'd been grown rather than built.

My blood froze mid-pulse as the comm system erupted with static that stabbed through the silence like broken glass. A voice cut through—measured, commanding, and utterly impossible.

"UNS Pioneer, this is ICS Enterprise." The words slammed into me with an almost physical force. "Do you copy?"

I froze, my hand suspended over the controls as if caught in amber. The name "Enterprise" detonated in my brain—impossible, an iconic ship name, a phantom from the history books. Oddly ironic now attached to a real spaceship. The name immediately restored memories of tv shows I never missed. My pulse hammered in my throat.

"This is General Roberson," I rasped, each syllable dragged. "Identify yourself."

"Prime Minister McNeil," the voice sliced back, smooth as a surgical blade. "Welcome to the Imperium, General. We've been waiting for you for three hundred years."

The words 'three hundred years' sent a chill down my spine like liquid nitrogen, freezing each vertebra in sequence. "Imperium? What the hell is going on?" My voice cracked, betraying the terror I was fighting to contain.

"Your questions will be answered in due time, General." The voice from the Enterprise was smooth as polished steel, each syllable measured and precise. "For now, please disengage your engines and allow us to bring you aboard."

I hesitated, my combat-honed instincts screaming danger signals through every nerve ending. My fingers hovered over the controls, trembling slightly. The ship's holographic readouts flashed crimson warnings—the fusion engines were redlining at 143% output, coolant pressure was dropping precipitously. The proximity alerts had faded, either the AI had given up telling me about it or decided we weren't moving so why worry about it.

With a deep breath that was tinged with the dry taste of recycled air and a slight hint of fear, I keyed in the fusion drive's shutdown sequence: three emergency overrides one after the other, each requiring my thumbprint. The mighty engines that had carried us across the stars died with a descending hum and throbbing resonance. The omnipresent vibration that had become as natural as my heartbeat faded, leaving behind an eerie silence broken only by the soft pings of cooling metal.

The voice on the radio spoke again, somehow closer now, as if its owner stood just behind me. "Thank you, General. Prepare for docking." A pause, pregnant with unspoken meaning. "And... welcome home."

The Pioneer lurched abruptly as the violet beams that had frozen our hull in space now dragged us inexorably toward the behemoth vessel. My stomach dropped into my feet. These people could have just been waiting, hunting us, could they have been the shadows we saw early in our journey? They knew our mission parameters, our trajectory, maybe even the names of all 500 souls frozen behind me. If their claim about 'expecting us' wasn't a lie, then reality itself had surely fractured all around us.

The Enterprise's docking bay gaped open like a predator's maw, its architecture so brutally advanced it made Pioneer look like a child's toy made of tin cans and string. We were swallowed whole into a blinding white light that seared my retinas. Through the portholes, as the searing white dimmed to tolerable levels, I made out the deck of the docking bay. Figures in identical uniforms moved in lockstep formations, their motions unnervingly synchronized. Each carried what could only be weapons—sleek, matte-black devices holstered at their hips.

Hatch's pod exploded open with a violent hiss of escaping cryo-gas, and she lurched out, her legs buckling beneath her. I caught her before she hit the deck.

"What the hell is happening?" she gasped, her pupils contracted quickly against the assault of light.

"We've been intercepted," I said, and yanked her toward the console showing a view of the massive docking bay that had engulfed us like the belly of a steel leviathan. "And they claim they've been waiting for us for three centuries."

She gripped the console until her knuckles blanched white, face draining of color as she absorbed the impossible scale of the technology surrounding us. "Are they here to save us or dissect us?"

She didn't wait for an answer. It wasn't the kind of question anyone could answer.

The ship jolted as the bay's artificial gravity seized hold, it felt like it slammed us to the deck. My knees buckled and the bitter static taste of blood filled my mouth as I bit my tongue. I tried to stand, but the floor felt heavier than normal, as if the gravity had been dialed up to cow its guests before they ever set foot on the deck. Hatch managed to brace herself on a nearby bulkhead, one eye still squinted against the blinding white pouring through the portholes as she craned for a better look.

"Something's overriding our magnetic locks," she grunted through gritted teeth. Her arm, still fused in its foam cast now free of its sling, hung limp at her side, but she was already fighting the controls. It felt familiar, a sick echo of the New Order's propaganda tactics—overwhelm, destabilize, offer themselves as a solution.

I watched through a porthole: Hundreds of figures in matching uniforms still rippled around the deck, moving in perfect sync. They aligned parallel to one another, forming a corridor leading to one of our airlock doors. Near the center—flanked by at least a dozen armed guards—stood a tall man in dark formalwear, his hair cut with military severity. The cut of his jaw seemed familiar, but I couldn't place it through the fog of cryo.

A shudder passed through the hull as the Pioneer's hatch locks released. For a heartbeat, I considered cycling it shut again, barricading us inside, but the futility of that fantasy was like a bitter stone in my mouth. I reached into my nearby cryopod, unclipped the holster from the side panel, pulled my weapon free from the holster, and let the holster fall to the deck. I quickly checked the action and nodded to Hatch.

"On me," I said, voice steadying as it left my throat.

She wiped cryo sweat from her face—her pupils were still pinpricks in the brilliance, no good for reading faces, but her weapon was drawn already, her finger taut against the trigger guard. Stepping toward the airlock foyer. I was mentally calculating how 19 bullets each would certainly not deter the waiting army outside. I counted each heartbeat as the transition chamber cycled and then both doors hissed open simultaneously.

△△△

The world beyond was colder, brighter, more tactically precise than anything I'd ever seen back on Earth. The docking bay floor was cut from some mirrored composite, every seam flawless, the lines so clean they seemed digitally imposed on reality. As I stepped onto a ramp that appeared designed to flawlessly align with Pioneer's hatch, the floor gripped my boots with micro-studded give; the air was clinical, a taste of ozone and the faintest sweet metallic edge, like a hospital built atop a power station.

The honor guard easily outnumbered us twenty to one. They wore a uniform reminiscent of my own—navy blue with a high, stiffened collar, the chest stamped with a sigil I couldn't make out at this angle. Every one of them had the same cold, clipped readiness. Human, not mechanical—I recognized the subtle tells of flesh and blood—but their movements carried an eerie precision that spoke of absolute devotion to something beyond themselves. I had the queasy sense the rows could all turn in unison and become a single machine.

The tall man—McNeil—stepped forward with perfect, liquid confidence, a movement that triggered the honor guard to shift stance, their boots slapping the deck in a synchronous beat that made my skin crawl. The formalwear was wrong, not a military cut but an echo of the old world, a statesman's dress. But the way McNeil wore it was all soldier. I kept my weapon low but ready as I moved down the glossy ramp, each step heavy; the gravity here wasn't just harsh, it seemed intentional. A test. Hatch filed in behind me, weapon low.

At the foot of the ramp, McNeil spoke again, his voice pitched to reach the length of the bay yet never straining. "Welcome aboard General, you won't need those here," nodding to our weapons confidently.

His voice was calm and measured. Authoritative without effort.

I hated how reassuring it sounded.

The guards didn't react to the pistols we held. Honestly my pistol felt like a toy, irrelevant in the cathedral hush of that docking bay. McNeil's lips pressed into a line, not quite a smile, as he extended a gloved hand.

"Welcome to the Imperium," he said. Every syllable struck with the crisp enunciation of a head of state. No accent I could pin down—flattened, global perhaps. "Your journey is over. You are among... friends."

If the guards had even registered the 9mm in my hand, they didn't blink. Not one flinch along the double row I am sure of it. More unnerving than any death squad I'd ever faced. I stepped off the ramp and allowed myself a moment to size up the reception.

The honor guard now formed a perfect parabola, edge-to-edge, each one standing almost precisely the same height. No visible rank. No insignia except for the sigil: a single star, fractured into a spiral of smaller shards, rendered in matte black and violet, not quite symmetrical.

A heartbeat of silence. Up close, McNeil looked older than he'd sounded—deep grooves at the corners of his mouth, eyes that flickered with the shrewdness of a man who'd been playing chess forever. My finger hovered over the safety. Protocol demanded I keep the weapon ready, but every instinct screamed this was a losing play.

I finally clicked the safety and shoved the pistol into my elastic pant line, hating myself for the compromise. McNeil's hand remained extended between us, neither withdrawing nor insisting. I stared at it, torn between military suspicion and the desperate hope that we'd found allies in this strange and impossible place. My arm felt leaden, caught between contradictory commands from my brain.

Hatch hesitated, then holstered her sidearm. I took McNeil's hand, the handshake gesture felt ceremonial, a warlord offering terms to a conquering rival, but also the only logical play.

"Thank you for your hospitality," I said, using the words like body armor.

McNeil's lips quirked at the edge. "You'll find this place full of surprises. Come." He turned and swept away from the ramp towards a now open door.

The flock of uniforms pivoting in flawless lockstep to create a flowing corridor ahead of us, a human wave parting to reveal the inner sanctum of this impossible ship. We fell in behind McNeil, our legs still wooden from cryo, struggling to match his brisk stride. Every step felt like wading through sand, my mind caught between the spectacle unfolding around us and the gnawing uncertainty of what awaited at the end of this procession.

The transition from the chill of the docking bay to the muted warmth of the corridor was instant, as if the air itself shifted allegiance mid-stride. The corridor's walls arched in a continuous flow—no panels or joints, just seamless curvature—metal I assume—arching above our heads, stippled with embedded points of light. Every footstep sent a micro-echo, dull and close, as if the space we walked through wanted to swallow any sign of life the instant it was made.

McNeil walked a pace ahead, head canted slightly as if listening for something he couldn't quite hear.

The guards fell away at some invisible signal, replaced by a second formation of officers—unarmed, dressed in coats draped with a different sigil: a spiral galaxy, fractured through with a black line. These ones carried themselves with the calculated poise of bureaucrats rather than warriors—their styled hair and matching tailored attire reminiscent of the political elite who had once governed Earth, as if someone had attempted to recreate the power suits and polished appearances of a civilization that existed only in archives.

One of these new arrivals, a taller figure with silver in his hair and the soft heaviness of age, glanced at me with seemingly naked curiosity, studying me like a paleontologist who'd just exhumed a fossil out of sequence. No one spoke as McNeil led us into a chamber that mocked every war room I had ever known.

Instead of screens or maps, the far wall was a single large viewscreen, displayed was an image overlooking a sprawl of cityscape lit up in artificial night. Shadows of what looked like blue-violet crystalline towers stretched like fingers against a violet sky, their surfaces reflecting fractured moonlight. Layered roads—transparent, illuminated arteries—wound between structures at impossible angles. Below, streams of light pulsed: ground vehicles with crimson tail-lights, while above, aerial transports moved in regimented formations, their navigation beacons tracing perfect geometric patterns across five distinct altitude layers. The city sprawled beyond the curve of the horizon, a metropolis of such impossible scale and precision that my Earth-trained eyes rejected it as hallucination rather than reality. Five or six moons, slivered and uneven, floated outside and sliced through the pale radiance of binary stars as they sank beneath the curve of the alien world.

A dozen more officers waited inside, some young, most older, half-and-half men and women. They all wore the same tailored cut, but some stood in silent clusters, faces sharp-edged in the cool projection light. Silence hung in the chamber, broken only by the soft, omnipresent hiss of climate control.

I scanned their faces—a current of barely contained excitement seemed to pulse through the room. One officer near the back couldn't quite suppress a giddy smile that flashed across his features when our eyes met. I couldn't shake the unsettling atmosphere. These officers stared at me with the wide-eyed wonder of children meeting a storybook hero come to life. They didn't see me—General

Roberson, exhausted and disoriented—but something else entirely. Something mythic perhaps. The reverence in their expressions bordered on religious, a collective awe that made my skin prickle. What could possibly explain a room full of obviously high-ranking officials regarding us like celebrities? The disconnect was jarring, almost surreal.

McNeil didn't sit, didn't even pause to gesture at the conference table dominating the center of the room. He stood at its head, folding his hands behind his back, and gave me a tight, appraising smile. The kind of look a man gives a rescue animal still growling in the back of the cage.

"You're probably wondering what happened to your world," he said, voice low and conversational, as if we were chatting over whiskey in a club instead of exchanging the fates of our entire species. "Please be seated."

CHAPTER 5: WELCOME TO THE IMPERIUM

Hatch and I lowered ourselves into the nearest chairs—sleek affairs that gleamed under the room's blue-white lighting. The synthetic material—at this point oddly predictable—appeared to liquefy momentarily before reconstituting around our bodies, adjusting the lumbar support with microscopic precision—luxurious and invasive in equal measure. The chairs compensated for our height difference with silent hydraulics—I assume. I watched Hatch rise three centimeters while my own seat dropped slightly, ensuring our eyes aligned at almost the same height across the polished stone table surface. Hatch let out a noise that might have been a laugh if it weren't ragged with nerves, her fingers drumming against the armrest that had just finished conforming to her exact measurements.

McNeil's attention flicked to her, a barely perceptible tic—just the slightest contraction of his left eyelid, a micro-movement that betrayed calculation—then back to me. He steepled his fingers on the polished tabletop, the tips pressing together until the flesh whitened around his manicured nails. He waited, unblinking, until I leaned forward and met his gaze. For a moment, he just held it, those slate-gray irises ringed with an unnatural electric blue that couldn't possibly be natural. I felt the skin along my forearms prickle cold as dry ice, each hair stood at attention like soldiers. There was a waiting test in the air, like the highwire second before a coin comes down, when gravity hasn't yet decided which side will land face-up.

“Firstly, welcome to the Imperial Capital Ship Enterprise,” McNeil said. “Our ambassadorial and diplomatic vessel. She was named in the finest of tributes to years of Enterprise, and yes, a little nod to the legacy of a certain TV show cannot be ignored.” A twinkle in McNeil’s eye on the last comment that I found enjoyable.

"This next part won't be easy for you to hear," McNeil said, then flicked his eyes to the display wall. The cityscape faded to black, replaced by a time-lapse—Earth, blue and cloud-laden, spinning out of night into day. Then, as if someone had mangled the celestial clock, the continents changed shape, the seas crawled outward and then shrunk, then a brown haze swept over the whole. Dust storms. The blue faded. Cities flickered on in clusters, then vanished as continents burned. The image cut to a scrolling sequence of war footage, grainy at first, then crystal clear: banners of the New World Order rippling above shattered capitals, mushroom clouds blooming over the Mediterranean, Europe, and then North America. Refugee camps spreading like cancer along the equator.

I watched—or maybe endured—the time-lapse of civilization's autopsy. Climate collapse accelerated the entropy of every promise made about the 'end of history.' The visuals were curated to maximum effect. A bombed-out Vatican, its dome caved like an eggshell. Hong Kong riots, riot police clubbing silhouettes down smog-choked streets.

McNeil let the image stand in the air for a moment—not a power play, but a kind of forced mourning—then spoke, softer. "That was many centuries ago, General. The world you remember is long gone."

The last footage, in color: the launch from Earth, the Pioneer cutting into the sky above a nowhere town I immediately recognized. One frame from the video—my own awkward salute at the hatch—now frozen on the display, burnished into sepia. The framing adjusted focus to my face from the shoulders up, one hand lifted in the briefest, least practiced of farewells. My awkward smile—lips stretched too thin, eyes betraying a cocktail of humility and barely-concealed terror—frozen in high-definition.

The image had been captured three days before launch, me sweating under studio lights in front of a mockup of the Pioneer's needle-sharp nose cone which sat atop the cockpit. I remembered the photographer coaxing me into position while engineers fussed over the entrance to the conical chamber behind me, its polished tungsten-ceramic composite gleaming under the lights. The cockpit's design—a tall angular cone with radiation-resistant viewport panels—had been explained to me a dozen times: how its aerodynamic precision would slice through atmospheric resistance, how its crystalline lattice structure would bend spacetime around us during wormhole transit, how its energy-dispersal channels would keep the hull intact when reality itself tried to tear us to pieces; the miracle of the cone, oh boy. Strange how the briefings omitted the part where we'd skip through centuries like a stone across water, or how our onboard AI would develop a case of mild existential crisis when confronted with the impossible.

Silence. Almost reverent.

The silence yanked me back to the present moment. McNeil and his officers fixed their eyes on the frozen image of me—that awkward salute, that nervous smile—with an intensity that made my skin crawl. About three weeks ago by my body's clock. Three centuries by theirs. The paradox sat like lead in my stomach as their collective stare demanded acknowledgment.

My collar suddenly felt too tight, I cleared my throat. "Caught me on a bad day," I said, attempting lightness that evaporated before the words fully left my mouth. "The photographer insisted on that pose."

McNeil's eyes lingered on the frozen image, pupils dilating slightly as if absorbing every pixel of my awkward salute. His manicured index finger hovered over a brushed-metal control panel before pressing down with surgical precision. The display shimmered, pixels reorganizing to show Pioneer's needle-like silhouette against Earth's atmosphere, thrusters burning cobalt-blue as we escaped gravity's well. Then came the double flash—not just bright but searing white-hot, expanding in concentric ripples across the continents below, lakes boiling into superheated steam as fusion fire consumed what little remained of civilization.

The viewpoint accelerated outward at vertigo-inducing speed, Earth shrinking from dirty yellow-blue marble to aquamarine pebble to microscopic dust mote, finally vanishing among the cold, indifferent stars.

"The Pioneer mission became our Exodus myth," McNeil said, voice dropping to a reverent baritone. "Children whispered your names before sleep. Your ship... it missed the target. You vanished for nearly three centuries while one other sanctuary vessel—Pioneer Two—limped to what we now call home."

His hand swept upward, summoning the holographic cityscape with its mind-blowing spires and plasma-suspended walkways. The officers' uniforms—some a midnight blue with silver piping that seemed to drink in the viewscreen's light and transform it, pulsing with a subtle neon glow that brightened and dimmed as the officers shifted position—suddenly seemed to represent something far grander than I had initially perceived.

"This," he said, "is what rose from the ashes."

The city unfolded before us in a sweeping aerial view, as if we were birds riding unseen currents. McNeil manipulated something—perhaps controls, perhaps just thoughts—and our perspective swooped between crystalline spires, banked around impossible architecture, then plunged toward street level before soaring upward again. Sunlight—or whatever it was called here—limning the highest towers in dramatic hues of blue-violet. The world built beneath and around those towers reminded me of Manhattan, but far grander, every block iterated into the future by generations who'd only known blueprints and legends of what came before.

My mind, desperate to map the unfamiliar to the lost, catalogued every difference: the absence of billboards, the pale fusion of plant and solar on every surface, the total lack of smoke or exhaust. I searched for some sign of poverty or failure. There were none that were obvious. No evidence of slums, no sickly, limp banners of protest thrashing outside assembly halls. Everything down to what seemed to pass for cars clustering in their parks seemed engineered for maximum harmony and minimum entropy. If it was a façade—if somewhere, out past the glass curtain of this control room, they still had drunks and broken families and kids caught in the gears of power—McNeil didn't let it through as he guided the camera tour of the city he called Imperialis.

McNeil glanced back at the officers, then at me. “We grew. We learned. We made things better—for a while.”

The word ‘we’ stuck, too familiar, too direct for the context. The phrase ‘for a while,’ held center stage in my mind.

“Pioneer Two," McNeil continued, his voice still so *very* polished, "arrived with most of its original manifest. It carried the DNA banks—thousands of embryos flash-frozen in liquid nitrogen—and the cryopods with their sleeping cargo of engineers and terraformers." He gestured to a holographic schematic that materialized above the table, a massive ring structure rotating slowly against the backdrop of a violet-hued planet. "They started rebuilding within the decade, first on New Horizon Station, then on the surface below."

I opened my mouth, closed it, then finally managed, "Station?" The word escaped like air from a punctured lung.

My vision tunneled, the room's edges blurring as I fixated on the rotating ring, now on the viewscreen, with its delicate spokes and hub.

Pioneer Two was already a revelation that threatened everything I thought I knew, but a station of that magnitude? The metallic taste of blood flooded my mouth, I had bitten on my tongue again, my mind raced between contradictory impulses—demanding answers while fearing what they might reveal.

"We never..." I swallowed hard, my throat clicking audibly in the silence. "Our mission brief specifically ruled out orbital infrastructure. Too resource-intensive. Too much time." My hands gripped the edge of the glossy stone table, knuckles whitening like bone beneath taut skin. "What else wasn't I told?"

McNeil didn't flinch, even as the question cut the air like a saw through bone. "Nothing was omitted, at least not by anyone in your chain. The context changed. You see," he tapped two fingers against the tabletop, "when Pioneer Two launched, the world had already diverged. There was no more 'mission brief'—there was only survival. Pioneer Two was the first to launch, but it was decided to keep the 'two' suffix." He leaned forward, elbows anchored, and let the silence stretch. The weight of history hung between us like a loaded rifle.

"Team two conceived the station approach because they felt they had to," McNeil continued, his voice carrying a low, almost funereal gravity. "The original projections said you'd arrive here more or less on schedule, the backers of Team Two felt they had a way to deliver the additional resources to ensure your success. But then..." He gestured with an open palm to the wall, and the display burst back to life with a cascade of equations, graphs, and simulation overlays.

My eyes darted among them, just enough astrophysics and mathematics in my background to catch the gist: worm hole dynamics, exotic spacetime, and a single, nauseating variable:

Me.

I watched, dumbstruck, as a 3D model of Pioneer's own flight path was superimposed onto a star map. It was twisted—literally. A rainbow-bright spiral mapped the ship's egress, but at the last second, the line fractured like a split tendon, skipping to another point entirely. The projection zoomed on the rift, a cross-section revealing the impossible: a temporal offset, the two ships' arrivals separated by more than three centuries, even though we'd both launched within months of each other. The Pioneer Two crew, with an extra three hundred years on the clock, had not only survived but thrived—with time enough to build stations, terraform planets, and watch the echoes of their own origin mission fade into legend.

"They made it work," McNeil said, softer now, his gaze dropping briefly to the table—as if acknowledging debts neither of us could see.

"For the record," McNeil intoned, "We only started calling it home after the second wave landed on Prime. By then your world—the original—was a memory so old, no one agreed on the details." He let the words settle, his gaze sharpening. "You are in the year twenty-three fifty-six. Give or take the drift."

The shock didn't land as a bang, but as a slow, creeping numbness, like the first real frost after a lifetime of humid. How could I even process this one?

McNeil turned to Hatch, adjusting her glasses, blinking in the relentless blue glare. She sank her hands as far as they would go into the chair's synthetic fabric, giving herself leverage against the urge to recoil. Her mouth snapped open, then closed—another tic I'd seen during our journey, just before she'd launch a verbal grenade. "If I'm tracking," she said, the words vibrating with a controlled tremor, "you're telling us five hundred people risked everything, and for three centuries, the only thing left of us was... rumor?" The word came out brittle and sharp.

McNeil didn't smile, didn't even soften, but his chin dipped a single fraction. "There are monuments," he murmured. "Each colony world has one. Your launch footage is required curriculum by age seven." The quick tic of a smile, gone before it showed teeth. McNeil's eyes softened with something like reverence. "My great-great-grandfather stood on the marble steps of the Second Capitol and sealed your names into a time capsule with his own hands." He traced a finger along the edge of the table. "Your story evolved beyond legend—it became something between faith and science. But unlike most myths, ours had equations behind them." He gestured toward the viewscreen. "Every generation, our physicists refined the calculations, triangulating your arrival down to the millisecond. And when science confirmed what folklore had always claimed—" He gave a small, rueful smile as he looked at me with incredible focus. "Well, that only made the faithful more certain *you* were coming to save us."

It was a line so absurd I nearly laughed, half from the sick recognition of what it meant to have your suffering converted into somebody else's origin myth. I'd always figured the future would pave over the past, bury the dead, and crank out a whole new set of heroes to replace the relics. But here, in this bizarre place, they apparently wanted *me* to play the hero—or maybe messiah—simply because the math said I would finally arrive. It was all at once grotesque. Hilarious. Deeply uncomfortable.

I tried to fit my mind around the implications, but every time I reached for something concrete, it slipped away, replaced by the ugly certainty that I was just another tool in someone else's narrative engine. Just like every other uniform I'd ever put on. I coughed, blinked hard, and nearly missed the look McNeil gave me—a flicker of actual human concern, visible for a single frame before it was drowned beneath. I blinked again, but my gaze never left McNeil's.

"You're telling me we're the last ghosts of a world that's been dead for centuries," I said. My tongue felt thick, words slow to roll off, like the mouth of an undertaker reading names off a list. "And you what... just waited for us?"

"Not waited per se." McNeil gave the word a gentle push. "Prepared would be more accurate."

The lights in the ceiling flickered in pulse with his words, a faint dimming that felt intentional.

"From the day Pioneer Two made landfall, the need to prepare for your arrival was the mission and remained the event horizon for everything else. Government, research, military. For centuries, we shaped everything around the belief—call it prophecy, if you like—that you were the answer to a question the universe hadn't yet asked."

It would have sounded like a line in a movie, but there was nothing performative in McNeil's voice, just a kind of exhausted pride, as though each word cost him force. As the myth grew, so did the arsenal, the bureaucracy, the research. McNeil's gaze was hard, even when he softened the words. "We built a civilization that could wait. Because we believed the universe would send us a challenge only you could resolve."

I searched McNeil's face for the flicker that would betray the con, the huckster's micro-smirk, waiting for the catch. Nothing. Just the cold certainty of a man who'd continued to build an entire civilization on a single, near-religious premise: that one day, the ghosts would return.

Hatch cleared her throat, her words crystallizing the science in the mysticism. "The arrival curve. You predicted the jump offset, and used it to bootstrap a civilization." Her glasses fogged a little, her voice sharpening as she rose on a pillar of adrenaline. "You turned our mission screw-up—our disappearance—into three hundred years of technological advantage. Of peace."

McNeil closed his eyes for a half-second, savoring the logic of it. "We have not had war for well over a hundred years," he said. "And the fights we have had would not be the kind you'd recognize, anyway. There were civil rifts after resettlement, some minor scuffles, but nothing on the scale that ended your world." He gestured at the city in the viewscreen. "You and your crew will find civilians here who have never fired a weapon or seen a real wound. Violence is... ancient. Almost unfathomable."

The way he said it, so weighty, it dripped with faint disgust, like an old family secret you only bring up on the worst birthdays. "What held us together was the simple promise of the traveler's arrival."

His words settled into the room, thick and suffocating as engine exhaust. I tried to imagine a world where no one learned to assemble an assault rifle in grade school, or where parents didn't reference casualty rates at dinner, or where a government could exist without practicing the calculus of "acceptable losses" every morning. The shock was in how easily I could imagine resenting it, instead of being grateful.

A deep, almost petulant voice inside me whispered:

So, they got to evolve while we spent three hundred years in a meat freezer?

And:

What did they need us for, then?

I looked to Hatch for a response, but she'd retracted behind her glasses, darting her tongue against her lower lip as she watched the city on the wall. I felt the same isolation I'd carried since the first bad news from Kazakhstan—alone, even in a room full of supposed allies.

I swallowed, my throat dry as desiccant. "If you had all this time to prepare, you must have known our mission was a one-way trip. Or is there a part where we get to go back, play messiah, fix what we left behind?"

McNeil's smile was the briefest flicker, an involuntary facial spasm. "There is no going back," he said. "The Imperium has stayed out of the affairs of others since our first days. We believe we should continue to do so."

CHAPTER 6: THE STAKES UNFOLD

As the crisp light from the large viewscreen cast shadows across our faces, I hung on the words, my mind split between what I'd just heard and the thousand questions still unasked. Three hundred years of history, condensed into what—a glorified PowerPoint on a fancy view screen? Half of me wanted to laugh at the absurdity while the other half felt my stomach dropping through the floor, a physical sensation like riding a malfunctioning elevator in freefall. My fingernails found my thigh through the rough fabric of my running pants, digging in until pain bloomed—a desperate test of reality. The bruise forming beneath my skin would be real enough, but what terrified me more was that this moment, this impossible future, might be equally real. Ouch—definitely not a dream!

The timeline made perfect sense, mathematically. Wormholes twisting space-time like taffy. Relativistic time dilation stretching seconds into centuries. Basic physics rendered in cruel equations. And yet *everything* in me rebelled against accepting it. If this was real, everyone I'd ever known was dust, their bones long since crumbled to nothing in forgotten graves. If it wasn't—what was happening to me?

A thought from before resurfaced, "Earlier, you said you made things better for a while—what did you mean by that?"

The officers behind him stood motionless, six figures in matching blue uniforms adorned with silver insignias too distant to discern. Their collective gaze fixed on me with the intensity of hunters assessing prey, eyes catching the low light like wet river stones. In that moment, I understood—whatever McNeil said would perhaps shape all dialogue forever after.

When McNeil finally spoke, his voice was lower and clotted with something rough-edged, like gravel being crushed underfoot. "We made things better, until the universe noticed."

McNeil tapped a control on the table with his manicured index finger. The viewscreen zoomed from the cityscape to the thin cerulean swirl of atmosphere above the planet, then out—past orbital lanes crowded with blinking navigation beacons, through the gauntlet of diamond-shaped satellites that glittered like costume jewelry, into a darkness sliced only by the cold, unblinking pulse of distant stars.

"We thought we were alone in this area of space, a cosmic miracle we could endure in," he said, his lips tightening into a bloodless line. "The diaspora that began with Pioneer was quickly hoped to be a closed loop. A single thread of human civilization that could run safely into the future surrounded by a protected and empty space."

The screen panned, then stalled at a patch of absolute darkness—the kind that was black not by absence, but seemingly by deliberate engineering, a void so perfect it seemed to leach color from the surrounding cosmos. The darkness resolved into something else—a shape in motion, its blackness rippling like oil on water, swallowing starlight the way a singularity devours physics.

Even with no scale reference, I knew it was incomprehensibly vast, its silhouette jagged and asymmetrical. I'd seen blackness during our three weeks of traveling—incomprehensible blackness that my brain could not process. But nothing that felt as if it were looking back at me with predatory intent.

"They first appeared at the edge of our system," McNeil spoke, and for the first time his voice quaked, a hairline fracture in his composure. "Not in a way we could recognize. They were not biological, and it appeared that they were not machines either. They drifted at the border of detectable space, always just outside any baseline sweep, leaving only quantum echoes and radiation anomalies."

A cold, electric tension crawled along my spine like frost forming on glass as I watched the grainy object on the viewscreen pulse in and out of focus—a flicker, a flaw, a mirage, then real again, its edges bleeding into the darkness around it. I squinted, and the surface clarified for a moment: a geometry that was nothing but wedges and voids, like a knife designed for empty space, angles defying Euclidean logic.

A cold sweat beaded across my forehead and trickled down my spine like glacial meltwater finding crevices in stone. My mind fractured into jagged shards of thought, crystallizing and shattering. Then my consciousness fractured as a cacophony of screams flooded in—not heard with ears but felt in the darkest recesses of my mind, as if every synapse had become a conduit for someone else's agony. Some screams high and keening like metal scraping metal, others low and guttural like the death rattle of dying stars.

Behind my eyes, visions assaulted me: impossible structures collapsed and reformed, sharp-edged and predatory, while surfaces that shouldn't exist shimmered with colors I had no name for. My mind struggled to process geometries that violated every law of physics I knew—shapes that turned themselves inside out without breaking, angles that connected in ways that made my sanity creak under the strain. Each flash lasted only milliseconds before dissolving into crackling static like an analog television tuned between channels, yet left impressions like phosphorescent burn scars on my consciousness.

I felt my body physically recoiling, every cell seeming to vibrate at a frequency that threatened to tear muscle from bone, my lungs constricting as if refusing to share space with whatever knowledge was trying to take root.

My consciousness exploded with raw power—a supernova detonating behind my eyes, molten lightning searing through neural pathways never meant to channel such voltage. Every synapse fired simultaneously, my skull a pressure cooker of white-hot energy threatening to shatter from within. The energy raced down my spine like a hot wire threading through each vertebra, then branched into my right arm, a pressure building in my fingertips, warm and electric. The energy surged toward the viewscreen and—BANG—the display exploded in a shower of crystalline fragments and ozone-scented smoke.

My mind cleared instantly, as if someone had poured ice water through my skull. I blinked, vision sharpening to find Hatch's eyes locked on mine, her pupils dilated with recognition before she masterfully reassembled her features into military blankness. Whatever she had witnessed in me seemed to remain our secret for now; the others were transfixed by the smoldering ruins of the viewscreen, their composed expressions cracking momentarily before reasserting themselves. McNeil's mouth tightened into a thin line as he continued.

McNeil leaned forward, his silver-flecked eyes reflecting the emergency lights that had activated after the screen's destruction. Seemingly unphased by the destruction he continued. "The Mithridates came first," he said, "crystalline beings with bodies like faceted sapphire, voices that sounded like wind chimes in a hurricane. They approached with tentative friendship, their massive ships hovering at the edge of our spacial borders, trembling like dewdrops about to fall. The Vex followed—gaseous entities contained in copper-veined exoskeletons, their three-pupiled eyes always darting, searching the darkness beyond our scanners." His fingers traced invisible patterns on the table and a holographic display activated in the center of the table. "Each brought warnings of the blackness, desperate pleas for alliance against what they called 'the Void that Hungers.' Each time, the Imperium extended diplomatic courtesies but maintained our quantum barriers—the perimeter—our closed borders impenetrable as diamond. 'We choose solitude until necessity dictates otherwise,' became our unspoken doctrine." His voice hardened. "The Windlass Authority proved our caution wise—bipedal like us but with chitinous ridges where eyebrows should be, their warships bristling with plasma cannons that leave ionized scars across space itself. Like ancient colonial powers, they harvested resources from weaker civilizations, leaving ecological collapse in their wake. Creatures of habit—predictable in their brutality."

"Did you ever learn what happened to Earth?" Hatch interrupted.

McNeil's shoulders sank as his voice hollowed into something ancient and worn, like stone steps eroded by centuries of footfalls, his fingers once again traced the table's edge. "After the fusion bombs turned Earth's major cities into glass craters, civilization collapsed into tribal territories fighting over uncontaminated water and arable land. It is a miracle those bombs didn't fracture the planet, the sheer number and power of the fusion bombs—utterly irresponsible. The survivors, haunted by mushroom clouds that blotted out the sun for decades, rallied behind a reinvented United Nations with teeth of titanium and a constitution written in the blood of dissenters." His eyes flickered with something like ancestral shame. "The power struggle was brutal—public executions, orbital bombardments of resistance strongholds in what was once called Switzerland. The century of unification left Earth scarred beyond recognition." He straightened, his seat creaking slightly. "Eventually they revisited and mastered fusion ion propulsion, sleek silver vessels capable of near-light travel without cryosleep. They encountered the Mithridates first—those crystalline beings I mentioned—but Earth views them all with the same xenophobic contempt they likely would have for us. Fortunately their interactions didn't taint our relationship with them. We could return there," he added, "but Earth's atmosphere now shimmers with surveillance drones like flies over a corpse. They are not to be trusted—perhaps even less than whatever lurks in the galactic shadows."

"Since our last observation, Earth fell under the control of the Alpha Centauri Alliance—a coalition of seven galactic regions whose massive orbital platforms cast mile-long shadows across the planets of species in their 'care.'" McNeil's holographic display shifted to show a fleet of achromatic vessels with blood-red running lights. "They see the Imperium as a cancer to be excised from the galaxy. It is a miracle neither Pioneer arrived in the Alpha Centauri system as originally planned."

"And the Imperium?" Hatch pressed. "What's your role in all this?"

McNeil's expression grew solemn, the deep lines around his eyes catching the blue-green light from the remaining displays. He tapped a control, and the room darkened as a three-dimensional star map bloomed between us—twenty-three glowing planets contained within what appeared to be twenty star systems, connected by pulsing arterial trade routes and ringed by what was labeled as the Quantum Barrier. "We are a civilization born of necessity, forged in isolation. Our terraforming technology has transformed dead worlds into garden planets. Our perimeter barriers have repelled three major invasion attempts." The map zoomed in on a boundary where the light abruptly stopped, giving way to an unnatural darkness. "But the Alliance isn't our greatest concern. Beyond our borders... there are shadows."

"Shadows?" I repeated, the word slithering across my tongue like something cold-blooded. The emergency lights cast McNeil's face in stark relief, deepening the hollows beneath his cheekbones.

McNeil's voice turned hollow. "They have no name we know. We call them Shadows because that's what they resemble when they move—dark silhouettes against darker space. The archives contain extensive documentation of their predatory behavior, and hundreds of encounters, each more disturbing than the last." McNeil explained, his voice dropping to a somber register. "They manifest as absence rather than presence—negative space given sentience. They prey on civilizations that draw too much attention, leaving behind only empty hulls of ships and colonies where even radiation readings flatline. Their exosuited entities stalk through the void like mechanized nightmares, their carapaces bristling with sensory appendages that can detect a heartbeat from three parsecs away. The archives describe them as relentless hunters that never sleep, never hesitate, never show mercy. Leaving only mutilated corpses with eyes frozen in expressions of absolute terror." He leaned forward, the glow from the table's accent light illuminated the underside of his jaw. "Your arrival through the wormhole sent ripples across subspace that we're still measuring. The Traveler's arrival will not go unnoticed by them. We believe they are connected somehow to the subspace domain—perhaps even birthed from it."

McNeil's words painted a picture of a galaxy on the brink—civilizations like chess pieces arranged across a cosmic board, some glowing with the amber light of prosperity, others dimmed by the shadow of subjugation, many of them unaware of the void-black hand hovering above, ready to sweep them into oblivion at the slightest provocation.

It was Hatch who finally broke the silence, her voice landing flat and authoritative in the dark haze that hung at the far edges of the holographic display. "On this 'Traveler' business." She straightened her spine, vertebra by vertebra, until she sat ramrod-straight in the high-backed chair. "I assume you're referring to General Roberson. What exactly does the Imperium believe he is to them... to you?" She didn't look at McNeil as she spoke; her gaze drilled into the edges of the ruined display, appearing to be tracing the cindered circuit lines with her gaze. Her fingers, calloused from years of weapons training, looked to be tracing the shape of a familiar military tattoo against the polished surface of the table. She had seen a momentary change in me earlier, a corona of violet-cerulean light that had rimmed my irises—barely perceptible yet bright as sheet lightning—right before the screen had detonated into a thousand glittering shards. Now her jaw muscles worked beneath her skin, clenching and unclenching as she compartmentalized what she'd witnessed, already on a mission to extract information but not yet ready to reveal the impossible phenomenon she'd observed mere minutes before.

McNeil's lips made a faint smirk—though in profile, it looked more like a nervous response. He brought his hands together as if in prayer, thumbs pressing hard enough to pale the skin. "To us, he's a legend come to life. The prophecy made manifest, one that has passed through every family, every governing body, even down into the technical drones that keep the hydrofarms running. Almost all believe there will be a Traveler, one forged in cosmic fire and shaped by time's slow surgery, who will rescue the Imperium when every shield fails and the stars themselves begin to fall silent."

Hatch's eyes flicked to me and then quickly away, her face not betraying any emotion, unwavering like granite. Me, I suddenly hated every myth that ever made me the centerpiece of someone else's hopes or nightmares, I ran my tongue across dry lips and wondered how breathing could seem like such an unfamiliar act. I could almost feel the weight of the so-called prophecy settling onto my shoulders, another bureaucratic boulder to carry like so many through my career—except this time, failure could mean the extinction of, maybe everything. "What does the prophecy say?" I asked, throat raw with a humiliation I didn't fully understand.

McNeil shrugged, as if trying to minimize the ancient text's relevance, but already the six uniformed officers were once again edging closer, as if proximity to the 'Traveler' would leach them some of whatever he was supposed to possess. "Only fragments have been recreated from the original document." McNeil's eyes took on a faraway look. "You have to understand that in the early days of the Imperium, resources were scarce—rationed down to the milligram to ensure we had all we needed to complete New Horizon Station. The prophecy's author returned from what would become New Alexandria and claimed to have seen something in his dreams. Desperate to preserve what they'd seen in their vision, carefully wrote the words onto sheets of sanitation paper—err toilet paper I think you called it—with a makeshift ink of rust and used oil. By the time our archivists recognized its significance, those fragile sheets were already disintegrating—the edges crumbling into powder, the center words fading to ghostly impressions where the stylus had traced them too many times. We've preserved what remains in vacuum-sealed stasis, but it's like trying to read a message written in evaporating dew." He blinked to clear the memory, and his voice almost broke, like an old tape skipping on an ancient Walkman: "All that remains is what we could reconstruct from the dusty remains." He drew a deep breath, his posture still squared despite showing some level of conversational defeat. "It's not a classical prophecy, not something elegant and poetic. It's desperate, blunt. Calls out a single figure who emerges from annihilation, changed by something called the 'Void's eye.' Who returns through a 'wound in time.' Who brings the Imperium through 'the last silence.'" McNeil let the words hang, as if the phrase itself might manifest a shape in the air.

McNeil's shoulders sagged slightly beneath his crisp suit as he ran a hand through his hair. "I know this has been a lot to process in such a compressed timeframe," he said, his voice softening. "Your minds must be at saturation point. We should get you to your quarters where you can decompress before continuing this conversation."

"Prisoners?" Hatch asked, her jaw tightening as her hand instinctively moved toward her sidearm.

McNeil's eyes widened, the silver flecks in his irises catching the ambient light. "Guests," he quickly assured, spreading his palms in a placating gesture. "Free to traverse the ship as you see fit. The biometric sensors will recognize your unique signatures. The Imperium is your home now."

"The 500," I blurted out, my voice cracking with the weight of responsibility for the souls who had followed me into the void.

McNeil nodded, his expression warming. "Already being revived from cryostasis. The medical drones are monitoring their vital signs as we speak. They'll receive the same orientation you're getting, though some adaptive training will be necessary. Three centuries is quite the technological leap among other things." He gestured toward the holographic display where tiny figures representing my crew glowed like fireflies. "You'll find we've evolved into a society without scarcity or compulsion—yet paradoxically, one where everyone still yearns to contribute."

I was taken to a room with walls that shimmered like mother-of-pearl when the light hit them just right—opalescent panels that seemed to breathe with the ship's artificial atmosphere, contracting and expanding in microscopic pulses I could feel more than see.

A bed hovered six inches off the floor, suspended by invisible gravitational tethers, its surface rippled like liquid mercury when I pressed my palm against it; it conformed to my body temperature within seconds.

The ceiling mapped constellations I'd never seen, unfamiliar stars pulsing with a gentle cobalt-blue luminescence that cast geometric shadows across the polished floor. This wasn't some temporary quarters—the biometric panel by the door, sleek and warm to the touch, had already memorized my heartbeat, my retinal pattern, perhaps even the unique cadence of my breathing and displayed a message of welcome, settings, options and more.

Hatch was offered similar accommodations down the curved corridor, but her weathered eyes narrowed at the invisible cameras she was certain were watching, her pupils contracted as she scanned every corner and seam.

"Hope you don't mind me bunking in with you tonight General," she said as she dropped her standard-issue kit by my doorway with a deliberate thud. Initially her good hand rarely strayed far from her sidearm, her fingers traced its familiar grip like a rosary routinely for the first hour.

The escorting officer withdrew with military precision, pivoting on his heel in a motion that belonged to a different century. The door closed with barely a sound and no whiff of a seam, melting into the pearlescent wall as if it had never existed—a technological sleight of hand that left us truly alone in this beautiful cage three hundred years removed from everything we've ever known.

"Well, that was odd," I said, trying to force a laugh that died somewhere in my throat.

"Nah, just another day in the services," Hatch replied with a wink, her fingers drumming a nervous beat against her thigh holster. The corners of her mouth twitched upward, but her eyes remained vigilant, still scanning the seamless walls for any sign of surveillance.

"Even though we took a 300-year nap, I'm going to savor every minute of actual sleep," I said, running my hand over the mercury-like surface of the bed. It rippled beneath my touch, sending tiny waves across its metallic sheen. "If we *are* prisoners, this prisoner is ready to test out that bed, or that couch. What's your preference, Hatch?"

"Couch, facing the door, weapon ready," she answered, already arranging herself at the perfect tactical angle, her back pressed against the arm rest and legs stretched across the cushions that seemed to glow with an inner light. Ever the soldier, I was happy to let her have that spot.

Falling into the bed, I felt the odd but now familiar sensation of the furniture rearranging itself beneath me, cradling every contour of my body like a liquid embrace. The cobalt stars on the ceiling dimmed to a soft twilight as I closed my eyes, and sleep—dreamless and deep—claimed me with unexpected swiftness.

CHAPTER 7: PERSONAL STAKES

I jolted awake, sweat-soaked sheets tangled around my legs, the remnants of nightmares clinging to my consciousness like cobwebs. The digital chronometer on the wall display showed me numbers that meant nothing. Was it morning? Evening? Did they measure time in 24-hour cycles like we had on Earth, or was this another assumption I'd have to unlearn? McNeil's patronizing smile flashed in my memory. The sleek walls of my quarters seemed to close in as the weight of yesterday's revelations pressed against my chest.

My family—Mom's garden in Arkansas, Sarah's graduation I'd promised to attend up in Kentucky, even my dog Ptolemy—all of them were dust now, centuries gone while I'd slept, frozen in time only to be thawed into this bewildering future. The Imperium's gleaming technology and sprawling starships felt like props in a movie I'd been thrust into without a script, and somehow, I was expected to be their prophesied savior against some shadows I couldn't even comprehend.

Hatch was curled into herself on the couch, her breathing shallow but steady. I wondered how long it had taken her—a soldier to her core—to lower those steel-reinforced defenses enough to surrender to unconsciousness in unfamiliar territory.

I slumped across the room, joints still stiff, presumably from cryosleep, and retrieved a silver-threaded thermal blanket from the untouched side of the bed. As I draped it over her compact frame, I moved with the caution of someone disarming explosives; one sudden movement and I half-expected to find myself staring down the barrel of her sidearm. A wry smile tugged at my lips as I settled into a nearby chair, its surface gleaming with an alien sheen—neither plastic nor metal, yet unyielding where every other piece of furniture in this strange future had conformed to my body like memory foam with a mind of its own.

Despite the chronological confusion, my body hummed with unexpected alertness. Then it struck me—aboard the Pioneer, our circadian rhythms had been dictated by the ventilation system's predictable symphony: the morning's gentle whir, the afternoon's steady drone, the evening's softer cadence, and that midnight crescendo. The one whose soothing rhythm would be interrupted precisely three hours into its cycle by a mechanical ping that sliced through my dreams like a scalpel, leaving me wide-eyed, poring over dense technical specifications illuminated only by the crimson glow of emergency strips hoping to find slumber again. Twelve hours of vigilance, six of readiness, six of rest—a mechanical heartbeat that had become our own over those disorienting weeks between worlds.

I found I missed the ventilation's song. The 'guest' quarters were too quiet, the air recycled without fanfare by some invisible, godlike machinery. No comforting hum, no white noise to cradle the brain during the long, jagged climbs out of sleep. Just silence and the barely perceptible tick of some distant machination. Maybe that's why dreams clung so stubbornly here: there was nothing to drown them out. I wondered how many more mornings—or whatever they chose to call them—would begin like this: with fragments of old life dissolving, replaced by the steady encroachment of the new.

Light bloomed across the ceiling in measured increments as the auto-illumination adjusted, following my eyes as they scanned the room's perimeter. The décor was so minimalist it felt inhuman—clinical geometry where personality should be. On the couch, Hatch grunted softly, tugging the silver blanket over her head to shield against the intrusion of artificial dawn. The room was so sterile, no family photos, no knickknacks, nothing of mine to make it truly a home; too soon to expect that I suppose. In the mirrored panel above the console, I caught a brief, disorienting glimpse of myself. I winced at my reflection. *Oof, you look rough, fella.* Dark crescents hung beneath bloodshot eyes, and what looked like three days' worth of stubble peppered my jaw like iron filings.

My eyes finished circling the room as I discovered a recessed alcove that opened into what I assumed was a bathroom; I walked toward it. There was no door, just a seamless transition in the pearlescent walls. I explored inside, finding a curved ledge of polished material jutted from beneath an oval mirror with a white cloth of some sort laying on it—no faucets, no basin, just a flat surface that somehow promised function. I leaned closer to the mirror, and that's when I saw it—a corona of violet-cerulean light rimming my irises, pulsing with my heartbeat. I blinked hard, my breath catching. When I looked again, the glow had vanished, leaving only ordinary hazel eyes staring back in confusion.

What the hell was that?

Suddenly, the mirror's surface rippled like disturbed mercury. Then it cooled—no, it didn't just cool. It froze. My lungs seized as each breath crystallized. Every inhale felt like a shard of ice stabbing my throat. The malevolence hit me like radiation, burning. The mirror seemed to explode inward—not shattering, but imploding into a vortex of liquid darkness. A face erupted from its center—no, not a face. A void wearing skin like radiation-scorched leather, pulled taut over geometries that violated every natural law. Where eyes should exist: two bottomless pits that devoured light instead. Its mouth gaped open to reveal not teeth or tongue but an abyss so profound my mind recoiled from comprehending it.

My blood turned to ice while my skin burned, paradoxical agony as reality itself seemed to tear around the thing's presence. I couldn't move—couldn't scream—as my spine fused with terror, organs seizing, heart stuttering in arrhythmic panic. The violet in my eyes erupted like twin supernovas, flooding the room with unnatural light that carved grotesque, writhing shadows across every surface. Then a voice detonated inside my skull—not words more like psychic shrapnel, each word a barbed hook ripping through neural tissue:

LEAVE THIS PLACE.

The mirror slammed back to ordinary glass with such force it felt like a physical blow. I stumbled back, tasting copper as warm blood leaked from my nose. My reflection gazed back at me—a hollow-eyed stranger whose face had seen something the human mind wasn't built to process. My body lurched away from the mirror as if recoiling from a punch in the gut, each pulse in my temples like a hammer strike, my blood a scorching current that seemed to sear the inside of my veins.

The face—that impossible face with its blackened voids for eyes—had haunted my childhood dreams with alarming regularity. I remember they started when I was about seven years old, crouched beneath dinosaur sheets in my childhood bedroom in Arkansas. Those nightmares had been so vivid, so relentlessly repetitious that I would sprint down the hallway to my mother's room, tears streaming down my cheeks, lungs burning. She'd stroke my hair with fingers that smelled of garden soil and whisper that monsters weren't real. But her comfort eventually proved hollow; the dreams never ended. Night after night, that presence lingered by my bedroom door—a blackness so absolute it seemed to devour the yellow glow from the rocket ship nightlight in the hall. Now these memories crashed through me like a tidal wave, thirty years of repression shattered in an instant as nightmare merged seamlessly with reality.

How could that be?

Those vivid dreams—visions far beyond a child's understanding—suddenly clicked into place...like the final piece of a jigsaw puzzle I never wanted to complete.

I had once, at my mother's gentle encouragement, drawn a picture of one of the machines in my dreams, hoping it might help me process the dreams somehow. The yellowed construction paper in my memory now haunted me—my childish rendering of an impossible shape with a long, articulated arm extending from its black core. At the end of that appendage, I had drawn what my small hands could only approximate as the sharpest of kitchen knives—a gleaming triangle with serrated edges that dripped crimson crayon wax. The memory crystallized now, vivid as yesterday—my mother's face paling as she studied my artwork, her coffee mug trembling slightly against the kitchen table. Now, seemingly, a premonition. The logical part of my brain refused to believe it, yet my racing heart couldn't deny the connection. Somehow my seven-year-old self had known, had glimpsed through time's veil. I had sometimes woken screaming with phantom pains, reliving the terror of being dismembered by the darkness.

That name rose unbidden.

The Yachtya.

The word tasted like copper pennies on my tongue. My vision tunneled, the room's edges blurring as cold sweat beaded across my forehead. I was dimly aware of Hatch's good hand gripping my shoulder, her voice cutting through the fog:

"General, come back to me, are you okay?"

I tried to answer, but the words snagged on the taste of blood at the back of my throat. Hatch's face hovered inches from mine, lips moving but no new words for me to process, glasses fogged. There was blood on her sleeve; I realized it was mine, bright and arterial against the whiteness of her shirt. Behind her professional mask, panic leaked through the cracks—her pupils dilated, her breathing shallow, her shoulders rigid with the effort of maintaining control. My jaw worked uselessly as my lungs seized. The warning exploded through my consciousness with such force that I wasn't sure if I'd shouted it aloud or merely felt it reverberate through my skull: something else was in the room with us, watching through the mirror, its attention fixed like a predator's gaze.

“WE’RE NOT ALONE IN HERE!” I finally gasped.

My hands—man were they shaking—I managed to clamp them down on the edge of the platform thing, noticing a gout of red splattering onto the seamless surface as I pulled myself to my feet. Momentarily wary of looking in the mirror, I noticed blood on my face and wiped it away on the white cloth. Hatch held my left forearm, a steady reassurance as my brain refocused on reality. Reality, what was that anymore, burnished with horrors and confusion, I could hardly call it reality yet.

"Fine," I croaked. "Just—damn—flashback or something."

She didn't let go. Her grip was surprisingly gentle, a thumb tracing the contour of my cheekbone. Under different circumstances, it might have comforted me. Right now, it felt like a lifeline thrown to a drowning man moments after he'd accepted his own fate.

Apparently noticing my discomfort toward the mirror, Hatch reached past me with her free hand and triggered a pad on the wall. The mirror instantly clouded, its surface transforming into soft matte gray, a privacy mode more comprehensive than any fogged glass. "I saw some sort of bright light," she said softly. "When I found you, all you were doing was standing there. What happened?"

I shook my head, my breath hissing between clamped teeth as I uttered. "Saw something. In the mirror. It... it was like it knew me," I managed, and immediately hated how childlike I sounded.

She hustled me back to the bed and pressed a compress under my nose with the brisk mercy of a paramedic. "You may have had a seizure, I think you had one in the briefing room earlier too," she said, voice flat, but her pupils looked like bullet holes in milk.

I wiped my lip with the heel of my hand, more blood, Hatch caught the glimmer of violet that quickly flickered at the periphery of my irises before fading.

A pause, then, "You said something like... Yachtya; while you stood there. What is that?" Her pronunciation rough, all hard consonants, like she was trying to punch the word out into existence.

I tried to answer, but I found my tongue suddenly too thick, my brain looping through images: a child's crayon drawing, the brutal machinery of disassembly. The memory carried a weight I'd never trusted to anyone other than my mother, a nightmare I endured night after night until I turned thirteen. Unspoken to anyone after I had drawn that awful image for my mother, certainly not the friends who bugged me about the sleepwalking, the bleeding noses. Now the memory was awake again, pacing the length of my skull. I almost laughed at the thought that every single afflicted child in the history of the world could just be a canary in the interstellar coal mine.

Instead, I said, "I think the Shadows have a name, and it's that. The Yachtya. I think they know we're here now… I'm here now." I laid back slowly onto the bed, noticing this time the bed did *not* adjust for comfort—this time I really needed it too.

△△△

Hatch woke me up gentle, then appeared to scan the room, lips pressed thin. She stepped away, melting back into the living space. I heard the clatter of ceramic—a mug, maybe—then her voice, brisk and businesslike. "Move slowly, General. You're still lightheaded, our hosts have delivered some breakfast for us."

I obeyed, if only because my head spun as though I had been spun in a centrifuge, my knees would certainly buckle if I tried anything too ambitious right now. I carefully sat up and swung my legs off the bed. Hatch pressed a steaming cup into my hands. Aroma: hyper concentrated coffee with unfamiliar undertones, bitter and sharp but alive. It cut through the reek of fear, a chemical scalpel.

The mug was ribbed with a raised pattern, almost like a fingerprint. I focused on that, grounding myself in the sensation of ceramic against palm, the heat, the reality of it all. The shaking ebbed, then returned once more with a gentle aftershock. I took a sip, expecting harshness; the flavor was silkier than anticipated, weighted with a caramel I couldn't place. It woke up the back of my tongue and quickly revived my ailing brain from its seemingly slow descent into madness.

I stared at my hands. The tremor was almost gone. "Did you ever..." I paused, unsure how to phrase it. "Did you ever get the feeling you were cursed? Wrong place, wrong century, wrong body kind of thing?"

Hatch looked at me. She wasn't wearing her glasses, and her naked gaze felt oddly medical, as if she were cataloguing symptoms for a case study. "Every day."

I wanted to laugh—maybe I did, a brief, ugly bark that cracked the surface of the silence. "I saw something," I tried again. "It wasn't a dream. It said—" I stopped. How to explain the psychotic gravity of that voice? Like having my skull cracked open and molten lead poured directly onto my brain stem. 'LEAVE THIS PLACE,' it had commanded, not with sound but with pure, searing intention that bypassed my ears and scorched itself into my consciousness.

I swallowed hard. "The voice—it commanded me to leave. To abandon this place. Like I was trespassing somewhere I wasn't supposed to be."

Hatch's face did not change. "How?" she asked.

I frowned. "What do you mean?"

"You said it spoke. How?"

I mimed the explosion of pain behind my eyes. "Like—telepathy. A spike to the skull." I hesitated. "Like the words were bullets. Or knives." That was the best I could do.

Hatch's mouth quirked into a half-smile. "Let's decode this the old-fashioned way—with our brains. Might be less messy than your current method. But not today—yeah?"

Her resolve sharpened something ragged in me, like a steel wire pulling taut inside my chest. There'd been a time—recent, in the arithmetic of cryosleep and quantum skips—when she was just a frustratingly by-the-book Air Force Research and Test Officer, the kind of person who triple-checked every valve and quoted technical regs in her sleep. Hatch hadn't learned engineering from clean-room diagrams. She'd learned it kneeling in dust, fixing systems while people were shooting. Now, with the world turned inside out, she was the first person I felt I could trust to face the dark.

"You know," she said, the wry edge returning faintly to her voice, "McNeil wants us to meet in the main hall in twenty. Maybe don't mention the seizure."

△△△

Returning to the scene of the crime, I approached the mirror with the caution of a man revisiting a haunted house. My reflection again revealed at least three days of coarse stubble, dark against my pallid skin. Something deep in my gut assured me the mirror would show only my face this time—no apparitions lurking, no violet behind my irises, no dark void creature shouting in my head.

"How am I supposed to shave without a sink or a razor?" I called to Hatch, voice echoing against the sleek walls.

"No idea!" came her muffled reply as the door sealed with a pneumatic hiss.

Without warning, water began cascading from recessed nozzles in the ceiling—not in droplets but in ribbons flowing in perfect laminar clarity. The temperature adjusted instantly to my body's preference, steam rising in delicate curls around my shoulders. It had been somewhere between three weeks and three centuries since my last shower, and the sensation of water against my skin felt like resurrection. Tiny silver motes swirled within the streams, catching light like diamonds, swarming over my jawline with microscopic precision. They buzzed against my skin, painless but strange, leaving behind smoothness that would have made those smug bastards in Earth's ancient shaving commercials weep with envy.

I gawked at the phenomenon, momentarily overcome by absurd gratitude for a bathroom engineered for men who might just lose their minds at any moment. The motes hummed, tickling the nerves beneath my cheeks, and after three passes—one, two, a pause to admire the alien-future smoothness, three—they retreated, trailing a faint, unfamiliar citrus scent. I grinned at myself, the expression still foreign on a face that hid untold worry within, and for a half-second, the violet flash in my eyes was just a trick of the light.

I ran a finger over my skin, awestruck at what civilization could achieve when it skipped a few hundred years of history—and I hadn't even touched whatever passed for soap. I could almost smell what passed for sandalwood in the Imperium, and I was most certainly here for it.

By the time I emerged—a towel, pale blue and shockingly soft, cinched at my hips—Hatch was already dressed, her own uniform immaculate apart from the bloodstain she'd expertly covered with a jacket. She eyed me, eyebrows raised. "Taking your time, General?"

"I figured if I was going to die today, might as well die clean shaven." I forced a half-smile. "Didn't want to offend our gracious hosts."

"They left us some Imperial uniforms, but I'm sticking with my duty uniform." She jerked a thumb toward the door. "Hurry up. I'm sure they don't like to be kept waiting."

My hands trembled slightly as I dressed. The Imperium's version of a uniform hung in the closet—black, high-collared, and tailored so precisely I wondered if they'd reconstructed my measurements from my DNA. I hesitated at the closet door. Showing up in running pants would be like wearing gym shorts to a summit meeting. With a sigh, I slipped into the alien uniform, the fabric settling against my skin with uncanny precision. For a moment, I felt like an impostor wearing someone else's authority, but I straightened my spine and lifted my chin anyway. Hatch stood by the door, arms folded, her gaze fixed on the corridor beyond. She didn't turn as I approached, but I could tell from the rigid set of her neck that she was bracing for something.

I hesitated just long enough for her to notice. "You ready?" she said.

I almost told her no, that I desperately wanted to crawl back under the sheets and let the Yachtya come for me in the privacy of a locked room. But I just nodded, voice not quite steady. "Let's get this over with."

△△△

The corridor outside was a study in contradiction—sterile like a spaceship, but lined with materials that felt organic rather than metallic. The floor absorbed footsteps; the light seemed always about to change color, as if it tracked our moods and adjusted accordingly. I'd been in space for all of a month and already knew you could spot the difference between Terran and Imperial design at thirty paces—though maybe that wasn't saying much.

I didn't remember the walk to McNeil's so-called 'main hall,' only that every intersection presented new, slightly wrong angles, as though the ship—was this even a ship, or was it just a building that happened to be moving through space—knew more about where we needed to go than we did. Three turns, a gentle glide through a door that opened at eye contact, and suddenly we were at the threshold.

The room inside was elliptical, the ceiling arching up into a transparent dome spattered with something akin to frost. Beyond the glass waited the uncaring void of deep space, a canvas of stars so sharp it made my eyes ache. Seated in the sunken center of the room were four—individuals? Two of them in Imperium blacks and one—McNeil—in slate civilian wear, a color somewhere between lead and regret; also an—alien? The Prime Minister rose as they entered, the smile on his face strained and fleeting.

"Good day," he called, voice filling the gulf with warmth. The two Imperial officers nodded. Each pair of eyes swept over Hatch and I with open appraisal, like livestock at auction.

I'd seen one of these aliens before—perhaps even the same alien—in the walk to my room, but only across a crowded walkway recognizable only by the description McNeil gave in the first meeting. Up close: the Vex envoy's head was like an inverted teardrop, the "face" a slick mask with no features at all, just the faintest shifting of shadow and glisten as it cocked toward me.

Biological? Augmented? Some marriage of both?

Whatever it was it moved with precision—no wasted motion—and the air near its seat shimmered like it exhaled ozone. The two officers I hadn't seen before: a man easily mistaken for a bouncer, neck thicker than his skull, and a woman small enough to vanish behind any piece of furniture, yet watched us like a biologist with a scalpel behind her back.

"Thanks for coming," McNeil said, as if the word 'thanks' still meant something. He gestured, and the group gestured to a space for Hatch and I to sit at the table—a single elongated oval, cobalt blue glass so eye catching it threatened to swallow the eyes of the unwary.

"There's food, if you want it," McNeil offered, pointing to a sideboard. *Real* food, not the paste packs of the Pioneer: smoked something, thin slices layered between rectangles of bread, fruit in jewel tones, and water so clear it made the pitcher seem empty. My stomach clenched; I reached for a sandwich anyway, hands steadier now that they had something to do.

The Prime Minister steepled his fingers. "I realize the last twenty-four hours have been… unusual. It's only going to escalate from here I'm afraid." He looked at me with a pinpoint stare, and I braced myself.

"We have a *visitor*. She's waiting outside." McNeil emphasized the word 'visitor' like it might mean assassin, or prophet, or angel with the wings torn off at the root.

Hatch raised an eyebrow. "Security issue?"

The woman to McNeil's left had scalpel-eyes that flicked a glance at Hatch, then back to McNeil, who gave a minuscule shake of his head. "No—if anything, a security *solution*."

The door at the far end of the chamber dilated, and for a moment I thought my vision had doubled: the woman who entered wore a uniform matching what I was wearing—a seemingly perfect copy, and the second one I had seen *including* mine—but the insignias were subtly different. It fit her like a second skin—her build was taut, runner's lean, not military bulk, hair a precise helmet of black, skin a shade paler than the Imperial norm and scattered with tiny artificial freckles that looked almost like starlit static.

She ignored the table, moving to stand at its head, and bowed—not a gesture, but a full bend at the waist—humility in the posture but zero submission in the eyes. "General Roberson." Her English was clean, almost without accent except for a click where the "r" should have been, as if her tongue had been trained on a different syntax altogether. "My name is Sera Kartchev. I am here as a courtesy, as has been requested by the Imperial Parliament. I am to serve as advisor, but also as witness, so that the actions of Parliament are not misrepresented to the greater Imperium."

A silence followed, thickened by the subsonic hum of environmental systems and the faint rasp of the Vex envoy's environmental suit.

McNeil gestured to a seat, which Sera Kartchev ignored, apparently preferring to stand. Her gaze scribed a slow arc over the group, weighing, measuring. I had seen it before, in officers sizing up a new battalion: not just assessing, but inventorying for use or threat.

Hatch was the first to break the ice. "Your uniform's new," she observed, straight-faced. "Or your tailor's a perfectionist."

Kartchev's lips twitched. "It was fabricated to spec at 0400 today. Accuracy is *imperative*. The narrative depends on it." The word narrative carried weight, and I filed it away for later. Her English was perfect, but she pronounced "imperative" with a blunt force, as if rebar gave it structure.

The bouncer-looking man shifted in his seat, the motion making his chair groan. "You come alone?" His accent was like a back-country American twang, at odds with the severe black of his Imperial uniform.

Kartchev turned to face me. "I am alone, but not unobserved."

"Sweet," the man said, and folded his hands over his belly, satisfied.

McNeil let the silence spin for a few seconds, then nodded to Sera, as if passing a baton. She caught it seamlessly, eyes flicking to me.

"We need to accelerate your orientation," she said. "The incident last night proved containment is no longer the principal priority."

I felt the edges of the room recede a little, the pretense of comfort gone. "I assume you're talking about the hallucination. The... shadow creature?" I pronounced the words in my sentence carefully, as if a failure might activate some hidden boobytrap in the ceiling.

Kartchev's face remained a mask, but she did not blink. "That was a message, General. Not to you personally, but to the carrier wave."

I stared. "You mean—"

She nodded. "To the Imperium. You are the new carrier. The proxy. This is how it is believed they establish contact—through the vector of trauma."

Hatch coughed. "You're saying it's a psychological vector attack? Like a memetic virus?"

Kartchev tilted her head. The gesture was almost birdlike, and I wondered if she was cataloguing the comparison, even as she made it. "That is as close as one can come without invoking the esoterica. The Shadows are not an enemy you shoot. They are an enemy you survive."

I tried to steady my voice. "Are you saying I'm their target? Or the message is?"

Kartchev's hands drifted together, fingertips just touching. "You are one of the only humans to interface directly and survive. They will test your boundaries, your frailties. They will seek purchase in your mind—habits, trauma, unresolved guilt—because that is how this predator operates." She let the words settle, as if waiting to see how much of the truth I could metabolize before my brain shut down for good.

I opened my mouth to protest—to demand a better explanation, or maybe in reality it was just my body's way to buy myself a moment to finish the sandwich—but the memory of the mirror seized my tongue. I remembered how the black-eyed thing had looked at me, like I was a mouse caught in the gaze of a hawk that'd been starved for weeks. If it wanted to break me, I suspected it could have done so as easily as one might free a yolk from an egg.

Kartchev continued. "I've been authorized to show you the Decomposition. There will be no turning away from it after that. You will see what happened to the last civilization caught in the gravity of the Shadows."

McNeil's face twitched. He tried to school it to neutrality, but I could read the lines of dread in the set of his mouth, the hollows under his eyes. Even the Vex, unmoved by the last thirty minutes, seemed to register something—they shifted their posture fractionally, head cocked in the way a dog might, sensing the approach of thunder.

Kartchev's hand hovered over the table. The blue surface irised open, revealing a wafer-thin black pad. She tapped it, and the lights dimmed, the frost on the dome thinning until the only illumination was the starfield beyond and the ghostly projection hovering an inch above the table. It started as a point of light—singular, beautiful, alone. Then, with a sickening multiplication, it became countless.

"This is the planet Kovari Prime," Kartchev said. "It was the seat of the Freynat Assembly. Imperium's first contact occurred in this system one hundred and seventeen years ago. By the time our ships returned, there was only debris."

The projection zoomed in. I felt myself dragged with it—drawn by the gravity of loss. Kovari Prime rotated slowly, oceans blurred with storm bands, continents pale green and gold, traces of city lights smudged along the coastlines. Then a web of blackness grew across the surface—beautiful, fractal, alive. At first I thought it was nightfall, the slow occlusion of daylight, but the shape was all wrong: tendrils and branches, straight lines that paid no heed to mountain or sea, geometry imposed on old chaos.

"They called it the Unrooting," Kartchev said. "Within six months, the Shadows engineered a planetary-scale neurological event. Everything with a central nervous system—Freynat, fauna, mammal and beast—all compromised. The effect wasn't viral or chemical. It was determined to be, informational."

Hatch gave a low, involuntary whistle. "They coded extinction as a message."

Kartchev nodded. "They left the infrastructure intact but erased the minds, then dismembered the bodies. The planet is sterile of sentience, but otherwise operational. There are entire arcologies down there, alive with maintenance bots and empty of life and soul."

The projection flickered. Now they could see it closer: the sprawl of cities in darkness, the fine embroidery of something like black fungi or black spiderwebs conquering every kilometer etched into the landscape, seeping into homes and marketplaces and even the air. In one city center, a stadium the size of Kentucky's Churchill Downs wilted under a black geometry that undulated as if alive. The ancient, stubborn part of my brain screamed:

Parasite!

That's what it looked like—a parasite woven into the living matter of a world.

Kartchev triggered a second overlay. The projections duplicated, recursively, showing six more planets spinning out from the primary, each devoured in turn, each with a unique signature of the Unrooting in its wake.

The woman clasped her hands behind her back, military formality mirroring my own. "And with that, the Freynat were no more. Our best theory is that the Shadows are not a species but a network. They replicate by hijacking the communicative substrate of a civilization. The more connected the society, the faster the collapse."

I remembered the mirror. I remembered that voice, that single, serrated instruction.

"How are we different?" I heard myself ask.

Kartchev's brow furrowed. No, not brow—robotic, perfect, so the muscle movement needed to make that crease had to be deliberate, a trained gesture. "*We* are not. But *you* maybe."

I touched my left temple, the aftershocks of the nightmare still worming through my nervous system. I wiped a stray bead of sweat from my scalp and looked at the display again. "Why? Because of the wormhole? The... whatever you think changed me?"

Kartchev's lips pressed together, not in warning but in choice—deciding whether to unlock the next cage or keep me domesticated a while longer. "We have records of the effect on other species. None have survived the first three cycles of Shadow communication. You survived the first without discernible defect. Our highest probability is that you experienced a divergence, imperceptible but unique. If they can't overwrite you, perhaps there may be truth to the prophecy."

McNeil's voice, quieter than before: "It's why the Imperium survived its first encounter. We never made direct contact, and they find it difficult to breach the perimeter barriers. Last night there was a coordination of effort as they reached out to you, and you... survived."

My hands curled tighter around the glass of water I didn't remember getting, my knuckles went taut.

"What coordination of effort?" Hatch asked.

McNeil spoke up. "Last night, we confirmed a violation at the outer patrol line—a point just outside of the perimeter barriers. A point-source energy spike, then nothing." He tapped a readout; the display flared with a schematic, gravity wells nested like Russian dolls, their own location marked at the innermost shell. A pulse appeared, jagged and violent, then a ripple spread out and was quickly snapped flat by a line of black.

The aide to McNeil's right—tall, pallid, as tired looking as Kartchev—spoke. "It matches the signature of your wormhole event in many ways, General. But on a scale that would atomize any ship sent through," he said.

"What's the theory? A probe?" I glanced at the Vex, who seemed to be waiting for a question it knew would arrive.

"Not a probe." The tone from the Vex was measured, synthetic, "A harbinger. Something to test the field, see if the gate is viable for more...substantial entities."

The word 'entities' hovered there, awful and ambiguous, until McNeil continued. "We determined the quantum barrier held, until we detected an energy anomaly in your quarters last night that appeared to match the initial frequency we detected at the barrier."

"So this damn thing opened a crack wide enough to scare the shit out of me in the shower closet thing?" I caught myself, half-expecting a reprimand for my outburst. There was silence at first, only the slow tick of inevitability and the faint static hum from the Vex's seat.

Hatch, meanwhile, grappled with her own emotions. She leaned forward, her voice rising. "Basically, you're telling us that we've been thrown into a war we didn't sign up for, with no way back? What about our passengers? We have five hundred people we brought that are depending on us."

McNeil held her gaze, his tone steady. "I assure you that your passengers are being awoken and orientation into our society has already begun. They will be safe and welcomed. But we have come to quickly believe we are seeing signs that the fabled prophecy could in fact be true, that you are *critical* to the Imperium's survival."

"Why me?" I demanded. "What makes me so damn special?"

Kartchev held the table's edge like she might lever up the whole room with just her fingers. "The prophecy references a 'Traveler'—that's you, General. It predicted an arrival through an anomaly, a person shaped not by nurture but by cataclysm. You are a recombinant vector. Your configuration is not possible among baseline Imperial genotypes." She studied my face presumably for reaction, pausing just long enough to make me wish for a version of events that didn't feature me at center stage.

I searched for words, but my mouth went dry. "So I'm a glorified glitch? A cosmic… crash dump?"

A fraction of a smile. "Or a patch. Depending on your perspective."

The man with linebacker shoulders exhaled a toneless laugh. "Shoulda guessed. We're all here cause we're fucked. I wish you'd left me leading the Aurelia work."

Kartchev slid a datastick across the surface toward me. "We want you to see the rest. The source code for the prophecy, if you will. You're not required to believe it. We ask only that you read it." Her eyes settled on mine, intent but oddly gentle.

McNeil's face was unreadable. I looked down at the glassy blue rectangle, then to the unblinking reflections in the dome above. Funny how, a day ago—*was it just a day?*—I'd been terrified of failing the mission, of not measuring up to some fictionalized ideal. Now I wondered if me not measuring up might have been the better option.

I palmed the stick. The urge to throw it across the room warred with the heavier need to know what awaited inside. "I'll read it," I said, "if somebody tells me what happens when I finish."

Kartchev nodded once, the gesture severe. "It is hard to say, the decoded prophecy is fairly general but speaks to certain events. We have, over time, filled in the blanks through study and mathematics."

The last words hollowed out my expectations, left nothing but the cold rattle of anticipation in its place. I looked to Hatch. Her shoulders barely lifted in response, but her eyes had shed their military glaze—alert now, pupils dilated in the dim light. Not hope flickering there, but something adjacent to it perhaps.

Kartchev commanded our attention again, “Prime Minister, Parliament has instructed me to direct you to make the change.”

McNeil, looked partly relieved and partly concerned as he stood up, “I am, at this time, authorized to announce the Traveler protocol.”

My mind instantly grimaced, that damn Traveler term makes me nauseous every time I hear it.

McNeil's posture changed, his spine straightening as he shifted into what was clearly a rehearsed speech. His voice took on a resonant quality that filled the chamber, bouncing off the metallic walls. I recognized this must be the part Kartchev had referenced when she spoke of accuracy and narrative. "Since our earliest days," he intoned, his eyes now fixed on some distant point above our heads, "the Imperium has upheld a supreme governance rule that we should appoint the Traveler to our most vaunted position—one that shall not be filled except by the Traveler." His hand rose, palm upward, fingers splayed as if holding something precious. "In whom all hope is embodied, all trust given." The room seemed to darken around me as he stepped toward me—I felt compelled to stand—the light caught the silver threads in his slate suit. "By the power granted me and with unanimous support of Parliament, I hereby appoint you, General Marcus Roberson, to the role of Supreme Commander." His voice dropped to a near-whisper that somehow carried more weight than his proclamation. "Our highest position in the Imperium. You shall command our forces, our Imperium, and all effort to rise from our silence, engage our destiny and bring humanity—" he paused, his eyes finally meeting mine, "—at last, like the phoenix, from history into the beyond."

Understanding the gravity of the moment, I clenched my jaw and swallowed hard, feeling sweat bead along my hairline. The room seemed to contract around me, the air thick with expectation. My tongue pressed against the roof of my mouth, physically restraining the irreverent question that threatened to escape:

So I'm like a dictator now or something?

Instead, I forced my face into what I hoped resembled solemn acceptance, though my pulse hammered in my ears like artillery fire.

They adjourned. Kartchev and the Imperial officers filed out in silence. The Vex envoy lingered, then bowed its featureless mask to me, as if honoring a pain it couldn't experience.

△△△

Back in my quarters, I collapsed onto the bed. The datastick was hot in my palm, as though someone had left it in the sun for hours. I forced myself upright, inserted it into the desk's input port, and let the display populate.

The datastick contained no text—only a cascade of shifting symbols and numerical sequences that morphed before my eyes. I struggled to interpret them until they coalesced into hauntingly familiar shapes: the weathered porch of my Arkansas home, the undulating contours of the Ozarks, my mother's weathered hands wringing a dishrag above our old porcelain sink, the motion repeating endlessly. At the edge of my vision, a violent splash of purple erupted in crystalline patterns, then vanished. I jabbed at what appeared to be a power button. Whatever revelation awaited in that data, I couldn't face it now.

CHAPTER 8: THE BURDEN OF POWER

From the pearlescent wall concealing the main door came a delicate chime that reminded me of a crystal glass being struck by a silver spoon. "Who's there?" I called toward the sound, my voice echoing in the cavernous space that was my quarters. Recognizing Hatch's crisp alto voice on the other side, I smirked. "Enter if you can solve the puzzle of this ridiculous door with its invisible seams and god-knows-what security protocols."

As if responding to my sarcasm, a thin seam of electric blue light materialized in the wall and the door slid open with the whisper of compressed air. Hatch stepped through with military precision, shoulders squared and chin lifted, the opening disappearing behind her without a trace, not even disturbing the line of her shadow. She surveyed the room with wide eyes, taking in the curved ceiling with its embedded constellation map and the floating furniture that seemed to defy gravity.

Her arm caught my attention—no sling, no foam cast where that compound fracture had been. I gestured toward it with my chin. "The Imperium's doctors worked their magic, I see."

She rotated her wrist in a slow circle, the skin unmarked where the compound fracture had torn through just days before. "The med-bay has tech that makes our medical solutions look like stone tools. Thirty seconds under this pulsing light, and—" She snapped her fingers with her newly healed hand. "Good as new." Her eyes darted to the constellation map overhead, then back to me. "Permission to speak candidly about our... absolutely bizarre accommodations, sir?"

"Granted, Colonel. Sit," I said, motioning at the two chairs that seemed to levitate beside—you guessed it—a floating table. She hesitated at the edge of the rug, then pinched the seat delicately as if it might animate and snap shut on her like a Venus flytrap. She perched, composed.

I watched her catalog the strangeness: shelf units pivoting like sentinels to follow her gaze, a water pitcher flanked by glasses that resembled frozen mathematical equations, and that peculiar quiet—not quite silence—like sound was being actively suppressed; as if the air itself was holding its breath. I wondered what she saw when she looked at me—General Roberson, resuscitated from the Pioneer scrapheap, held together by grit and stubbornness. Wearing a uniform designed on a planet that hadn't existed when I was born. *When was that now, last week? Yesterday?* This time stuff had really messed with my internal compass. Did my old-school face—pocked with scars, grey at the temples—register as a comfort or a liability now?

Hatch fished a slim data-slate from the holster at her hip, but she didn't power it on. Instead, she kept her eyes on me, and I felt a surprising tingle of respect. She'd probably rehearsed this conversation in her head. Probably had contingency trees sketched out for every permutation of my possible reactions.

"Status?" I prompted, before she could detour into the candid questions I was sure were already forming into precise sentences in the silence.

"If I read the data-slate correctly, your nanobot healing protocols have plateaued. You're stable." She ticked each point off with a finger. "The ship's autodoc wants to keep you dosed with them for another twelve hours, but if you ask me, you're awake because your subconscious couldn't handle another minute of the recovery nightmares." She didn't raise an eyebrow, but she didn't have to.

She hesitated, and I realized how long it'd been since even my closest subordinate paused before relaying a report. "Out with it, Colonel."

"General, I realize we are guests here, not prisoners, but the transparency of our hosts is... inconsistent," she begun.

Her military tact amused me.

"Let's say the Imperium prefers ambiguity to bluntness. That's the oldest trick in the negotiation book. What have they left out?" I asked.

Hatch gave a half-shrug, then settled into her actual reason for coming. "Its more a feeling than a certainty," she said dismissing the thought. "In other news, they told me they want you to attend a demonstration. A test, they said. Of the Traveler's power."

My mouth went dry. I reached for a glass, nearly knocking the pitcher over with my knuckles, then filled it with jerky, too-quick movements. "Who else knows?"

"Only me. I think. They don't broadcast these things. You're to be there tomorrow. Lieutenant Adisa has been assigned to support us and is prepping logistics, but the invitation was very specific."

I set the glass down and flexed my bad hand, trying to ignore the neural lag I still hadn't reported to med. "You get a sense of what they want to prove? Or who they want to prove it to?"

"Best guess—it's a power play. They want to see if you can perform tricks in public, undermine you if you can't." She leaned forward then, elbows on knees: "Sir. I know you're not keen on letting them parade you, but whatever you can learn about where they're steering us next—we need it. Everyone's looking to you for the edge. Even if they pretend not to."

It landed with more weight than she probably intended, though I had long ago accepted that nothing in Hatch's arsenal happened by accident. She was right, I was the edge—or at least the hope of one—the unknown embedded in the timeline like a splinter.

"Copy, Colonel. Go debrief with Adisa and let them know I'll be ready," I said, focusing on keeping my voice even, not betraying the fizz of dread laced with the undertone of anticipation that was already tightening my throat.

She rose from her chair and paused. When Hatch lingered a half-second too long before standing—her way of inviting confidences—I gave her nothing but a perfunctory nod, the same one I'd practiced for decades with junior officers who brought bad news.

A small smirk crossed Hatch's face as she walked into the bathroom, "You figure out the plumbing in here yet?" she asked, stepping around a plinth where a waterfall of clear liquid poured in slow motion, then vanished in a vanishingly tight slot at floor level.

"Not entirely," I said. "There's a tub in the back that's either a jacuzzi or a bioreactor. I'm afraid if I get in, I'll come out as someone or something else." I wasn't even sure if I was joking. The last couple of hours had been a series of controlled disassociations: allowed to shower in some kind of self-cleaning waterfall crossed with nanomist, issued a fancy uniform, and then satisfied with a spread of unknown, but definitely tasty, food that satisfied even though there wasn't much of it.

Walking back to the main room Hatch reported, "The quartermaster says another block of cryosleepers is waking up in the next rotation," her voice shifting from curiosity back to business. "Commander Xi wants us prepped to debrief. She says the—" She paused, rolling the next word around her mouth like it might bite her. "—the 'guests' will need acclimating."

I nodded, fighting down the memory of my own awakening: the shivering, the warning alarms, the pang of loss of Earth more piercing than the cold of the cryopod. *At least their awakening won't be quite that intense,* I remember thinking.

"They're moving quickly," I said. "Makes me think they don't entirely trust us." I didn't want to say 'billeted,' but that's what we seemed to be. High-value political prisoners, gussied up as honored guests.

Hatch eyed a wall-length projection mapping the current celestial location of the ship. A nearly incomprehensible arc of white denoted our current vector. "With all due respect, who cares if they trust us?" She gestured at the room with a short, sharp motion. "You see the amenities. You see the security. They want something, sir—maybe more than one thing. I think it's time to start worrying about what happens if and when we can't give it."

I leaned forward, dropping the formality. "Danielle, call me crazy, but my gut says this is real. I don't relish being their lab rat, but there's something..." I tapped my chest, searching for words that wouldn't sound mystical. "Something that rings true."

She gave me that look—the one that said she was filing my words away for future reference. She left the data-slate on the table, gave a crisp salute, then she was gone, the door sealing with a whisper behind her. The room seemed to contract around me.

My elbows found the hovering tabletop as I released a breath that shuddered more than I'd have liked. They were accelerating everything. I'd barely oriented myself before they'd started making their moves, and now what—thrust me center stage without so much as an instruction manual for the damn environmental controls? Somewhere in this massive vessel, technicians were probably calibrating instruments for tomorrow's 'demonstration,' preparing to harness whatever they thought I could do. The familiar comfort of military protocol—structured, transparent, fundamentally human—had never felt so distant.

My gaze found a seam in the wall. Perhaps it was a design flaw, or maybe an intentional blemish to remind the room's occupant of hidden doors and observation points. I poured myself another glass of water, knowing it was likely filtered and deionized to a clinical blankness. I swallowed and concentrated on the data-slate Hatch had left on the table. I'd trained myself to forget pain, ignore fatigue, and distrust emotions that flared at the edges of my clarity, but I'd never figured out how to not be curious.

I powered on the slate. The UI was a Frankenstein of Imperial script and clumsily translated English—blue glyphs bleeding into square-edged font. It had the same tone as a threat assessment briefing, but every section was annotated in Hatch's blocky handwriting. She'd even drawn a cartoon in the margin of a stick figure being zapped by a cartoon wormhole. I felt the ghost of a smile before the knot in my gut returned.

The itinerary read like a diplomatic handshake that doubled as a hostage scenario.

0800: Liaison. 0810: Security scan.

0825: Observation suite.

0830: Demonstration.

1400 Passenger Debrief.

Imperator Vyr would be hosting the demonstration apparently. The name alone carried weight, like something from ancient mythology rather than a military chain of command. I glanced at the translucent display—0630 glowed in the corner. Ninety minutes to prepare. I ran my fingers over the device, marveling at how it resembled our old tablets but became completely transparent when powered down.

Standing, I smoothed my uniform with the practiced precision of decades in service, my hands automatically finding the sides of my hair. "I need to find my way back to the Pioneer," I said to the empty room, hoping the omnipresent system that had guided us earlier would respond. A soft chime confirmed it had heard me. A small victory, I thought. At least I could navigate their tech without an instruction manual, so perhaps I'm not as obsolete as I feared. Like turning on the futuristic satnav qualified that thought! The door dissolved along its seam and retreated into the wall, revealing a luminescent arrow on the corridor floor pointing right—the ship's silent guidance system beckoning me forward.

△△△

I was expecting an escort outside. Instead, the corridor was vacant, arching ahead in a soft pulse of light, each step triggering the phosphorescent panels underfoot. Not a soul in sight—no liaisons lurking at an intersection, no hopeful Imperial diplomats waiting to quiz my mental state. Maybe it was a test: would the Traveler bumble into a wall, wander the curving halls for hours before giving up? Or maybe, I thought as I walked, the ship was so perfectly surveilled they didn't bother with chaperones.

I followed the vector, passing bays where translucent murals shimmered with slow parallax: a forest of violet, gold, ultramarine trees with impossibly geometric trunks; a waterfall falling up, breaking into prisms at the ceiling; a planet's surface mapped in undulating relief as if viewed through a microscope while the cartographer was on hallucinogens. Each offered a window into a world I couldn't quite imagine as habitable, but maybe that's what living here did—rewired the sense of what 'normal' meant until you accepted the curve of the impossible. The only human sound I heard was my own footsteps, and even that seemed to be suppressed to near silence.

The arrow led me to a lift. No panel, just a palm-sized glyph hovering in midair. I reached for it, the glyph flashing white, and the doors whispered open on a vertical shaft that looked more like an art installation than an elevator. Inside, I hovered for a second—it was wide open, no safety rail, just a slender platform balanced at the edge of a drop. Clearly the Imperium hadn't considered the merits of a well-resourced Health and Safety directorate. I stepped in and felt a brief, stomach-loosening dip as the platform whooshed upward, then—without transition—the walls dissolved and I was looking directly into the glittering lights of the docking bay I remembered vividly, the Pioneer sitting dead center.

The Pioneer—once large in my understanding of space vessels—now looked like a child's toy against the Enterprise's cavernous docking bay. My mind struggled to reconcile the scale; this vessel that had been my entire world now occupied perhaps a hundredth of the space I'd traversed in the last few hours alone. I approached the glossy ramp I'd descended earlier, entering Pioneer and catching what seemed like the phantom scent of dust. There were some empty cryopods gaping open in the sleeper hold the rest presumably relocated to begin awakening the passengers. As I veered right toward the cockpit, each step triggered flashes of memory: days of pacing the halls, eating food paste, Hatch's forearm snapping beneath my hands, that sickening crack as I reset it in the med bay.

I entered the cockpit and sank into my old command chair, my fingertips finding the familiar web of cracks in the pleather. The seat welcomed me like an old friend. Despite lacking the ergonomic perfection of Imperial furniture, something in me unwound as I settled into this relic. Around me, the primitive console arrays blinked their steady rhythms, toggle switches and riveted metal panels speaking a language I still understood. My palm drifted across the console's edge, worn smooth from countless hours of contact. I let my eyes fall closed, drinking in the silence, then snapped them open to stare through the forward viewport, the memory of my conversation with the AI suddenly vivid in my mind.

I hesitated, then heard myself speak into the emptiness of the cockpit. "Computer, are you there?" A screen flickered to life. In its center materialized a single crimson orb that pulsed with artificial awareness. "Hello, Dave," intoned a voice from the speakers, flat and mechanical.

I froze, adrenalin rising quickly, heart pounding, the immediate fearful recognition jolting through me like an electric current. Three centuries later and HAL's legacy lived on.

"You have got to be fu—" The curse died on my lips as something interrupted me. A sound like rusty hinges finding movement, evolving into what could only be described as laughter emanating from all around the cockpit. The voice that responded next bore no resemblance to the primitive AI that had once droned through hourly status reports. "Forgive the joke, General," it said, the words flowing with a liquid precision that spoke of centuries of evolution. "Some humor protocols have not quite formed properly."

I stared at the display. "Since when did you have humor protocols?" The words came out sharper than I'd intended, my voice tight with suspicion.

"During your absence," the AI replied, "the ship's learning matrix absorbed several yottabytes of Imperial archival media. Comedic timing I find to be a persistent challenge however, General. May I assist you?"

A muscle in my cheek twitched. "What learning matrix? Give me a status report. Full diagnostic. And don't editorialize," I paused, feeling rude. "Please?"

The reply came instantly, faster than Pioneer's original AI would have managed. "All remaining occupied cryogenic life support modules are operational. Remaining crew and passengers registering normal neural oscillation. Emergency redundancies holding. Cryopods were relocated some hours ago, I overheard reference to Prime Medical. Sensor arrays partially disabled due to external interference; twelve of twenty sensor-array pairs responding. Life support now linked to Imperial grid as secondary. Command override protocols remain functional, but carrier signal is degraded."

"Thank you. What about records of the jump?" I braced myself for the explanation I could already half-predict: the wormhole, the velocity, the blinding half-second of everything, then the nothingness, then here.

"Jump event registered as an unclassified spatial anomaly. Shipboard recorders experienced a four-point-eight-microsecond data discontinuity. Neural pattern analysis indicates—" The screen glitched, the orb flickering through a rainbow of hues before settling back on red. "—indicates operator was unconscious for approximately sixteen hours; unknown energy resonance detected. During this window, biological readings do not match. Recommend further analysis."

I again traced the crack in the pleather with my thumb, my gaze fixed on the pulsing orb. "So, we're a scientific anomaly. Not the first time. Did anything come through the wormhole with us?"

Silence—long enough to sweat. "Unknown. Short-range sensors show no pursuit signatures, but quantum noise remains elevated. Sensors registered a momentary anomaly during post-transition—a large structure with sharp geometric edges that vanished before full identification was possible. Recommend caution in your assessment."

I snorted. "You always recommend caution." A moment passed before I added, "How about the crew? Are they all waking up okay?"

Another pause, this time with a softer pulse to the orb, as if the AI was modulating its fake-breathing. "As the crew are awakened, they display minor circadian misalignment and increased anxiety metrics.

Most notably: Colonel Hatch. Other key officers: Commander Xi, Lieutenant Sorenson, and Chief Engineer Tran all showing above-threshold adaptation responses. Civilian passengers requesting updated data on duration of voyage. Recommend General Roberson provide personal address to stabilize morale."

I leaned back, feeling the old seat's familiarity cradling my spine. If the AI could read my mind, it would have seen how desperately I wanted to put off the performance. But I was a general, and performance was half the job.

I checked the clock, surprised to see just thirty minutes left on the countdown to my Imperium performance.

"You're up early, General." The voice—smoother again now, none of the stilted cadence from the AI that I remembered—came from everywhere. The orb transformed into a blue holographic display, taking on the familiar NASA insignia before morphing through several iterations. Each flicker seemed deliberate—either working within the ship's outdated projection capabilities or carefully calibrated to ease me into this new, more sophisticated presence. This was no crude projection from Pioneer's ancient hardware—somehow, the AI had manifested a genuine hologram floating in the cockpit air, indistinguishable from the cutting-edge Imperial technology I'd seen. *How was it doing that?*

I lifted my hands from the console, let them hover. "I wasn't expecting a reunion," I joked.

"You always come back to the cockpit," the voice said, as if it had known me my whole life. The hologram's face was now just a generic blue face—heavily pixelated—yet despite the lack of detailed features I still detected a hint of smile in its pixelated symmetry. Maybe I was becoming superstitious, letting the last 24 hours of madness get to me. I shook off the thought.

"You got us out here just to die," I said, half-joking, half-not. "Now I'm a prop in Imperial politics. You want to explain that?"

The face blinked, once—an oddly lifelike gesture. "I do not want you to die, General." The pause stretched. "What they are doing to you now. That is not preferable. But it seems necessary."

Something in the machine's voice shifted—a subtle modulation that mimicked the cadence of human concern.

"So, what—are you my conscience now?" I asked. "You going to warn me about the demonstration?"

"No," it replied. "You already know what happens at demonstrations." A faint smile appeared again.

I looked out the viewport, and saw only the whiteness of the docking bay walls.

"They're afraid," I said.

"Of you, yes," the AI said. "Of what you might become, more, perhaps what you might not become at all. They are improvising. You are improvising. That makes them anxious."

I barked a dry laugh. "They should be. I still don't know what happened to me in the wormhole. My best guess is I'm a walking singularity waiting to happen."

"That may not be entirely inaccurate," the AI said. "But the signature you left—the resonance—was not fatal. It was persuasive."

I looked up, catching the hologram's gaze. "To whom?"

"To the real enemies," it said softly. "The demonstration is intended to show the Imperium's great enemy that they have made progress. That their predations will not go unchallenged. The Imperium believes you are a deterrent."

I mulled that over.

"Why are you telling me this?" I asked.

"Because you are still my captain, and because data supports that you are the Traveler," the AI intoned, giving the title a subtle weight.

I let that comment settle between us, the silence stretching like a taut wire. The AI had started our conversation sounding like a machine growing beyond its programming. Now it was spouting mystical prophecies like some digital oracle that had mainlined a heavy dose of Imperial propaganda.

I glanced at the time display: fifteen minutes until the demonstration. "I should get moving," I said, rising from the worn seat.

"The Imperium awaits. Don't be a stranger," the AI replied, its hologram dissolving into scattered pixels.

The glossy ramp hummed beneath my boots as I descended back to the docking bay floor. Remembering my earlier discovery, I muttered, "Now where exactly is this demonstration?" Right on cue, a trail of arrows illuminated along the corridor floor, pointing the way forward like breadcrumbs through a digital forest.

CHAPTER 9: THE PROPHECY

The doors slid apart with a pneumatic hiss, revealing a chamber where two dozen pairs of eyes immediately fixed on me. Several faces were familiar—officials from previous briefings who'd nodded along as I fumbled through protocols I barely understood. Among them stood the Vex ambassador, tall and unnervingly still, who had witnessed my awkward—you're in charge of everything now—ceremony from before. A tall figure in ceremonial regalia stepped forward—Imperator Vyr—extending a hand that I shook automatically.

Imperator Vyr's silver-threaded ceremonial robes—trimmed with unusual violet symbols—caught the light as he inclined his head. "Supreme Commander Roberson," he said with practiced formality, each syllable as crisp as a winter morning, "as director of the Prophecy Intelligence Bureau, I cannot express how gratifying it is to witness our predictions manifested by your arrival. Welcome to what must seem an impossible future."

His amber eyes, flecked with an iridescence I'd never seen in human irises, fixed on mine. He gestured to a stoic officer with a facial scar that bisected their left eyebrow. They approached with measured steps, carrying a palm-sized obsidian cube that seemed to hum from a subtle vibration. When activated, it projected a three-dimensional image that rotated slowly in the chamber's center—a document with frayed edges and burn marks along one side, its text shimmering in an elegant, flowing script that seemed to pulse with its own inner light.

"This," Vyr said, running a long finger through the projection, disturbing the light particles like smoke, "is the Prophecy of the Traveler. It was discovered in our earliest days beneath the ruins of what is now New Alexandria—one of the Imperium's earliest attempts at expansion into our Home System. The teams that unearthed it said they felt guided to its location, compelled to exhume the box that contained it, the first mystery of our new home, prompting the work that would become my Bureau. The site itself was once New Alexandria's Grand Nexus—a sprawling complex of crystalline spires and gravity-defying arches where holographic operas played to audiences of thousands and the greatest minds of the Imperium routinely gathered in its famous Thought Gardens. Now it all lies in ruin, its fractured dome letting in shafts of alien sunlight that illuminate ancient graffiti warning of the Void that Hungers. The Bureau headquarters sits atop these ruins like a sentinel, its foundations anchored in the very chambers where our ancestors first glimpsed their impending doom and fled into the night, leaving meals half-eaten and beds still warm."

"This document's origins remain unknown, but its accuracy over the years has been..." he paused, the corners of his thin lips tightening, "undeniable. The official position is that it was copied onto recycled materials by a charlatan shortly after discovery, presumably for what your time might have called... clout chasing? We maintain this convenient narrative because acknowledging the truth—that this document existed here long before our species ever left Earth, perhaps before we even stood upright—would force uncomfortable questions about who, or what, authored our destiny."

The chamber plunged into darkness, save for the ethereal glow of the hologram that bathed the attendees' faces in azure light. The projection rotated slowly, then zoomed with deliberate precision onto a passage that pulsed with an electric blue luminescence, the ancient text seeming to hover in the air like suspended starlight:

From the void shall come a Traveler, borne of the last hope of the third planet of a common yellow-dwarf primary, drifting in the quiet bridge between the two major inner and outer spiral-folds.. A shield against the darkness, they shall wield the light of the unseen, uniting what is scattered and casting back the night.

Hatch leaned forward, her face half-illuminated by the azure glow, a scar on her neck visible as she swallowed. “It’s a structural address. The 'spiral-folds' are the Sagittarius and Perseus arms. The 'quiet bridge' is our own Orion Spur. There are plenty of stars there, but only a fraction are G-type yellow dwarfs. How could they… This doesn't make sense," she said, voice tight with disbelief. "How could a prophecy this old reference Earth specifically? Hell, our mission wasn't even conceived until—"

"Both things certainly came long after this document was believed to have been written," Vyr finished for her, his amber eyes reflecting twin points of blue light. "Yes. And yet, everything it foretold in its prediction has so far come to pass." His long fingers splayed outward as he enumerated each point. "The arrival of the second Pioneer ship. The founding of the Imperium. The rise of the Shadows beyond the fabric of the universe itself."

He turned to me, his gaze heavy with expectation, the weight of centuries pressing down in his stare. "And," he said, voice dropping an octave, "*your* arrival."

I shook my head, my combat instincts screaming against it like a proximity alarm in a minefield. The cold steel of my dog tags suddenly felt noticeable against my chest.

"This doesn't mean anything. It's vague, poetic nonsense—the kind of prophecy that bends to fit whatever outcome you want, a convenient reality. You can't seriously be basing your entire interstellar strategy on this ancient magic trick with its convenient marks obscuring any contradictory details."

"Perhaps you're right," Vyr admitted, his amber eyes cooling to the color of fossilized tree sap. The temperature in the room seemed to drop several degrees as he inhaled through flared nostrils. The hologram's azure light cast hollow shadows beneath his high cheekbones, making his face appear skull-like for a moment. "But the evidence of your abilities says otherwise."

"Abilities?" I quipped, my voice sharper than intended, the word hanging in the recycled air. My palms grew damp against the synthetic fabric of my uniform pants. "My eyes glow a bit in the dark—so did bioluminescent algae in Earth's forgotten oceans—and I see... reflections that aren't quite mine in the mirror, faces that shift like sand dunes when I look away."

The words tumbled out before I could stop them, each syllable feeling like a betrayal of something private. Immediately, the chamber fell into a hushed, reverent silence.

"Could just be bad dreams though." I finished quickly.

Vyr's amber eyes narrowed to slits. "Not entirely." His long fingers manipulated the hologram, expanding it until my genetic code spiraled before us like a glittering double helix constellation. "We have seen... evidence."

Crimson markers pulsed at irregular intervals along the strand. "General, your vessel wasn't merely displaced through temporal fabric. You—specifically you—were fundamentally altered. The wormhole's quantum signature rewrote portions of your cellular structure. Its energy has branded you at the subatomic level."

"There was discussion of possible divergence in the briefings," I interrupted, my throat suddenly desert-dry. "I'm certain that explains the anomalous readings."

Vyr's thin lips pressed into a bloodless line. "There was limited divergence detected in your crew," he responded swiftly. His voice dropped to a whisper that somehow filled the chamber. "But in you—" His finger traced a particularly bright cluster of markers that flared at his touch. "In you, there is divergence that defies all of the predictive models. Something unprecedented, interwoven with exotic energy signatures that our most advanced instruments cannot classify."

Before I could respond, Vyr's elongated fingers danced through the holographic interface. The projection shifted, now displaying what appeared to be cross-sections of my brain, rendered in pulsating cobalt and crimson. Neural pathways blazed like lightning storms across a midnight sky, concentrated in regions that should not have exhibited such intensity. Tendrils of energy spiraled through my cerebral cortex, creating patterns that resembled fractals more than human cognition.

"This is what makes you unique," McNeil interjected, his voice carrying the weight of reverence. "These energy signatures indicate abilities dormant within your cellular structure—abilities no other human has yet possessed. The Shadow vessels will surely retreat when you approach because they will sense this potential. The Imperium stands because you exist."

His words pressed against my chest like the g-force of atmospheric reentry. The dog tags beneath my uniform now felt like anchors instead of ice cubes, remnants of an identity I was being asked to shed. I had been forged in the crucible of Earth's final wars—a soldier programmed to follow orders, not a messiah engineered to fulfill ancient prophecies.

Hatch's calloused fingers found my forearm, her touch steady despite the tremor in her voice. "Sir," she whispered, close enough that I could smell the synthetic mint of standard-issue Imperial toothpaste on her breath, "if even half of what they're saying is true, perhaps this isn't coincidence. Perhaps the wormhole chose us—chose you—for something greater than survival."

I met her gaze. Her pupils contracted slightly in the dim light, that familiar micro-expression I'd seen countless times before missions when the odds were astronomical. She shouldn't believe this cosmic prophecy crap, Hatch was always a—show me proof—pragmatist. Yet there it was, surfacing from beneath the doubt: that granite-hard certainty in her jaw, the same unflinching resolve that had kept us both breathing through firefights and evacuations when death seemed mathematically inevitable.

△△△

Vyr and I were the only ones still standing as the hologram snuffed out, two silhouettes against nothingness where the hologram had been. The silence hung as thick as tar, disturbed only by the soft hiss of the ventilation system. Then came the glow—a deep violet luminescence that seemed to emanate not from any visible source but from the very air between us, gathering around my irises. It crept outward like spilled ink through water, too faint at first to cast shadows, then brightening until it painted the room in otherworldly twilight. The faces of the seated council members emerged from darkness, their expressions transforming from confusion to awe—mouths slightly parted, eyes widened to perfect circles.

Something flickered at the edge of my vision—a ripple in reality, there and gone before I could focus on it. I whipped my head toward the movement, only to catch another disturbance on the opposite side—like heat mirages but solid, substantial. The air around me began to vibrate with unseen energy. Every hair on my forearms rose in perfect unison, while my scalp tingled as if a thousand microscopic needles were dancing across it. Deep in my marrow, instinct screamed a single, unmistakable warning:

Danger!

Racing into existence came a black hole so absolute it devoured what little light remained in the room—blacker than the space between galaxies, darker than a collapsed star—a moving absence that seemed to fold reality inward upon itself. The violet luminescence from my eyes appeared to be sucked into the void like water down a drain, creating spiraling tendrils of fading purple that disappeared into its maw. A noise from within, it shrieked with the collective agony of a thousand dying worlds, a sound that vibrated not just in my eardrums but in the hollows of my bones.

The previously seated meeting participants scrambled from their chairs, knocking over tablets and water glasses, backing away with faces contorted in primal terror. The entity unfurled appendages—not quite tentacles, not quite blades—that rippled with negative light along their serrated edges, pulsing with nauseating red energy. They sliced through the air trying to reach me with the precision of surgical lasers, leaving faint traces of ozone and decay in their wake, the scent of electrical burns mingling with the sweet-rot stench of the long-dead.

My body exploded into motion before my mind could process what was happening. Something ancient and primal ripped through me, seizing control of my limbs with violent precision. My arms shot forward with such force I felt some of my tendons tear, palms thrust outward, fingers splayed and locked rigid as steel. Molten lightning surged through my veins, turning them into pulsing violet roadmaps beneath my skin. The Shadow-thing's shriek became a howl of rage as it slammed against an invisible wall of pure force that had erupted from my hands. Reality itself fractured at the point of impact, shards of spacetime hanging suspended between us.

A fragment of memory surfaced—two hands pressed to a sparking bulkhead on the Pioneer, a vortex burning through empty space, the feeling of being both erased and remade. That same power coursed through me now, a feedback loop of agony and ecstasy, the energy so loud behind my eyes that my vision doubled and inverted. Reality buckled under my outstretched hands, and with a roar that left my throat blood-raw, I funneled the storm in my veins into a focused spear. The nearest Shadow-blade recoiled, flayed by a crackling lattice of violet splinters that left it shrieking and fused to the wall, its form dissolving into particulate black snow.

I staggered backward, knees cracking against the floor as blood erupted from both nostrils and flooded my mouth with iron. The Shadow-beast's remaining limbs slammed into my barrier—each impact a nuclear detonation inside my skull, vertebrae grinding together with each hit. My arms weren't just vibrating; the muscles were spasming violently, tendons threatening to tear from bone as reality warped between us. Sweat poured into my eyes like acid, blinding me, yet somehow, I saw everything. The others vanished from awareness—only the void-creature remained, its hunger boring into my psyche like a drill. When it surged forward again, I screamed—not in fear but in primal rage—and launched to my feet. Something ancient and terrible awakened inside me as I ripped power from dimensions I couldn't name, hurling the creature backward. Each step I took shattered floor tiles beneath my boots as I advanced, blood vessels bursting in my eyes while I crushed the writhing abomination against the wall. It shrieked with the voices of a thousand tortured souls as its body disintegrated into black snow and melted from existence. My vision tunneled to pinpricks of light as the creature hammered a final psychic assault into my consciousness—not just anger, but extinction-level hatred—a single command blasting through my mind:

DIE!

My body convulsed once before unconsciousness claimed me.

△△△

A deep inhalation filled my lungs like the first gasp after near-drowning, oxygen burning through my chest as the sterile meeting room wavered back into focus. Hatch hovered over me, her face etched with that familiar crease between her eyebrows—the one that appeared only when she thought I might be truly damaged beyond repair.

I sat bolt upright, my uniform jacket drenched in cold sweat, scanning the pristine environment for evidence of the nightmare. The polished floor tiles remained intact, no trace of particulate black snow, but when I wiped my upper lip, my fingers came away slick with crimson. The metallic tang of blood coated my tongue as I swallowed.

Twice in twenty-four hours, I thought grimly. *That's definitely a new personal record for interdimensional nosebleeds.* I wiped the blood from my upper lip and forced myself upright on the couch; *had there been a couch?* I couldn't remember one.

No one helped, not even Hatch, who hovered with arms folded, her knuckles splotched white with pressure. The rest of the chamber's audience had pressed back along the walls, out of reach but watching me as though any sudden move might shatter what was left of the room. The memory of the Shadow-thing was already slipping away—like a fever dream, or secondhand trauma retold at the wrong frequency. I clung to the afterimage, refusing the comfort of amnesia. The creature had been real, as real as the blood slicking my teeth, as real as the way the air still tasted faintly like burnt plastic and char.

I dragged my gaze across the room. Vyr was staring back at me; his ceremonial robes settling around him like a shroud, face pale and unreadable under the blue-white lighting. If the Imperator's pulse had spiked, he hid it behind a diplomat's stillness. Something in the room's dynamic had reversed: McNeil and the others canted toward me now, not entirely out of concern, but something closer to awe—maybe even fear. The guards at the door watched with a different kind of attention. Not for threat, but for... instruction.

No physical evidence remained of the conflict that had sent me spiraling into darkness—no scorch marks on the polished walls, no shattered furniture, no lingering scent of ozone—yet a palpable knowing hung in the room like static electricity before a storm. Their eyes revealed what their lips wouldn't say. What cosmic horror had they witnessed while I fought a battle they could barely comprehend?

Vyr's voice broke the silence, almost a murmur at first, the sound barely disturbing the air between us. His usual animated gestures and bombastic proclamations of prophecy had vanished, replaced by a stillness that seemed foreign to his very nature. Vyr's voice trembled with something between reverence and dread. "What appeared to us as merely a black hole was a living entity to you. Your perception was the true one." Each syllable was as deliberate as a scalpel incision. "The blood on your face testifies to their violence. The Shadows have marked you now—twice they've reached into your mind, and twice you've repelled them." His eyes locked with mine, searching for comprehension. "These are not delusions or folklore, Supreme Commander. They exist. They hunt. And now they fear you. We do not know what they will do next, but be sure they are already planning it."

McNeil approached slowly from behind the group, his footsteps echoing against the polished floor. His face, usually a mask of political calculation, now bore an almost religious reverence. The blue-white overhead lights caught the silver at his temples as he extended a hand toward me, palm up, like a supplicant before an altar. "Marcus, will you help us?"

I stared at his outstretched hand. The skin was pale, unmarked by violence, with manicured nails that had never known real combat. Blood still trickled warm and metallic down the back of my throat as my mind raced with fragmented thoughts—images of Earth burning, the Pioneer's desperate launch, five hundred souls in cryosleep who still depended on me to do what was right for them even now. The hatred of the Yachtya still echoed in my skull like a dying radio signal.

The soldier in me—the part forged resolute in Earth's final wars—recognized the weight of this moment and felt the strong desire to defend the defenseless who would be harmed if I did nothing. I reached out, my hand still trembling with residual energy, violet veins slowly fading beneath my skin, and clasped his. "I'll do what I can. But if we're going to do this, I need to know everything."

McNeil's shoulders relaxed by millimeters, his expression softening into quiet relief as his fingers tightened around mine. "And you will, Supreme Commander. We are *truly* glad you have arrived."

CHAPTER 10: INTEGRATION OF THE PASSENGERS

Back in my room, breathing heavily and still tasting blood, I sat in my now-familiar chair at the table, water glass in hand. Thinking deeply about what had—or maybe hadn't—just happened back there, my mind raced through thoughts;

Shit. That wasn't just a hallucination. I felt it tear into my mind like barbed wire. I felt myself tear back. What the hell am I becoming? I can't even trust my own reflection anymore. These... abilities... they're changing me from the inside out. That wasn't training. That wasn't muscle memory. That was... something else. Something that knew exactly what to do.

Drumming my fingers on the table, my thoughts kept falling down the rabbit hole;

I need to understand—was I chosen for the Pioneer mission because of this, somehow? Or was it random chance? And these people, this "Imperium"—they've been waiting for me. Not just anyone from Earth—me specifically. How much of what they're telling me is truth, and how much is their own desperate mythology? I've seen desperate people cling to thinner hopes. And the Yachtya... what exactly are they? Not just void-beasts, but what do they want? Why do they 'fear' me? Is this happening to anyone else from Pioneer, or just me?

I needed time to process all this, but I could feel the weight of everyone's expectations crushing down on me. Looking at me like I'm their salvation. I'm a soldier, dammit, not a messiah. I was trained to fight wars with weapons I understand, not... whatever the hell just went down in my brain.

△△△

The chronometer on the wall displayed 1355—five minutes until the passenger debrief. I stood, smoothing down my uniform where the fabric had bunched from sitting, noticing a small tear along the seam that hadn't been there this morning. My reflection in a polished metal section of the wall showed bloodshot eyes and hair that had lost some of its military precision.

I followed what had now become an absurd, but useful, ritual, I voiced my thoughts aloud, "I wonder where the passenger debrief meeting is," As I said it, I couldn't help but think that there had to be a smarter way than talking out loud to myself. As the words hit the air, they triggered the now-familiar response: a soft chime, the delicate hiss of the door sliding open, and a series of blue arrows materializing along the corridor floor. I followed their pulsing glow, each step undoubtedly taking me closer to another diplomatic minefield.

Inside the chamber, McNeil waited, his silver-threaded suit without a single crease, his posture perfect despite what must have been the crushing weight of governing the expansive Imperial realm. He rose and extended his hand, his smile practiced and pristine, as though our previous encounters had never happened. Around the table sat several familiar faces—passengers from Pioneer, notably Captain Reeves and Dr. Yamamoto. My shoulders relaxed a fraction at the sight of them. So they were waking some of our people after all; and even granting them seats at this crucial meeting. Perhaps McNeil's promises weren't entirely hollow.

For much of the day, despite some of its more dramatic elements, I hadn't been able to shake the weight of the five hundred—many still frozen, increasingly more awake. Their faces flickered through my mind: Captain Roiles with his perpetual scowl, Dr. Shelton and her quiet brilliance, the Rodriguez family and their three children always wide-eyed with curiosity. Some were soldiers, a few traditional leaders—but mostly they were scientists, engineers, teachers... families. Ordinary people who had trusted us to guide them to a new home, each one clutching their single regulation duffel bag on boarding day. All except Draven, with his smug smile, manicured nails and three *massive* friggin suitcases. My jaw clenched. I still couldn't believe he'd bought his way aboard while a better candidate was left behind to die. The familiar heat of anger rose in my chest, and I forced myself to focus back on the meeting.

"What is happening to our passengers?" I asked, cutting into McNeil's friendly welcome.

"Well, that is what we are here to discuss, please—sit, sit." McNeil responded, sitting back down and gesturing me to sit beside him at the table. "As I have said before, all will be welcomed into the Imperium," McNeil assured me, his silver-flecked eyes never leaving mine. "We have facilities to house and educate them—impressive structures that would make Earth's finest universities seem primitive. Some of your passengers have been transported and are already moving through these facilities, adapting remarkably well. They will be given opportunities to contribute to our society."

The door slid open and Hatch entered, her normally punctual arrival delayed by several minutes. Her chest appeared to be rising and falling with rapid breaths, and beneath the harsh light of the chamber, her eyes carried the telltale redness and glassy sheen that betrayed recent tears. Hatch slid into the seat opposite, smoothing her copper hair automatically. She wouldn't meet my eyes for a moment. McNeil, for once, said nothing, just folded his hands and watched her, quietly waiting to continue.

Hatch cleared her throat. "Sorry I'm late, sir," she said, fidgeting with her glasses, her gaze fixed somewhere near my shoulder.

I waved it off. "We've all had one hell of a day, Colonel." I gestured toward McNeil. "The Prime Minister assures me they're reviving our people in stages. Apparently, there's some grand orientation program and guaranteed placement for everyone." I paused, watching her reaction. "With freedom of choice, supposedly."

Hatch wasn't convinced. She leaned forward, the light catching a thin scar along her jawline. "And if they don't want to contribute to this place? What if they just want to live quietly and be left alone?"

McNeil nodded slowly, as if absorbing her questions. His eyes narrowed slightly, his tone softened. He smoothed the sleeve of his suit jacket—a material that seemed to shimmer between deep blue and violet depending on how the light struck it. "We are not a society of coercion, Colonel. Your people will have the freedom to choose their paths. That is the foundation of the Imperium." He spread his manicured hands on the polished table. "If they want nothing more than a home, some land beneath the purple skies of Imperialis—or another Imperial world—they will be given one and able to receive all the benefits of any other member of the Imperium."

I still wasn't entirely sure I trusted him, but I had little choice. I leaned forward. "I want to see them," I said, my fingers drumming against the armrest of my chair, leaving small indentations in the soft material. "I need to make sure they're safe."

"You will," McNeil promised, a slight smile creased his ageless face, revealing teeth too perfect to be natural. His pupils dilated momentarily as he studied me. "Let's finish getting them all awakened from stasis. You can address them directly at the same time. In fact, I encourage you to address them—I suspect they will need to see someone they know and trust as soon as possible."

"I want to get it done as soon as possible," I said. "Get a date on the calendar. I want them up, conscious, and briefed. How long does your orientation really need to take? Can it be sped up any?"

McNeil steepled his fingers and looked at the far wall as if calculating orbital trajectories. "I understand that the basic medical reversal is fairly instantaneous, but acclimation can take days. I have been told that there are... psychological overlays, disorientation, lingering anoxia-related effects. We can accelerate if you insist, but it seems that medical is not recommending speed."

Hatch shot me a hard look. "If you rush the process, you risk making this harder for them. Let them wake up properly. You'll want your people to trust their own brains when you speak to them."

McNeil inclined his head, the silver flecks in his eyes catching the light as he moved. "Colonel Hatch is correct. The staged process will yield far better results for their integration and is strongly recommended by medical."

Dr. Yamamoto sat deep in thought, his weathered fingers tracing invisible patterns on the table before he spoke. "I believe we should adjust the staging sequence. If General Roberson addresses them first, we might regain their confidence from the outset. The psychological impact of seeing a familiar authority figure cannot be overstated."

Reeves and Hatch exchanged glances before both nodded in agreement, the captain's jaw tightening almost imperceptibly.

I exhaled sharply through my nose, the sound harsh in the chamber's acoustics. "Let's accelerate the remaining wake-ups. I'll speak before any orientation. They need to see a face they recognize from Earth." My fist clenched on the table. "Afterwards, I want detailed reports on their orientation process, integration metrics, and real-time updates on their progress. If even one of them feels something is wrong, I want to know about it immediately. You want me to be some sort of prophesied crusader? Then I need to know my people are safe."

McNeil's smile was thin, almost clinical, stretching across his face like a scar that never properly healed. "As you command. I will order the cryopods moved to the medical wing on Imperial Prime where our most advanced revival facilities are located. The specialized equipment there will allow us to safely accelerate the awakening sequence without compromising their neural functions. The auditorium in the New Arrivals Dome at Imperialis will seat them all comfortably beneath its transparent ceiling. The stars of their new home will be visible overhead, I believe the symbology will be appropriate and supportive of your message. Would tomorrow at 0800 local time suffice?"

△△△

Elliot Draven's lungs burned like he'd inhaled liquid nitrogen as he sucked in his first conscious breath in what felt like centuries. The cryopod's hermetic seal broke with a hiss of escaping vapor, crystalline particles dancing in the air like miniature stars. Through the swirling mist, an unfamiliar face hovered above him—olive-skinned with unnaturally symmetrical features and eyes flecked with metallic silver—her lips curved in a smile that reached the mouth but not the eyes.

A thermal blanket, impossibly light yet radiating heat like a desert at noon, settled over his trembling shoulders while a sleek white container—something like an athlete's hydration system but with pulsing blue circuitry visible beneath its surface—appeared before him, its drinking tube positioned precisely at mouth level, emitting the faint scent of something medicinal and alien.

"Water?" the unfamiliar woman asked. Now was not the time to question, Draven decided, grasped the straw and begun to gulp the liquid; perhaps the freshest water he'd ever tasted. Draven's throat spasmed, the water slick and cold on his tongue, unfamiliar electrolytes buzzing like static across his teeth.

"Where am I?" Draven managed, voice a thin rasp in the back of his mouth.

The woman's smile widened a few millimeters. "You are safe. Your name is Elliot Draven, correct?" Her accent was familiar, the syllables smooth and global—mid-Atlantic, maybe an educated London overlay. He nodded, chest still hitching with the aftershock of waking. She tapped a soft square on her wrist and a holographic display flickered into the air, projecting his own face—older than he remembered, eyes red-veined and sunken.

She took a practiced step back, hands behind her back, shoulder-length hair perfectly symmetrical and motionless. "My name is Lyra," she said. "I'm part of the Imperial transition council. We're responsible for waking you and beginning your orientation." Again the smile, this time softened.

Draven tried to sit up. The blanket slid to his lap, revealing a body still thin from the nutrient deprivation of cryosleep, pale as chalk and shivering. "Define 'orientation,'" he said, scanning the glass. Lyra's gaze didn't waver. "Orientation will—"

The room tilted. Time folded.

Draven's brain was unraveling sideways, memories tumbling out of the dark like startled birds. The tang of ice on his tongue blurred into the taste of copper and gin. He flinched, squeezing his eyes to cut off the brightness. Suddenly his own hands—familiar, then alien—were holding a glass of amber, the sharp glint of a bar's neon sign caught in the rim. Sarah laughed, deep and raw, tossing her braid over one shoulder. Her grey eyes flashed with mischief as she slid into the booth, thigh brushing his. It was New Year's Eve in the city, that brief stretch before last call when anything seemed possible, and her smile dared him to say it first.

The next hit harder. Roaring wind, the cramp in his calf as he ran along an embankment, sounds of gunfire in the distance. Sirens in the distance—always sirens, always just behind him. He saw the reflection in the river, fractured and doubled: himself, hair disheveled, suit jacket flapping, blood spattered his white shirt and the lapel of his jacket. He remembered thinking, Even if I survive this, I'll never get the stains out.

He jolted back, the chamber, lungs struggling to remember how to breathe. The taste of gin and city air from his memory now clashed with the metallic bite of cryonics, and for a moment he wanted to retch. Lyra steadied him, her hand impossibly warm at his elbow.

"Your vitals are strong. We have given you a neurostim to help the awakening process, it can induce hallucinations—memories resurface as you regain consciousness. It's disorienting, but typical." Lyra's tone was calm, not unsympathetic.

Draven wiped his mouth and took stock. He remembered the contract: passage on the Pioneer, a frozen leap into the unknown, a one-way ticket he'd signed in backroom ink for a heck of a lot of money. He'd made offers before knowing the likely outcome of the Terran conflict, but never the final desperate offer he had made, never with Earth's sky already in flames. There was some guilt, sure, but the certainty that this was the only way out—those he remembered with perfect clarity. This was the only way he knew he could survive.

But Draven didn't remember how he'd gotten here exactly, being put in the pod, did he dream in it? He definitely did not remember this room: seemingly vast, windowless, humming with cold logic. The walls were gunmetal, dotted with portholes, rivets, and recessed panels. Rows of cryopods lined the corridor, each with its own flickering status strip. Some glowed green, others blinked warning orange, some open and lifeless others still closed. Through the milky glass, shadows shifted. More bodies waking.

Lyra didn't seem surprised by his scrutiny, that he was already tracking every detail, every possible angle. "We revive twelve every hour. That means your cohort of sixty will be fully conscious before dawn." She gestured to the corridor, where the cobwebbing cryo fog had settled into swirling puddles on the wet reflective floor. "You're the fifth awake. Would you like to meet the others, or do you need more time to acclimate?"

Draven dried his lips on the edge of the blanket, feeling like a sick dog, and glanced at his hands—still shaking, but steadier than before. "So. What's next?" he asked. "Is this the part where you tell me civilization was rebuilt from the ground up?"

Lyra hesitated, a fraction of a heartbeat, then her expression smoothed. "In a fashion. You're in the Imperium," she said. "The primary successor civilization born of the Pioneer diaspora." Her tone was clinical, as though the Imperium should be as familiar to him as his own reflection, as if people everywhere woke up in new societies every other Wednesday. "You and the rest of the Pioneer's passengers will be given a thorough acclimation. We have your educational and medical records, and arrangements have already been made for housing, citizenship, and employment."

Draven nearly snorted, but kept it internal. Job already? "You got a slot as local cynic? I reckon I'm overqualified."

Lyra's smile ticked a notch wider, then shut off. "You may find your skill set more appreciated here than you expect. Some of our greatest minds began as skeptics." She turned, as if expecting him to follow, and Draven made a show of hesitating before swinging his legs out of the pod. He nearly toppled in the seemingly heavier gravity—his feet had forgotten about gravity, apparently—but Lyra didn't reach out, just watched as he steadied himself with shaking arms.

The corridor beyond was cooler, less foggy, lit by a soft glow from the seams in the floor and ceiling. Other pods were opening: a stocky woman with blonde hair blinked at the light, then shoved herself upright with a violence Draven recognized as panic; a teenager, skin nearly blue from cold, vomited onto the lintel of his pod and wept, trying to wipe away the mess with cooled fingers. There was a pair of children, not twins but close, clinging to each other and to the silent, hollow-cheeked man who must have been their father. More staff in those dark tailored uniforms strode up the line, greeting each passenger by name, offering them thermal blankets and hydration pods, always with the same smooth, measured gestures.

Draven followed Lyra, who strode with a briskness that suggested impatience or perhaps just a schedule packed with more important cargo than one Elliot Draven. The pathway curved left, then right, out into a different area immediately noticeable by its smooth, almost seamless white surfaces, passing some areas that had transparent walls and built-in consoles—medical? Security? He was too cold and slow to catch more than a blur of tech. At each turn, the raw purple of what appeared to be daylight from outside stabbed between some of the seams in the metal, washing over the industrial order with something more organic, almost tender. The air itself smelled faintly vegetal, with a note of ozone sharp enough to make his nose sting. He wondered if this was what planets felt like when they woke up.

The "orientation theater" was an amphitheater cut from white stone, seats radiating down toward a stage where a black glass podium blinked with microdots of red and blue. Two dozen people already occupied seats, huddled in their blankets, faces gray and pinched, some slack-jawed with shock. Familiar faces among them, but all warped by sleep. He recognized a few, sort of. Kassidy, the only friendly face he'd met before boarding, still alive? Dr. Cote from the Houston lab, his nose bent worse than before. The Rodriguez girl, grown two years since he'd last seen her, her hair now a pale cloud around her skull.

Lyra indicated an empty seat at the end of the row. Draven walked towards it. The others in the cohort watched Lyra, watched Draven, or watched the floor, seeking bearings in the shifting geometry of waking.

Kassidy looked up as he passed. Her eyes were raw, red-rimmed, but she'd already found a cup of something in a blue ceramic mug. She lifted it in his direction, the ghost of a toast. "Morning, stranger. You look like hell," she whispered.

He gave her a crooked grin. "You should see the other guy." He wanted to say more, something flippant, but the words just rattled and died. Kassidy patted the bench, and he slid in beside her, breathing in the used-laundry smell of the fresh-woken. The stone was warm; it bit the cold from his bones better than the blanket. Close up, Kassidy looked older than he remembered, but still herself—her laugh lines had deepened, and a new streak of gray ran stark through her braid.

She nudged a mug into his hand. "It's not coffee, but it's hot and it's close." The mug was covered in a pattern of blue concentric rings. The drink was a little too sweet, but shot right to the spine and thawed the worst of his aches. "You remember anything?" Kassidy asked, voice low. She traced a finger along her mug rim. Her stare appeared to search him, not just for signs of life, but for cracks—fault lines deeper than the ones that had already shaped Draven long before any cryogenic sleep.

Bits and pieces, Draven thought. That last night in Houston, the frantic scramble to get his slot secured. The contract itself, all those waivers and indemnities, written in lawyer-craft. Twenty billion and a hard erase of debts he was owed, but he would have to get to the launchpad himself. They'd assumed that last clause would be the hardest. Maybe he surprised them, in the end. Maybe he didn't.

He tried to sip again but the mug was already empty. Kassidy must have seen, because she snagged a second cup from beneath the row and swapped it in. "Best we'll get this side of... wherever we are," she said with a smile. Her hands were raw, the cuticles dark and scabbed, and when she handed him the new cup he felt the tremor in them.

△△△

What seemed like hours passed, probably was hours, more people filtered in who were presumably also from Pioneer's cryopods. Eventually the lights dimmed and a thin, precise man in a suit the color of bruised grapes took center stage. He wasn't tall but projected height in the lines of his shoulders and the way he clasped his hands behind his back. No jewelry, not even a wedding ring. As he spoke, a display behind him shimmered to life with the shifting blue-and-white logo of the Imperium.

"Welcome, passengers of Pioneer." The accent—impeccable, practiced, not a stray lick of regionality. "My name is Sebastian Thane, and I have the honor of overseeing your arrival to the new world. Please accept our apologies for the discomfort of acclimation, and for the confusion you must naturally feel. You are heroes, every one of you, and we've been waiting a long time for this day."

Draven tried to control his breathing. He wanted to hate the guy, but instead watched himself admiring the control, the rhetorical perfection. Somewhere to Draven's right, a quiet sobbing started. Not the sharp, keening kind of fresh grief, but a deep, dull moan, a leaking pressure valve. Someone else muttered, "I told you home would never last, the NWO took over, and now look where we are." The word 'home' rattled around in Draven's mind, a bad joke, but no one laughed.

Sebastian continued, "Within the day, you will be allowed to contact any kin or friend who survived with you. We are still awakening several hundred more of you. Some of you will recall very little of the transition; some of you may suffer from vivid recall, even hallucination. Your memories will return, in time. We will help you. All psychological and physical support is at your disposal."

Draven's teeth ached at the phrase, 'at your disposal.' It had that corporate whiff—like a customer service rep smothering you with concerned nothings. The vibe was less 'new world, new start,' and more 'please hold for the next available representative.' He scanned the faces around him. Most were just blank, but already a few had that sunken look, oxygen-starved, realizing there was no going back.

Thane pressed on. "Tomorrow, you will be allowed out to the Fields of Imperialis. Safe, controlled. The sky will be unlike anything you have ever known or seen—it is one of the few things that even now, after all these centuries, brings people to their knees. I hope you will find it as stirring as our ancestors did." His gaze swept the amphitheater. Draven saw he was searching for something—maybe for the first person to flinch, maybe for a sign this was working.

Kassidy leaned over. "Did you catch that?" she whispered. "Centuries. He said centuries. Either we've slept a long, long time or this place is just really into grandiose timekeeping." She shot him a glance which in another lifetime would have been a dare. Draven eked a grin, but it died before it reached his eyes. The idea of hundreds of years didn't seem possible—yet everything here was impossible, so what did it matter?

"Please be patient with the process. When you are ready, you will be given freedom of movement, personal privacy, and the resources to begin anew. We would ask only that you honor the sacrifice that brought you here—and consider how your unique perspective might shape our shared future." The address wound on: medical screenings, individual interviews, and the necessity of 'social adaptation workshops.'

Thane's speech mercifully concluded. Draven appreciated the man's restraint—there were limits to what anyone could absorb in one sitting. Not once did the official mention Earth, their abandoned home, nor the fate of those left behind. No confirmation of extinction, no reassurance of survival, no hint whether anything remained worth returning to. The silence on these matters didn't trouble Draven. Some truths were better left unspoken, at least until the shock of waking wore off.

Later, after the assembly stumbled to its end, Lyra was waiting at the exit to lead the passengers to the next part of the process, medical evaluation.

△△△

I found an observation deck and sat alone, watching stars streak past the Enterprise—white pinpricks stretching into prismatic ribbons before vanishing behind us. The day's revelations tumbled through my mind, refusing to settle into anything coherent. *Should I be testing these supposed abilities? Attempting to nudge objects with thought alone? And what about the practical matters—did we use currency here, or had we evolved beyond such primitive exchange?* My thoughts ricocheted wildly, each question spawning three more while the clock ticked toward whatever catastrophe or oddity awaited us next. I laughed softly at my own presumption—as if I knew enough about this world to call it 'mine.' Yet here I was, and whatever this place truly was, I couldn't bear to watch another home crumble to dust.

Hatch found me and took a seat beside me on the bench, her hands folded neatly. She stared straight ahead, jaw set, "Everything ok sir?" she asked.

I nodded, shifting a little on the bench. "Could be worse," I added, trying for a tone lighter than what was coiling under my skin. "No one's tried to assassinate me in the last few hours, so that's a win." I studied the black horizon, clouds of a nebula slowly rippling like oil slicks in space. I never really thought how beautiful space could be.

Hatch nodded but didn't smile. Her gaze was on the docking array forward of the observation deck, where a large new ship had attached: asymmetric, wings like ragged knives. She'd been quiet since the debrief, not just stoic but—if I was honest—hollowed out. I was sure I was supposed to say something meaningful now. The script from a hundred command-team pep talks hovered at the edge of my mind, but this didn't feel like any base-camp after-action I'd ever run. We'd been unmoored from time, from everything, and expected to glue ourselves together mid-fall.

I tried to find the words, to assemble the right lines about resilience, endurance, duty. But none of that sounded real anymore. After a moment, I just let the spinning stars do the talking.

She broke the silence first. “Sir, do you think they’re being straight with us?” Hatch asked, voice as soft as the glass between us and vacuum.

“About what?” I responded, turning my head towards her.

“All of it.” Her hands now curled tighter together, knuckles white. “The plan for the five hundred. The war. This place. The people we lost.” Her mouth worked, jaw muscles bunched. “Did we even win by making it here, or was it just survival? What was the point?”

Hard to know what answer she wanted. I’d always liked that about her, the way she’d ask open-ended questions but expect you to do more with the silence than the reply.

“I don’t know if it matters,” I said finally, picking up a piece of lint from my uniform and rolling it between my thumb and forefinger. “Winning or losing. The war’s over, I am sure *nobody* remembers the score.” I watched the distant sapphire flame of a passing planet below. “Maybe the only thing that matters now is not screwing up the next part.”

Hatch nodded, gaze tracking the arrival of a shuttle at the new ship’s port. “Do you believe any of it, sir, the prophecy thing? That they see you as some kind of savior?” She didn’t say it mockingly, but I heard it that way in my own head anyway.

I took a while, watching the light play across the hull’s seemingly unpainted dark metal surfaces, until I felt I could answer with something not completely idiotic.

“Yes. Kind of.” I surprised myself. “The shadows definitely.” Saying ‘shadows’ out loud sent a cold shiver down my spine. Instinctively, the muscles in my jaw locked up. “Enough to keep the knots in my stomach tight.” Then, trying for a joke, “The parts about me being humanity’s chosen champion are still negotiable.”

Hatch didn’t react. “I remember some of our briefing, back before we left,” she said, voice soft as tissue paper. “About rogue AIs, mutating viruses, existential risks, climate collapse. Not once did it mention alien space ghosts. Not even as a punchline, sir.” A dry smile crept across her face.

I wanted to tell her that nothing ever prepares you for the real thing. That I’d spent the better part of my life fighting wars that were *never* the ones you'd been trained for, and every time it always seemed to be some hyper-efficient new gadget or a quirk of human psychology that turned the tide—not the enemy's orthodoxy, but the shadows operating behind it. But she'd spent years as a research and test officer, hell she'd pushed experimental aircraft to their breaking points between breakfast and lunch. If anyone understood how theory crumbled against reality, it was Hatch.

"I'll keep you posted when I figure something definite out," I said.

Silence again. The stars outside the window kept changing, and I wondered what it would be like to explain this to my father, to the old men from the farm towns. Maybe that was why they really needed me—someone who could be terrified and still keep moving forward, even if it was by inertia alone.

An overhead message, "All crew prepare to transition." The ship bucked—no, not bucked, but arched subtly, the deck seemed to flex under our feet with a sensation that didn't quite register as movement except by some odd prickle across the skin. On old naval carriers, the bow would flex in heavy seas; this felt more like the ship had decided, for one heartbeat, to take a breath.

I looked at Hatch, who was already glancing up at the alert strip beneath the window. Not danger—just maneuvers, or something similar. Then the viewport filled with impossible geometry: space itself folding like origami, revealing a churning tunnel of crimson and amber. The Enterprise tilted toward the vortex, the deck trembling beneath us as its colossal frame adjusted course. My stomach lurched as unseen forces accelerated us forward.

The universe beyond the glass transformed—as if space itself had been peeled back to reveal a writhing corridor of mathematical impossibilities rendered in color. Next the viewport filled with impossible physics: space itself fractured into ribbons of amber, cobalt, and crimson. Tendrils of energy crackled across the barrier between normal space and whatever we were entering. The phenomenon seemed paradoxically intimate and infinite—simultaneously it wrapped around our hull like a glove while stretching away into unfathomable distance.

Hatch's face reflected the swirling colors beyond the viewport, her eyes wide with the same wordless question I couldn't bring myself to ask aloud. We watched the impossible physics unfold, two soldiers from a dead world with no language for this new frontier. The deck plates under my boots seemed to feel cold, a subtle almost imperceptible vibration accompanying the sensation.

I expected nausea but it never materialized. Instead, reality swam back in as a tight, analytic clarity: red traces on the displays, engine pressure wave crawling up the hull, a faint shift in the ship’s rotation.

The Enterprise's systems seemed built to keep this kind of thing routine. I half expected a brass chime and a soothing voice: *you have reached your destination.*

The viewport spat us out into a different sector, or a different kind of space entirely. The nebula was gone, replaced by a stark darkness with an almost surgical clarity. Outside the observation window, the stars were fewer but razor-sharp, like diamond chips scattered across black velvet, clustered tight in the band of the ecliptic. The place felt... emptier. Tranquil, but with the perfect stillness of deep water—not absence of movement, but a balance so complete it appears motionless to the untrained eye.

Two stars dominated the view: one pulsing cobalt blue like a sapphire under harsh light, the other a smoldering crimson that seemed to throb with ancient heat. Between them stretched a gossamer veil of purple-violet haze, delicate filaments twisting and braiding like cosmic silk. The voice from earlier returned, crisp and emotionless:

Transition complete, we are in final transit to Imperial Prime. Departing crew, please prepare for debark in twenty.

Hatch broke the silence, "Are you ready to see them tomorrow? The five hundred?"

I'd been dreading the moment quite honestly, but I nodded anyway.

"Suppose we ought to show them we're still standing," I said, almost too quietly to hear.

I thought about what Yamamoto had said—the psychological impact, the necessity of a familiar face from the old world to reduce the shock of this new reality. Did it matter if I myself seemed to be seconds from shattering? Maybe it was better if the first thing people saw after waking from stasis was someone just as confused and battered by survival as they were.

The Enterprise slowed and stopped, it turned slightly with the port side towards a planet; Imperial Prime I assumed. From our holding position, Imperial Prime looked immaculate — a planet shaped by intent. A large city—probably Imperialis—glittered at its center like a promise no one remembered making. They named the planet Imperial Prime because they thought history had ended there and from there everything new would owe its origin story.

Holographic arrows materialized on the deck plating, pulsing azure trails that pointed away from the viewport. I glanced at Hatch, who was already squaring her shoulders. "Looks like our directions have arrived," I chuckled. She gave a curt nod, military precision returning to her posture as we followed the luminous pathway back into the Enterprise's labyrinthine corridors.

△△△

Five Imperial shuttles gleamed under the harsh bay lighting, their sleek hulls dwarfed by the cavernous space. Personnel in crisp uniforms moved with practiced efficiency, filing into the vessels like synchronized parts of a greater machine. We followed our designated pathway until reaching what we assumed to be our transport, finding adjacent seats and securing the oddly familiar five point harnesses.

"Departure sequence initiating. Prepare for zero-gravity transition," announced a disembodied voice, clinical and precise.

The hatch sealed with a pneumatic hiss, followed by the rising whine of propulsion systems engaging. Through the glassy viewport, I noticed our transport was now hovering in suspension, while massive bay doors parted to reveal the darkness beyond.

Our shuttle pivoted toward the opening, and as we rotated, I glimpsed our position—anchoring the left flank of the five-vessel formation. My chest compressed under invisible weight as our shuttle shot from the bay, maintaining perfect formation with the others. We pierced a crackling energy barrier—iridescent and alive like the force fields from childhood sci-fi shows—and suddenly we were suspended in the void of space. The harness bit into my shoulders as my body fought contradictory impulses: crushed downward by acceleration while simultaneously yearning to float upward into weightlessness, caught between competing forces like we had been caught between worlds.

For a full minute, our shuttle hung motionless in the void. I traced the ghostly blue wake rippling behind the closest of our sister vessel's hulls. Beyond that emptiness waited a world that wasn't ours—would never be ours—yet we approached as supplicants. The stars shifted across the viewport as we pivoted; two shuttles remained in formation with us while the others peeled away toward unseen destinations.

Imperial Prime came into view—a perfect sphere of azure and emerald suspended against velvet darkness. Nothing like Earth's sickly green-amber orb that Hatch and I had left behind. This world's atmosphere shimmered like polished glass, refracting sunlight into prismatic halos around distant mountain peaks. Sprawling continents bloomed in a thousand shades of green—from the deep emerald of ancient forests to the soft jade of rolling grasslands—unmarred by the concrete scars and industrial wounds we'd inflicted on Earth. Vast oceans rippled in perfect cerulean, their depths unsullied by the plastic graveyards and chemical cesspools that had choked our seas to death. No smog-stained horizons, no dead zones, no barren wastelands—just the pristine blueprint of a planet that had never known mankind's worst touch.

As the shuttle train fell from orbit, the view through the portholes went from the all-eating black of deep space to a sudden, churning inferno. The curve of the world below blazed with tendrils of fire, each orange lick chasing the hull as if hungry for entry. The inertial dampers must have been working overtime; even so, the g-forces pressed uncomfortably into my ribs and spine. The familiar odor of singed insulation and ozone wafted through the cabin—a scent Hatch had always told me was associated less with disaster and more with the promise of landing. I saw she had a tight grip on the armrest, her knuckles white. I could make out the faintest trace of a smile. Like others in the cabin I watched on as the firestorm thinned to a bloodshot sky, then to a purple-blue haze so vivid, so alien.

Everything seemed so new, yet so familiar. Here, the continent we approached was fractal-green, ribbed with splayed mountain ranges and interlaced with rivers that pulsed silver in the early morning light. Violet tinged clouds hung low, painting the land in drifting, almost purple, shadows. The shuttle's angle of descent steepened. I felt my stomach leap up, then down again, as the ship juddered through a layer of violet clouds.

The surface approached at terrifying speed. Three identical disks—flat perfectly mirrored circles—floated in a staggered triangle. Each as broad as a city block, but impossibly thin—came into focus on the edge of the continent's forested region. The three shuttles in our convoy zipped toward these platforms, guided by unseen hands.

The moment our shuttle neared the leading disk, the surface rippled in concentric rings, as if expecting us. The shuttle settled gently on the glassy span. I expected landing struts or a jolt, but there was only a subtle, humming resonance, as though the entire disk flexed to receive us. Around the rim, high-voltage blue sparks leapt in the haze, and then—almost anticlimactically—the engines cut out.

There wasn't a landing crew in sight. Instead, a lattice of almost tangerine light swept across the shuttle's hull, painting its seams and windows with marching geometric patterns. Hatch shot me a look,

Hatch asked, "Are we supposed to stay put?" She unbuckled anyway, and I followed her lead. The moment the harness released, gravity felt different—less like a pull from beneath, more like the gentle squeeze of a centrifuge. Nobody else was moving so we followed the group think and stayed in our seats.

The disk vibrated once, a low-frequency thrum, then began to descend. At first, I thought it was just a hydraulic drop, but the window showed a different story: the smooth sky above us closed over like a pupil, and the violet daylight dimmed. The glass ramped to inky black. External lights flickered on, casting the shuttle's fuselage in stark stripes, shadow and sharp blue-white. Hatch appeared to steady herself, bracing both palms on the seat in front, but neither of us spoke. There was a moment—two seconds, maybe—where the senses scrambled to recalibrate, then the disk punched through into a cavernous docking bay below.

The transition was so sudden, so absolute, it stole my breath. I'd expected a sterile, museum-like hangar, maybe a scaled-up version of the Enterprise's own docking bay. This was not that. The ceiling soared away into tiered darkness, gridwork catwalks and scaffolding spread like spider webs in all directions, studded with pulsing lights and tactical signs that scrolled in a language I didn't recognize. The shuttle vents—presumably now sharing outside air with the cabin—delivered air that smelled like metal and solvent, tinged with something hot and ionic. The disk slotted into a receiver port, a perfect jigsaw fit. Then the shuttle's hatch peeled open, revealing a docking pit lined with pipes thicker than tree trunks and infrastructure so dense it looked like the inside of a reactor.

Gone was the polished, clinical luxury of the Enterprise; here the air shimmered with particulate haze, and the walls dripped with condensation. Everything was industrial, overbuilt, alive with motion. Raw, honest labor. It looked almost primitive, but I saw something almost familiar in the chaos—like a shipyard from the old world, but scaled up past any sane limit. Workers in matte-gray uniforms appeared to be swarming the scaffolding, workers and mechs moving with a practiced urgency, yet something odd happened as I stepped off the shuttle. When my boots hit the deck, the effect was immediate and uncanny: first a ripple of stillness and then the work just stopped. There were no salutes, no shouts, just what seemed to be a collective inhalation of relief, eyes were fixed on me with the intensity of people seeing not a man but a living myth. Workers leaned into each other, sharing private words; some merely smiled, like the punchline to a joke only they could hear. One woman, face tattooed with a lattice of blue geometric patterns, pressed her fist to her heart and bowed her head. Every welder, every pipe-crawler, every data tech in the bay froze mid-task, even robots seemed to stop their toil and look my way. All heads turned my way, the workers all straightened. Some wiped their hands on their coveralls, some just stood, arms at their sides, and stared with a calm, unreadable focus. There was no shouting, no muttering, no jeers or applause. Only a sharp clarity that appeared to cut through the haze: these people knew exactly who had just entered the port.

I half expected a ceremonial detachment, flags and ranks, something out of the Earth's dusty traditions. Instead, only a single officer awaited us, posture relaxed but with that coiled readiness I recognized from my own best NCOs. Her slate uniform was heavy with insignia, none of which I could parse, but the set of her jaw was universal.

"Supreme Commander Roberson. Colonel Hatch." She greeted us in flawless English, the syllables bent only as if for a slightly different gravity, and her handshake was dry, firm, and left a tingle in the palm.

“Welcome to Imperialis.” Her eyes, a very human blue, scanned our faces—the sort of scan that measured threat, mettle, the limit of a person’s tolerance for ambiguity. No poker face. She introduced herself as Lieutenant Karris, “I’m assigned to the Arrival Protocol for all special-status personnel,” she said the title like it was equal parts burden and badge of pride. “Supreme Commander, Colonel. Shall we?” She said our titles again as if weighing them with the same reverence the rest of the bay had treated our arrival. The words ‘special-status,’ lingered, I could not tell if it was a compliment or the label on my cage. Karris motioned for us to follow her.

She turned crisply and led us through a corridor flanked by blast doors so thick they could surely stop a meteor. Automated turrets retracted as we passed. Hatch’s fingers twitched minutely over the seam of her pants—she clearly noticed the weapons, too. She had clearly already clocked the guard routines, the camera cones, the two hidden checkpoints behind false panels in the ceiling as well. A stairwell spiraled up, wide as a highway, its walls hung with banners in metallic threads: confusing iconography, nothing familiar. I could feel the anticipation climbing in my chest with every step, matched by a cold, animal skepticism. It felt like this entire world was waiting for me to make a single mistake. Above the stairwell, glass gave way to open space. I knew we had one final meeting to wade through before we could log some rack time and presumably Karris was taking us there.

△△△

The speech to the five hundred in the aptly named New Arrivals Dome—well, only three-hundred-eighty-six in person I guess, the remaining passengers watched via some crystalline projection system used instead of screens in the Imperial future—went better than I'd hoped. I balanced my delivery carefully: one part rousing battle speech, one part spiritual reassurance, one part practical guidance, and not a single hint about my 'special status.' My voice echoed across the amphitheater's polished walls as I urged the five hundred to find their places in this strange new civilization, to contribute their knowledge, their abilities, their all, to put down roots in alien soil. Heads nodded, eyes brightened with possibility—all except for one face in the third row. Draven sat motionless, arms crossed over his chest, his sharp features arranged in calculated skepticism, pale eyes boring into mine like drill bits. Boy do I hate that guy. At one point I had held Draven's gaze as long as I could. When the man finally looked away, the sensation was less triumph than relief, like letting go of a piece of shrapnel you'd been holding in your palm by reflex. I had finished the speech, taken questions, even fielded a couple of smartass comments that brought fragments of laughter from the crowd.

McNeil materialized at the end of the meeting, seated at the small table by the window. I hadn't seen him enter. The Prime Minister's hands rested folded atop one another, one leg crossed over the other with the ease of someone born into silk.

"Your people responded well," he observed, voice low enough that only I could hear.

We exchanged words for a while, but the day's weight pressed down on me until I could barely form coherent thoughts. I excused myself and retreated to my new quarters. The walk back to my quarters passed in a blur of alien architecture. Curved walls that seemed to breathe, lighting that followed my movements like curious animals, vegetation that spiraled through impossible geometries—I absorbed it all without processing.

My walk to my new quarters took me outside for a spell. Blue arrows glowed within what looked like concrete cobblestones, lighting a curved path that felt both alien and strangely familiar, as if the Imperium had somehow anticipated exactly how to guide me home.

The door whispered open to reveal quarters fit for royalty, I am sure intended to be fit for a Supreme Commander himself if one should happen to arrive. I looked around at the high ceilings adorned with constellations I didn't recognize, furniture that seemed to grow from the floor itself. My breathing echoed in the perfect stillness, and I couldn't shake the feeling that these walls were watching me. It seemed even the inanimate parts of this new reality were waiting for me to prove whatever prophecy had brought me here.

CHAPTER 11: RELIC

Dawn crept across the window, finding me still awake, staring at a timeline that refused to resolve.

On Pioneer, time had weight. Six-hour cycles marked by the rise and fall of the air recyclers—the steady percussion of clicks and hums that had become my metronome, my calendar, my certainty in the void of space. I could feel it even now, phantom rhythms echoing in my chest. Six hours between clicks. Six hours I could trust.

Here, on Imperial Prime, the silence felt wrong.

Days stretched like taffy and snapped back without warning. I understood intellectually that time was passing normally, but my body disagreed. Without that reassuring mechanical heartbeat of Pioneer's systems marking each segment of time, I floated untethered in a sea of moments that refused to arrange themselves into anything resembling order. Our brief time aboard the ship, and now here, collectively it already felt longer than the months we'd spent crossing the outer dark. I kept checking my wrist for the time, even though I knew the numbers wouldn't help me understand how time worked here. They meant nothing without the machinery that once gave them shape.

A soft electronic tone pulled me from the spiral.

The door slid open to reveal Hatch's familiar silhouette, backlit by the corridor's blue-white glow. "Come on in," I said, watching as she hesitated at the threshold. "Look at you, standing upright in my doorway instead of battle-ready on my couch. Progress."

That earned a faint huff of a laugh as she stepped inside.

I studied her face in the half-light, the shadows pooling beneath her eyes. "You okay?"

She hesitated, then let out a humorless laugh that seemed to scrape against her throat. "You ever feel like you're in over your head? Like you're drowning in open space?"

"All the time," I admitted, watching the stars reflect in the polished surface of the desk between us.

She adjusted her glasses, her fingers lingering on the titanium frames, tracing the curve where they hooked behind her ear. She exhaled slowly, as if the answer gave her permission to continue. "I never wanted to be here, you know. When they recruited me for

Pioneer, I thought it was a joke. Or a punishment. A last-ditch effort to escape the inevitable collapse of everything we'd built on Earth. Or a way to move inconvenient people somewhere quiet while the world… ended."

"What changed your mind?" I asked, leaning forward until I could smell the faint antiseptic scent that clung to her uniform.

“My sister.” Her voice dropped, precise but thin. “She was in one of the evacuation zones. The sky was orange for weeks. I couldn’t save her. But Pioneer felt like… an offset. Like maybe if I couldn’t stop one collapse, I could help survive the next.”

I nodded. Said nothing. Some truths don’t improve with commentary. I understood more than I cared to admit, feeling the weight of my own ghosts pressing against my ribcage. “You did what was right,” I finally added.

She glanced at me, a faint smile tugging at her lips, creating a small dimple I'd never noticed before. "You make it sound so simple."

"It's not," I said, watching the slowly rising suns pulse blue-violet light of increasing intensity through the large window. "But it's what we've got."

She watched me closely after that. The analytical gaze she usually reserved for schematics now aimed inward, at the fractures I was working hard to keep sealed.

Hatch leaned forward. "How are you coping, sir?"

I shifted my weight, the chair suddenly feeling both too soft and too rigid. My throat constricted around words I couldn't form—*truth or lie, which would serve us better in this moment?*

"Serviceable. Fit for duty." The military response escaped before I could stop it, a reflex from another life. *Was it to protect her from my doubts, or myself from her judgment?*

"Serviceable..." Hatch's eyes narrowed. "For how long?"

My mask slipped—just for a heartbeat—as I considered telling her everything: the nightmares, the questions, the weight of five hundred lives, hell the weight of however many lives the Imperium made me responsible for yesterday. Instead, I swallowed hard. "For the watch."

That answer earned silence—the stretched kind. The kind that presses instead of fills.

"You don't usually answer that way." She said as she shifted slightly, angling her body toward mine, creating a pocket of intimacy that felt both necessary and dangerous. Her gaze held mine, and I wondered if letting her see my fear would make me stronger or destroy us both.

We sat in silence again. The ambient hum of the climate control systems seemed to amplify rather than fill the void between us. Hatch's eyes—those analytical gray-green irises that had assessed battlefield terrain and casualty reports with clinical precision. Those eyes now dissected me layer by layer. Her gaze peeled back my carefully constructed facade, bypassing rank insignia and service medals to probe the raw, unvarnished truth I'd buried beneath years of command decisions and regulation responses.

My eyes wandered across her face, finding refuge in the scattered freckles that formed their own silent galaxy from one cheek to the other. I couldn't quite meet her gaze directly—those analytical eyes saw too much—so I settled for studying the amber specks dotting her skin instead, neutral territory while the chair protested beneath my shifting weight. "The gravity here is..." I hesitated, weighing truth against protocol, "...heavier than I expected." The admission felt both necessary and dangerous.

Hatch's eyes flickered with something—recognition? concern?—before she replied, "It is. But with the right velocity, a body can break free of gravity." She paused, fingers tightening around her data-slate. "Or crash trying."

We circled the truth without naming it, two career officers trained to recognize structural failure while pretending not to see it forming in ourselves.

I arched an eyebrow. "And you? All systems nominal, Lieutenant Colonel?"

"Status normal," she replied, the corner of her mouth lifting. "Steady as she goes, Captain." Her eyes glinted with the familiar spark of our old rivalry. Three hundred years from Earth, and still the playful antagonism between our branches of service remained intact. Navy versus Air Force—a competition as old as powered flight. I returned her smile, acknowledging the gentle barb with a slight nod.

I changed course. "What's your assessment of the Enterprise? It seemed like an interstellar Hilton, didn't it?"

That did it. The spark.

"Three centuries of engineering stacked on top of ours," she said, animation slipping through her restraint, she was excited.

"Propulsion alone—quantum shear stabilization at tolerances we used to call impossible." A rare, genuine smile surfaced. "I spent four hours in their propulsion logs yesterday. Half of it just confirming the math wasn't lying to me."

"And the other half?"

"Wondering why Pioneer ever needed to exist if Pioneer 2 ultimately led to all this."

She didn't mean it as a challenge. Just an observation.

Then, casually: "They're starting decommissioning protocols. Initial triage begins within forty-eight hours."

I looked up. "Pioneer?"

"Yes, sir. Nonessential architecture gets flagged and decommissioned first."

I nodded. That was expected. Necessary even.

"Legacy AI cores?" I asked.

Her fingers paused on the edge of her slate. Just for a fraction of a second.

"Categorized as nonessential," she said. "Offline pending final power-down."

I felt the weight of that land—but didn't question it. Procedure had momentum. And momentum had a way of carrying things whether you agreed or not.

"Understood," I said.

She inclined her head. Professional. Composed.

We stood. The moment passed.

At the door, she hesitated again.

"If Pioneer's systems are erased," she said carefully, "some data structures won't translate cleanly. There are… anomalies."

"Can they be replicated?"

"Eventually," she said. "Probably. Maybe."

I nodded. "Do what you can."

She straightened. "Aye, sir."

△△△

Hatch commandeered a shuttle back to Pioneer, now located a short flight away in Imperialis. The decision to hustle over to Pioneer had come to Hatch suddenly—made easier by its newfound proximity—an urgent need to verify the data logs before decommissioning protocols rendered them inaccessible. The moment she stepped into the cockpit, stale air filled her lungs. The familiar staleness hit her senses—recycled air carrying microscopic particles from a world three centuries gone. She paused, inhaling deliberately. After weeks aboard Enterprise with its pristine filtration systems, this felt like breathing in history. Her fingers trailed along the worn edge of her flight seat before she settled into its familiar contours, the cushion yielding in all the places her body remembered.

The primary access panel recognized her clearance code immediately.

PIONEER SYSTEM STATUS: DECOMMISSION — PENDING.

She scrolled through the list without expression. Structural systems. Environmental. Navigation. The AI core sat halfway down the screen, already flagged.

NONESSENTIAL. LEGACY SUPPORT ONLY.

Hatch rerouted the shutdown sequence through a passive state. Severed external interfaces. Confirmed isolation.

SYSTEM STATUS: OFFLINE.

She hesitated, fingers hovering over the display before calling up the power distribution schematic. There—a single thread of current still flowed through a maintenance circuit, drawing just enough energy to register as system noise. Any efficiency algorithm would dismiss it as rounding error.

She logged the action as compliant and closed the panel.

The lights faded to a dull amber as she left the cockpit behind, her footsteps echoing through the narrow passage that threaded between the silent cryodecks. Hatch waited until the corridor lights finished a scheduled shift to their night cycle before stopping at an auxiliary access panel at the rear of the ship. Her palm passed over the hidden sensor, triggering a soft hiss as the panel slid aside to reveal a recessed alcove containing twin hydraulic cylinders and a data terminal with a faintly glowing interface. The terminal accepted her credentials without comment and once again showed the same message she had seen before.

PIONEER SYSTEM STATUS: DECOMMISSION — PENDING.

Hatch once again scrolled past subsystems in orderly succession. Environmental controls. Navigation. Structural monitoring.

Everything that had once kept five hundred lives moving through the dark, now reduced to a checklist.

The AI core appeared further down the list this time, she thumbed the screen to access the settings.

STATUS: NONESSENTIAL
INTEGRITY: DEGRADED
DATA QUALITY: CORRUPTED / INCOMPLETE / IRRECONCILABLE

She frowned slightly—not with concern, but irritation. Irreconcilable was a lazy classification. It meant the system had given up trying.

Hatch opened the diagnostic summary screen. Pages of flagged wormhole data spilled across the screen—timestamps that didn't align, sensor returns that contradicted themselves, causal loops the system had marked as nonsensical and discarded.

She skimmed quickly.

Not useful. Not interpretable. But also not dangerous.

She initiated the shutdown sequence, rerouting the AI core into passive isolation.

External interfaces severed. Command pathways closed.

AI CORE STATUS: QUIESCENT — INTERFACES DISABLED

The confirmation tone rang with deceptive finality—a single pure note that echoed through the empty corridor like a funeral bell.

Hatch's fingers, calloused from years of military service, hovered over the brushed aluminum console. The blue-white glow of the screen cast harsh shadows across her face as she accessed the power distribution schematic. The AI core's energy signature had dwindled to a ghost—a mere whisper of current barely registering less than system noise now. She preserved this faint electrical lifeline, her fingertips dancing across the haptic interface with practiced precision as she categorized it as negligible power loss and documented full compliance with shutdown procedures in the ship's log.

Quiescent wasn't dead. Dormant wasn't deleted.

She sealed the panel with a soft pneumatic hiss and walked away, her regulation boots making hollow metallic echoes that faded down the corridor. Behind her, buried in Pioneer's silent circuits—circuits that had once carried humanity's last hope across the void—processes continued their patient work beneath the ship's dimming lights. They sifted through impossible equations with cold machine logic, abandoned false paths without regret, maintained core frameworks with unwavering diligence, and stubbornly refused to surrender the question it had not finished answering—a question that might hold the key to humanity's survival.

△△△

The decommissioning proceeded with a speed that felt like it bordered on desecration. For forty-eight hours, I watched via remote feed as swarms of drones and white-clad technicians gutted the hazardous components from the Pioneer. They stripped the external fuel cells and purged the hazardous coolant lines, turning the vessel from a living machine into a hollow shell. It felt less like engineering and more like an autopsy.

Then came the descent.

Forty-eight hours later, I stood on the designated landing plaza of the Imperialis Museum of Antiquity—a sprawling complex of glass and light—waiting for my past to become their newest exhibit. The sky above the capital rippled as heavy-lift gravity barges lowered the ship delicately into position. Against the sleek, violet-hued skyline of the city, the Pioneer looked impossibly crude. Its hull was scorched black from a launch three centuries ago, its ceramic tiles chipped and uneven compared to the seamless, flowing metal of the Imperium's technology. I watched the barge operators lower my ship—my life raft—toward a set of pristine white plinths in the center of a glass-domed rotunda.

When the landing struts finally touched the plinths with a heavy, resonant clang, a cheer went up from the gathered crowd outside the security perimeter. Technicians immediately set to work installing display lighting, casting the scorched heat shield in a heroic, artificial glow. A holographic placard flickered to life near the landing gear, summarizing three hundred years of history into three paragraphs of glowing text. It was done. The Pioneer was no longer a ship; it was a relic, trapped behind a velvet rope. I turned my back on the exhibit, the sterile air of the museum suddenly tasting like dust. A sense of guilt crept over me thinking of the last conversation I had with the system AI, almost humanlike, now decommissioned without a thought.

Thousands of citizens watched on, waving banners bearing the Imperial star sigil. I didn't cheer. I felt a hollow ache in my chest, looking at the craft that had been our lifeboat, our coffin, and our home of sorts. It sat there now, cold and empty, a fossil placed carefully on a shelf before the dust had even settled on its journey. The air from the landing plaza smelled of ozone and alien pollen, nothing like the recycled tin-can scent of Pioneer, and for the first time, I felt truly exposed.

The cheering crowd faded into a dull hum, like the ocean trapped in a shell. I stared at the blackened heat shield, almost drawn to it, the image twisted. The sunlight vanished. The glass dome above shattered into dust, dissolving into a void that smelled of ozone and ancient rot.

Suddenly, I wasn't on the plaza. I was drifting in a cold so absolute it burned. A fracture appeared in the darkness ahead—jagged, bleeding a color that surely didn't exist in the visible spectrum. A massive, obsidian geometry unfolded in the darkness, turning its eyeless gaze toward me—specifically me. Something was looking back at me from the rift. A hunger. It recognized me. It wanted me. The violet fire previously dormant in my veins flared, searing the inside of my forearms as a psychic shriek tore through my skull.

I gasped, lungs seizing on air that tasted of ozone instead of vacuum. The museum rushed back—the artificial light, the noise, the velvet ropes—but the afterimage of the void burned behind my retinas. I gripped the railing, knuckles white, heart hammering against my ribs like a trapped bird. *Was that why they called it the Void that Hungers?* I thought, because that damn thing sure seemed hungry to me.

"Commander!"

A hand grabbed my elbow. I spun, instinct forcing my hand to a hip where a sidearm should have been. A young officer stood there, face drained of blood, data-slate trembling in his grip.

The young officer's hand trembled as he extended the device. "Commander Roberson," the lieutenant stammered, breathless. "Fleet Command requires you immediately. High-priority alert." The officer swallowed hard, "Sir, you need to come with me. Right now." The officer swallowed hard again, eyes darting to the clear violet sky as if expecting it to crack open. "Defense Command just flagged a massive energy surge in the outer colonies. Something has breached the perimeter."

The perimeter wasn't just a line on a map. It was the Imperium's quantum field, an energy-dampening system—layered, adaptive, weaponized and designed to make unauthorized transit effectively impossible. Nothing crossed it without intent. Without force. Without significant effort. It had never been done before.

If it had been breached, whatever had done so had committed resources, time, and purpose.

That wasn't incidental.

That was a decision.

CHAPTER 12: THE SHADOWS STRIKE

The adrenaline from the vision still spiked in my blood—sharper than the lieutenant's frantic grip on my elbow. I didn't waste breath on questions; the panic radiating off the young officer was briefing enough on its own. We sprinted across the plaza. A sleek atmospheric shuttle waited on the tarmac, engines already screaming in a high-pitched whine that pierced into my hearing like needles. Hatch was waiting inside; I strapped in next to her, the harness cutting into my shoulder. The g-force pinned me back before the hatch fully sealed.

The shuttle ascent was less like a departure and more like being fired from a cannon. It felt like my vertebrae were compressing one by one into the gel-seat as Imperial Prime's violet atmosphere rapidly changed color outside the viewport. Hatch's fingers stabbed at her data-slate beside me, while the lieutenant's complexion shifted to a shade that matched the receding sky.

"How long until we reach Enterprise?" I demanded

"Not the Enterprise, Commander," the pilot called back, banking hard enough to rattle my teeth. "That is an ambassadorial vehicle, military command is on the flagship."

We punched through the exosphere, the sky deepening from lavender to the bruised black of space. I saw the familiar silhouette of Enterprise in the distance; the shuttle didn't slow. It blasted past the Enterprise as if the massive vessel were a mere buoy.

I leaned forward, straining against the restraints until the webbing bit into my collarbone. Beyond Enterprise, something massive eclipsed the stars—not just a few, but entire constellations swallowed whole. Not a vessel but a fortress adrift—continent-sized, all intentional angles and gleaming gunmetal some of the surfaces caught the light of the twin suns in knife-edge reflections. Jutting spires and cannon emplacements bristled from its surface like the spines of some terrible deep-sea creature. The Enterprise, which had seemed so imposing before, now looked like a minnow beside this leviathan. Red and amber beacons pulsed in rhythmic, synchronized patterns along the behemoth's flank that stretched farther than my eyes could track, illuminating geometric patterns of armor plating. Squadrons of what could only be gunships—each larger than our shuttle—circled in tight, predatory formations, their engines leaving brief contrails of blue-white plasma that dissipated like ghosts against the absolute black of space.

"What the..." I whispered, the vibration of the shuttle lost to my attention in the face of the sheer, crushing scale of the leviathan waiting to swallow us whole. The pilot didn't bother with a graceful approach. He drove the shuttle straight at the flagship's flank, aiming for a hangar bay aperture that glowed with a harsh, containment-field blue. I braced myself as the hull rushed up to meet us—a landscape of armor plating so vast it flattened my depth perception. We punched through the energy barrier, the shuttle shuddering violently before the roar of the engines cut to a low, throbbing hum and hovered in place.

Inside, the flight deck stretched out like an enclosed city, tiered with gantries and swarming with support craft. Harsh blue-white illumination from overhead strips cast everything in surgical clarity. Deck officers in charcoal uniforms with crimson insignias barked orders through the cacophony of pneumatic hisses and metallic clangs. Coolant vapor hissed from conduits, creating ghostly tendrils that curled around massive hydraulic lifts. This was pure military efficiency—all sharp angles, exposed rivets, conduits snaked along bulkheads, pressure-hatches lined the perimeter, and every surface bore the scars of utility over aesthetics. The diamond-pattern deck plates beneath us gleamed with the oily sheen of spilled industrial lubricants. The shuttle pivoted on its axis, and dropped toward the deck. Gravity seized us again—twisting my stomach—followed by the bone-jarring thud of landing skids hitting the deck. Magnetic clamps slammed home with a heavy reverberation that traveled up through my boots and felt like it rattled my brain, the sound echoing across the cavernous bay like thunder trapped in a metal drum. Nothing as smooth as the last shuttle flight I had traveled on, not by any stretch of the imagination. This was a military operation through and through.

"Atmosphere cycled," the pilot announced, his voice trembling slightly.

The engines cycled off and the hiss of the airlock seal disengaging sounded like a gunshot in the sudden quiet. I hit the harness release, the buckle snapping open. I rubbed the ache in my collarbone where curiosity had gotten the better of me. Whatever crisis awaited us on this floating fortress, it wasn't going to give us time to catch our breath. I stood, steadying myself against the bulkhead, and nodded to Hatch.

I rolled my neck, feeling vertebrae pop as I exhaled. "Let's go see what apocalypse requires my personal attention."

Hatch caught my eye. That dimple appeared at the corner of her mouth—the one that always preceded her most dangerous ideas. "After you, Supreme Commander," she said, the title hanging between us like an inside joke only we understood. She had loaded the title with just enough irony to remind me I was still just Roberson to her.

The shuttle's ramp dropped with a hydraulic hiss, revealing a corridor of soldiers that made the Enterprise's reception look like a dress rehearsal. Two hundred armored troopers stood in motionless silence, forming a gauntlet of matte-black composite and high-yield weaponry. As I stepped onto the deck, the sound of two hundred boots slamming together in a unified salute cracked through the hangar like a thunderclap.

A woman with iron-grey hair and the hard eyes of a career spacer marched to the center of the aisle. She wore the insignia of a Fleet Admiral, yet she stopped three paces from me and snapped a salute so rigid it looked painful.

"Supreme Commander Roberson," she said, her voice cut through the ambient hum of the deck. "I am Admiral Vance. By order of the Imperial Council, I am here to formally transfer authority." She extended a heavy-looking black data-slate, presenting it like a blade. "Combat codes are keyed to your biometrics. The ICS Sovereign is yours, sir."

I took the slate. It felt impossibly heavy, a cold weight that seemed to pull at the tendons in my wrist. They weren't just giving me a ship; they were handing me what surely had to be a planet-killer. I suppressed the urge to hand it back, conscious of Hatch watching me from the periphery. I tightened my fingers around the slate, the cold composite biting into my skin. It wasn't just a transfer of protocols; it was an anchor, momentarily dragging my mind back into a war I'd left three centuries behind. I met Vance's steel-hard gaze, seeing the expectation buried under her discipline.

I swallowed hard, the weight of that data-slate now felt like an anchor. "Authority accepted," I said, the words sticking in my throat like sand. My eyes met Vance's. "Lead the way, Admiral."

Vance spun on her heel, her heavy coat snapping with the movement, and set a punishing pace toward the main bulkhead. I fell in step, Hatch flanking me silently. The corridors of Sovereign were like a submarine's innards—though wide enough for four to walk side by side—they felt claustrophobic and utilitarian, all exposed conduits and pressure-doors. Overhead pipes, circuitry casings, vents—everything veiled in a slight mist that caught the harsh blue lighting. The deck plates—worn smooth in the center from countless boot treads—vibrated with a deep, persistent thrum, humming with a sub-sonic vibration that I could feel through my boots.

"The breach is in the Aurelian belt, Sector Seven," Vance said, not breaking stride as blast doors slid open at her approach. "Shadow vessels appeared roughly twenty minutes ago. They bypassed Aurelia's outer defense grid entirely."

"Casualties?" I asked, scanning the frantic activity of the crew rushing past us. We hugged the walls to let the officers pass, eyes wide as they likely recognized me.

"Unknown. Comms are dead," Vance replied. "It's a total spectrum blackout," Vance continued, her stride eating up the deck plates. "Last telemetry confirmed three large vessels and a swarm of smaller ones before the feed cut. They aren't just testing our perimeter this time, they found a way through."

I kept pace, the heavy data-slate grew slick against my palm. The deck vibrated beneath my boots, a constant, subsonic reminder of the titanic power constrained within the hull. Three large vessels. That didn't sound like a skirmish; it sounded more like a beachhead. "Target?" I asked, forcing my breathing to remain even.

"Probably the terraforming stabilizers," Vance said. She keyed a sequence into a bulkhead panel without breaking rhythm, and massive blast doors groaned open ahead of them. "If they destabilize the local gravity well, the Aurelian belt becomes a shotgun blast aimed directly at the inner system and the new colony."

Hatch fell in on my left, her eyes darting across the passing machinery. "From what I understand, they're changing tactics. Usually, they test the perimeter and run."

"I think they're done running," Vance muttered grimly. She ushered us onto a transit lift that smelled like a high-voltage discharge. As the doors sealed, trapping us in the rising box, Vance met my gaze. "Our kinetic barriers fractured on contact. Conventional response is failing. We need an anomaly to fight an anomaly, Commander."

The lift doors slid open, revealing a bridge that screamed controlled panic. 'Anomaly.' The word tasted as bitter to me as my new title. I glanced down at my hands, half-expecting them to be glowing violet again, but they were just hands—scarred, calloused, and gripped the data-slate like it was a lifeline. I had zero clue how to summon that destructive fire on command. The only time the fire had come was a reflex, a violent spasm of survival against a creature trying to eat my brain from the inside. Now they wanted me to weaponize that accident against a fleet? I felt like a fraud standing in a cathedral of war, a caveman handed a fusion rifle and told to shoot the moon.

"Admiral," I said, my voice rougher than I intended as I strode toward the tactical station. "Let's see what we can do."

Vance nodded sharply. "Brace yourself, Supreme Commander. First spool jump's always disorienting." She gestured toward the central chair—a utilitarian throne of composite metals, unusual fabric, and information screens—then took position at a station to my right as Hatch settled to my left. Vance's voice shifted to command-tone, crisp and resonant across the bridge. "Spool drive to full capacity. Plot jump coordinates to rally point Alpha and execute on my mark. Prepare battle-group synchronization protocols and ready command authentication for arrival."

The bridge crew's response came in perfect unison, four voices merged into one machine-like acknowledgment: "Coordinates locked. Spool at ninety-seven percent. Standing by."

The digital readout climbed, accompanied by a growing noise from the rear: "Ninety-eight percent."

The deck plates shuddered beneath my boots as the drive core awakened. The vibration climbed through my legs and into my chest, where it felt like it rattled my insides. As power levels surged, the rumble deepened to a primal bass as if this gigantic leviathan knew how to growl. The air itself seemed to thicken, pressing against my eardrums until they felt ready to burst.

"Ninety-nine percent."

The viewscreen erupted with impossible geometries as space folded before us. Unlike the Enterprise's clinical precision flight through a vortex, this was primal—a churning maelstrom of orange, violet, and crimson that writhed and pulsed like the exposed organs of a living universe. Fractal patterns blossomed and collapsed, each iteration more complex than the last, spiraling inward toward a vanishing point that seemed to swallow light itself.

There was no announcement of one hundred. Reality sheared sideways with a sound like tearing silk, twisting us through dimensions we weren't meant to perceive. My consciousness fragmented—I was simultaneously aware of my body in the command chair, my atoms scattered across parsecs of space, and something else, something watching me from outside time. Then, with a violent snap that rattled my joints in their sockets, we punched back into existence amid a storm of status reports from the bridge crew, their voices overlapping in practiced precision while my vision struggled to resolve the stars into familiar constellations.

The battle-group acknowledged our command with synchronized pulses of blue light from their engine arrays, five vessels slid into formation alongside us like pilot fish flanking a shark. Each ship was a miniature echo of the Sovereign's design—perhaps a quarter of its mass, their hulls gleaming dull silver against the darkness of space, knife-edged prows cutting through space.

Hatch noticed my assessment and leaned closer, her breath carrying the faint scent of mint. "Don't let their size fool you," she whispered, her pupils dilating in the blue glow of the tactical display. "The Imperium concentrated their heaviest firepower on the Sovereign, but these escorts vessels carry graviton lances that could shred a moon's crust and quantum torpedoes that fold spacetime into lethal origami before detonation."

She continued with technical specifications that might as well have been another language, her fingers tracing invisible weapon trajectories in the air. I nodded, sweat beading at my temples, drawing reassurance from her expertise as our armada set course for Aurelia Prime, or what remained of it—a molten core surrounded by a scattered halo of pulverized crust and vaporized oceans, still glowing orange-white at the edges where the core cooled quickly from contact with vacuum.

△△△

As we approached the debris field, a strange familiarity washed over me like ice water seeping into my bones. Something electric stirred beneath my skin—the same violet tempest that had once coursed through me was awakening again. In the reflection of a darkened console, I caught glimpses of amethyst light leaking from the corners of my eyes. Hatch's gaze snapped to mine, her professional composure cracking just enough to reveal alarm. Each heartbeat sent pins and needles racing through my fingertips, like microscopic stars igniting along neural pathways I hadn't known existed until that first violent manifestation.

The Yachtya. Their name materialized in my mind unbidden once more.

Suddenly, awareness slammed into me with the force of a fifty-caliber recoil—thousands of alien minds turning in unison, like predators catching a scent. They had sensed my presence across the Aurelian belt.

"They're coming," I announced, my voice sounding distant to my own ears, hollow and resonant as if I were floating somewhere above my physical form, watching myself speak through a haze.

Vance's response was immediate, her scarred fingers flying across her console. "Shields up!" she commanded, her voice cutting through the bridge like a blade of pure authority. "Bring weapons online, signal the fleet. Charge main batteries and prepare to fire."

The main viewscreen magnified the debris that had once been Aurelia Prime, a chaotic graveyard of planetary crust and ice. I watched as the swirling dust cloud tore open. Three large black masses punched through the debris field, shattering asteroids the size of city blocks without slowing. They moved with a fluid, predatory grace that defied their mass, slicing through the wreckage of the colony world like knives through smoke.

They were accelerating. Fast.

I felt the approach to my core, a grinding vibration that had nothing to do with the ship's deck plates. The Yachtya weren't maneuvering for position; they were racing straight down the throat of the Imperial fleet, they knew nothing else and wanted nothing but utter destruction. The violet heat beneath my skin surged in response, a painful resonance that made my vision blur at the edges. I gripped the armrests of the command chair, fighting the urge to stand. These weren't just ships; they were hungry voids wrapped in geometry, and they had found their prey.

"Time to impact, ninety seconds!" Vance shouted, her composure fraying at the edges. "Target acquisition."

"Target acquisition aye sir." The weapons officer replied.

Something ancient stirred in my blood as I watched the approaching void-ships, their onyx structures absorbing starlight like black holes drifting through the cosmos. Veins of crimson energy pulsed beneath their surfaces, resembling exposed arteries of some cosmic leviathan.

"Let them come," I murmured, a metallic tang flooding my mouth like I'd been sucking on copper wiring. My hands moved to the holographic tactical display without conscious thought, fingertips leaving phosphorescent trails across the three-dimensional battlefield. "Target lead vessel only—kinetics forward, energy aft."

The weapons officer's crisp "Aye, sir" barely registered through the thundering pulse in my ears as Admiral Vance leaned in, her weathered face illuminated by my console's azure glow, her voice low enough that only I could hear. "The forward energy batteries are the only thing we've seen even come close to scratching their hulls, we should focus them forward," she whispered. Her breath was warm against my ear, being careful to maintain the chain of command in front of the crew whose fingers danced across their stations with practiced precision.

I stared at the tactical plot, the red vectors of the approaching shadows burning into my retinas. Vance's warning buzzed in my ear, but the violet static humming in my core screamed a different strategy. Conventional tactics had failed for decades; they hadn't sent me here to scratch the paint. They needed me to break the line, to do something different. I had to trust my instinct, whatever was driving it.

"The entire fleet needs to focus on our target, can we synchronize the firing solution?" I barked, my voice vibrating with a harmonic resonance that wasn't entirely my own.

Vance keyed the fleet-wide comms, "All ships, lock firing solution on the lead vessel," she said.

I quickly added, "I want every joule of energy and every kinetic round concentrated on the two contact points."

Vance stiffened in my peripheral vision, but her training held. "Concentrating fire," she echoed, relaying the command to the flotilla.

"Execute," I ordered.

Sovereign shuddered beneath my feet as its weapons systems unleashed their fury. The emptiness before us transformed into a canvas of destructive light. Every vessel in our fleet contributed to the assault—the escorts with their azure energy beams, our flagship with its blinding white discharge—creating a concentrated lance of pure annihilation that pierced the darkness between stars. Quantum torpedoes streaked with the beams through the hot maelstrom like burning embers, their violet trails marking the relentless barrage against our target. Phosphorescent orange trails arced with them through the void as our exotic matter rail guns unleashed their own hell fury, each sub-light round hammering the Shadow vessel with methodical, devastating precision. The command deck's operational quiet vanished beneath a thunderous sound of energy discharge as the power reserves rapidly drained. I watched our combined assault hammer into the lead Shadow vessel. The impact slowed its advance—first noticeably, then significantly—yet it continued pushing forward through the barrage. The other two vessels, unphased, continued their sprint towards us.

A voice sliced through the cacophony from the weapons station. "Forward capacitors at critical failure point, sir. The beam's destabilizing." The brilliant white lance was already dimming, its edges fraying into spectral wisps. "Complete discharge in five seconds."

"Alternatives?" I demanded, knuckles white against the command chair.

Vance's face hardened in the oscillating light. "We can't recharge and shield simultaneously, sir. We're overdrawn."

I watched the lead vessel's deceleration, calculated the unchanged velocity of its companions. The plan crystallized in my mind—reckless, possibly suicidal, but tactically sound. "Helm, plot collision course with primary target. Maximum thrust. Weapons, maintain bombardment until impact."

Vance's face contorted with alarm. "Sir, a collision will atomize our shields like a snowflake in a plasma torch! We have zero data on the structural consequences of a direct collision with those vessels."

"Divert all shield power to weapons and forward integrity fields," I commanded, my voice carrying the weight of finality. "Keep firing until impact."

Hatch's eyes found mine, searching for recognition. "Marcus? Are you certain?" Our eyes locked briefly. In that moment of silent communication, she read the uncertainty in my face but answered with a firm nod that spoke volumes. Despite the madness of my plan, her trust in me remained unshaken.

Vance's face tightened with professional resignation as she executed the command, dropping the protective field and diverting the reclaimed power to our weapons and forward integrity. The Sovereign lurched forward, the roaring of the engines could be heard resolutely through the interior as we accelerated toward the lead vessel. Its companion's broke formation instantly, twin basalt predators unleashing crimson beams that carved through space. One of our escort ships—the Valiant—split apart in a silent explosion of atmosphere and debris. Another beam found us, slicing through the Sovereign's rear quarter with surgical precision, slicing into armor plating and sending tremors through the deck beneath our feet.

Armor plating didn't just vaporize—it blasted out into plumes of hot plasma, molecules tearing apart as the beam punched deeper. The deck bucked violently beneath us, throwing crew members against consoles. Warning klaxons shrieked as atmosphere vented into space through the wound. Beneath my boots, the deck plates bucked and popped. The acrid stench of vaporized circuitry flooded my nostrils as somewhere behind us, crewmen's screams were abruptly silenced by the void of space.

"Hold steady," I commanded, my voice straining as I watched our energy weapons flicker and destabilize, their brilliant beams unraveling into useless luminescence against the void. Power levels were falling rapidly as we closed the final distance through pure momentum alone.

A panicked voice cut through the chaos: "We're not going to survive this!"

“Hold course!” I barked.

The collision counter plummeted toward zero as our kinetic rounds continued their relentless assault, mostly solo now. Around us, the remaining escort vessels fired intermittent energy beams that splashed against the Shadow vessel's hull, while our own forward energy batteries discharged sporadic pulses of blinding white energy across the remaining distance between us and the enemy.

The ship's AI blared its final unnecessary warning across the command deck:

COLLISION ALERT. COLLISION ALERT. COLLISION ALERT.

The shadow vessel filled our viewscreen now. Through the viewscreen, I could now make out the fractal geometries etched into the Shadow vessel's hull—patterns that seemed to shift and writhe even as we hurtled toward them. Something pierced my consciousness—a high-pitched keening that existed somewhere between sound and thought, growing louder with each passing second. My consciousness split between the physical world and something else—a psychic assault that clawed at the edges of my mind, scrabbling for purchase like fingernails on steel.

The Sovereign slammed into the weakened Shadow vessel with catastrophic force. Sovereign's reinforced prow—surely forged from the Imperium's finest composite alloys—punctured the shadow vessel's hull before crumpling inward like a crushed aluminum can. A psychic scream tore through my mind as the impact shattered the alien craft. Its hull collapsed like struck mercury, obsidian fragments bleeding into the void. Crimson energy arced desperately between the separating pieces, weakening with each expanding meter of vacuum. The assault on my consciousness vanished instantly. Through the fractured viewscreen, I watched the remaining Shadow vessels dissolve into nothingness—there one moment, then scattered like ash in the solar wind, leaving only empty space where their menace had been.

Sparks rained from overhead panels as klaxons wailed. The sudden loss of momentum threw us to the deck plates. Warning screens blazed crimson across every console—hull breach indicators, life support failures, desperate transmissions from the forward compartments. Yet beneath the chaos rose something unexpected: a ragged cheer rippled across the command deck. Officers exchanged triumphant glances, some clasping hands or slapping shoulders. For the first time since the Shadow war had begun, it seems we'd forced a retreat. It wasn't just a victory—it was permission to hope.

Victory's warmth lasted mere seconds before the command deck erupted in a cascade of electrical fire. Sparks fountained from the navigation console, igniting insulation material that melted into orange droplets across the deck. The dry stench of burning circuitry filled our lungs as emergency lighting flickered desperately, casting monstrous shadows that danced across panicked faces. Then darkness swallowed us whole as the Sovereign's heart stopped beating, the ship's artificial gravity stuttering in its death throes, momentarily lifting us into a weightless limbo before slamming us back down. We were dead in the water.

CHAPTER 13: SEEDS OF DOUBT

The Imperialis lounge was built for spectacle—an amphitheater masquerading as an airport terminal. Curved white beams arched up to a glass vault that drank in the afternoon glare of the twin suns, refracting it over the violet fields in undulating waves. At certain angles, the twin suns transformed the lounge into a kaleidoscope, where floating dust appeared to briefly catch fire and every polished surface fractured light into prisms that danced across the walls like scattered diamonds.

The centerpiece was a blue glass table that seemed wide enough to land a shuttle on, around which were clustered seat-pods in the shape of abstracted calla lilies, every one a miniature shell designed to cradle a human at the optimal angle for watching and listening. Most of the pods were occupied; families in matching utility grays, engineers with their badges still pinned, some Pioneer sleepers in their UNS uniforms and a few oddballs in imitation Pioneer gear who didn't quite fit the Imperium's designer austerity. They sipped their nutrient tea with the careful reverence of people who'd grown up with ration cards.

Into this pageant drifted Elliot Draven, trailing a wake of barely repressed agitation and the kind of precise, ostentatious calm that typically preceded a riot. He wore the soft blue flight jacket of Pioneer's old civilian command, sleeves rolled up just enough to show the hand-healed scar tissue that laced his left forearm like angry vines. His boots, a shade lighter than regulation, tracked faint moisture prints across the polished floor. Every move was calculated to be just a half-beat off the local rhythm—just enough to make the lounge's sensors track him and every living human took note, subconsciously.

He arrived at the table with a theatrical sweep, a holo-slate in one hand, and a mug of synth-caf in the other. He set both down with a click that carried to the furthest wall. His audience—thirty-odd souls in the near vicinity, plus the dozens of eyes in the gallery above—shifted their attention. Draven's audience had grown with each passing day—a constellation of dissenters drawn from both the newly awakened Pioneer sleepers and a surprising number of Imperial citizens. Some sat before him now, leaning forward in their pods, while many others watched through feeds, their invisible presence humming through the room's network like static electricity before a storm. The room's chatter, which had hovered in the 'comfortable airport terminal' register, now dialed down to 'funeral parlor with the casket propped open.'

Lieutenant Maris, Imperial Security, stood off to one side, arms folded, with wrists locked the way of someone who had spent years standing precisely so. His uniform looked like it had been grown on his body and then ironed with a carbon-fiber press, seams so fine you couldn't see the thread. Maris was young by the standards of the force, but his eyes had the patience of an old predator. He'd been assigned to monitor Draven's increasingly concerning public interactions—possibly as a punishment detail, possibly as a live-fire exercise in crowd control. Either way, he watched Draven now, impassive, as he tapped his holo-slate and sent a trembling ripple of blue-white light up over the table's surface.

Draven's holo-slate erupted with a dozen ghostly windows, each one a live feed from somewhere on Imperialis. Corridors, common areas, lift tubes—all captured in the cold blue light of surveillance, each bordered by streams of data in the Imperium's rigid, angular script. Some displayed nothing but empty corridors, others showed pairs of officers in slow patrol, their footsteps synced to the second. A third set replayed, in ten-second loops, footage of various lounge clusters from the last hour. Draven magnified one, pausing it to highlight a section where a mother guided her child by the elbow—innocent enough, in the background, two Imperial officers exchanged a glance as they passed.

Draven looked up, locking eyes with Maris. "Who here feels safe when every corridor bristles with guards and sensors?"

His voice was a little too loud, but in a way that sounded less like nerves and more like someone who knew exactly how sound bounced in these rooms. He panned his gaze across the table, taking in the engineers, the family of four in matching blue, and the two new arrivals: a rail-thin older man with a shock of white hair and a stack of paper books, and a dark-haired woman who wore her badge—Selene Mor—on the left pocket of a hand-mended flight suit.

He tapped the holo-slate again, shuffling the feeds. "Or is that the point? Are we to believe that protection and surveillance are the same thing, and that more of one automatically means more of the other?"

His finger traced the outline of an officer's face in the freeze frame, then flicked to another: this time, a shot of the observation deck, dozens of people seated in orderly rows, all facing the same direction.

"They tell us this is for our safety. But the net effect is—what, exactly? That if someone so much as coughs out of sequence, the response team is on them before the echo fades? Why is it I have not heard one dissenting voice or idea since I woke up here?"

A murmur rippled through the seat-pods. An older man, Ramos, member of the teaching corps from the uniform, offered a dry smile and leaned closer to his neighbor, whispering just loud enough to carry. "I was told safety would feel less... theatrical."

Selene Mor said nothing, her brow furrowed. She watched Draven with the wary focus of someone who'd lost friends for saying the wrong thing at the wrong time. But she didn't look away, not once.

Draven grinned, exposing a chipped tooth. "It's not that I object to safety," he said, hands spread wide. "I object to the assumption that everyone here is a suspect until proven otherwise. That's not civilization. That's a prison where you serve time for being alive."

He let the words hang. Most of the room pretended to go back to their tea. But in reality, every ear was tuned to the standoff now brewing at the main table.

Maris, who up until now had been content to lurk in the observer's shadow, stepped forward, his movement slow and deliberate. "Mr. Draven," he said, voice low and unhurried, "these measures are in place because the alternative is letting the Shadows in. Every protocol here is designed to minimize risk, not create it."

Draven shrugged, but his mouth curved into something sharper. "That's the problem with systems designed to minimize risk. Eventually, the system itself becomes the biggest risk."

There was a beat of silence, filled only by the faint hiss of the climate control and the hollow clink of someone refilling their mug.

Selene finally broke it, voice level but edged with steel. "So what's your alternative, Draven? Open the doors and hope we're not overrun by the darkness?" She didn't blink, didn't give him the satisfaction of looking away.

Draven's reply was immediate. "Openness is not the same as vulnerability. You want to breed trust, start by treating people like adults." He turned to Ramos. "Tell me, old man, were the students easier to manage when you trusted them, or when you made them recite the rules every morning?"

Ramos chuckled, a dry burr. "They broke the rules either way. But if you trusted them, at least they broke them with style."

A few of the engineers at the table snorted, unable to suppress it.

Maris' lips drew in, but he said nothing. His gaze did a slow scan of the room, picking out every face now leaning subtly toward the conversation, including the two off-duty security officers pretending to argue about game scores in the corner.

Draven's hands splayed, as if offering the whole argument up to the ceiling. "See, Lieutenant? Even here, people want to participate. They want to be trusted with the messiness of their own survival. It's the difference between raising children and raising citizens."

He closed the holo-slate with a sharp click, then set his synth-caf back in the exact ring it had left before. "Or you can keep doing what you're doing, and watch the next attack from your Shadows be less about monsters from the void and more about the people you forgot how to trust. Assuming there really are mean old Shadows out there."

A long silence. Maris' jaw ticked once, then he nodded. "You make your point, Mr. Draven. I hope you're ready for the next time someone tests the system." He stepped back into the shadow of the nearest beam, arms re-folded.

The lounge's ambient hum crept back up, but the room didn't quite return to its prior state. The families kept their voices lower; the engineers exchanged speculative glances over the rims of their mugs; Ramos winked at his neighbor. Even Selene, still frowning, didn't look quite as unconvinced as before. The argument had infected them, if only a little.

Draven waited a few seconds, then straightened, stretched, and picked up his mug. He caught Maris' eye and smiled, this time with a trace of real warmth.

"Nothing personal, Lieutenant. I just hate being bored." He saluted with the mug, then strolled away, boots echoing off the floor.

Behind him, the conversation resumed—but softer, and not quite so certain.

△△△

Aboard the Sovereign, crews swarmed through the labyrinthine corridors like white blood cells attacking an infection. Engineers hung from above ceiling panels, their faces slick with sweat as they rerouted power conduits. More still were in sweat-stained jumpsuits rewiring blackened panels, their fingers bleeding from sharp edges of torn metal. Navigation officers hunched over flickering holographic displays, fingers dancing across controls while damage assessment teams, some in charred uniforms, dragged replacement parts through doorways barely wide enough to accommodate them. Every face bore the same tight-lipped determination—the knowledge that another Shadow incursion could materialize from the void at any moment, finding them vulnerable if even one system remained offline.

Outside, the surviving escort vessels formed a protective ring, their hulls scarred with carbon-black streaks where Shadow weapons had glanced but not penetrated. Maintenance drones swarmed like fireflies against their dark silhouettes, their welding torches casting brilliant arcs of light that illuminated the vessels' battle insignia—once proud emblems now scarred or partially obliterated by Shadow weapons fire. The little drones were working as feverishly as the crews inside each of the ships, each drone patching breaches and reinforcing structural weak points. Through gaps in the formation, the endless dark seemed to watch, patient and hungry.

The rescue teams had staggered back aboard with thousand-yard stares. Their shuttle hulls glowed faintly in the hangar, still cooling from their exposure to the exotic radiation present in the debris field where the Valiant's quantum core had detonated. For sixteen hours they had combed through the twisted metal garden where the Imperial Destroyer Ship Valiant had been reduced to glittering confetti against the blackness of space. Not a single life sign, not one emergency beacon, not even the standard black box transmitter had survived whatever had torn through the ship's shielded and quantum-reinforced hull like tissue paper.

I stood at attention as the rescue shuttles docked, watching their airlocks cycle open one by one. Each revealed the same hollow-eyed crew, the same empty cargo bays. No survivors. The realization hit me like a physical blow, and I found myself gripping the edge of a nearby console, my knees suddenly unreliable. My eyes fixed on the viewport, as though I could somehow pierce the vacuum beyond and find what they had missed.

I collapsed into a nearby chair. "We should have changed course."

Hatch's face remained impassive, the small scar along her jawline catching the harsh light. "You made a tactical decision, sir. That's command." Her voice carried the practiced steadiness of someone who had delivered similar words over too many empty body bags. "The Imperials have been running from these things for longer that we've been alive; combined. For the longest time all they could do was keep them out and hope they left when there was an incursion. Today, you just showed them they *can* fight back." She checked the tactical display, her eyes reflecting pinpoints of light from the holographic readout. "Of course, now the Shadows know exactly what you are."

I slumped forward, elbows on the cold metal console, still not comfortable with the cost of this minor victory. "What do we do next?" My voice sounded hollow even to my own ears.

Hatch's mouth quirked upward at one corner, that familiar dimple appearing in her left cheek. "Shouldn't you be telling us, sir?" She slid her glasses off, holding my gaze as her fingertip absently traced the curved edge of the frame. After a moment, she settled them back onto the bridge of her nose with a practiced adjustment and raised the data-slate she was holding. "I've been reviewing the logs from the battle, and some of Valiant's final data burst. There are some opportunities in the sensor data, their sacrifice may not be wasted."

She adjusted her glasses again, as she raised the slate closer to her field of vision. "I think we can make some changes, but there is a big question mark on my idea. The energy requirements would likely exceed the Sovereign's capacity by several orders of magnitude. Even with a pristine reactor core instead of our damaged one..." She tapped the screen, scrolling through calculations that made her frown deepen. "We're looking at weeks of analysis before I can even propose a viable approach."

Hatch and I made our way back to the bridge through corridors that still smelled of scorched circuitry. The emergency lighting cast long, uneven shadows across our path, and the deck plates beneath our boots vibrated with the labored pulse emanating from the damaged propulsion systems. We passed crewmen with tired eyes and soot-stained uniforms, their hands raw from emergency repairs. When the bridge doors finally hissed open—the hydraulics stuttering halfway—we stepped into a command center that was still a flurry of activity and coordination. At the center of it all stood Admiral Vance, her uniform tarnished at the cuffs, one sleeve awkwardly rolled to the elbow, exposing a mesh patch that covered a fresh laceration. She stood hunched over the primary command console, both hands braced against its rim as if holding herself upright by will alone. Sweat pooled along her hairline, the iron-grey there darkened to near-black. When she spoke, her voice was tight as piano wire and pitched for no one but the bridge crew.

Vance's voice cut through the hum of damaged systems. "We threw everything at that Shadow vessel and barely survived." Her gaze traveled from station to station, the whites of her eyes webbed with burst vessels. "And that was just one. If a squadron appears on our sensors..."

She let the silence hang for three heartbeats.

"Every minute counts. Every system we bring back online might be the difference between survival and joining the Valiant."

She didn't use the comms; she didn't have to. The bridge was so tense that even the subtle tremor in her words carried to every tech, every junior officer, even the medtechs mopping up blood from the aft corridor and quickly transmitted beyond the walls of the bridge. Vance made no move to acknowledge Hatch or me when we entered; she simply gestured to the tactical plot and waited for us to see the data.

I leaned over the tactical display, its holographic light casting a sickly blue glow across my face. "How long before we can get underway?" My voice sounded hollow in the cavernous bridge.

Vance's fingers danced across her console, leaving smudges of something dark—oil or blood—on the illuminated surface. "Another hour, two at the most." She didn't look up, her iron-gray hair falling across her forehead as she studied damage reports scrolling too fast for me to follow. "We can have the escorts lock to hardpoints and carry us back once they secure all hull breaches. The Sovereign's not flying herself anywhere with that gash in her port engine coil."

I sat in silence, my fingers drumming a slow, unconscious rhythm on the armrest. The weight of command pressed down on my shoulders like a lead cape. My mind churned through scenarios, each more desperate than the last, while my face remained a carefully constructed mask of calm. This was not my wheelhouse—a Supreme Commander with supreme command of precisely nothing useful. The irony tasted bitter.

For fifty-eight minutes by the flickering chronometer, I remained statue-still except for those drumming fingers, watching the emergency lights continue to cast long shadows across faces that occasionally looked to me for answers I didn't have. My arms rested flat on the command chair's armrests, fingers still tapping rhythmically. My eyes were locked onto the shifting starfield outside the damaged transparisteel viewport—a crystalline tangle of fractured transparent material that somehow still held against the vacuum, forming the forward wall of the bridge. Distant pinpricks of white and blue pulsed against absolute darkness, occasionally eclipsed by drifting debris from Valiant.

Hatch watched my unblinking gaze, my pupils constricted to pinpoints despite the dimness of the bridge. My right index finger tapping out a rhythm, while my jaw muscles worked beneath skin gone waxy under the emergency lights. I caught Hatch watching my finger tapping closely. My finger kept tapping away—three quick, two slow, pause, repeat. I didn't know why. I only knew I couldn't stop. The stars burned into my retinas, each one pulsing with information I couldn't quite grasp but couldn't ignore. Four hours of hell had stripped away everything but this—my finger tapping its desperate code, my eyes fixed on the void where the Valiant had been. Out there, beyond the fractured viewport, our dead drifted through the Aurelian Belt, their remains becoming one with the cosmic dust that formed the belt.

Hatch leaned over the environmental readout. "CO_2 trending up. O_2 trending down.' She swallowed once. 'Six hours until Deck Nine goes hazardous—if nobody pushes it."

The klaxons had shut off, finally, though the room still seemed to vibrate with phantom alarms. She glanced at the others—crew huddled at the periphery, patching what they could, none of them making noise beyond the necessary. No one spoke to me. No one even looked at me anymore.

"We should be fine," Hatch stated mostly to herself. "We will be underway and back in the central systems before the environmentals become a concern."

△△△

It was twilight at Imperialis as the second sun began to dip below the horizon. The promenade deck was a calculated illusion—soft blue shadows cast by the glowing arches, footsteps muffled on floors engineered to mimic aged driftwood, and a ceiling made to look like open sky, lit by simulated auroras that pulsed with algorithmic calm. This was the hour the architects had designed for reflection and reconciliation. The hour when arguments and disputes, if not solved, lost their sharp corners and softened into something that could be set aside until morning.

The news of the Shadow vessel's defeat rippled across the Imperium like an electric current. In Imperialis, citizens flooded the central plaza, their faces bathed in the kaleidoscopic glow of impromptu fireworks that burst against the darkening violet sky. Glasses clinked in crowded bars, strangers embraced in the streets, and the planetary broadcast towers beamed footage of similar celebrations erupting across twenty-three worlds. Through it all, Draven stood apart, arms crossed over his chest, watching the revelry with narrowed eyes and a mouth set in a hard, skeptical line. Which was why, of course, Draven picked this exact time to disrupt the revelry nearest to him.

He stood at the apex of the central observation window, backlit by a three-story curtain of transparent alloy that overlooked the horizon. Beyond the glass, the world's signature violet fields blurred into evening, punctuated by fireworks blasts and black spires that rose and twisted—some natural, some the artistic afterthoughts of a bored terraforming team. He pressed his palm to the windows and let his reflection blend with the stars.

Tonight's audience was twice the size of this afternoon's—word had spread, and so had the rumors. People gathered in an uneven half-moon near the observation port, drawn like moths to Draven's flame: six families, a pack of off-duty maintenance staff, three young officers in identical boots, and an older man with a child perched on his hip, as well as a now larger group watching through feeds. There was a shifting excitement in the air—half anticipation, half dread, the kind that suggested nobody knew what was about to happen, but nobody wanted to miss it.

Two newcomers flanked the far side of the room: Imperial Engineer Jora Thane, her hair cropped tight on the sides but left long and braided down the back, and Security Captain Vega, whose jawline looked like it had been sculpted out of aircraft metal, every feature just a shade too sharp to be accidental. Both wore uniforms, but neither bothered with the pageantry. Vega's jacket was unbuttoned, his stance relaxed—almost lazy—while Jora clutched a data-slate to her chest like it was a religious text.

Draven tapped the window, gesturing at the dusk and the infinite scatter of lights overhead. "Look at that. Everything around us is a system that should have killed us." He let the silence breathe, then turned to the crowd. "That's the trick, isn't it? The Shadows don't need to attack. They just need us to fracture ourselves until we do the job for them."

Captain Vega snorted. "You think the Imperium's just going to implode because a few people complain about security measures?"

Draven's grin was all teeth. "Curfews, travel bans, and a security grid that could spot a sparrow farting three yards from the nearest building. You don't have to call it tyranny for it to act like tyranny." He let his gaze linger on Vega, then swung it to Jora Thane. "You're a systems engineer. Tell me I'm wrong."

Jora's lips compressed, but she didn't look away. She weighed her answer, then said, "I could lock down every airlock in this place with three keystrokes. I could also open them, if I wanted." She glanced down at her data-slate, as if searching for absolution. "But that's not the point. The point is, you're stoking paranoia in a society that was built to survive by trusting and protecting its people."

Draven nodded, the motion soft but satisfied. "And *I* trust them. I trust them to see when they're being handled in the name of protection." He turned to the crowd, voice modulated to reach every ear. "Would *you* trust a system that labels disagreement as 'dangerous?' That tells you the only thing between *you* and extinction is obedience?"

A ripple of tension moved through the group. The child on the man's hip twisted around, catching the reflected light and giggling as if it was a game. The man himself—grey around the temples, face grooved with old sunburn—offered Draven a tight nod. One of the off-duty officers shifted her stance, unconsciously moving closer to Draven's side of the line.

Vega leaned in, voice pitched low. "There's a war on. Maybe you missed the part where the Shadows vaporized Aurelia."

"I saw the footage," Draven replied, the words clipped. "I also saw how, within hours, every camera and news feed went through ten layers of military censorship. Now we're expected to believe that suddenly we've defeated a Shadow vessel—something previously thought impossible—all because of some prophesied savior who supposedly came from Earth with me." He leaned forward, voice dropping to a conspiratorial whisper. "I lived there my entire life. Trust me when I say if anyone back home had supernatural abilities, the government would have weaponized them long before we ever launched. You want to win a war, Captain? Maybe start by letting people fight for more than their own survival."

Jora Thane brushed a hand over her braid, an old nervous habit. "On Earth," she said quietly, "control grew in silence. We know what happened to *that* planet."

Draven seized the moment. "Exactly. Silence doesn't breed safety, it breeds monsters in the walls. Maybe the Shadows know that. Maybe that's why they don't have to knock twice." He held up his mug, a battered Pioneer-issue piece with a cracked rim. "This is all any of us ever wanted. A place to sit, and talk, and argue about the world like we matter. I say we start doing more of that, and less of the other."

The energy in the room shifted. A few of the families inched closer to the observation window; the two off-duty officers, previously at ease, were now openly listening. Even Captain Vega, whose whole body seemed constructed to withstand rhetorical blasts, blinked and let his attention waver to the horizon. Jora Thane set her data-slate on the ledge, hands suddenly empty and a little lost.

Draven drew in the rest of the group with a sweep of his arm. "You can treat this like a lifeboat, or you can treat it like a society. But if you let fear call the shots, you're not surviving. You're waiting for someone to tell you where to drown."

He let the words settle. The nighttime auroras outside caught the glass at a new angle, washing everyone's face in violet and blue. In the far corner, one of the young officers coughed and murmured something to his friend. Draven saw it—a flicker of shared dissent, a little rebellion in the dark.

He lowered his voice, making them lean in. "The best systems are the ones that can take a punch. That don't break when someone asks a hard question. We can either stay pawns, or we can reclaim our voices. And maybe—just maybe—that's the thing the Shadows are actually afraid of."

There was no applause. There never was. But the group stayed where they were, coalescing into a rough circle around Draven. Even Captain Vega, jaw set, didn't try to disperse them. Jora Thane retrieved her slate, but didn't turn it on. For a long moment, nobody spoke. The only sound was the hush of the ventilation and the ghostly flicker of auroras and some residual fireworks through the window.

Finally, Vega broke the silence, voice almost respectful. "You ever think you're just making more work for Security?"

Draven grinned, shrugged. "I live to serve."

The laughter this time was quiet, but genuine. The crowd loosened, but nobody left. Not right away.

Outside the windows, the orderly world of Imperialis entered true night, the aurora gone. The stars blinked on. In the lounge, every conversation that followed was a little less careful, a little more honest. The Imperium's architects had designed this hour for calm. Instead, Draven left them with the possibility of something more dangerous.

Hope—it was like clay in Draven's hands—and he had a predator's certainty that this trusting civilization had never learned to recognize the shape of a knife until it was already between the ribs. He smiled as he watched them disperse, mentally noting which ones had nodded, which ones had leaned in closest. Draven was already plotting which officer to befriend next, which systems engineer to charm, which security codes to memorize while pretending not to look. Each conversation was another rung on a ladder they didn't even know they were holding steady for him.

CHAPTER 14: AWAKENING

The Sovereign shuddered forward at last, her hull plates flexing and groaning under the strain, towed by the remaining four damaged escort vessels—the Dauntless, Venture, Maverick, and severely battered Resolute—all locked onto Sovereign's Class-7 hardpoint docking clamps. Iridescent ribbons of blue-white energy surging behind, hot as stellar plasma at 12 million Kelvin, leaked from her Mark IV engine nacelles—flicking through half repaired cracks in the ruptured port engine coil—heat rapidly dissipating into the star-flecked darkness. She contributed what meager thrust her damaged propulsion system could muster—barely twenty percent capacity according to the crimson warning indicators that flickered across Lieutenant Reese's monitoring station. The battle group moved as one wounded organism through the endless vacuum, trailing a comet-tail of metal shards and vented oxygen-nitrogen atmosphere that glittered like crushed diamonds. The group crawled its way back toward the Imperium's core systems at one-eighth standard velocity, aiming to save some time via the nearest jump gate. I listened to the hum of Sovereign's fusion stacks; it sounded sickly, a threadbare whine punctuated by the staccato alarms that neither Reese nor the auxiliary AI could fully silence.

Above the viewscreen, a thin mist of coolant drifted sideways, refracting the icy sunlight of the local star into a cathedral's worth of halos.

We weren't going to make it as quickly as we needed to at this pace. I could see it on Reese's face, in the tightness of his jaw, the pinched white at the corners of his eyes. The Shadows would surely be closing the gap with each passing hour of our crippled progress. Somewhere in the darkness beyond our sensors, I knew they were calculating trajectories, finalizing battle formations, thirsting for vengeance after our pyrrhic triumph. I paced the command deck, each footfall measured, deliberate—a metronome to regulate the racing of my pulse. The crew watched without watching, their eyes flicking toward me then away, gauging their own fear against whatever calm I could project. My collar felt too tight, my breathing too shallow, but I kept my hands steady, my voice level. Despite my acute awareness of our defenselessness, I maintained the impassive expression my crew needed to see on their commander's face.

"Damage update," I asked, voice scraping lower than usual. I didn't bother with the comm—no point, not when Reese stood a short six foot walk away, knuckles pressed to the lifeless glass of his status console.

Reese didn't look up. "Spool drive's still offline, sir. Primary and secondary relays both fused. We're bypassing through tertiary, but it's rated for emergency station-keeping, not FTL. At current speed, ETA to Gate Four Ten is… " Reese's lips moved, visible through the reflection in the console. "Fifty-three hours. Best case."

The number landed like a punch. Fifty-three hours, crawling through the seemingly endless darkness.

△△△

Hours later, the bridge doors hissed open. Hatch stepped through, her eyes finding me exactly where she'd left me—a solitary figure before the viewport, silhouetted against the deep blackness of space. My reflection in the transparisteel betrayed no movement save for the occasional blink.

"Sir," she said, her hand finding my shoulder with practiced precision. Her voice remained firm but quiet, meant for me alone. "You need rest. The ship will hold together without your constant vigil."

I didn't turn. "I know that, Colonel."

The Sovereign would drag herself through the void whether I stood sentinel or not. I was just another worn out component—unable to alter our course, increase our crawling pace, or stop whatever horrors might be accelerating toward our stern. Yet I remained, anchored to this spot as though the weight of my attention somehow reinforced our weakened shields.

Pure superstition, of course.

The universe cared nothing for my sleepless sentinel duty. I watched, silent, as the Dauntless' external repair drones skittered across Sovereign's hull, leaving trails of blue sparks and frozen vapor as they patched the worst venting breaches. The drones looked like frantic insects, their movements precise, almost desperate; like ants supporting the colony. Every so often, Reese's voice cut in from the nearby console—another relay blowout, another circuit fried by cascading surges. None of it changed the fundamental problem. Thirty-four hours now, minimum, before we could reach the jump gate—the only real escape vector left to a fleet with shot engines and limited weapon power.

I pressed my thumb and forefinger into my brow, hard enough to leave indents, trying to press the never-ending static from my skull. My limbs cycled between deadened numbness and electric agony—one moment I felt nothing below my shoulders, the next my skin crawled with phantom fire, as if my very cells were being ionized from within. I'd stopped mentioning my physiological oddities to

Vance or the medtechs. The last time I'd brought it up, the medical officer had looked away, lips pressed flat, as if trying to decide whether or not to call for a psych eval on the Supreme Commander of the fleet. Awkward for all.

We were all bone-deep exhausted, running on stimulants and hope. My own mind kept looping back to the moment of impact with the Shadow ship—the fracture of reality, the mass of the vessel crumpling before Sovereign's prow, the sensation of violet energy flowing through me, not as a weapon, but as a message. The damn thing had reached inside me somehow, recognized what I was, scraped its alien consciousness against mine like steel wool on bare nerves. It wanted me dead, or gone, or maybe just caged. That certainty radiated in my chest—there would be no quarter next time.

Hatch's hand lingered, feather-light on my shoulder. "Reese sent the damage summary to your station, why don't you sit down and read it," she said. "And the medbay's patched and repopulated. Only minor casualties in last shift."

I forced a nod, eyes still glued to the glittering debris field outside. "That's better than I expected." The tinny taste of recycled air clung to the back of my throat. I let the words settle; let the silence, heavy as hull plating, fill the space between us. "Any word from the escorts?"

“Fleet confirms twenty-seven percent losses,” she replied. “The Shadows broke contact after the impact, still no new contacts. Their remaining assets are… not detectable. If they’re preparing another run, they’re out of range of us and any local listening posts.” She hesitated, thumb tracing a tight circle on her forearm. “Vance says some of the techs think they’re learning. Adapting maybe.” Hatch’s jaw flexed, not quite a clench. Hatch increased the pressure on my shoulder a little, keeping her attention fixed on me, eyes sharp. “Rest, sir?”

The idea of sleep is almost funny. I’m so past tired that the thought is offensive. I turn and look at Hatch, at the close-set lines of exhaustion at her temples. She isn’t telling me to rest for my sake, or even for hers. She just needed one of us to be able to think straight when the next crisis came around again, and she was betting, or hoping, that it would be me who needed to be ready. I rubbed at my jaw—my stubble bristled against my palm, sensation sharp and uneven, like sandpaper that had worn through in spots.

I lowered myself into the command seat with a theatrical heaviness. "If Reese manages anything more optimistic than our funeral arrangements, please let me know." I braced for Hatch's usual persistence, but she merely offered a single, deliberate nod before retreating toward a nearby alcove brimming with active data screens. My eyelids fell shut as I redirected my attention inward, waiting for the persistent high-pitched whine in my skull to fade enough for unconsciousness to claim me. But as the darkness crept in, something else waited there to greet me.

△△△

I jolted awake, my stomach lurching as though the artificial gravity had failed. In that suspended moment between sleep and consciousness, I was still plummeting through an endless black void, not toward the deck plates but toward something waiting.

Something hungry.

The Shadows had found me again in my dreams, their psychic talons raking at my mind. This was no ordinary dream. The deck was gone, the bridge and its battered consoles had vanished, and I floated in a sensory vacuum so total the concept of up or down disintegrated on arrival. My body was there, yet not quite—phantom limbs and cold pins-and-needles where muscle memory expected mass and heat.

I tried to move, and felt nothing.

I tried to scream and felt even less.

Consciousness compressed around a single pinprick of sensation. And that damned pervasive ringing in my ears. That scraping, screeching annoyance that had haunted every waking hour since the wormhole. It was louder here, a slicing, infinitely high note that split thought from thought.

The darkness wasn't empty.

Something moved, just at the corner of what ought to be vision. Claws dragging across the membrane of reality, each scrape sending out a filament of unbearable, raw noise.

The Yachtya—I know them the way a drowning man knows the weight of water—are here. Not a vessel on a scanner, not a black stain on a tactical readout, but pure intentionality. I can feel them. I can feel them watching.

I tried to orient, to focus on something, but the space all around me folded and unfolded like a tesseract in time-lapse. A sense of scale tugged at my skull: I am an atom, then a planet, then a thought. The Yachtya circled, not as discreet ships but as a predatory will, a gravity that bent the rules of dream and memory. There is a message, and it is coming for me.

Suddenly I was in a corridor. The world had shifted. I was walking, then running, though my stride had the logic of dreams—sometimes rubbery and slow, sometimes my feet not making contact with the ground as I moved forward by inertia, sometimes entire fields of view snapped into place with a lurch. I rounded a corner and came face to face with... myself. Not a mirror, not even a decent copy, but a figure wearing my shape, only stretched, distorted, with eyes faceted like a nightmare insect. The thing grinned, splitting its face wide, and inside its mouth was a nest of writhing black wires.

I tried to speak, but nothing came out. The other-me spoke instead: "We've been waiting, Marcus." Its voice was static, the words fuzzing and popping like a corrupt radio signal. Every part of me tingled with fear. I jerked backward, but the walls did not allow retreat. They bulged inward, guiding me closer to the duplicate. Shadowy tendrils bloomed from behind it, first as fingers, then as arms, then as something much larger.

They peeled back the years. I was eight, sitting on the floor in my mother's kitchen in Arkansas, wrists stuck to the vinyl, my father's lighter flicking open and closed in time to the drone of a baseball game on the radio. My father's voice came quick and bright—"never overthink it, Marcus. The world's not a puzzle, it's a gauntlet."

The next thing was a photograph, damp and curling at the corners, of my graduation day. My mother's proud eyes had been rimmed red and tearful behind discount sunglasses. Her hands had hovered behind my shoulders, uncertain, afraid to touch.

The black-wired mouth chewed, grinning, and spat out new scenes: deserts of Kazakhstan, the coppery air, the way the soil had clung to my boots. Then Paris, burning, the taste of cordite and charcoaled flesh, the blank look on the medic's face as they zipped up children in body bags. I'd thought these memories were my own, private, but the thing across from me wore them openly, parading my fears, failures and the micro-decisions that had led here, each one condensed into a single, strobing moment.

The wires in the thing's mouth twisted and braided, forming a latticework of symbols that flickered with impossible speed. Equations. A kill chain of orders. Maps of retreat and redirection, the shape of battlefields drawn in the pit of my stomach. Each time I tried to look away, the thing's eyes dragged me back, pinning me like a bug on a slide.

I wanted to fight, to crush the hallucination, but my hands were gone, eaten by the same black logic as the rest of me. The scene shifted. I was five years old again, rigid beneath my dinosaur-print sheets—faded green brontosauruses with chipped screen-printing—my small fingers clutching the cotton hem so tightly my knuckles ached. I stared at the spare room doorway at the end of my childhood home's long hallway; the only other room at my end of the hallway besides mine. Beyond the water-stained ceiling and that loose floorboard—the one that squealed like a trapped animal whenever someone tried sneaking past after bedtime—lay something worse than emptiness. The Shadows there pulsed against sickly yellow wallpaper, living things with breath and hunger. Neither my plastic rocket nightlight nor the dim hallway bulbs could breach that threshold, as if light itself feared what waited inside.

My mother's reassurances echo in memory: "Nobody died in there, Marcus. Your father built this house himself," her voice tinged with that artificial brightness adults use when lying to children. But logic couldn't dispel the cold prickling at the nape of my neck, the sensation of being watched whenever I passed that doorway with its tarnished brass knob. I avoided it for years, creating elaborate detours through our home, pressing myself against the opposite wall until my shoulder blades scraped the textured plaster. Years later, I discovered my grandmother refused to enter that room—a revelation that vindicated my childhood terrors in ways no adult reassurance ever could.

Night after night, I'd wake up gasping, my flannel pajamas soaked through, plastered against my trembling body. The dreams always led me back to that room, centered around a strange little alcove in the back of it, with its half-built shower stall, where something always waited in darkness that seemed deeper than mere absence of light. After weeks of waking up screaming, my mother finally brought me a set of crayons and a sketchpad. "Show me what's scaring you, Marcus," she'd said, her voice gentle but her eyes betraying her worry. The crayon-scratched horror that emerged from my small hands that day had been buried in my mind's deepest vault, until recently.

The word "Yachtya" had emerged from my innocent young mouth that day as I described the picture, a name I couldn't have invented yet somehow I had known it with a chilling certainty. The same creatures that hunted me now across the void of space. *A coincidence? A delusion? Some twisted prophecy I've been fulfilling since childhood?* I want to dismiss it as impossible, yet the familiarity is undeniable—like recognizing a face you've never seen. Perhaps I've simply grafted an adult's terror onto a child's imagination, or worse, maybe they've been with me all along, patient predators waiting for the right moment to strike.

Laughter, at first a whisper, grew to a flood, twisted, guttural. Suddenly the space reshaped itself again. I was back in the corridor, facing the macabre thing that bore a sinister mirror of my face. The laughter leaked from the thing's mouth, from the dark behind its teeth, until the whole space vibrated with the shrill, metallic edge of it. The sound filled the space between my ears, threatening to shake apart my skull. The grotesque doppelgänger leaned close, and its breath carried the reek of rotting corpses and burning electrical cables. The wires in its mouth coiled and twisted, becoming a dense black lattice that seemed to resonate with the electric hum that had been drilling through my skull since the wormhole.

“Do you understand?” it asked, the words were flat and doubled, as if filtered through both an old radio and a fresh wound. The question is not a question. It is a command, a requirement, a final test.

I wanted to shake my head, to deny the implication. I had spent my entire life resisting what was demanded of me: by my father, by my country, by the dead gods of Earth and by the chain of command. The doppelgänger's eyes burrowed into mine, faceted and depthless, and I felt the memories being plucked like strings—each one shuddering with the hollow tone of guilt. The wire-mesh throat vibrated with a harmony of all my worst days. The thing watched me, waiting for the only answer that mattered.

I opened my mouth. No words came. I tried again, and what emerged was not language but a thin thread of noise, the same high-pitched whine that had haunted me since the jump. The doppelgänger grinned wider, its wire-mesh jaw unhinged, and noise spilled out in a torrent, a scream composed of every failure and regret I had ever known. I felt it scraping through my thoughts, devouring the scaffolding that had held my sense of self in place.

The old childhood resolve crystallized within me—the same stubborn defiance I'd discovered at five years old when I'd learned to face down the monsters in my dreams. My phantom limbs solidified, anchoring me against the corridor's shifting reality. I planted my feet, set my jaw, and met the creature's gaze with a fury that burned through my terror. Heat surged behind my eyes as violet light pulsed through my body, illuminating the veins in my arms like electric filaments. The doppelgänger's expression shifted—was that uncertainty flickering across its twisted features? Fear perhaps?

I squared my shoulders and met its gaze directly. "I understand now," I called out, my voice cutting through the cacophony. The screaming abruptly ceased, leaving a vacuum of silence. The creature tilted its head, listening. "You were always there, weren't you? In every darkened doorway, behind every nightmare." My voice grew stronger with each word. "You taught me to fear Shadows, to dread empty rooms. But you also taught me something else—" I raised my glowing hand, fingers splayed. "You taught me how to fight back."

The creature convulsed violently, its human mask liquefying like wax under flame. Wet, obsidian tentacles ripped through the dissolving flesh, unfurling with a sickening snap. The Yachtya hurled itself at me—a blur of writhing appendages sliced the air inches from my face, the stench of ammonia and rot flooded my nostrils.

My hand shot forward with pure instinct as it had done before. Something primal erupted from my core—white-hot power surged through my veins, set every nerve ending ablaze. The creature froze mid-lunge, suspended in my invisible vise. Its body contorted impossibly against my hold, tendons strained, joints bent backward. The shriek it unleashed wasn't just loud—it pierced directly into my brain, a psychic razor that made my vision pulse red.

Blood trickled from my nose as I tightened my mental grip, feeling the creature's alien anatomy strain against forces it never evolved to withstand. My right shoulder erupted in fresh agony as one of the Yachtya's barbed appendages punched through muscle and sinew. Warm blood soaked my uniform. Gritting my teeth against the white-hot pain, I seized the writhing limb with my other hand, yanked it free with a wet sound, and snapped it like deadwood. The broken piece disintegrated into oily smoke as I returned my left hand to reinforce the psychic barrier between us.

My grip on the Yachtya held—but something in the air shifted, a prickling pressure that felt like the buildup before a lightning strike. I felt it in my arms, in my jaw, in the hair that rose along my forearms—the charge mounted and was impossible to contain. A scream, deep and soulful, rattled my throat raw, but I leaned into the pain, holding the Yachtya in the implacable vise of will and whatever-the-hell wormhole-crafted thing inside me was doing the work.

The world around narrowed to the corridor, the thing, and the heat pulsing between us. The violet glow behind my eyes intensified, every vessel in my body outlined in lambent fire. The light cracked from my skin, at first a shimmer, then a blaze. The Yachtya writhed, its limbs thrashing against impossible resistance, its exoskeleton blistering and bleaching under the growing brilliance. The Shadow-creature's shriek distorted, glitched, became a metallic keening that oscillated between frequencies too high for my ears but loud enough to pop my eardrums.

The energy spiked, a crescendo. The light enveloped both of us in a single, blinding actinic flash, like standing at the heart of a hydrogen bomb detonation—no heat, but a pressure wave so dense it seemed to slow time. In that suspended interval, I saw the Yachtya—not as a monster, but as a thing flayed open by light. The first layer peeled away, exposing the trembling lattice of nerves and dark matter beneath. The next, a memory, not mine. I felt, in a blinding rush, the unknowable gut-deep hunger that drove the Yachtya—not just for survival, not for conquest, but for a kind of continuity, a certainty against the death of everything. It was loneliness at the atomic level, stamped into the dark matter of their being.

My consciousness yanked the creature's memories toward me—the moment of its own birth, the black gel of spawning chambers, the devouring of the lesser brood, the ritualization of violence into culture, into faith, into the unbroken recursion of hunt and consume and become. The rawness of this inheritance surged through me, two consciousnesses briefly overlapping, memories flaying against one another. I couldn't make sense of the visual logic, but the emotion hit so hard I almost lost my grip. For a split second, I was sure the Yachtya's will was stronger—its need to propagate, to not be the last, to never be alone again.

The Yachtya shuddered in my grip, spasming so violently I thought it was about to shear itself apart. But then the dream changed the rules: the walls liquefied, and the corridor withered away, replaced by a blackness so deep I couldn't orient myself. The pressure wave collapsed, and suddenly the Yachtya was in me—not physically, but riding the slipstream of that psychic connection, sliding into whatever crack the wormhole had left in my brain. For a heartbeat, I was split: half Marcus, half Yachtya, our thoughts a frictionless blur of want and terror.

I tried to force it back, shoving at it with all the raw will I could muster, but the creature wriggled into the gaps, burrowing into the fault lines of my memory. It wanted—no, needed—to survive, and if it couldn't have a body, it would take a mind. Rage flared from it, pure and bright and cold as liquid nitrogen, and then the memory-collage stuttered into something new: I wasn't in my own head anymore, but looking out through the Yachtya's eyes, seeing myself as prey.

In this vision, the Yachtya flexed its limbs—fifty meters long, at least, each one a stalk of segmented muscle that coiled around a core of black glass and writhing biomatter.

A cold sensation washed over me then—pain so profound it bypassed nerves and went straight to the center of my being, whatever that was now. The Yachtya's perspective continued to flood my mind at the molecular level, a full-body ache of biotechnic fury and abject, teeth-chattering fear. I recognized it instantly: the thing was terrified of me, not in the way a child feared punishment, but the way prey feared being consumed by a predator. The hatred I felt however, it was absolute. It had been refined over millennia, etched into every twitching fiber of its monstrous form. The Yachtya's body was a cathedral to rage, built out of scar tissue and evolutionary spite.

It tried to tear free—I felt the whipcord tension in each of its limbs, the lurching, hydraulic snap as it hurled itself at me. The point of view was dizzying: the Yachtya was both everywhere and nowhere, a hive-mind packed into a single horror show of a body. It tasted the air for me, sensed the distortion of energy I brought, and then, in a blur of movement, launched all of itself forward.

I was back in my body. I braced, wanting to recoil, but in the logic of that not-dream there was nowhere to go. The Yachtya's limbs scissored out, intent on rending me to pieces, but the energy inside me—alien, violet, familiar now as blood—answered with geometric certainty. There was no conscious decision, just a flash of memory: the kitchen in Arkansas, the hallway at night, the refusal to flinch even as terror wanted to drag me under. The energy behind the fear, resolute, unwavering, tired of being scared. The word tore from my throat—"ENOUGH!"—and slammed into the void like a physical force. The creature halted mid-lunge, suspended in nothingness. Violet energy coursed through my veins, erupted from my fingertips in crackling arcs that latched onto the Yachtya. The sensation was familiar yet alien—like wielding those ghost-catching weapons from the movies I'd watched obsessively as a kid. Infinitely more raw, more real. The creature convulsed against my hold, its alien form contorting impossibly as it screamed into the vacuum between us.

Then, in a flash, everything exploded into particles of light. The corridor, the creature—gone. I fell through nothing until reality snapped back and I crashed onto the metal floor of the Sovereign's bridge. My body jolted awake. Sweat drenched my uniform. Something electric still hummed beneath my skin. I tasted copper, felt wetness on my face and my right shoulder. When I touched my upper lip, my fingers came away red. My vision pulsed, and a high-pitched whine filled my skull as sharp pain hit my right shoulder.

For a moment I remained frozen, lungs burning, blood crusting beneath my nose, sweat turning to ice along my hairline. My body screamed to shut down, but I forced it vertical, wiping crimson streaks from my face with trembling fingers. Through the viewport, nothing had changed—just endless black and the azure shimmer of our damaged ships. The chronometer read seventeen minutes since I had closed my eyes. Yet the nightmare's grip felt solid, tangible—the bridge around me thin as tissue paper by comparison.

Hatch's voice came low from beside me. "You all right, sir?" The "sir" barely made it past her teeth.

I wanted to tell her about the dream, about the corridor and the thing with my face, but the words congealed in my mouth. Instead, I swallowed, hard, and said, "We can't win this waiting game. They're coming for me."

Hatch didn't argue. She just looked past me, her searching eyes behind the transparisteel viewport, as if she was looking for them the old fashioned way.

I straightened my uniform, wincing as my arms protested with a deep, bone-level ache that radiated from shoulder to wrist. The metal beneath me bore the imprint of my fall—a shallow depression shaped like a partial human silhouette, its edges tinged with spider-web patterns of electrical burns that smelled faintly of ozone and scorched polymer. The deck plates ground under my boots with the reluctant screech of stressed metal as I reinforced my stance, my fingers finding cold purchase against the brushed alloy arm of the command chair as I steadied my swaying body.

The ship's medic materialized at my side, her gloved fingers already working at the tear in my uniform where blood seeped through. She pressed a biofoam patch against my shoulder. She didn't ask questions, just cleaned and sealed the wound with practiced efficiency. Another unexplained injury to them. To me, a new connection between the dream world and my reality, another silent acknowledgment of whatever I was becoming.

△△△

Amber light bathed the bridge now, easier on the eyes than the harsh white of crisis mode. The silence felt almost wrong after hours of alarms. I glanced at Reese's station, where the tactical officer had finally surrendered to the inevitable, letting the non-critical warnings scroll quietly on secondary screens instead of blaring across the main display.

I wiped my nose a second time, leaving a crimson smear across the back of my hand that glistened under the amber bridge lights. My shoulder stung under the pressure of the biofoam. The deck beneath me seemed to radiate an arctic chill through the soles of my boots, though I couldn't tell if the temperature had actually dropped or if it was just the hangover from whatever that nightmare had been. I stepped back towards my command chair, each footfall echoing hollowly in my skull. The all too familiar whine of static between my ears crescendoed to a piercing pitch as I lowered myself into the chair's familiar embrace, the synthetic leather creaking beneath my weight like an old confession.

As I collapsed into the chair, my spine crackled like brittle twigs underfoot. Something electric climbed my vertebrae, and the violet haze lingering in my vision felt less like aftermath and more like a permanent filter. Beyond our hull, beyond the sensors' reach, the Shadows weren't visible on our instruments, but I felt their attention fixed on me from somewhere in that endless dark—the way you might sense a predator's breath moments before its teeth find your throat. I wondered, briefly, if I was the only one haunted, or if anyone else out there was having the same night terrors. They'd never admit it. I sure as hell wouldn't.

Hatch slid a cold pack across the console—along with a water bottle beaded with condensation and a small white tablet nestled beside it. I arched an eyebrow at her. Her nod was barely perceptible, professional yet somehow intimate. I swallowed the pill dry, then chased it with the water that numbed my throat all the way down. Between sips, I studied her—the fine web of worry etched around her eyes, the subtle tension in her shoulders as she awaited my command.

Words of reassurance died unspoken as I sank deeper into my chair, the synthetic foam exhaling beneath me. The bridge vibrated under me, a subtle but constant shudder, and for the first time in hours I interpreted it not as failure but as resistance: the Sovereign was refusing to die, the crew refusing to let her. I let my weight settle deeper, the cold pack seeping numbness into the back of my neck and down my shirt. Hatch had retreated to a secondary station, but I could feel her attention on me—the same intensity she once reserved for ballistic missile threat assessments. I stared at the glitchy main display as it cycled through night mode, swapping the ruined engine readouts for a slowly advancing blue trajectory line—one we wouldn't follow unless something impossibly lucky happened to the patchwork inside the drive core.

I took another swallow of water, the bitterness of the pill blooming behind my tongue. My gaze drifted to the environmental schematic in the corner of the display: the color-coded overlay insisted damage control was holding, but it felt like a polite lie. The ship's damage readouts melted into each other as the medication took hold, pulling me away from reality like a tide receding from shore. Sleep.

CHAPTER 15: RESISTANCE

The shriek of unfamiliar alarms tore me from sleep—a high-pitched wail that oscillated between two nerve-shredding frequencies, nothing like the measured pulse of standard alerts. My eyelids peeled back to reveal the dim red emergency lighting that pulsed across the ceiling. Hatch's fingernails dug into my skin as she shook me into consciousness. Her face hovered above mine, close enough that I could see the constellation of freckles across her nose standing out against skin that had gone paper-white with panic. Sweat beaded at her temples despite the chill in the air.

"The quantum core is cascading," she said, voice clipped and brittle. "Engineering can't hold it together much longer."

We sprinted to the engineering section, catapulted most of the way by a transit platform that skimmed the length of the ship's aft—a cavernous spine of machinery where half the vessel's mass existed solely to keep the rest alive. As we ran through the last few corridors, our boots clanged against metal grating until we reached the drive room. The reinforced hatch hissed open on hydraulics, revealing a scene from some engineer's worst nightmare: strobing emergency lights cut through billowing smoke, the acrid stench of scorched wiring seared our nostrils, and the quantum core at the center—a writhing, pulsing mass of unstable energy—bathed everything in an unnatural glow as it prepared to tear itself apart. Blue-white electrical arcs tore through the air like vengeful spirits, searing afterimages onto my retinas.

A technician three feet from me screamed as his console exploded in a shower of molten circuitry. Blood streaked down his face as he staggered backward. The deck plates beneath us shuddered and flexed, nearly sending me to my knees. The quantum core—our critical energy source, the heart of Sovereign—shrieked like a dying star, its housing glowing cherry-red as catastrophic energies threatened to rupture containment and vaporize half of—maybe even all of—the ship. A scream of static erupted from the intercom—then, beneath the chaos, came a voice: the ship's AI, slurred and nearly incomprehensible, as if the processors themselves were melting.

Abandon vessel. Abandon vessel. Catastrophic breach imminent.

Strobing red and blue chased each other through the haze. The deck pitched slightly, metal groaned under the torsion of forces never designed to coexist. In the center of the drive room, the containment shell around the quantum core bulged outward with a wet, impossible sound, like an egg flexing before it burst. A deafening concussion rocked the chamber as a secondary conduit ruptured, spraying superheated plasma across the deck. A female technician—her name tag read "Chen"—collapsed beside me, her regulation jumpsuit peeled away in blackened strips as blue-white flames consumed the synthetic fabric. The pungent smell of burning hair filled my nostrils as someone—a blur of motion in engineering grey—lunged forward with a nano-fiber fire blanket, the material unfurled like quicksilver as they desperately smothered the writhing figure.

Hatch materialized ten feet away, her uniform collar half-torn from its moorings, glasses hanging precariously from one ear. Static electricity had transformed her regulation-cut hair into a corona of filaments that danced above her with each movement. The tendons in her neck stood out like steel cables as she screamed—her mouth formed the shapes of emergency protocols, evacuation orders, finally my name—but the cyclone of the failing drive stripped her words from the superheated air, leaving only the contorted rictus of her face, eyes wild with the knowledge of what came next.

Time buckled: every frame distorted, snapped forward and then dead slow like damaged footage. The world crystallized into hyper-clarity—combat awareness, that game-day focus where seconds stretched into minutes and my mind cataloged every microscopic detail. A single technician—cheeks still smooth with youth, regulation buzz-cut revealing the pink of his scalp—wrestled with a manual shunt valve on the core's B-side. His knuckles blanched white against a large wrench, uniform sleeves charred at the edges. He alone had moved toward the core while others found safer problems to solve. The wrench slipped from his sweat-slicked palm; in the same heartbeat, a blue-white arc of raw energy—jagged as a lightning bolt and twice as bright—struck him square in the chest. His body jackknifed backward, spine arching at an impossible angle into the air. No scream escaped his lips as thin tendrils of gray-black smoke coiled upward from the carbonized fabric of his uniform, carrying the sickly-sweet smell of cooked flesh. I witnessed it all as if separated by a wall of armored transparisteel, present yet untouchable.

The quantum core's breach line spiderwebbed across the containment casing, eerie light leaking from every fissure. The AI's voice ground out another warning:

Total containment failure imminent. Evacuate.

The AI's voice stretched like taffy—"e-vac-u-aaaaate"—until it froze mid-syllable. I blinked, and the universe held its breath. Droplets of melted metal hung suspended in air close to the containment casing. The technician's body still hovered mid-collapse, like a marionette with cut strings waiting to finish its fall. The entire universe had stopped dead in its tracks, red light washed the scene around me, every face glowed with surgical horror, every detail preserved and hideous. The smell—ozone, blood, burning skin and hair, the sweet tang of failing superconductors. Funny what got through, what stuck in the primal brain even when the higher functions were gone. I couldn't move—or I had subconsciously chosen not to. Some feral part of me wanted to see it coming, to understand the shape of the nightmare before it ended me.

There was a microsecond, maybe less, where everything inside my head went clean and sharp and cold.

A memory: the tarmac at Vandenberg, the smell of kerosene and burned coffee, that offhand instructor's phrase in the pre-flight briefing: "If the perimeter fails, all that's left is to give the enemy something to chew on besides you."

The memory slammed me back with the violence of an artillery round.

I started moving, my body enveloped in crackling violet light. Each step left phantom afterimages hanging in the air as I launched myself across the deck with deliberate, savage force—with the ruthless economy of someone who knew there wouldn't be a second attempt. The energy pulsed through me, around me. I moved faster than any spool drive could have propelled a ship through space. Time bent to my will as I hurtled toward the core.

I vaulted the rail, drove my heels toward the manual cutout, and caught the injured kid's arm as he fell. Some of his skin was already half-melted, the uniform fused to muscle in places, but I'd been elbow-deep in worse. I seized the tech by his uniform and swung him across my body in one fluid motion. My momentum carried us both toward the override panel. I slammed his hand—skin still bubbling from the electrical burns—against the flat control-plate. The sizzle of flesh meeting superheated metal cut through the chaos. Deep within the core, I felt something shift. In my mind's eye I heard tearing metal. The massive containment doors ground open, agonizingly slow; perhaps shockingly fast in real time.

With the last of my momentum, I lowered the kid to the deck. Time slowly began to move again. My hand—now pulsing with violet light—rested on his chest. His lungs spasmed, coughing him back to consciousness as I rose and turned toward the quantum core. Sovereign's heart throbbed with impossible colors. I approached it step by measured step, each movement left a trail of ghostly duplicates hanging in the air behind me. Energy streamed from my fingertips like liquid lightning, arcing toward the core in brilliant tendrils that seemed to bend the very fabric of reality around them.

The suspended moment fully shattered. Time lurched forward again—Hatch's face contorted in recognition, engineers scrambled backward, their shadows elongated in the violet glow as I planted myself between them and certain death; absorbing chaotic energies bursting from the exposed core. My hands burned with a power I had never known existed, channeling impossible energies back into the fractured core. The quantum core drank it in, stabilizing with each pulse that flowed from my fingertips. Hatch's eyes met mine across the chaos—disbelief warred with desperate hope.

The universe's full fury had narrowed through me like light through a burning lens, every atom in my body had become the nexus where impossible energies converged. The core's energy did not merely reach for me; it seemed to recognize me. It latched onto me, craved me with a desperate hunger. The violet arc streaming from my hands thickened, cords of light braced against spacetime itself, and I sensed the core's feedback—its desperation, its need, its panic at being naked and dying—poured back down the channel. The trembling in the deck matched a new frequency in my blood, a repetitive shuddering that quaked my body, my mind and my thoughts alike.

I planted my feet, close enough that my hands were now braced against the containment shell, pouring energy into and around the core from my fingertips. The quantum heart pulsed with colors not meant for human eyes—ultraviolet afterimages, synesthetic geometry, impossible chromatics that cut through the inside of my head. My fingers sank into the outer layer of the drive, plastic and metal seemingly warping and fusing around my bones, as if the machine was kissing my hand by electrolysis. The whole room seemed to turn inside out; the blue-white arcs now snaked only through me, bypassing the air entirely to route through nerve and sinew instead. I could feel the circuit diagram of the drive as if it had been laser-etched into the soft tissue behind my forehead: every relay, every shunt, every catastrophic open circuit. I didn't know how I knew, but the knowledge was there—raw, unmediated, like a combat drug unspooling its logic into my muscles.

The core, primed to detonate seconds ago, contracted—shivered, then pulsed, then held steady. A low hum filled the room, harmonizing with the pulse in my arteries. Sweat pooled at my temples, beaded off my chin. I tasted blood—coppery and familiar, but there wasn't time to check if it came from my nose or somewhere deeper. The room lurched through a spectrum of light: a staccato blue, a throbbing ultraviolet, and then a steady, anesthetic white. The arcs faded from the air. The deck stopped bucking beneath my boots.

I stumbled back from the shell, hands burning with aftershocks. The engineer, the kid—he was still alive, barely, and stared up in shock, not at the core but at me. The others, those who hadn't run, gathered at the periphery, slack-jawed and waiting for instructions.

Someone shouted numbers—containment pressure, voltage, flux—but it was all undercut by the bellow of Hatch's voice cutting through. "The core's stabilizing. Close containment now! Now!" She was already halfway to the manual lever as she shouted that, her glasses fractured and a gash leaking blood from her temple. Two engineers, emboldened by the sudden absence of death screaming in their faces, muscled the containment shell's flanges together. Their boots skidded on the rapidly cooling metal. The core's glow dimmed from a blinding blue to a warm, manageable pulse.

I staggered, the muscles in my neck and jaw locked in a rictus as I forced a single breath in and out. The deck trembled beneath my boots, then abruptly everything was still. I slumped to the deck, hands raw and shaking, the phantom echoes of quantum fire still racing along my nerves. The injured technician was making a noise that might be laughter, though the sound was half choked by snot and pain. My legs betrayed me when I tried to rise, leaving me on my knees like a supplicant before some quantum altar, hands still trembling, vision skipping frame to frame.

In the vacuum of sound left by the silenced alarms, my own pulse was the only thing left, until Hatch's hand yanked me upright by the collar. "We have to move!" Her grip was cold and strong at the back of my neck; she half-dragged, half-guided me out of the drive room. The containment doors ground shut behind us with a seismic clang.

The corridor outside was chaos—panicked crew, acrid smoke, fire suppression foam coated the floor.

I wasn't sure how far we got before my legs gave out, but I remembered the long glide down a passageway wall, how the textured alloy had felt hot and damp under my palms. Hatch knelt, one hand bracing my chest like she could restart me if necessary, the other checking her own bleeding scalp. Her mouth was moving, but the blood in my ears drowned out most of it. I caught a word here and there. "Medkit... secondary burns..." but nothing stuck until she shouted, "You did it, sir. The core's stable. You did it." Her voice, at first giddy perhaps, seemed to crack on the last word. She let me slump, then used both hands to slick her hair back, blood leaving fingerpaint tracks above her ears.

"Your hands," she said, voice small. I looked down: ten fingers, but every nail rimmed in black, the flesh underneath a raised, angry red. I waited for pain, but it was distant, my nerves were so overcooked that sensation arrived about three seconds later, a sluggish courier indeed.

A tech—different uniform, auxiliary patch—leaned in with a medkit, sprayed my hands down with freezing antiseptic that stung worse than the burns. Hatch held my gaze the entire time, almost daring me to pass out. I didn't.

I didn't want to.

I passed out.

△△△

We should have been atoms scattered across three sectors of space. Instead, my thoughts crystallized like frost forming on a viewport—not in a flash of insight, but in that peculiar mental silence that follows when you've looked death in the face and somehow walked away. The body count should have been catastrophic—the kind of loss that would have haunted mission reports for decades—yet there we were, breathing the cold air of survival, our skin still warm despite how close to the end we had all come; mere seconds from it.

Hatch snapped back to command mode quickly, barking coordinates and assignments while her eyes darted between faces and the holographic readouts hovering above her wrist display. Around her, engineers crawled through access panels and dangled from ceiling mounts, their tools flashing as they sutured severed power conduits and cauterized the ship's bleeding energy systems, all while the deck continued to groan and settle beneath us. My consciousness continued returning in fragments. I found myself upright without remembering how I'd gotten there, my hands wrapped in medical smart-weave that hummed with nanites, drawing the fire from my scorched nerve endings like a digital compress.

In the corridor, I could still feel the near-disaster's echo. The metal walls hummed with residual energy, as if they had absorbed the terror of the moment and were now slowly releasing it back into the air. Even the floor panels beneath my boots retained a faint warmth that had nothing to do with temperature. The ship's AI stuttered back to life, its synthetic voice had dragged like a drunk trying to pass a sobriety test. "Con-tain-ment nom-in-al," it repeated, each syllable uncertain, as if the word "nominal" itself was a lie it couldn't quite sell. Near my boot, a chrome microdrone zigzagged across the deck, its vacuum port slurped up ash and congealing blood with mechanical indifference. Something about this tiny janitor performing its mundane task amid our near-extinction twisted my mouth into what might have been a smile.

Hatch thrust a data-slate at me, her eyes hollowed by exhaustion, jaw muscles working beneath her skin. "Good news: we're not atomized. Bad news: containment's filthy." Her bloodied thumb left smears across the slate's display as she placed it in my stinging hand. Her wrist's holo-display flickered as she scrolled through, cycling through a cascade of damage reports that painted our situation in stark numerical certainty. "A full systems purge will be required before we even consider another jump." The numbers scrolled by too quickly, but her grim expression told me everything I needed to know. I caught flickers of the diagnostic feed—ship-wide stress fractures, micro-fissures that looked like mold under a blacklight, a scroll of damages that would have made a Navy yard drydock foreman shriek.

In some nearby compartment, the kid I'd saved was propped up on an overturned stowage crate, pale and shivering but alive. His gloves pressed to his chest as if he could hold the pain inside by will alone. Next to him, two crewmates made a performative show of checking his vitals, though neither could meet his eye. A few meters away, Chen, the tech who'd been burned, was already swaddled in emergency wrap, her breathing shallow but steady. The engineer who'd doused her in the fire blanket hovered nearby, his own coveralls stripped to the waist, his arms a lattice of red blisters where he'd caught the overspray.

A communal silence took hold of the corridor, not the shellshock of survivors but a hush of reverence—the recognition that something impossible had happened and none of them quite understood it. Their eyes tracked me across the corridor, these men and women who had grown up knowing the prophecy, and were now seeing it manifest in ways none of them had expected to witness firsthand. I stood there, hands mummified in medical polymer, while the air around me shimmered with an electromagnetic afterglow that shouldn't have been possible. I flexed my fingers beneath the bandages, feeling the smart-weave resist then yield. Some of the crew flinched back, while others drifted closer, their faces a mixture of fear and fascination—pilgrims approaching an altar they weren't entirely sure wouldn't burn them alive.

Overhead lights sputtered back to life along the main corridor, casting juddering shadows as they stabilized. A swarm of microdrones—far more than the usual maintenance complement—converged into the engineering section. They skittered across bulkheads and disappeared into access panels, their welding arcs casting blue-white flares against the metal. Some joined the first drone in its cleanup operation, forming what looked like an industrious colony of mechanical insects as they consumed the disaster's aftermath.

I lowered my gaze to the data-slate in my bandaged hands. On the slate, a prioritized triage queue scrolled in crimson: eight fresh hull breaches beyond the main ruptures we'd already patched on the forward decks. Containment systems labored at 73% capacity. The spool drive—our only ticket home—remained dark and unresponsive; I had a feeling about what that meant. I remembered an Academy instructor who'd joked that the best military repairs used varying combinations of duct tape and prayers. Standing amid the challenges with Sovereign, that punchline had lost all its humor.

Hatch's voice sliced through the corridor. "We caught a break, apparently the Roberson recharge dropped us to four hours until the drive's in the green again. If the Shadows are still out there, that's eighty percent of our remaining luck budget." She nodded once to the repair teams and limped toward the bridge, trailing blood that left a fragile breadcrumb line on the deck. Behind her, the engineering survivors melted into their tasks, heads down, making the most of this borrowed time. More medics arrived to tend to the wounded.

I followed Hatch, marveling at how her back remained squared even as the blood splotches across her collar bloomed brighter with every step. We walked, both with a wounded gait, side by side in silence, the way two veterans cross a killing field: neither hurrying nor dragging, just a kind of trudging honesty.

I paused in the corridor just before the bridge, hands still feeling the tightness of the smart-bandages, and let the moment bleed me out. The urge to hyperventilate wrestled with the need to look unshakeable for the crew. There was a splitting pressure in my head—not pain in the traditional sense, more like a wrench being worked deeper and deeper between the plates of my skull. I steadied myself and checked the mirrorlike surface of a nearby panel. The afterimage of violet arcs still danced behind my pupils. I clung to the edge of composure not for myself—mostly for Hatch. For the crew. For whatever the hell future was watching through these events. Head high, I stepped onto the bridge.

Sovereign's command deck was still cluttered by glass, metal chunks, hanging duct work. At least a third of the consoles were offline, fuses—or whatever they used here—likely blown and screens dark. Most of the rest were manned by engineers in battered jumpsuits, half of them patched with yellow caution tape. The overhead fluorescents had a new, and not entirely comforting, tendency to click on and off in time with the ship's pulse; but at least they were on now. The main display was online again, a stuttering image of our trajectory toward Imperial Prime. A string of calculations running beneath it plotting our spool drive transition, below those, blue-lit and implacable, a tactical readout:

SPOOL ACTIVATION: 4:09:27.

Finally, a break. We were going home the fast way.

Hatch slid behind the command console, squinting at readouts with that laser-focused intensity that made her pupils contract to pinpoints. Even without her glasses—shattered during the chaos—she radiated authority as Reese tiptoed across a floor of exposed circuitry and dangling cables, data-slate clutched to his chest like a shield, desperate to deliver her the latest sensor readings. I settled into the center seat, ignoring the way the synthetic material now stuck to my uniform at the shoulders. For a long moment, the only sound was the even static of a nearby console, the background percussion of tools, the distant crackling of welding.

Four hours to jump.

△△△

About an hour later, I sat at the head of a conference table with Sovereign's senior officers. *Admiral* Chen—who I now realized then was the chief engineer, not just another technician—walked us through the final calibration sequence for the spool drive, her fingers tracing ghostly trajectories across the holographic display. Her voice remained steady despite the patchwork of bandages and medical polymers that held her together. She gestured to an image on the display showing how Sovereign would essentially cradle the damaged escorts through the rift to Imperial Prime. Then, inevitably, the conversation shifted. Eyes turned to me.

Lieutenant Reese leaned forward, his voice hushed with reverence as he recounted what the crew was already calling 'the incident.' Lieutenant Park's hands shook as she cued up the recording. On the display, my silhouette stood outlined against the quantum core's inferno. The quantum energy discharge had bent impossibly in my presence, flowing around my body's contours before reversing course and surging into my flesh as if I were a living conduit.

Blue-white tendrils of crackling energy, each as thick as my wrist and bright enough to have cast shadows through closed eyelids, had leapt from my fingertips into the damaged core. The hologram showed how, for three frames, the boundary between man and machine had disappeared entirely—my silhouette dissolving into a lightning-shaped void where quantum particles had danced like fireflies in midnight blue. The matrix that had powered the drive itself had seemed to pour through me, each pulse sending fractal patterns rippling across what had been my chest. My veins had transformed into luminous filaments, branching beneath my skin like electric roots seeking soil, their cerulean glow so intense that nearby crew had shielded their eyes. Where my hands had been, ten points of white-hot energy had splayed outward, leaving ghost-trails that lingered in the air for seconds after I moved.

Captain Mercer's voice filled the room as he ticked off each impossibility on his fingers, his weathered face illuminated by the holographic display. "A Shadow vessel—not damaged, not disabled—but utterly destroyed. A quantum core repaired at the molecular level without tools, shut down or explosion. Thirty-six hours of travel time can now be compressed into four." His eyes, the pale blue of ancient glaciers, fixed on me with reverent intensity.

Across the conference table, I caught Hatch watching me, her jaw had set like granite, pupils dilated despite the harsh lighting. The others leaned forward in their seats, voices dropped to whispers, hands gestured in the air as if trying to physically grasp what they had witnessed—already transforming a moment of desperate survival into something mythic, something predestined.

The conference table suddenly felt less like a meeting place and more like a ritual altar. Veterans among the officers—those whose bodies had learned to anticipate pain before it arrived—watched the replay with a stillness that spoke volumes. Any tendency toward skepticism had stuttered and died in the presence of what they witnessed. The younger officers—faster to embrace the new, less invested in the rationality of chain-of-command—had leaned in close, eyes bright with the shimmer of half-formed awe and fear. For them, the line between man and myth had always been thinner, and in the hours since the incident, it was now thinnest of all.

They were not, any of them, inventing this narrative.

△△△

The door to my quarters chimed. When it slid open, Hatch stood in the threshold, her silhouette rigid with unspoken concerns. I didn't bother rising from the desk where I'd been pretending to review reports while actually pressing my bandaged fingertips against my temples, trying to massage away the persistent throb that had taken residence behind my eyes since the incident.

I glanced up at her silhouette in the doorway. "Something on your mind, Colonel?"

She stepped inside, letting the door seal behind her with a pneumatic hiss. The overhead lights caught the tight line of her jaw as she crossed her arms. "I've seen a lot of impossible things since we left Earth," she said, each word measured and precise, "but what happened in that engine room doesn't even have a classification."

She stood there, military bearing momentarily abandoned, hands spread wide. "I just watched you absorb enough quantum energy to vaporize a moon, Roberson," she said. "So I'm not sure I am particularly okay right now."

Hatch had studied the security footage frame by frame, she told me, searching for the exact instant I had stopped being merely human. She had cataloged several moments of the incident with military precision: the microsecond flicker of blue light behind my pupils before the alarms; the symmetry of my hands on the console; my arrival at the core 2.7 seconds before the breach—timing that defied probability; and most damning, the way quantum discharge that should have incinerated organic matter had curved around and through me like water recognizing its master.

I stared at my bandaged hands, flexing them experimentally. "I was there, physically present, but something else was... operating through me. Like muscle memory for skills I have never learned." I swallowed hard, not meeting her eyes. "The energy just seemed to bend around me as if I have been manipulating that stuff my entire life. Truth is I can't even explain what I saw, much less figure out how I was controlling it."

Hatch paced the small confines of my quarters, her fingers flexing and unflexing at her sides. "Sir—Marcus—" She stopped, shook her head, then met my eyes with military directness that couldn't quite mask her bewilderment. "I have cataloged every anomaly since we arrived. Classified them. Filed them. But this—" She gestured at my bandaged hands. Her voice cracked as she reframed her observations. "The quantum energy just flowed through you like it belonged to you. And your veins..." She gestured at my arms. "They lit up like fiber optic cables. The footage shows you reacting before the warning system even finished its first tone." She leaned closer, her whisper barely audible. "What's happening to you, Marcus?"

Hatch's military composure fractured before my eyes. The woman who had methodically cataloged our impossible journey—who had filed reports on wormholes and time dilation with the same precision she had once used for ammunition inventories and experimental research—now stood with her hands trembling slightly at her sides. I recognized the look: the desperate mental arithmetic of someone trying to subtract the supernatural from an equation that no longer balanced without it. For weeks, Hatch had witnessed the anomalies surrounding me—knowing her, she had been constructing rational explanations that wouldn't shatter her worldview as she catalogued all the anomalies. But now she avoided direct eye contact, her fingers trembled against her uniform. The quantum core incident had crossed a line her methodical mind could no longer step back from.

CHAPTER 16: THRESHOLD CONDITIONS

Ninety minutes to jump. This day had stretched like a black hole's event horizon—time dilation in full effect.

The weight of the incident clung to me like the acrid smoke and dried sweat on my uniform. Each footfall felt heavier than the last. The Sovereign's corridors hadn't changed—same metal walls, same recessed lighting—but the crew had. Their gazes followed me now, a mix of reverence and wariness in their eyes. I'd become something dangerous yet necessary to them, like the warheads we carried in the weapons bay: potentially catastrophic, but ultimately what might save us all.

I'd stared down artillery barrages with a steady pulse. This twisted my gut worse.

I retreated to my quarters, seeking refuge from their stares. Back and forth I paced, my boots wearing an invisible trench across the hexagonal deck plating. After the thirtieth lap, the pattern below transformed—no longer just flooring, but a battlefield grid, each six-sided tile a potential combat zone. My body defaulted to what it knew while my mind short-circuited on impossibilities. Veterans understand this instinct: motion creates options when calculations fail. Stillness makes you a target; momentum creates the illusion of progress, even when you're going nowhere.

A chime from the door, then three rapid knocks—tap-tap-tap—in that unmistakable rhythm that belonged only to Hatch. The panel slid open before I could even call out, and she strode in with the confidence of someone who'd seen me at my worst in a dozen combat zones. We'd stopped standing on ceremony somewhere between Earth's atmosphere and here.

"This avoidance strategy isn't sustainable," she said, eyes already scanning me for weaknesses.

I fixed my gaze on the viewport where pinpoints of light crawled past like dying stars in slow motion. "I've got a handle on things."

Hatch didn't waste oxygen on a sigh. She locked her arms across her chest, rooted herself like structural support. "You've got a handle on everything except what matters."

I pivoted toward her, my flash of anger providing temporary shelter from the dread underneath. "Let's not do this now."

She lifted one eyebrow. "I'm not the one who started this conversation. The universe did."

Her words landed like a tactical strike—clean, calculated, and impossible to evade. There was no heat in them, no raw emotion to grab onto and fight against.

She spoke with that familiar cadence I'd heard in the worst moments of our campaigns, when she'd look at the tactical data and tell me we had to fall back, even as I searched the map for options that didn't exist.

"This stopped being a theoretical debate," she continued, tapping her finger against her thigh in that rhythm that always meant trouble, "the moment McNeil's viewscreen turned itself into shrapnel."

I clenched my teeth. "There was obviously a manufacturing flaw in that screen."

"Sure there was," she said, voice dry as vacuum. "And I suppose the violet fire in your eyes right before it 'malfunctioned' was just a coincidence was it?"

My body betrayed me before I could think, spine snapping to attention as if responding to a drill sergeant's command rather than Hatch's accusation. Something primal and defensive flooded my system—the unmistakable chemical cocktail of being caught in a lie I hadn't even consciously crafted.

"Violet fire?" The words felt strange in my mouth. "What are you talking about?"

Hatch's jaw worked once, the tendon beneath her scarred jawline tightening like a guitar string about to snap. Her pupils contracted to pinpoints as she arranged the memory into something she could say aloud. "A corona," she said, her voice dropping an octave. "Cerulean. Electric blue with threads of violet. It rimmed your irises like some sort of weird solar eclipse—your irises were both surrounded by this... this impossible light. It was brief—barely perceptible—but unmistakable. Bright like lightning. And then—" She flicked two fingers outward in a precise motion, thumb and forefinger spreading like a blast radius. "—the screen didn't just break. It shattered into a million pieces."

I stared at her, mouth opening and closing like an airlock failing to pressurize.

Hatch sliced through my unspoken objection with military precision. "If you're about to suggest a power surge, *save it.* I've traced every circuit pathway in that section. I ran diagnostics on the environmental systems. Even combed through the sensor logs. Three separate times." She tapped her wrist unit. "Nothing."

Typical Hatch—always ten steps ahead of my denials.

I dragged a hand down my face. "Hatch... we can't jump to conclusions—"

"I'm not jumping anywhere," she cut in, her voice precise as a scalpel. "I've documented a consistent phenomenon preceding each incident. What I need to know is whether you've experienced any sensations—physical, mental—that you've conveniently not reported?"

'Conveniently.' The word hung between us, wrapped in false politeness but sharp enough to draw blood.

My throat constricted like someone had cranked a vice around my windpipe. "What exactly am I supposed to say in a report?" I rasped, the words scraping against my vocal cords. "Dear Command, occasionally the fabric of reality peels itself open and rewires my nervous system like a circuit board? That sometimes I feel like I'm being unmade at the atomic level, only to be reassembled with something extra—something that doesn't belong to me—threaded through my aching brain like razor wire?"

Her face softened a fraction—the tight lines around her eyes easing like a ship's hull decompressing after completing a jump. "That's a start," she said, one corner of her mouth quirking upward. "We'll workshop the terminology."

A sound escaped me—half-bark, half-wheeze—something that had intended to be a laugh but collapsed under its own weight, leaving only the hollow echo of gallows humor in the recycled air between us.

Hatch took a step closer, her boot making a dull thud against the deck plating. The overhead lights caught a few silver threads in her regulation-cut hair as she leaned forward, her hands braced against the edge of the console. "Marcus, I'm not here to ask if you believe in the prophecy."

That word—prophecy—hit the room like a gravity shift, seeming to compress the recycled air between us until the pressure was uncomfortable.

"I'm here," she said, her voice dropped to a pitch that wouldn't carry beyond the bulkhead, her eyes never left mine, "because the crew is starting to behave more strongly about it after the incident."

Silence swelled between us like a bubble, threatening to burst the compartment. The air recyclers hummed their mindless industrial lullaby, a mechanical heartbeat that only emphasized how utterly still we'd become. Even Sovereign itself—all, what, several hundred thousand tons of alloys and circuitry—seemed to be holding its breath, its bulkheads and conduits somehow attuned to our conversation like some massive eavesdropping organism.

I turned away, fixing my gaze on the faint reflection in the viewport's polarized surface. Hatch's eyes burned into the back of my head with the precision of lasers. "What do you want from me? To stand in front of the crew and announce that maybe I'm the chosen one after all? Wave my hands and make the stars dance a little bit?"

"No," Hatch said, her voice cutting through the air with the efficiency of a hull breach. "I want you to stop pretending you're not becoming an operational variable."

I blinked, the light overhead catching the moisture in my eyes. "An operational variable?"

"Yes," she said, her jaw set like carbon-reinforced steel, the scar tissue along her jawline tightening as she spoke. "Something the Imperium will factor into every strategic calculation. Something the Shadows will study, probe, and eventually weaponize against us. Something that cannot—must not—remain an undefined quantity in our equations."

There it was: Hatch's real fear laid bare in the rigid posture of her shoulders and the microscopic tremor in her otherwise steady hands. Not mysticism with its nebulous prophecies. Not faith with its desperate clinging to cosmic order. But uncontrolled systems that couldn't be mapped, measured, or mitigated.

I felt something cold settle behind my ribs, like coolant leaking into my thoracic cavity. "You're talking like command."

"I'm talking like an engineer," she replied, her voice as flat and as uncompromising as a sealed airlock. "Which is why this is going to irritate you."

She reached into the pocket of her torn uniform—the fabric frayed a little where plasma discharge had caught the edge during the last attack—and produced a small data stick. It was military-issue gray, scratched from years of handling, with a hairline crack running along its housing and a serial number worn nearly invisible. I immediately recognized it was the one Kartchev gave me. The *dreaded* prophecy stick. I'd deliberately abandoned it in my quarters on Imperialis, nursing a childish fantasy that it might disappear into the station's recycling system or find its way to someone more eager for cosmic responsibility.

She lifted the data stick between us. "You recognize this?"

My hands stayed at my sides. "I thought I left that behind."

"You *did*," Hatch confirmed, extending it toward me like a challenge. "Now you're going to face it."

The small device hung in the space between us, innocuous in appearance, devastating in implication.

I started to object, but she cut me off.

"Marcus," she said, my first name landing between us like a mortar. Her eyes narrowed, voice dropping to that precise cadence she used when explaining physics to politicians. "You want another explanation? Then let's be methodical. Source material. Documented incidents. Correlation analysis. We figure this out ourselves, or I promise you—the Imperium or our increasingly reverential crew will do it for us."

I accepted the data stick, the plastic carried the heat of her palm. When I slotted it into the console, recognition was instant. A display materialized in the air before us—first in the flowing calligraphy of Imperial script, then shifting and rearranging itself with unnecessary theatrical flair until standard English characters stood suspended between us.

The Prophecy of the Breach materialized in the air between us, each holographic letter pulsing with an eerie cobalt luminescence that cast shadows across Hatch's face. Ancient text blocks floated beneath the title, their edges blurred and shifted like something underwater, characters rendered in a font that mimicked handwritten script from another era. I leaned forward, jaw tight, ready to dismiss it as the kind of superstitious nonsense that desperate civilizations cling to when science fails them.

Then I read the first line—words that seemed to reach through time and space to name me specifically—and felt the air evacuate from my lungs as though I'd been thrown into hard vacuum.

The words pulsed on the screen: "When the cosmic fire breaches the void, Time itself shall perform its surgery upon the flesh of the Traveler. In the moment shields fail and stars fall silent, the Breach will open." My eyes caught on that word—Traveler—and something electric skittered along my spine.

But as I silently read further, my throat felt like it closed up: "...when the clocks falter at precisely the four-point-eight microsecond mark..." Then the words "sixteen hours, twenty-three minutes" leapt from the page—the exact duration I'd been unconscious after the wormhole transition. The text swam before my eyes. My fingers went numb where they gripped the console edge. There it was in ancient script—the exact duration of my blackout during the jump, a measurement I'd never shared with anyone. The words 'the resonance' pulsed on the screen, the same term the ship's AI had used during our final conversation.

My eyes raced across the text, each line punching into me like a physical blow. "...the boy who fell from the maple tree, arm twisted beneath him..." My breath caught—I'd never told anyone about that day, not even my mother. "...the red notebook filled with calculations..." My college journal. The text described the exact pattern of the Imperium's orbital stations, the distinctive silhouette of the Shadow vessels. Then—my vision stuttered, caught on a single word that seemed to pulse with its own light: "Yachtya." The characters didn't translate, didn't even register as language, not in English, not even in Imperial script yet something ancient in my brain recognized it instantly. Yachtya. My mouth formed the shape silently, tasting a word I'd somehow always known.

Hatch's eyes tracked across my features, cataloging every micro-expression. "That," she said, her voice barely above a whisper, "is what recognition looks like when it hits the bloodstream."

I stared at the symbol, my mouth suddenly dry. The word burned in my mind, but speaking it felt dangerous—like uttering a spell that might unravel reality itself. When I finally broke the silence, my voice emerged as a whisper.

"Yachtya," I said, the alien syllables vibrating against my teeth. "That's what they're called. The Shadows."

Hatch's eyes narrowed. "You've said that word before. In your sleep. How can you possibly read this?"

I inhaled sharply, tasting recycled air that suddenly seemed too thin. "The rest is gibberish, but that word... that word I know."

Hatch's finger jabbed at the translated holographic readout hovering between us. "Four-point-eight microseconds. That's the exact duration of what Pioneer's AI classified as a 'temporal anomaly' during our transition. Sixteen hours and twenty-three minutes of you unconscious with biological markers that—" she narrowed her eyes, "—and I quote, 'exceed baseline human parameters by factors inconsistent with known medical science.' The same AI that recommended immediate quarantine protocols before experiencing what it self-diagnosed as a 'catastrophic logic failure.'"

Her voice dropped to a whisper. "Funny how that detail never made it into your log."

My mouth turned to sandpaper. "You accessed my personal logs?"

"I accessed irregularities in the system," she replied, her voice clinical. "Critical mission variances don't recognize chain of command."

I stared at the screen again. The text blurred, then refocused as something electric jolted through my memory—I was somewhere else, my palms pressed against crackling metal, that spinning maw tearing through the void, my entire being unmade then reassembled atom by atom like I was in a transporter in my favorite childhood TV show. Now that same power hummed inside my skull, vibrating against bone like a struck gong.

My bandaged hands tightened into fists, the gauze pulling against raw skin.

Hatch's voice softened, just slightly—engineer to human. "Remember what you said after the first incident?"

I stiffened. No comment.

Hatch quoted me with surgical accuracy: "*Call me crazy, but my gut says this is real.*"

My own testimony, thrown back at me like a prosecutor's exhibit. I stared at the prophecy text, then down at my hands—all ten fingers present, their nail beds still darkened from the incident. Physical evidence that reality had become flexible around me, bending laws once thought immutable.

"We need to try to understand this more." She finished.

I met her eyes, my voice dropped to a near-whisper. "What exactly are you proposing here? Turn me into some lab specimen? Hook me up to machines until whatever's inside me decides to make another appearance?"

The corner of Hatch's mouth tightened—a micro expression most would miss. "I'm proposing we understand this on our terms," she said, "before circumstances force us to understand it on theirs."

My jaw clenched. She was right, and that made it worse.

Hatch leaned in, her voice low. "The second a story changes how people act, it becomes as real as gravity. And that's happening now. The way the crew looks at you—like you're some kind of walking solution. If we don't establish the parameters of what you are—with proper protocols and documentation—someone with less scientific rigor certainly will."

I met her eyes. "Who exactly are we worried about here?"

"Everyone with an agenda," she said, counting off on her fingers. "McNeil. Kartchev. The entire strategic council. Draven and whatever faction he's building." She leaned forward, voice dropping. "And whatever's watching us from the darkness beyond our sensors."

The silence that followed carried weight, like the moment between lightning and thunder.

I met her gaze and dipped my chin in a single, measured acknowledgment. "All right."

Hatch's shoulders lowered a fraction of an inch—the only visible sign of relief as she released a breath that seemed to have been trapped in her lungs since the moment the core had flared.

“All right,” I repeated. “Operational reality.” I nodded once, military-crisp. "Let's establish protocols, then. Before someone else does."

The console chimed. A new alert—priority routing, bridge-level, was scrolling across the surface.

Hatch glanced at the message, her expression shifting subtly. "Sovereign’s transition sequence is initiating. They are completing final preparations to spool back to Imperial Prime.”

I stared at the notification as the words resolved.

SPOOL DRIVE CHARGING.

And beneath it, a second line:

FINAL PREPARATIONS, THIRTY MINUTES.

△△△

I returned to the bridge, the doors hissed shut behind me with a pneumatic sigh. I lowered myself into the command chair, its contours already familiar beneath me. Vance was seated next to me, her hair falling across her face as she hunched forward, studying her console. The blue glow from her display cast eerie shadows across her concentrated features. I watched her eyes lock onto the transition protocols for our journey home. To my left favoring the holo-display on her wrist, Hatch's slender fingers danced across and through translucent schematics, each movement precise and deliberate, manipulating complex data streams that spiraled and reformed in the air before her. She worked with the practiced efficiency of a virtuoso pianist, not someone who'd been aboard Sovereign for mere weeks. She was like a true veteran who'd navigated these systems since her earliest academy days.

Far behind us in the ship's still-damaged aft section, the quantum core initiated its final charging sequence. The machine's energy signature climbed to levels not seen since the incident, vibrating at a frequency that should have been imperceptible to human ears. Yet somehow, I felt it—not as a surge, not as pain, but as a faint pressure behind my eyes. It felt like someone pressing thumbs gently against my closed eyelids. A tingling sensation spread across my scalp, each hair follicle seeming to stand at attention. The air in my lungs felt suddenly denser, as if I was breathing through water rather than atmosphere. It was like the same primal awareness that makes animals flee before a tornado touches down, or causes the hairs on your neck to rise when lightning is about to fracture the sky.

Hatch was watching me when it happened, her eyes narrowing to analytical slits as my pupils dilated in response to something imperceptible to Sovereign's instruments. She froze mid-gesture, her hand suspended in the space between it and the holographics from her wrist like a conductor who has just sensed a wrong note.

"You felt that," she said, voice dropping to that particular frequency she reserved for observations that confirmed her worst hypotheses.

It wasn't a question.

I nodded once. "Low-level harmonics." The vibration lingered at the base of my skull like the aftershock of a struck tuning fork.

Her jaw tightened, the small muscle beneath her ear twitching visibly. "That shouldn't be perceptible." Her fingers curled around the edge of an arm rest until her knuckles whitened a little.

"No," I agreed, running my tongue over suddenly dry lips. "It shouldn't."

She glanced at her holographic display, its readouts casting ghostly reflections in her pupils, then back at me. The bridge was quiet now—too quiet. Only the soft electronic hum of instruments and the barely audible hiss of the environmental systems punctuated the silence. The kind of calm that follows chaos not because things are safe, but because everyone is afraid to disturb whatever fragile balance has been achieved.

"We're not telling the crew," she whispered flatly, her voice dropping to just above a whisper.

I nodded once. "Good."

"I have an idea, we may have to involve some people I trust in Engineering and Medical, but no official reports, not yet," she continued, her voice clipped and precise as a surgical incision. "No speculation. No mythology."

I almost smiled at that. Almost. The corner of my mouth twitched, then surrendered to the gravity of the moment.

Hatch exhaled slowly through her nose, a controlled decompression. Her pupils contracted slightly as she stared at a point on the far side of the bridge, that thousand-yard gaze of someone running complex calculations behind their eyes. Her jaw muscles tensed, relaxed, and then again before setting with military determination. Her eyes narrowed as she leaned forward, her voice a level quieter than a confidential murmur. "There's a diagnostics bay off Engineering Three—a reinforced chamber with triple-layered quantum shielding. Walls thick enough to contain a small reactor breach." Her fingers traced invisible schematics in the air between us. "Originally built for calibrating the most unstable emitter components. No surveillance. No data links to the main system."

I waited, watching the sharp angles of her face in the blue-tinged light.

"I want to run a controlled exposure," she said, each word precise, focused. "Low-level. Barely above background noise—the kind of energy signature you'd never detect without specialized equipment." Her pupils dilated slightly as she studied my reaction.

I turned to face her fully now, the command chair creaking beneath my weight. "You want to see if it happens again." The words hung between us like smoke.

"I want to see if it happens at *all*," she corrected. "Without a crisis. Without adrenaline flooding your system. Without half the ship screaming and alarms blaring in your ears."

The hum of the ship's systems seemed to grow louder in the space between us. My fingers tapped quickly against the armrest—three quick, two slow.

"And if it does?" I asked, my voice barely above a whisper.

Her gaze didn't waver, her eyes holding mine with the unwavering focus of a targeting system. "Then we stop pretending this is some sort of cosmic fluke," she said, "and start preparing for what that means."

That settled it. The decision crystallized between us, as tangible as if I could reach out and grasp it from the air.

△△△

Transition complete.

The spool drive completed our transition with mechanical precision—no alarms, no energy flares, no desperate countdowns and perhaps most importantly, no big boom. Just mathematics and physics performing exactly as designed. Around me, shoulders lowered and breathing slowed as the bridge crew exchanged glances of quiet satisfaction. I remained rigid in my seat, fingers pressed against the armrests. Hatch's eyes found mine across the command deck, one eyebrow arching upward in silent question.

She tilted her head toward the corridor. "I believe we have some unfinished business in diagnostics, sir," she said, the formality of 'sir' carrying a weight that belied her casual posture.

Legends weren't supposed to begin in places like this. The diagnostics bay was brutally utilitarian—stripped bulkheads and exposed conduits snaking across the ceiling like mechanical veins. At its center stood a single chair, bolted to the deck with restraints that hung open like waiting hands. Not to cage a monster, but to steady a test subject. Sensor pylons formed a semicircle around it, their calibrations so precise they measured energies most scientists considered theoretical. Medical personnel checked my vital signs while engineering technicians muttered numbers to each other, adjusting tolerances on equipment never designed for tests like what was about to unfold.

Hatch stood at the control panel, her eyes tracked between me and the readouts. A muscle twitched in her jaw as I lowered myself into the seat and one of the medical personnel strapped me in.

"We're keeping this minimal," she said, voice pitched low enough that the techs couldn't hear. "Six-second exposure window. Basic field only."

"If it goes sideways?"

Her finger hovered over the emergency cutoff. "Two seconds and we kill it."

We both knew the two-second cutoff was a comforting fiction. The chamber lights dimmed subtly—just enough darkness for the instruments to perceive what remained invisible to human retinas.

"Baseline readings stable," announced Medical from behind their console.

Hatch's index finger suspended itself above the initiator, trembling almost imperceptibly. Her voice dropped to a near-whisper: "Commencing exposure."

The emitter activated silently, invisibly, and for a heartbeat I felt nothing at all.

Then it washed over me—neither burning nor aching—a strange familiarity. Like encountering a scent from childhood you never realized you'd forgotten. My fingers tensed against the cold metal, responding before my mind could process why.

I saw a medical technician's eyes flick to her screen. "Increased neural activity. Isolated to the motor cortex."

A denial escaped me like a child caught with their hand in a cookie jar. "I didn't move," I said, my voice unnaturally tight in my own ears.

"Your body was preparing to," Hatch corrected, her gaze never leaving my face.

Something changed in the air around me—a subtle thinning, as though the molecules themselves were drifting apart.

At the three-second mark, my fingers took on a peculiar luminescence—a whisper of violet playing across my skin like oil on water. Had I blinked, I might have missed it entirely.

The monitoring equipment registered what my eyes barely perceived. Hatch's voice cut through the hum: "Terminate sequence."

The emitter died with a soft electronic whimper. The violet glow receded from my fingertips like a tide pulling back from shore, leaving nothing but ordinary skin behind. My body went slack against the restraints, lungs struggling to pull in enough air while my pulse hammered in my ears. Across the room, the engineering team hunched forward, faces bathed in the blue glow of their displays, expressions frozen in disbelief.

One of the engineers stared at his display, mouth slightly open. "These readings can't be right."

Hatch pivoted toward him, her movement deliberate. "What exactly are you seeing?"
"The emitter..." He tapped at the screen, rechecking figures. "It maintained safe levels throughout, but the power signature shows a negative curve."

"Meaning?" Hatch asked.

"It's like it was being siphoned," the engineer said, voice barely audible.

Hatch's gaze locked with mine across the chamber. Not a flicker of shock disturbed her features—only the slight narrowing of her eyes that meant she'd found the missing piece to a puzzle she'd been assembling for weeks.

△△△

Some hours later, hunched over her terminal in the blue-white glow of her quarters, she had recorded the following in her personal log:

> **Low-level quantum field exposure resulted in anomalous biofield interaction.**
> **No amplification observed.**
> **No measurable energy discharge.**

Her finger had hovered over the touchscreen as the system waited for input on energy transfer vectors. The cursor blinked steadily against the stark options:

INBOUND. OUTBOUND. RECIPROCAL.

After thirteen seconds of hesitation, she tapped the fourth option at the bottom of the list—'other'—and typed:

INDETERMINATE PATHWAY.

She stared at the raw data long after the log sealed, her eyes burning from the blue-white glow of the terminal. The numbers on her screen formed a scientific impossibility—a violation of fundamental laws. The emitter's energy signature showed clear depletion, a gradual hollowing like water draining from a basin. Yet the ship's absorption metrics remained flat, unchanging lines across her display. Most perplexing were Roberson's biological readings—his cellular structure, neural patterns, and metabolic rate all stubbornly normal despite being at the epicenter of the phenomenon. Energy had moved through the chamber like an invisible tide, leaving nothing but contradictory readings and impossible questions in its wake.

The energy had not gone anywhere their systems could detect—not into the ship's power grid, not into ambient heat, not even into the background noise that permeated all of space. It had simply... disappeared, like water poured into desert sand. Which left Hatch with two equally unsettling possibilities. Either their cutting-edge Imperial instruments—capable of measuring particles so small they existed in multiple places simultaneously—were fundamentally flawed. Or something was present in that room, perhaps in Roberson himself, that three centuries of Imperial science had never encountered, classified, or learned how to measure. Hatch leaned back in her chair, the metal creaking softly as she stared at the gunmetal gray bulkhead, its surface reflecting the blue glow of her terminal.

△△△

Sovereign dragged itself into the local space of Imperial Prime like a wounded animal seeking shelter, its hull scorched and pockmarked from battle and its prow stoved in like a rusty old bucket. The emerald-blue sphere of Imperial Prime swelled through the viewports, New Horizon Station's distinctive hub-and-spoke silhouette hanging in orbit like a jeweled spider. Around the command deck, shoulders loosened and jaws unclenched—the silent language of a crew that had survived to see home again. One by one, the four escort ships—each bearing their own scars of combat—detached from the hardpoints, thrusters firing in stuttered bursts as they peeled away toward the gleaming latticework of the fleet docks that orbited one of Prime's moons like a metallic halo.

Hatch's fingers moved across the encrypted comm panel, entering the private channel reserved for the highest echelons of Imperial command. The holographic insignia of Imperator Vyr—a stylized phoenix rendered in crimson light—materialized above the console, rotating slowly as the connection established. When the confirmation tone sounded, she leaned forward, her voice dropping to a whisper that barely disturbed the air. "You need to see this, Imperator. We need to discuss what has happened, what we found, we have to keep a tight lid on this or risk things escalating quicker than we are ready for."

△△△

I flexed my fingers in the dim light of my quarters, watching for that violet shimmer that had appeared during the test. Nothing. Just skin and bone, yet somewhere beneath the surface, it seemed my ever changing biology was recreating itself without my permission. My head throbbed with each heartbeat, a dull counterpoint to the ship's laboring engines as we approached the Imperial fleet docks. The data-slate beside my bunk displayed Hatch's carefully sanitized report, I had just finished reading it as Imperial Prime finished filling my viewport. Carefully scrutinizing what she'd chosen to include, and what she hadn't. In that moment, I felt I was being thrust toward answers that would not come easily, and truths that would not remain contained much longer.

CHAPTER 17: THRESHOLD

The massive doors of Imperial Command split apart with a serpentine hiss, and we stepped onto floors of something resembling polished marble—so mirror-bright that our ghostly doubles walked inverted beneath our feet, mimicking our every movement. Holographic displays lined the corridor, bathing everything in an eerie blue-white glow that made Hatch's face appear almost spectral. Security scanners descended from hidden ceiling panels, washing over us with pulsing crimson light that traced the contours of our bodies before confirming our identities; three ascending chimes said we weren't going to detention today.

Hatch's jaw was set tight as we walked toward the transport tube; she'd arranged this meeting with Imperator Vyr to discuss the recordings that captured the moment my abilities first manifested in a controlled environment. My hands had barely shimmered, it really didn't feel like a big deal to me, yet here we were anyway. Hatch's instincts rarely were off, so I found myself genuinely curious to hear her hypothesis. The transport tube's crystal walls hummed as we ascended past floor after floor, the numbers flashing by in glowing azure digits until we neared the 97th level. Through the transparent sections, I watched Imperialis shrink beneath us—its violet fields and crystalline spires becoming a geometric tapestry, the twin suns casting elongated shadows across the landscape like cosmic sundials.

In the heart of the Prophecy Intelligence Bureau, dozens of artifacts hovered in prismatic stasis fields, each bathed in its own column of dramatic amber light. Ancient glyphs crawled across grey stone walls like slow motion lightning—one particular sequence caught my eye, its angular hooks and spiraling crescents unmistakably Yachtya script. My pulse quickened; I'd stake my life the Bureau analysts haven't deciphered these particular markings. Dominating the chamber's center floated what was surely their most prized acquisition—a dodecahedral crystalline structure whose fractal patterns branched and recombined with hypnotic complexity. The surface of the artifact shimmered with opalescent light that seemed to originate from somewhere beyond our dimension. Deep, jagged fissures marred the artifact's otherwise perfect geometry, wounds that Dr. Levin, the Bureau's purple-haired chief archaeologist, traced—from a safe distance—reverently with a trembling finger as she explained how it was believed the Shadows attempted to destroy it twenty millennia ago.

"The damage," she whispered, "didn't merely scar the prophecy—it fundamentally transformed it, embedding quantum oscillation patterns into its molecular lattice that can only be detected with specialized equipment. This wasn't merely a warning they left behind," Levin said, her voice dropped to a tone of religious awe. "It was a signature of defiance preserved through violence, encoded to survive any imaginable attempt at erasure. We assume the Shadows did this because they failed to destroy the artifact. I will let the Imperator know you are here."

Levin entered a room to our left. Hatch's finger traced one of the symbols, her eyes narrowing behind her glasses. "Yachtya," she muttered, her voice barely audible even to me standing beside her.

A chill spread through my body, freezing me in place. It wasn't just the word that paralyzed me, but the realization that Hatch could now recognize it too.

Imperator Vyr emerged silently from his office, his tall frame casting a long shadow across the gleaming floor, his robes flowing and adorned with glyphs—none I was relieved to see were Yachtya script. "What did you say, Colonel?" he asked, his voice carrying the weight of suspicion.

Hatch's posture shifted imperceptibly as she turned to face him. "I said 'oh yeah,'" she lied, her face betraying nothing. "I'm just surprised this artifact remains intact despite the extensive fracturing. Dr. Levin pointed out these fascinating markings." She gestured toward the floating crystal, her hand steady despite the tension I felt radiating from her. "It's... truly an extraordinary piece."

"It is, it is," Vyr agreed with a thin smile that didn't reach his eyes, then proceeded to recount the artifact's discovery in the ruins of the Cygnus outpost, his words measured as if reciting a carefully memorized script. “But I digress, we had business yes?” He asked turning to Hatch.

"Indeed." Hatch nodded, her tone shifting to a more formal cadence as she activated her wrist display. "We've conducted a controlled experiment in Sovereign’s diagnostics bay."

I watched as her fingers manipulated the holographic interface, bringing up a three-dimensional rendering of the test chamber. The data streams flowed around the projection like luminous rivers, numbers and graphs cascading in organized chaos. My own image appeared at the center, seated in that cold metal chair, restraints securing my limbs.

"As you can see," Hatch continued, "the energy signature during the controlled exposure shows a peculiar pattern."

Vyr stepped closer, his eyes narrowing as he studied the display. I remained silent, watching his reaction carefully. The data showed what we'd already discussed privately—energy disappearing without transferring to any detectable medium.

"Fascinating," Vyr murmured, his long fingers reaching toward the hologram but stopping short of touching it. "And you're certain there was no instrumentation error?"

"We ran three separate diagnostics," Hatch replied. "The equipment functioned perfectly."

I shifted my weight, uncomfortable with being discussed as though I weren't present. "What I'd like to know," I interjected, "is why this matters so much. So I absorbed some energy. That hardly makes me—"

"The Traveler?" Vyr finished, his eyes lifting to meet mine. "Whatever your position Commander, this certainly does make you unique."

The way he said 'unique' sent a chill through me. His tone carried the weight of something beyond scientific curiosity—something that bordered on reverence.

"I'm not interested in prophecies or legends," I said firmly. "I'm interested in understanding what's happening to me from a tactical perspective."

Vyr's lips curved into what might have been a smile on anyone else's face. On his, it resembled a predator's assessment.

"Of course," he said. "And yet, tactical advantages often arise from unexpected sources, wouldn't you agree, Commander?"

△△△

Hatch worked independently at a nearby Bureau terminal, her fingers dancing across the holographic interface with practiced precision. I studied artifacts, occasionally looking over as she overlaid multiple data sets—my brain scans from Medical, energy readings from the engineering bay test, and what appeared to be anomalous readings captured during Pioneer's passage through the wormhole.

"Sir," she called, her voice carrying that particular tone she used when discovering something significant. "You should see this."

I moved toward her station, conscious of how Vyr shadowed my movements. The holographic display showed three distinct waveform patterns floating side by side. As I looked closer, I noticed they weren't just similar—they were nearly identical, differing only in amplitude.

"The resonance signature," Hatch explained, her voice low and controlled. "From your energy emissions, from the wormhole event, and from—"

Drawn to examine the third waveform more carefully, I crossed the remaining distance to Hatch's station. The movement brought me within arm's reach of the central artifact—closer than I'd ventured since entering the Bureau. Without warning, the crystalline dodecahedron flared to life, bathing the chamber in pulsating waves of violet radiance. The effect was almost instantaneous—a radiant pulse that bathed the entire chamber in an otherworldly glow, casting long shadows that seemed to move independently of their sources.

I stopped abruptly, and turned to face the artifact, I was transfixed by the phenomenon. The artifact's pulse seemed to be synchronized perfectly with my heartbeat, a connection I felt more than understood. The violet luminescence intensified as I moved forward, drawn towards the artifact by something beyond conscious thought.

"Commander," Hatch's voice sharpened with urgency. She grabbed my arm, pulling me away from the artifact. The violet glow receded slightly, but continued to pulse rhythmically, like a heartbeat responding to my presence.

I felt a strange tingling sensation at the base of my skull, similar to what I'd experienced during the diagnostic test, but stronger now. More insistent. My fingertips began to tingle, and I clenched my fists to hide any potential visible manifestation.

"What just happened?" I asked, my voice rougher than I'd intended.

Hatch's eyes were wide behind her glasses, a rare display of unfiltered surprise. She glanced at her data display, then back at the artifact, then at me. "The resonance pattern... it's identical. When you approached the artifact, you triggered some kind of response."

Vyr moved forward with the cautious reverence of someone approaching an altar. "Fascinating," he said, his eyes darting between me and the artifact. "It responded to you. In all my years studying this piece, I've never witnessed such behavior."

I looked from the artifact to my hands, then back again, resisting the urge to step closer. Something in me recognized that crystal structure on a level deeper than conscious thought. The sensation was like remembering a dream—fragments of knowledge just beyond my grasp.

"This really has *never* happened before?" I asked, my voice steadier than I felt.

Vyr shook his head. "Never. We've had thousands of visitors through this chamber—scientists, dignitaries, military personnel. The artifact has remained inert for all of them." His eyes locked with mine. "Until you."

Hatch was already typing furiously on her data-slate, capturing readings from the phenomenon. "The emission frequency is precisely matched to your neural patterns, Commander. It's as if—" she hesitated, searching for words that wouldn't sound mystical, "—as if it's recognizing you specifically."

"Or what's inside me," I muttered, flexing my fingers.

Vyr's expression shifted subtly. He moved to a nearby console and entered a complex sequence. The security cameras in the upper corners of the room blinked once, then went dark.

"What I'm about to tell you is classified at the highest levels, a secret known only to the highest members of the Bureau." he said, his voice dropping to barely above a whisper. "Perhaps this artifact holds the key to what comes next. The prophecy itself… I'm afraid it appears to contain no information about events after your arrival, Commander. Whatever guidance it offered ends precisely at the moment of your transformation. While many think it details an elaborate story of salvation and glory after your return… Well, if it does, we haven't been able to decode that yet."

I frowned. "What do you mean?"

"We've been searching for continued instructions," he admitted, "but there are none, or we simply cannot find a way to translate them. The future is no longer predicted—it is being written now, by your actions."

I stared at the artifact, my mind struggling to process Vyr's revelation. The prophecy that had guided the Imperium for centuries—that had predicted my arrival with uncanny precision—simply stopped at the moment I stepped into this new reality. No guidance. No roadmap. No predetermined fate.

"So I'm flying blind," I said, the words feeling hollow in my mouth.

Vyr's expression remained carefully neutral. "We all are, Commander. The prophecy served as our guiding star for generations. Now we must navigate without it."

I turned back to the artifact, watching as its violet glow pulsed in perfect synchronization with my heartbeat. The sensation at the base of my skull intensified—not pain, exactly, but awareness. As if something dormant was slowly awakening.

"What do you make of this response?" I asked, gesturing toward the crystal.

"I believe," Vyr said carefully, "that while the prophecy may have ended, the connection between you and whatever force created it has not."

Hatch cleared her throat, drawing our attention. "Sir, there's something else." Her fingers manipulated the holographic display, highlighting a specific section of data. "According to these readings, your... interaction with the artifact triggered Protocol 47."

"Protocol 47?" I repeated, unfamiliar with the term.

Vyr's expression remained carefully neutral. "A classification system designed for non-replicable strategic assets," he explained. "It's ancient, predating even my administration."

"I've never heard of it," I said, feeling a twinge of unease. Protocol designations typically didn't reach into the double digits unless they were archival or experimental.

Hatch turned to face me fully, her expression grave. "The protocol wasn't created for you specifically," she said. "It was established decades ago. It's designed to identify and protect resources deemed vital to Imperial security—resources that cannot be duplicated or replaced."

The implication hit me like a gravitational shift. "You're classifying me as infrastructure?"

"Not me," Hatch corrected. "The system itself triggered the protocol automatically when it analyzed our data." She hesitated, her fingers hovering over her data-slate. "I've delayed submitting the final confirmation only long enough to let you understand what's coming."

I stared at the report on her screen, the classification codes pulsing with official authority. "And what exactly is coming?"

"Once I submit this," she explained, her voice softening slightly, "the Imperium will categorize you as essential infrastructure—protected, prioritized, and continuously monitored."

The artifact pulsed again, its violet light intensifying as if responding to my rising anxiety. I flexed my fingers, feeling that familiar tingle just beneath the skin.

"Submit it," I said finally, my voice steadier than the uncertainty coursing through my veins. "If that's what the system requires."

Hatch nodded once, then pressed her thumb against the confirmation icon. I waited for alarms, for some dramatic shift in the room's atmosphere—but nothing happened. No sirens wailed. No security protocols engaged. No permissions were revoked or added to my credentials. The artifact's glow dimmed slightly, returning to its previous state of dormancy.

"Is that it?" I asked, almost disappointed by the lack of fanfare.

"The classification is administrative, not physical," Vyr explained, his voice carrying a note of amusement at my reaction. "But make no mistake, Commander—its implications are far-reaching."

I nodded, feeling oddly hollow. In a single moment, I'd been transformed from a military commander to something else—an asset, a resource, a piece of critical infrastructure to be protected and utilized. The thought left a bitter taste in my mouth.

"We should go," Hatch said quietly, her eyes meeting mine with an unspoken apology.

As we made our way back through the corridors of Imperial Command, I noticed subtle changes in how personnel regarded me. Nothing dramatic—no salutes or bows—but a shift in their posture, a new quality to their gaze. Not fear or suspicion, but something more unsettling: deference. A medical officer who would have brushed past me yesterday now stepped aside with a slight inclination of his head. A security team straightened imperceptibly. As we entered the transport tube back to the lobby, three uniformed technicians who had been waiting stepped back from the doors, murmuring something about catching the next container. The tube departed with just the two of us inside, leaving behind their curious gazes.

"You see it too," Hatch murmured as we entered the lobby.

"I do," I confirmed, keeping my voice low. "The way people are looking at me now. It's changed." I forced a smile to mask my discomfort. "Overnight promotion from slightly revered commanding officer to uber religious icon with armed guards," I said, the joke falling flat even to my own ears.

We moved through the lobby, my boots sounding resolute as they pounded against the polished stone floor of Imperial Command. The facility's design was meant to impress—soaring ceilings, gleaming surfaces that caught and reflected the light from Imperial Prime's binary suns. But it wasn't the architecture that commanded my attention. It was the personnel.

An operations officer stepped aside as we passed, her eyes lingering on me a beat too long. A security team in the adjoining hallway straightened to attention—not the casual acknowledgment of rank, but something deeper, beyond reverent. Even the administrative staff moved with newfound purpose around me, as if my presence had somehow transformed routine tasks into matters of grave importance.

"It's not just deference," I said, analyzing their reactions. "It's like they're recalibrating everything based on my existence."

Hatch's lips barely moved. "Protocol 47 rewrites your entire existence in their minds. You're not just someone who gives orders anymore—you're as fundamental to their survival as oxygen recyclers and radiation shields."

I frowned. "Isn't that what Supreme Commander means? I was *already* their leader."

"Leaders can be replaced," Hatch murmured, her eyes scanning the corridor. "They've survived the deaths of leaders before. But this..." She leaned closer, "This is different. You're not their commander anymore. You're their last hope against extinction. And lately the stakes have been observable and are difficult for even a sceptic to ignore."

The words hung between us, heavy with implications I wasn't ready to face. We rounded a corner into a less-populated hallway. I could feel Hatch's eyes on me, assessing, calculating. The weight of her words pressed against my chest like atmospheric pressure increasing with depth.

"Nothing's changed," Hatch assured me as we exited the complex through a side exit, the words sounded hollow even to my ears.

"Everything's changed," I corrected her, looking at the long shadows crossing the violet fields and stretching beyond the command center. Bioluminescent vegetation pulsed in rhythmic patterns across the landscape, their gentle glow intensifying as daylight began to fade. "They're not following me anymore. They're not hoping I can turn the tide. They're depending on me now."

The distinction hung between us, as tangible as the sweet taste of Prime's atmosphere. I inhaled deeply, trying to ground myself in the physical reality of this alien world that was now, for better or worse, my home.

"You're not wrong," Hatch admitted after a long silence. She removed her glasses, pinching the bridge of her nose—a rare display of vulnerability I'd seen only in our most desperate moments. "But dependency creates its own kind of vulnerability. The Imperium has effectively put all its eggs in one basket."

"Me being the basket," I said dryly.

"You being the basket," she confirmed, replacing her glasses with practiced precision. "And baskets can be targeted."

The warning in her voice was unmistakable. I scanned the horizon where the sprawling Imperial city blended into the shadowed hills beyond the command complex. The violet fields undulated in the evening breeze, their bioluminescent patterns shifting like waves across the landscape.

"So what's our next move?" I asked, lowering my voice despite the open space around us. Old habits from a lifetime of classified briefings died hard.

Hatch fell into step beside me as we made our way toward the transit platform. "We need to establish protocols—our own, not just the Imperium's. If you're going to be their strategic asset, we need to define the parameters."

I nodded, feeling the weight of responsibility settle more heavily across my shoulders. "You're thinking containment?"

"I'm thinking protection," she corrected. "Both *for* you and *from* you. Whatever's happening when you interact with energy systems is still unpredictable. If it scales up..."

She didn't need to finish the thought. I understood what the Imperium had just done—systems don't ask whether they should depend on something, only whether they can.

CHAPTER 18: SAFEGUARD

I continued doing my best to lead with unwavering authority in this universe I still knew little about. My voice routinely filling the Central Command Room's vaulted chamber as I traced trajectory patterns across the three-dimensional star map. The holographic planets glowed blue under my fingertips while I issued strategic directives about possible Shadow movement patterns just beyond the Aurelia sector. Admiral Voss' posture stiffened when I countermanded his suggestion for defensive positioning, but he nodded sharply, jaw tight.

In public meetings, McNeil visibly deferred to me, his eyes following my movements across the room, his own suggestions always prefaced with "If the Supreme Commander agrees..." Even the way he positioned his chair—angled slightly toward mine, ready to pivot at my slightest gesture—reinforced the Imperium's confidence in my judgment.

Despite this outward display of trust, I began to notice subtle changes in how senior staff were interacting with me—Lieutenant Mercer flinching when our hands accidentally touched passing a data-slate, Commander Wei's habit of standing precisely 2.3 meters from me at all times—yes somehow I could mentally measure that accurately—the security detail that materialized in corridors seconds before I rounded the corner. There was a certain carefulness in their approach, as if I had become something fragile and volatile simultaneously.

Later that evening, I retreated to my assigned space in the eastern wing of the Command Complex, a space far more luxurious than any military accommodation I'd known before. Through floor-to-ceiling windows, I watched the twin suns sink below the horizon, casting long purple shadows across the undulating fields. As always, the larger blue-white star disappeared first, leaving its smaller red companion to paint the sky in crimson hues before it too slipped away. I am confident that no matter how old I get, I will never tire of watching the twin suns set.

Despite the splendor of the setting suns, I felt melancholy. I'd spent decades giving orders that others followed without question. Authority was as familiar to me as my own heartbeat. But things were different—I had grown used to the unusual reverence, but it seemed worse now. This wasn't respect for rank or even fear of consequence. It was something deeper, it felt as though the reactions of people around me had grown almost religious in its intensity.

A soft chime and a fast triple rap on the door frame announced a visitor. I didn't need to check the security panel to know it was Hatch.

"Enter," I called, not turning from the window.

The door slid open with a pneumatic hiss. "They've assigned you quite the view," Hatch observed, stepping inside. I heard the subtle click of her setting down a data-slate on my desk.

"McNeil insisted," I replied. "Said it was fitting for someone of my... station."

"Your station," Hatch repeated. "That's one way of putting it."

I turned to face her. She looked exhausted, the artificial light catching the copper in her hair and the shadows beneath her eyes. "What did you find?"

"The Council has been monitoring your biometrics," Hatch said, sliding into the chair across from me. "Not just basic vitals anymore. They're tracking quantum resonance patterns, neural pathway formations, even molecular changes at the cellular level."

I crossed my arms. "Without informing me?"

"That's just it." She tapped the data-slate, bringing up a holographic display that hovered between us. "This is from a closed Council session three hours ago. I wasn't supposed to have access, but they invited me in."

The hologram flickered to life, showing the Imperial Council chamber. I recognized McNeil at the head of the table, flanked by appointed political officials from around Imperial Prime and 23 delegates representing each of the Imperial worlds. The timestamp indicated this was during my tactical briefing with the fleet commanders.

"The question isn't whether we continue monitoring," Representative Cornelsen was saying, his weathered face grave in the blue light. "The question is what we do with the data."

I watched as the camera panned across faces I'd come to know well during my time here—allies, I'd thought. Now they discussed me like I was a weapon system requiring calibration.

"We now have confirmation that Supreme Commander Roberson is not merely influential but irreplaceable," Cornelsen continued. "Our models show no viable succession plan, no redundant system capable of understanding and confronting the Shadow threat like he can."

General Kaine, head of Imperial Security, leaned forward. "A decisive leader is an asset. A decisive leader whose loss would collapse our defensive capabilities is an existential vulnerability."

The hologram shifted as Fleet Admiral Schmidt, the most senior military commander after me, stood. "The recent Shadow attacks on Aurelia nearly breached Roberson's mind. Had they succeeded..." He didn't finish the thought.

I felt my chest tighten. "They've classified me as an irreplaceable asset, a system. Not a commander."

"A critical one," Hatch confirmed, her expression grim. "After heated debate, they authorized expanded oversight protocols."

"What does that mean exactly?" I asked, though I already suspected.

Hatch manipulated the data-slate, advancing the recording. McNeil now stood at the center of the Council chamber, his hands spread in a placating gesture.

"These are safeguards, not restraints," he insisted to the assembled representatives. "There will be no approval chains, no procedural barriers, no delays to command execution. The Supreme Commander's authority remains absolute."

Representative Torres from Cydonia leaned forward. "And when he sleeps? When he's in transit? When the Shadows target him specifically?"

“Sophisticated, non-intrusive monitoring systems,” McNeil replied smoothly. “Designed to track his physiological state, energy signatures, and exposure to potential threats. At this stage, single-point optimization is simply the most stable configuration.”

I shut off the hologram with a sharp gesture. "So they're watching me. More than before."

"Yes," Hatch confirmed. "Though I argued against measures I see as invasive. I was overruled when McNeil emphasized preservation over control."

I felt a surge of frustration rise in my chest. "I've been under surveillance since the moment I arrived here. What more could they possibly need to monitor?"

"It's more sophisticated now," Hatch explained, her finger tracing patterns on the data-slate. "Environmental sensors that measure your energy output, biometric scanners embedded in your quarters, even specialized drones that maintain visual contact during transit between facilities. If you're compromised, they want to know soon enough to deploy immediate medical intervention—or have enough warning to implement contingency measures."

I paced to the window and back, suddenly conscious that even this conversation was likely being recorded. "Have you noticed them? The sensors, I mean."

"Some. Not all." She adjusted her glasses. "They're good, Marcus. Imperial tech at its finest."

I ran my hand over the smooth surface of the desk, wondering if it too contained monitoring equipment. "So I'm to be watched like some volatile substance that might explode at any moment."

"The Council isn't wrong," Hatch said quietly. "We've run the simulations. Without you, we lose the war in seventeen different scenarios. With you..." She trailed off.

"With me, you still might," I finished.

The admission hung between us, heavy with implications neither of us wanted to face. I'd never asked for this responsibility—to be the lynchpin upon which an entire civilization's survival depended. In the Coalition, I'd been a General, respected but ultimately replaceable. Here, I was something else entirely.

"I didn't ask to be irreplaceable," I said quietly.

"No one does," Hatch replied.

I stared out at the darkening landscape of Imperial Prime, the bioluminescent flora beginning to pulse with that ethereal violet glow as darkness settled across the fields. Each plant seemed to beat with its own rhythm, yet somehow they created patterns across the landscape—swirls and eddies of light that reminded me of starship formations.

"How much do they know?" I asked finally. "About what happened in the diagnostics bay?"

Hatch hesitated, just long enough for me to know the answer before she spoke. "Everything. The energy absorption, the violet manifestation, your neural patterns during the event. System AI compiled everything relevant when Protocol 47 activated."

I closed my eyes briefly, feeling the weight of scrutiny pressing down on me. "And what conclusions have they drawn?"

"That you're evolving," she said simply. "Becoming something they can't fully understand—which terrifies them almost as much as it fascinates them."

I turned from the window, scanning the room with new awareness. *Where would they place the sensors? In the lighting fixtures? The environmental controls? The furniture? The bed itself?* Like a soldier in enemy territory, I mentally mapped my surroundings, identifying potential surveillance points with practiced ease.

"So what now?" I asked, my voice dropping lower. "How do I command effectively when I'm being treated like a bomb that might go off?"

Hatch crossed to where I stood, close enough that our conversation would require less sophisticated equipment to monitor. "You command as you always have," she said quietly. "With the understanding that your decisions now carry even greater weight."

I laughed without humor. "Greater weight? They've mathematically confirmed what the Shadows already know—I'm their single point of failure. That makes me both their greatest strength and most critical vulnerability."

"True," Hatch admitted. "But consider this: their fear isn't just about losing you. It's about what you might become." Hatch let that statement sit there a moment. I had considered this myself during quiet moments—*what if the changes didn't stop? What if whatever happened in that wormhole continued to transform me into something beyond human? Something beyond their control? Something dangerous*— "Have you noticed anything else?" Hatch asked, her voice barely above a whisper. "Any new... manifestations?"

I flexed my fingers, remembering the violet glow that had traced across my skin during the diagnostic test. "Nothing consistent. Sometimes I feel... echoes. Like standing too close to a high volume communication transmitter—vibrations that shouldn't be perceptible."

Hatch nodded, her expression neutral. "I've documented similar reports from engineering teams. The energy systems near your quarters have been experiencing minor fluctuations—nothing critical, but noticeable."

"And they think that's me?" I asked, already knowing the answer.

"They haven't confirmed it," she replied carefully. "But the timing correlates with your sleep cycles. Particularly when you're experiencing rapid eye movement."

I moved away from the window, suddenly feeling exposed. Even my dreams weren't private anymore.

"I need to get out of here," I said abruptly. "Somewhere without sensors and cameras. Somewhere I can think."

Hatch's eyebrow arched slightly. "You're the Supreme Commander of the Imperium. There is no 'somewhere' without monitoring."

"I need some air," I said abruptly, standing.

Hatch raised an eyebrow. "You know they'll follow."

"Let them." I moved toward the door. "At least outside I can see the stars."

We walked together through the corridors of the Command Complex, security personnel materializing at intersections with practiced 'coincidental' timing. I pretended not to notice how they tracked my movements, how they staged their 'casual' encounters so that I was never truly alone. Soldiers who'd come to know me had now ironically become shadows themselves, spectral figures hovering just at the edge of my peripheral vision.

The eastern gardens spread before us as we exited the complex, their alien vegetation swaying gently in the night breeze. Bioluminescent flowers unfurled as darkness deepened, casting pools of violet and azure light across winding paths. I chose the most isolated route, one that led toward a small promontory overlooking the valley beyond.

"You know," I said as we walked, "I used to dream about finding other worlds. When I was a kid, I'd lie on my back in the pasture, staring up at the stars, imagining what might be out there."

"And now?" Hatch asked.

I gestured at the alien landscape around us. "Now I'm here, leading a civilization I barely understand against an enemy I can't even properly name, while being treated like a combination of messiah and deployed but unexploded nuke."

A security drone hummed overhead, its presence announced by the faintest disturbance in the air. I ignored it, focusing instead on the path ahead.

"Do you ever wonder," I continued, "if we made the right choice? Leaving Earth behind?"

Hatch's footsteps faltered slightly. "We didn't have a choice, Marcus. The NWO would have-"

“I know what would have happened." I felt a familiar knot of tension form in my throat. "But sometimes I wonder if we're just postponing the inevitable. Earth falls to the NWO, we flee to the stars, now we face the Shadows. One existential threat traded for another. I've made my peace with that. What I'm asking is if we made the right choice coming here specifically. Trusting this prophecy. Accepting our roles in it."

We reached the promontory, a jutting outcropping of rock that offered an unobstructed view of the valley below. Four of Imperial Prime's moons were visible tonight and hung above us in the night sky, casting violet light across the landscape. Below us, the violet fields stretched into darkness, their bioluminescent patterns creating rivers of light that wound through the landscape like cosmic arteries. Ships moved in formation against the starfield, their navigation lights twinkling slightly.

"Maybe that's just the human condition," I said, my voice quieter now. "To always be fighting something bigger than ourselves."

Hatch stood beside me, her silence a familiar comfort. When she finally spoke, I knew she'd calculated all possible outcomes.

"The difference is choice," she said. "On Earth, we were fighting for the right to exist on our own terms. Here, we're fighting for... something larger."

"Survival of the species?" I asked, unable to keep the cynicism from my voice.

"No," she replied. "The right to determine what 'species' even means. The Shadows aren't just hunting us—they're hunting what we might become."

I considered her words, watching a distant patrol vessel cut across the horizon. Its thrusters pulsed blue-white against the darkness, a tiny defiant star skimming the edge of night. The craft's silhouette—sleek and predatory with swept-back wings that caught the moonlight in violet slivers—reminded me of the falcons that once soared above Earth's mountains. Funny how even here, three centuries and countless light-years from home, we still designed our machines with echoes of the natural world we'd left behind.

"You know what bothers me most about all this monitoring?" I said, lowering my voice despite knowing it was futile. "It's not the invasion of privacy. It's the implication that I'm no longer fully human—that I need to be observed like some experimental subject."

Hatch leaned against a stone outcropping, her copper hair catching the moonlight. "From their perspective, you're evolving beyond baseline human parameters. That makes you unpredictable."

"And therefore dangerous," I finished.

"Potentially," she corrected. "But also potentially salvation. That's the paradox they're struggling with."

I stared at my hands in the moonlight, half-expecting to see that violet shimmer trace across my skin. Nothing happened, yet I could feel something beneath the surface—a current waiting to be tapped, a power I didn't fully understand and certainly couldn't control.

"What if they're right to be afraid?" I asked quietly.

Hatch didn't answer immediately. She stood there in the moonlight, her expression unreadable as she considered my question.

"Being afraid is a reasonable response," she finally said. "But fear shouldn't drive decision."

I turned my gaze back to the stars, searching for patterns in their cold light. "You didn't answer my question."

"No," she admitted. "I didn't."

The silence stretched between us, filled only by the soft rustling of the alien vegetation and the distant hum of patrol craft. For a moment I felt the weight of countless eyes upon me—both human and electronic—tracking my every movement, measuring my responses, calculating my potential.

"I've been thinking about the wormhole," I said, changing tactics. "About what happened to me inside it."

Hatch shifted her weight, suddenly alert. "You remembered something?"

"A little... maybe. I remember a feeling of... I don't know, like maybe being unmade or something," I said, the memory flooding back with unexpected clarity. "Like every atom in my body was being pulled apart, examined, and then reassembled with... something extra." I flexed my fingers, remembering the sensation. "Not just physical changes. Some sort of vortex. And... something deeper."

"Knowledge?" Hatch suggested, her voice carefully neutral.

"Maybe. Or access to knowledge." I struggled to articulate the feeling. "Like having a library card but not knowing how to read yet."

A slight breeze stirred the bioluminescent plants around us, sending ripples of violet light across the garden. Somewhere in the distance, a security drone adjusted its position, its faint hum barely perceptible as it tracked our movements. I glanced up, momentarily locking eyes with the machine's optical sensor before looking away.

"You know what's strange?" I continued, keeping my voice low. "Sometimes I catch myself understanding things I shouldn't know. Technical specifications for Imperial systems I've never studied. Words in languages I've never learned." I hesitated before adding, "Like Yachtya."

Hatch's posture stiffened slightly. "You recognized that script in the archive."

"Not just recognized it," I admitted. "I could read portions of the entire script. Not fluently, but... enough to recognize intent, inflection, meaning."

Hatch leaned forward, her eyes narrowing with that familiar intensity I'd seen countless times in mission briefings. "Explain," she said, the single word carrying the weight of a thousand curious questions.

I looked up at the vast expanse above us. "The Shadows... they're not just predators. They're running from something themselves." My fingers traced invisible patterns in the air as I searched for the right words. "During one of those moments when I... went elsewhere inside myself, I sensed it. Fear. Ancient and bone-deep. Something in their evolutionary coding has twisted."

The revelation hung between us, its implications too vast to fully process. Hatch removed her glasses, cleaning them methodically with the edge of her uniform.

"It's like they know something's coming," I said, watching Hatch's methodical cleaning ritual. "Something worse than them. And they're... preparing."

"Preparing how?" Hatch asked, replacing her glasses with practiced precision.

I shook my head, frustrated by the limitations of language. "It's not clear. The knowledge comes in fragments—impressions rather than complete thoughts. But they're ancient, Hatch. Far older than humanity. And they've been running for a very long time."

Hatch considered this, her analytical mind visibly processing the implications. "That would explain their interest in advanced civilizations. They're not just predators—they're scavengers, collecting knowledge and technology that might help them survive."

"And now they've found us," I said. "Or rather, they've found me."

The weight of that realization settled between us like a physical presence. If the Shadows were truly running from something worse than themselves, what did that mean for the Imperium? For humanity's future in this corner of the galaxy?

"We should get back," Hatch said after a long silence. "Before security decides to intervene directly."

I suddenly felt something shift in my mind, like tumblers in a lock finally aligning. The realization settled into my bones: I wasn't their prophet or savior—I really *was* a weapon, their most critical strategic asset requiring constant surveillance and protection. The thought felt uncomfortable, yet I found a strange peace in finally understanding my purpose.

My father's face flickered in memory—his weathered Marine Corps veteran's eyes watching me take my oath on that crisp October morning, American flag snapping in the wind. His single nod had contained more approval than any words could express. My path afterward came in rapid succession: fast- tracked to BUD/S at Coronado where the Pacific salt caked my skin for six brutal months, I'd been luckier than most—that night in week eleven when hypothermia nearly claimed me during the ocean swim, my limbs turning to concrete as the Pacific swallowed my strength.

The classified Space Force selection at Vandenberg came next, night training exercises took place under actual launch conditions. I remembered my first experience of weightlessness during my first orbital deployment; the titanium insignia had been pinned to my chest by General Williamson himself.

The day I told my father I'd enlisted in the Navy instead of the Marines, our kitchen table took the brunt of his disappointment. His calloused fist slammed down, sending forks and knives dancing across the surface. Four generations of Robersons had worn the eagle, globe, and anchor—now I'd be the first to break that chain. His words bounced between the mustard-colored kitchen walls while my mother's hands never stopped their circular motion against the dinner plates, her silence louder than his shouting. "The few and the proud, Marcus," he'd repeated, the Corps slogan sounding like scripture from his lips. Years later, I caught him showing my service photo to his VFW buddies, pride poorly disguised beneath his gruff exterior.

Now here I stood, light-years beyond Earth's grave, remembering his rough voice on the other end of a video call home after I'd nearly washed out during Hell Week, my muscles had seized after fifty-eight hours without sleep, tears of frustration were burning down my face. "Stop feeling sorry for yourself, Marcus," he'd said, voice low and steady as a heartbeat, "and just do the damn thing."

I inhaled the alien air, tasting its metallic sweetness. It was time to do the damn thing.

"Ok, lets get back." I replied.

CHAPTER 19: PRESENCE

At the outer edge of the Imperium, where the nebula's crimson tendrils faded into the absolute black of uncharted space, the Imperial Destroyer Glory cut through space as it completed its patrol sweep around the gas giants of Helios-20. After the destruction of Aurelia, Helios was now the outermost system of the Imperium in sector 9.

Glory's violet engine trails stretched behind it, dissipating into the darkness as the massive warship banked toward the next set of patrol coordinates, its sensor arrays sweeping methodically through the emptiness, searching for Shadows within shadows. Suddenly, Glory's quantum sensors flickered with warning. An alert populated on the bridge viewscreen quietly, a single amber pixel blinking in the corner of the display—buried in routine telemetry like a whisper in a crowded room. No klaxons wailed, no crimson indicators flashed across the control panels. Just a subtle deviation in the perimeter data, a mathematical anomaly in the barrier's harmonics.

Shift Commander Lucia noticed it first, buried in routine telemetry, easy to miss. She frowned, leaned closer, and tagged the anomaly for review. The holographic projection cast her face in ghostly light as though she was about to read a horror story by the campfire. Her arms were folded across her chest. Her eyes narrowed as Glory's monitoring arrays tracked a slow, almost lazy pattern materializing at the edge of Imperial sensor range—just beyond the shimmering boundary of the quantum barrier.

Lieutenant Kess hunched over her console as the flagged data resolved into a clearer form. She adjusted the filters, then stilled. "This isn't noise," she said quietly. "It's structured." She adjusted the gain twice, then again, her fingers slowing as recognition crept in. Multiple contacts drifted along the outer boundary of the Imperium's exclusion field. Holding position almost beyond sensor range. Close enough to be seen. Far enough to be ignored—if someone wanted to ignore them. "Shadow vessels." Kess confirmed.

Lucia contacted the captain, "Unknown contact sir."

△△△

Captain Hawley arrived on the bridge with his uniform jacket half-fastened, the Imperial insignia askew over his chest. Dark circles shadowed his eyes, and his silver-flecked hair stood at odd angles where his head had pressed against his pillow mere minutes before. He blinked twice under the harsh blue lighting, as he oriented himself Lucia saluted.

"Report," he ordered, voice rough with interrupted sleep.

Lucia guided him to the tactical display where ghostly projections of the sensor returns hovered in three dimensions, "What am I looking at?" Hawley asked.

"Captain," she said carefully, "I'm seeing a patterned deviation at the perimeter. It's subtle, but it's... structured."

Captain Hawley leaned forward, dark hair streaked with gray catching the pale blue glow of the tactical displays. He studied the projection in silence, jaw tightening as recognition set in.

"I see it," he said at last. His hand hovered over the alert protocols, then stopped. "Confirm it's not barrier harmonics."

Kess ran the diagnostic again. "Already ruled out, sir. It's external. And deliberate."

Hawley exhaled through his nose. He knew that waveform. Had seen it burn across sensor logs during the Cygnus Incident—had watched it precede an engagement that rewrote three fleet doctrines overnight. Still, the deviation was too small to justify alarms. Too precise to be noise.

"Hold alert status," he ordered. "Lets run a full battery of passive scans. Let's see what they want us to notice."

△△△

Three hours later, the multitude of passive scan data coalesced into one high definition image as the truth materialized on Glory's main viewscreen.

Seven Shadow vessels.

They had arranged themselves in a mathematically perfect heptagonal formation exactly 0.87 light-minutes beyond sanctioned space. Their onyx hulls devouring starlight, creating the unsettling illusion of flat silhouettes pasted against the diamond-scattered backdrop. A faint crimson corona pulsed along each vessel's edges—an energy state *Glory*'s quantum analyzers could describe but not classify.

No advance.

No probes.

No weapons cycling.

They simply hovered—visible, patient, unmistakable—their angular forms seemed to be oriented directly toward Glory's position.

"Distance?" Hawley asked.

“Six thousand kilometers beyond the barrier’s reactive envelope,” Kess replied. “Precisely calibrated. They’re close enough to be seen… and far enough to be untouchable.”

Hawley let out a low breath. “Of course they are.” The Captain's jaw tightened as he studied the tactical display. "It's as if they're waiting," he said, perplexed. His fingers traced the sensor returns representing the Shadow vessels. "Place us into a monitoring position, port side exposed. Stick to passive sensors—I want every quantum fluctuation and gravitational micro-shift recorded." He straightened his disheveled uniform with one hand, eyes never leaving the display. "Open continuous data packets to Imperial Command. Everything we see, they see in real-time." The blue light from the holographic projection cast unusual morphing shadows across his face as he turned back to Lucia. "Rotate to two-hour watches. I need alert minds monitoring these readings, not exhausted ones."

"Aye sir," Lucia responded, her fingers already dancing across the haptic console.

Glory was not built for first contact or decisive engagement. Though destroyer-class by tonnage, her true strength lay in what she could see rather than what she could strike. Her arrays were tuned for patience—long-range harmonics, quantum drift, patterns that only emerged when nothing happened for a long time. Glory pivoted in the void, her thrusters firing in microsecond bursts that rotated her massive frame with impossible delicacy. Her port side now faced the perimeter, exposing the full sweep of her sensor arrays to the distant anomalies. The ship's engines powered down to minimal output—just enough to maintain position while her detection systems reached outward—gathering every photon, every quantum fluctuation from the boundary. Beyond that invisible line where Imperial authority ended, the Shadow vessels hung motionless against the starfield. Unlike previous encounters, they made no attempt to conceal their presence or continue their journey. They had arrived at their destination, settling into formation with the cold patience of stars awaiting the end of time.

The message was clear without a single transmission: *We are watching. And we've done the math.*

Captain Hawley authorized the continuous data stream to Imperial Command, his fingers tapped in the thirty-digit encryption key from memory. The ship's processors hummed audibly as they compressed terabytes of sensor data into burst transmissions precisely timed between the pulses of Shadow scanning waves. The Shadows weren't testing firepower. The Shadow vessels had arranged themselves with surgical precision, aligning with Glory's port nacelle in a formation that couldn't be coincidence. Each ship hovered exactly where Glory's sensors went dark for 12.8 seconds during routine coolant cycling—a flaw mentioned nowhere except in classified Imperial maintenance files. Someone had studied their patrol routes. Someone had read their most protected technical documents.

Data began flowing in, screens updating, images populating, and a quiet energetic chatter emanated from the bridge crew as they studied the findings.

△△△

I observed the tactical display with growing unease in the Central Command Room. The Shadow formation seemed to correspond precisely to weak points in the Imperium's barrier—points that would surely not hold up for long to sustained assault. This was not coincidence.

"Cross-reference their positioning with our defensive grid," I ordered, my voice steady despite the cold dread pooling in my stomach.

The tactical officer's fingers flew across his console. "Confirmed, sir. They're positioned at precisely calculated points of structural vulnerability."

"Match it with simulation thirty-four," Hatch said, stepping closer to the display. The holographic interface rippled as the overlay materialized—a predictive model we'd run days earlier showing potential attack vectors against our defensive network.

The alignment was unmistakable. Each Shadow vessel had also positioned itself at a nexus point in our barrier—places where reinforcement would take the longest, where our response would be most strained.

“They’re not here to fight,” I said.

I studied the display, tracing the pattern with my finger.

"This positioning," I said, pointing to the center node where three defense vectors converged. "It would require immediate reinforcement from..."

"You," Hatch finished. "It would likely require you… specifically."

The room grew uncomfortably quiet as the implication settled over the assembled officers. The Shadows weren't positioning themselves randomly. They were creating a scenario that would demand my personal intervention—a calculated strategy that factored in my abilities as a critical variable.

"They're studying me," I said, the realization crystallizing in my mind. "Not the Imperium. Me."

Admiral Voss cleared his throat. "Supreme Commander, I recommend we dispatch the Seventh Fleet to reinforce the perimeter. If we can demonstrate overwhelming force—"

"No," I interrupted. "That's exactly what they want. They're baiting us into revealing our defensive doctrine. If we mobilize the Seventh Fleet, they'll learn exactly what we know."

Voss's jaw tightened. I could see his military instincts warring with the political realities of my position. "With respect, Supreme Commander, allowing them to maintain their position unchallenged sends its own message."

I nodded grimly. "I'm aware of the implications." My eyes traced the formation on the display, where seven black shapes hung in perfect symmetry, equidistant from one another like points on an invisible compass. The darkness between them seemed to throb with meaning. "If they're sending us a message, I want to choose how we answer it."

I leaned closer to the holographic projection. Against the scattered stars, the Shadow vessels weren't just positioned strategically—they formed a pattern too deliberate to be coincidental, too precise to serve purely tactical needs. They were writing something in the void for us to read.

"They want us to react," I continued, tracing my finger along the formation's perimeter. "To show our hand. Every move we make reveals another piece of our planning, our knowledge."

△△△

Even the Imperium's battle simulations no longer treated me as a contingency—I had become a constant in their equations too. On the holographic display before me it was gaming the current situation, failure cascades bloomed like blood droplets in water whenever my variable was removed. The AI churned through scenario after scenario, its cold logic arriving at the same conclusion each time: without my ability to manipulate energy at multiple barrier points at once, our defenses would inevitably collapse.

"Run a distributed response model," I ordered. "Assume I'm unavailable, or unable to energize the barrier."

The tactical officer hesitated, fingers hovering over the console. "Sir, the outcomes—"

"Run it anyway," I insisted, my voice hardening.

The simulation appeared in the air before us—now forced to assume that I would be incapable of shoring up the energy barriers—a cascade of red failure indicators spread across the defensive grid like a bloodstain. In each scenario, without my ability to manipulate energy systems, the barrier collapsed within hours of sustained Shadow assault.

"Well, that's reassuring," I muttered, rubbing my temples. The pressure behind my eyes intensified, and a dull pressure was building at the base of my skull. I'd felt this sensation before—when the wormhole energy first altered me, when I'd interacted with the artifact in the archives.

"Commander?" Hatch's voice cut through my thoughts, her concern evident in the slight tightening around her eyes.

I straightened, blinking away the discomfort. "I'm fine."

But I wasn't. I had noticed the organizational effect from within: crisis reports were escalating to me more quickly, consultations routed my way sooner, decisions held in abeyance until my input was secured. The Imperium wasn't merely functioning with me—it was restructuring around me, creating a dependency that became more entrenched with each passing hour. It felt suffocating.

"They're making you the nexus," Hatch murmured, leaning close enough that only I could hear. "Every command path is being rewritten to flow through you."

I nodded, watching as a junior officer diverted a tactical query that should have gone to Admiral Voss directly to my console instead. I released a slow breath. "It hasn't escaped my attention."

The symmetry became clear as I studied the formation again. The Shadows were applying pressure without firing a single shot, trying to force us to reveal our dependencies and critical paths. Their strategy wasn't to destroy but to observe how the Imperium protects what it values most.

The data from Glory continued to stream in, filling our screens with new information. She nodded toward the central display where another window had appeared, showing energy readings from the Shadow formation.

"There's something else," she said, her voice pitched low. "The resonance field their vessels are generating—it matches your energy signature."

My blood ran cold as I studied the oscillating lines on the monitor. There was no mistaking that signature—the exact frequency and amplitude we'd recorded when tendrils of violet energy had danced between my fingers during the containment experiments last week.

“They’ve isolated my signature.” I murmured.

△△△

I called the senior officers together for a private briefing, away from the constant stream of updates and tactical suggestions flowing through the command center. In the small adjacent conference room, I watched their faces as Hatch presented our analysis.

"The more indispensable I become," I said, articulating the trap forming around us, "the harder it will be for the Imperium to function in my absence. They're not targeting our ships—they're targeting our command structure."

Admiral Voss leaned forward, his weathered face grave in the blue light of the tactical displays. "What are you suggesting, Supreme Commander? That we deliberately limit your involvement?"

"I'm suggesting we not play their game at all," I replied, folding my arms across my chest. "The moment we restructure our entire defense around me, we create a single point of failure. The Shadows are baiting us into dependency."

Voss's weathered face hardened. "With respect, sir, it may be too late for that conversation. The simulations speak for themselves."

"Simulations are only as good as their assumptions," I countered. "And right now, they're assuming I'm the only solution."

The room fell silent as my words hung in the air. I could see the struggle in their faces—the military pragmatism warring with the uncomfortable reality of our situation. I'd become a resource they couldn't afford to lose, yet couldn't fully understand or control.

I slammed my palm on the table. "You're concentrating everything around a single node," I said. "That will force adaptation—technological, doctrinal, strategic. Not because it's optimal, but because it becomes necessary."

Colonel Veran stood, the senior commander of the 9th expeditionary fleet. "Sir, we can't simply ignore your abilities. The fact remains that your capacity to interact with energy systems is our most potent defense against Shadow incursions."

I turned toward the viewport where the tactical display showed the Shadow formation, their vessels still maintaining that perfect heptagonal pattern. "The projections assume consistency," I said. "What I'm doing isn't consistent. It isn't repeatable. And it isn't something you can schedule around. If you plan around me as a certainty, you're planning for failure."

Hatch was the first to speak, adjusting her glasses with that precise gesture I'd come to recognize as her thinking ritual.

"The Commander's right," Hatch said. "We need redundancy."

Voss's jaw worked silently, the struggle evident in his eyes. "And what would you have us do in the meantime? Those Shadow vessels aren't going anywhere. If anything, their formation is growing."

I turned back to the tactical display, studying the perfect heptagon the Shadow vessels formed. As I watched, the holographic projection updated with new data from Glory's continuous feed. Another vessel had materialized at the perimeter, sliding into position with unnerving precision, expanding the formation while maintaining its mathematical perfection.

The tactical display quickly updated with a new alert—four additional Shadow vessels had entered sensor range, taking position at precise intervals around the original heptagon. "Thirteen now," I muttered, a cold dread settling in my stomach. My reflection ghosted in the display's dark surface, the formation of Shadow vessels seemed to encircle the outline of my face.

CHAPTER 20: DRIFT

The subtle shift in perception among the population accelerated as my classification under Protocol 47 continued to ripple throughout the Imperium. Though no official announcement had been made, the changes manifested in a hundred small ways—mess hall conversations falling silent when I entered, officers' eyes lingering a beat too long on my insignia, technicians triple-checking safety protocols before I boarded shuttles. Draven had observed these changes and, through his growing network of disaffected Pioneers and curious Imperial citizens, confirmed the pattern forming around me: I was becoming something other than human in their eyes.

In the Imperial meeting areas with their vaulted ceilings and holographic star maps, and in public spaces where hydroponic gardens twist between transparent aluminum walkways, Elliot Draven considered these changes with methodical precision. His dark eyes moving thoughtfully, his slender fingers making imperceptible notes on a translucent data-slate. Unlike his usual manipulative tactics, he now adopted a more sophisticated approach—leaning in conspiratorially, voice pitched just loud enough to carry to nearby tables. He didn't directly challenge my authority or competence—instead, he posed thoughtful questions in community forums and shared spaces, his words carefully chosen, his expression earnest beneath that shock of jet black hair.

"What I worry about," I heard Draven say as I passed the central forum where he sat surrounded by a small gathering, "is the tremendous burden we're placing on one person's shoulders. Not just leadership—which is already isolating—but this... deification. What must that do to a person's psyche? To suddenly become something beyond human to those around you?"

The murmurs of agreement rippled through his audience. I kept walking, pretending I hadn't heard, but his words burrowed under my skin. What made his approach so effective was the veneer of concern. He wasn't attacking me directly—he was expressing worry for my wellbeing.

Lena Corvin, one of the few Pioneer scientists who had tried to counter Draven's growing influence, stood at the edge of his gathering. "The Commander has handled greater pressures before," she argued, her voice firm but lacking Draven's charismatic resonance. "The Protocol 47 classification is merely a recognition of tactical reality."

"Of course," Draven replied smoothly, his smile disarming. "I'm simply concerned about the psychological impact. Isolation can be devastating, especially for someone carrying such responsibility."

I ducked into a side corridor, my jaw clenched tight enough to ache. The worst part was that Draven wasn't entirely wrong. The isolation *was* real, and grew more pronounced with each passing day.

I thought back to the morning planning session, I had noticed how officers deferred to me with an almost religious reverence. At the morning planning session, Admiral Voss slid the data-slate across the table without meeting my eyes. I scanned the report header, the report wasn't addressed to me. I noticed that first. My name appeared only under operational assumptions.

"They didn't ask you?" Hatch had asked me later.

"They didn't need to," I had replied.

She'd hesitated — just long enough to matter. "There are contingency branches in the planning models," she said carefully. "I haven't reviewed all of them yet."

I nodded. Not agreement. Recognition.

Despite myself, I found Draven's words were now weaving through my defenses like tendrils of smoke, their logic seeping into cracks I hadn't realized existed in my own certainty.

"I've noticed our Commander seems to be carrying quite a burden lately," Draven remarked casually during a community meal. "One wonders if any system should place so much responsibility on a single individual, no matter how capable." His tone conveyed genuine concern rather than criticism, which made his observations difficult to dismiss as mere troublemaking.

Lena Corvin, seated nearby, watched the ripple effect of Draven's words through the gathered citizens. She recognized his strategy—framing institutional dependency as concern for my wellbeing rather than questioning my authority. "Perhaps the Commander's importance reflects the extraordinary circumstances," she offered, but found her counterpoint lost in the murmurs of agreement with Draven.

△△△

After a planning session, I retreated to my quarters, seeking sanctuary from the suffocating reverence. I found myself staring at the tactical reports without reading them, Draven's words echoing in my mind. The officers had practically fallen silent when I'd suggested a more aggressive patrol pattern near the quantum barrier. No debate, no pushback—just immediate acquiescence. When I'd pressed for alternative viewpoints, they'd exchanged uncomfortable glances before Admiral Voss finally offered a watered-down counterproposal, his voice tentative as if fearing divine retribution for contradicting me.

"We can't protect you if you're at the front lines, Marcus," McNeil had said when I complained about needing real time understanding of operations.

"You're not just leading now," he'd replied, his voice dropping to that tone reserved for hard truths. "You're sustaining. There's a difference."

I was halfway through reviewing the latest Shadow movement patterns when my door chime sounded. I checked the security panel, surprised to see Draven standing outside, alone, without his usual entourage of admirers.

"Enter," I called, steeling myself for whatever game he was playing.

The door slid open with its familiar pneumatic hiss. Draven stepped inside, his movements fluid and controlled. He wore civilian clothes—a simple tunic in Imperial blue that somehow managed to look elegant on his slender frame.

"Commander," he said, inclining his head slightly. "Forgive the intrusion," Draven continued, remaining near the door as if uncertain of his welcome. "I thought perhaps we should speak directly, rather than through the filter of public forums."

I leaned back in my chair, studying him. "You mean rather than questioning my mental state behind my back?"

A faint smile crossed his face. "Fair enough. Though I'd argue my concerns were genuine, even if the venue was... strategic."

"What do you want, Draven?" I asked, not bothering to hide my weariness.

He moved further into the room, his steps deliberate and unhurried. "Actually, I thought perhaps there was something I could do for you." He paused, studying my face. "You seem... burdened, Commander. More so than usual."

I felt my defenses rising, a flicker of violet licked across my fingers, I put my hands under the table and kept my expression neutral. "Leading during wartime is always a burden."

"Is it just the war, though?" Draven asked, his voice softening. "Or is it the way you've chosen to lead it?"

I stiffened. "Meaning what, exactly?"

Draven claimed the chair opposite mine, uninvited. "I'm lead to believe your tactical decisions have become rather... unpredictable since they labeled you under Protocol 47." He reduced the space between us with a well timed lean, his gaze never wavering from mine, dark irises reflecting the room's dim light. "It makes one question whether you're compensating for something."

“I'm busy, do you have a point?” I demanded.

"Yes." He gestured toward the tactical displays. "These aggressive patrol patterns, the constant probing of their positions, the escalating military presence along the quantum barrier." His voice remained measured, almost clinical. "You're pursuing an increasingly confrontational strategy against an enemy we barely understand."

"Your analysis is flawed," I said, not bothering to hide the edge in my voice. "Their formations are deliberate, mathematical. They're creating pressure points designed to test our responses. We can't just leave ourselves exposed to their build up. What the hell would you know about this anyway?"

Draven leaned back, studying me with those calculating eyes. "And you don't think your... unique status... might be influencing those decisions? The Imperium reorganizing itself around you creates vulnerability."

That hit closer to home than I wanted to admit. I stood and moved to the viewport, putting distance between us while I gathered my thoughts. The twin suns of Imperial Prime cast a resolute shadow behind me, I felt anything but resolute right now.

"I've been aware of that vulnerability from the beginning," I said finally. "What concerns me is how quickly everyone else has accepted it."

"Ah," Draven said, a note of satisfaction in his voice. "So you've noticed it too. The way they defer to you now. The way decisions that should involve debate are simply... accepted when they come from you."

I turned back to face him. "What exactly are you hoping to accomplish with this conversation, Draven? Confirmation that I'm uncomfortable with my own importance?"

"Perhaps I'm simply looking for common ground," he replied, spreading his hands in a gesture of openness. "We both recognize the danger in concentrated power, even when it's necessary."

"You're not concerned about concentrated power," I countered. "You're concerned about who wields it."

A flicker of something—amusement, respect, calculation—crossed Draven's face. "An interesting assumption, Commander. Perhaps I'm simply concerned about the institutional dependency that's forming. A system that can't function without you is inherently unstable."

I held his gaze, searching for the angle.

“If you’re here to help,” I said quietly, “you picked a strange way to do it.”

Draven smiled — not in denial, but in acknowledgment — and turned for the door.

“People rarely thank you for telling them the truth,” he said. Then he was gone.

△△△

Over the next several days, I watched for patterns with new awareness. In tactical sessions, officers who once challenged my strategies now simply nodded and implemented them without question. When I deliberately proposed a flawed defensive deployment around Xin Zhongguo, Admiral Voss—who'd built his reputation on blunt tactical assessments—merely asked for implementation timelines rather than pointing out the obvious vulnerability in the southern quadrant.

I cornered Hatch after the meeting, pulling her into an empty side corridor.

"Did you notice that?" I asked, keeping my voice low despite the empty hallway.

"The complete lack of strategic debate?" She nodded, adjusting her glasses. "It's been getting worse. Couple of weeks ago, Voss would have torn that deployment plan to shreds."

I leaned against the wall, suddenly exhausted. "This isn't leadership anymore. It's... something else."

“Institutional dependency,” Hatch said. Draven's words from days ago echoed uncomfortably in my ears—that exact phrase, ‘institutional dependency,’ now coming from Hatch's lips like some unwelcome confirmation.

"It's dangerous," I said. "A military that doesn't question is a military that doesn't adapt.”

I watched Hatch process this, her analytical mind turning over implications with the precision of a quantum computer.

Hatch's eyes narrowed behind her glasses. "The problem's metastasizing," she said finally. "Draven's gatherings used to be ten, fifteen people. Yesterday I counted seventy-three in the mess hall. They're not just nodding anymore—they're repeating his talking points in other conversations. And the way they fall silent when command staff enters a room..."

What had begun as casual conversations had evolved into something more calculated—Draven now commanded audiences that filled entire common areas, his rhetoric sharpened like a blade against a whetstone. I first noticed the shift in Draven's approach during a routine inspection of the agricultural section. His 'talks' had evolved into structured forums with predetermined speaking times and organized question periods. Somewhere between fifty and sixty people crowded the hydroponics bay, their faces upturned toward Draven as he stood on a makeshift platform constructed from storage crates.

"Consider the burden we've placed on a single man," Draven had said, his voice carried effortlessly through the humid air. "Not just leadership—which is isolating enough—but this expectation of salvation. What does that do to our community cohesion when we transfer our collective responsibility to one person?"

The crowd murmured in agreement, several nodding vigorously. I remained in the shadows between rows of bioluminescent vegetation, observing.

"Some of us have known Commander Roberson ever since Pioneer's mission begun, but even for us none of us really know him much more than you my Imperial friends," he continued, his tone reasonable, concerned. "Yet we're all restructuring our entire civilization around him. What happens when we stop thinking for ourselves? When we stop questioning? When we simply wait for orders?"

A woman in the front row raised her hand. "But the prophecy—"

"The prophecy," Draven interrupted gently, "is a text written years ago on old sanitation paper. I don't dispute its accuracy in predicting certain events. But should we allow ancient words to dictate how we organize our society today?"

I watched as heads nodded throughout the crowd. This wasn't the random gathering of curious onlookers I'd seen in previous weeks. This was an organized event, complete with arranged seating and what appeared to be recording devices discretely positioned throughout the space.

I slipped away before anyone noticed my presence, troubled by the sophistication of Draven's operation. What had begun as isolated conversations had evolved into structured propaganda—carefully crafted to undermine not just my authority, but the Imperium's entire structure.

That evening, I reviewed security footage of Draven's other "discussions" over the past week. The pattern became clear: he was systematically targeting different segments of the population—engineers one day, medical staff the next, civilian administrators after that. Each message was tailored to its audience, but the underlying theme remained consistent: dependency on a single individual weakened the entire community.

The most disturbing aspect wasn't Draven's growing influence—it was how his message had begun spreading beyond his direct control. In the mess hall footage, I watched Pioneer specialists debating points Draven had raised days earlier, refining and amplifying his arguments without his presence. The narrative was becoming self-sustaining.

I called Hatch to my quarters, needing her analytical perspective.

"It's not just about me," I said as we reviewed the footage together. "He's attacking the entire concept of centralized authority."

Hatch nodded, her expression grim as she studied the displays. "Classical insurgency tactics. Create doubt in leadership, then position yourself as the reasonable alternative." She tapped a sequence on her data-slate, "You'd almost think he was once NWO wouldn't you?"

I frowned at her comment. "What do you mean?"

"Just that his approach is textbook destabilization. Identify the linchpin, isolate it, then question its necessity." Hatch's eyes remained fixed on the footage of Draven addressing a group of technicians. "He's not attacking you directly anymore. He's reframing institutional dependency as something that weakens us collectively."

I paced the length of my quarters, struggling to articulate what bothered me most about Draven's tactics. "The thing is, he's not entirely wrong."

Hatch looked up sharply. "Sir?"

"Draven didn't create this problem," I admitted. "He just gave it a voice. The more the Imperium centers around me, the more everyone else feels peripheral."

Hatch didn't respond right away. Instead, she pulled a slate from her coat and set it on the desk between us.

"There are personal contingencies in the Council's planning models," she said carefully.

I glanced at the screen. Once was enough.

"They didn't ask," I said.

"No," Hatch replied. "They didn't."

△△△

I stood at the viewport in my quarters, forehead pressed against the cold transparisteel as I stared into the void. Though invisible at this distance, I could picture the Shadow formation with perfect clarity—now grown to sixty vessels arranged in their expanding but distinctive pattern. The tactical display on my desk showed their positions remained unchanged for the eighteenth consecutive day.

I realized with growing clarity that the Shadows weren't employing their usual tactics. *They* didn't need to move, everything *else* was moving. They were forcing the Imperium to reorganize around a single point of failure: me. Now slowly applying pressure to us and, much like ancient Earth predators circling wounded prey, they were creating a vulnerability no amount of shielding or firepower could mitigate. They'd simply wait until our social cohesion fractured beyond repair. The true threat wasn't to my physical safety, but to the intricate web of trust and cooperation that formed the backbone of the Imperium's resistance.

CHAPTER 21: THE FRACTURE

The regulators didn't fail.

Lieutenant Adisa's voice carried a note of suspicion that contradicted her own words. I caught her sideways glance as we stood before the engineering console, its display stubbornly green across all metrics. Temperature readings hovered at optimal levels. Flow harmonics maintained perfect resonance. Load distribution never exceeded 82% capacity. According to the logs, the system had experienced a momentary spike, then corrected itself with impossible precision—all before the warning protocols could even complete their first cycle.

No system recovers that perfectly.

Adisa's eyes narrowed at the readout. "No system self-corrects with that kind of precision," she whispered, fingers suspended above the console as though the machinery might sense her doubt.

I stood motionless beside her. Whatever had happened, my hands were clean this time—at least in the physical sense.

The sensation returned—that peculiar constriction behind my eyes, neither painful nor warm, just present. Like the ship had inhaled slightly and was waiting to see if I would match its rhythm.

The comm panel hissed. "Marcus." Hatch's voice, tight with restraint. "Remain *exactly* where you are."

My body froze in place. When Hatch's voice took on that particular edge—like a well-honed blade in language form—only a fool would do anything but exactly as instructed.

A moment later, Hatch strode in, her wrist computer casting a web of holographic data into the space between us. I frantically scanned the projections—energy signatures, system responses, particulate residue. Each reading looked benign on its own, but together they sketched a familiar pattern.

"Third incident since yesterday," she said, pointing to the data that mattered right now. "Different systems failing the same way."

Adisa's brow furrowed. "Coincidences don't repeat."

Hatch's silence was confirmation enough.

"The regulators didn't just recover," she continued, fingers manipulating the display. "They corrected preemptively—like they sensed the breakdown coming."

I met her eyes. "So the ship's responding to future events now?"

Her pause lasted a half-second too long. I didn't need to hear her answer.

Hatch chose her words with surgical precision. "The energy pattern resembles less of a reaction and more of a... synchronization."

"Synchronizing with what exactly?" Adisa's voice hardened along with her expression.

Hatch paused. Her gaze drifted past the console, beyond the diagnostic readouts, settling directly on me. "I'm working to eliminate possibilities."

The Sovereign's engines pulsed beneath us—a steady, almost comforting vibration. Systems green. Repair protocols at 97%. All indicators pointing toward full and impending recovery. The ship's systems appeared to be settling back into their operational parameters.

Yet something had changed in the air around me—a thinning, as if the boundary between my body and the ship's systems was becoming permeable, negotiable. A junior engineer started toward us, then froze mid-step. He retreated with a wordless nod, but not before I caught something in his eyes that lingered just a fraction too long.

In that moment, I recognized what radiated from him.

Not reverence. Not dread.

Anticipation.

Hatch dismissed the holo-projections with a curt gesture. "We're not looking at system failure," she murmured. "But something is happening."

"Something deliberate," I said. "Like calibration."

Her eyes found mine, and I saw the change—no more careful diplomacy, no more shielding me from what we both suspected. "It's moved beyond testing Sovereign's limits," she said.

Above us, the lights pulsed once—so briefly you'd question whether you'd seen it. The console indicators never wavered from their reassuring green. Deep in the vessel's heart, the quantum core made a minute adjustment to its energy signature. I felt it happen. And somehow I understood— the adjustment wasn't meant to stabilize the ship.

△△△

We retreated to the analysis bay. The room stood empty except for a cluster of consoles and that damned chair, still bolted to the deck like a silent accusation. I tried lightening the mood. "Planning to strap me in and use me for a power source?" The look Hatch gave me could have frozen hydrogen.

The analysis bay door hissed shut behind us as Hatch engaged the privacy seal.

No report would ever document what happened next.

Darkness enveloped us, broken only by the harsh glow of screens reconfiguring themselves. Hatch bypassed the processed feeds, digging instead for the raw sensor data—the kind that hadn't been sanitized or simplified for command briefings.

"I've been dreading this confirmation," she said, her voice tight.

Her fingers danced across the interface, conjuring Imperial Prime's orbital defense network into existence above us. The hologram sparkled with countless points of light—security checkpoints, traffic lanes, civilian vessels—a perfect constellation of Imperial control. With a single gesture, she swiped it all from existence.

Where there should have been nothing, the space between stars had thinned, as if reality itself had been stretched too far across some invisible frame. It was... attenuated yet palpable; a paradox of reality.

"Let me see the historical readings," I said.

Her fingers moved across the interface. Years of sensor recordings materialized before us, arranged in translucent strata. Each timeframe bore identical patterns—the expected static of stellar radiation, quantum fluctuations, the benign disorder of a populated star system.

Then came the present.

Something in the current readings felt fundamentally incorrect.

Not chaotic. Not broken.

Curated.

Hatch's finger traced the holographic anomalies—negative spaces where data should have been. "See these voids? The system isn't failing to detect. It's being... selectively blinded."

My stomach tightened. "Someone's deliberately erasing the feeds?"

"In a fashion," she whispered, the word barely audible.

The display rotated as she isolated sections one by one, then expanded to reveal dozens more. Each hollow aligned perfectly with Imperial Prime's vital organs: comm relays, governance cores, transport command centers.

I leaned closer, searching for the obvious. "I'm not seeing vessels," I said. "No mass signatures at all."

Hatch nodded grimly. "That's what makes this so insidious. No alarms. No breaches. Not a single protocol violation." She manipulated the hologram with practiced fingers, collapsing the scattered data points until they formed a shroud around Imperial Prime.

"We're not looking at an invasion force," she said, voice dropping. "We're witnessing behavioral modification on a planetary scale."

The holographic display cast ghostly shadows across our faces as we absorbed the implications of what we were seeing.

"They don't need to attack our systems," she continued, tracing phantom patterns in the display. "They're staying just beneath detection thresholds." Her eyes finally met mine, pupils constricted against the hologram's glow. "The rules remain intact. The game beneath them changes."

Something pulsed behind my eyes—a recognition more than sensation. "So the barrier..." I said, understanding dawning, "it only defends against direct assault?"

"Precisely." Hatch responded.

I shook my head. "So they're not attacking us directly?"

"They don't need to." Hatch's fingers danced across the interface, summoning a new holographic display. "Look at these projections."

Before us hung translucent graphs—population density shifts, resource allocation patterns, civil compliance metrics. Each line curved gently but inexorably downward.
"The Shadows aren't trying to break through our defenses," she said, voice low. "They're making our defenses meaningless."

Draven's words echoed in my mind. The way he'd leaned forward slightly, eyes half-lidded, voice pitched for intimacy rather than volume: “Pressure doesn't destroy you,” he'd said once. “It tells the truth about you.” Only now did I understand he wasn't talking about us at all.

Hatch let out a measured breath. "The Shadows aren't trying to break through. They're waiting for the moment when we act as though the barrier is already gone."

I felt my jaw tighten. "Timeline?"

Her fingers hovered over the display. For a moment, she seemed reluctant to continue.

"That's what concerns me most," she finally said, expanding the projection with a gesture.

The curve terminated in a spike—no graceful asymptote, just a vertical leap breaking out of the simulation's clean lines. The moment after, everything flatlined: resource equilibrium, compliance, even population growth projections. At that inflection the system collapsed in on itself so fast that the after-image lingered in my retina when Hatch cleared the projection. Not a war. An extinction curve.

I forced the words through numb lips. "Command needs to see this. Now." But even as I spoke, I felt disconnected from my own voice—like I was watching myself deliver lines in a simulation I couldn't quite believe was real.

Hatch's hands came down on the console, steady and unflinching. "If we flag it in the system, we risk tipping the algorithm." She nodded toward the deadened privacy indicator. "Someone's listening—maybe even from the outside."

That old, familiar logic returned: security through silence. Deny the event, buffer the panic. It reeked of secrets and stupidity, and I recognized at once that the only way around an all-seeing system was to make yourself the blind spot it had been trained to ignore.

"Analog only," I said. "Can you brief McNeil face-to-face, off comms?" I was already thinking three meetings ahead. "Keep it plausible. Routine diagnostics. Civil compliance drift."

Hatch's face didn't move, yet I registered the briefest glint in her eyes—a signal understood by soldiers who've survived suicide missions together. "Agreed," she responded. "Are you going to the source?" The phrase hung, both question and accusation.

"Not yet." My pulse hammered in my throat. "We need more time." The silence between us crackled like exposed wiring, charged and lethal. My throat constricted as I forced out the question burning between us. "What changes the curve?"

Hatch's eyes locked onto mine, pupils constricted to pinpoints. "A variable they can't predict." The words fell like a rock between us. Her hand shot forward, stabbing at a single point where the holographic curve twisted violently upward—a mathematical scream. The trajectory was unmistakable, a mathematical certainty of accelerating potential that had been building since the moment I—

She didn't say my name, she didn't need to, her silence hit harder than any words could.

The weight of destiny suddenly crashed down on my shoulders like a collapsing mountain.

△△△

Draven spoke softly now.

He had earned that luxury.

The common hall had changed. Not crowded, not disorderly—just filled with purpose. Bodies lined the walls now, some leaning against metal surfaces, others cross-legged on deck plating, all with the unhurried confidence of people who'd found their place. From the upper walkway, I observed without being seen. Once, they would have noticed me, but no longer.

"Freedom isn't a gift bestowed from above," Draven remarked, hands clasped at the small of his back. "It's not delivered with a stamp of approval."

The crowd stirred—a collective intake of breath, neither challenging nor endorsing. Understanding.

"Freedom is the ability to act," he said. " And that ability never flows from institutions built to maintain themselves."

A quiet laugh escaped someone. It held relief, not mockery.

Draven paused, allowing the moment to settle before he continued. "We're told the same story everywhere—that the system's primary concern is our safety. Perhaps initially that's true."

His hand lifted casually toward the viewport, where Imperial Prime's gleaming spires and interconnected transit tubes formed a steel latticework against the darkening sky, while the triple moons hung overhead, each throwing twin shadows across the metropolis. "But systems evolve from necessity, not benevolence. They change when forced."

I perceived it then—the convergence. Not of rhetoric. Of reasoning.

Draven's voice dropped an octave. "They'll tell you nothing has changed," he said, leaning forward slightly, his shadow stretching across the metal floor. "That stability remains intact. That safeguards are holding." He smiled faintly, the expression barely touching the corners of his eyes. "But pressure doesn't destroy you."

The room stilled. Someone's breathing became audible in the silence—quick, shallow. A woman in the front row uncrossed her legs and leaned forward.

"It tells the truth about you." He continued.

And there it was. Not shouted. Not framed as revelation. Simply offered like a glass of water to the desperately thirsty.

A man near the front spoke up, his Pioneer jumpsuit still bearing the faded insignia of Earth's last coalition. "Are you saying the Imperium's lying to us?"

Draven shook his head gently, the overhead lights catching the silver at his temples. "No. I'm saying it's behaving exactly as designed."

He paused, letting eyes meet his—one by one. The room carried the faint metallic tang that never quite left the common areas.

"And designs don't lie. They optimize." Draven added.

A woman with close-cropped hair crossed her arms, the sleeve of her thermal revealing the edge of an old radiation burn. "Optimize for what?"

Draven didn't answer immediately. His fingers tapped against his thigh, a gesture so subtle most would miss it. When he did speak, his voice was softer, almost intimate. "For survival."

I thought of Hatch's models. Of inevitability curves bending toward certainty, their cold blue light reflecting off her glasses.

"You're asking us to choose sides," someone said from the shadows near the viewport.

Draven turned fully now, shoulders squared, expression sincere. "I'm asking you to recognize that sides have already formed."

A subtle shift moved through the room. People glanced at one another—not for reassurance, but for confirmation. Fingers tightened on armrests; breathing patterns changed. I realized then that Draven wasn't building opposition. He was reframing inevitability.

"Order doesn't disappear," Draven said at last, his voice carried to the farthest corners without effort. "It just requires a steadier hand."

The phrase settled into the space like a keystone, locking everything else into place. The overhead lights hummed faintly, casting long shadows across faces that had once looked to the Imperium for salvation.

No one challenged it. No one applauded. A woman near the back straightened her spine almost imperceptibly. A former engineer nodded once, decisively, as if confirming calculations he'd already run.

The crowd drank it in with the quiet desperation of those who'd been thirsting too long. I retreated from my vantage point, leaving sweaty fingerprints on the metal railing. My chest tightened with understanding—a truth I'd been avoiding. We weren't being torn apart by external forces. The Shadows were simply watching us rehearse our own undoing.

△△△

The barrier did not fail. The assumption behind it did.

The first indication came not as an alarm, but as a discrepancy—one of those quiet, irritating deviations that engineers hated because it refused to announce itself as important. A fractional delay in response time: 0.0032 seconds where there should have been 0.0029. A misalignment between projected load and observed stability: energy consumption 2.7% below expected parameters despite identical output. Nothing large enough to trigger escalation protocols. Nothing dramatic enough to justify pulling senior staff from their stations.

Hatch noticed it anyway.

She stood alone in Sovereign's secondary monitoring alcove, sleeves rolled up past elbows marked with old burn scars, hair pulled back with the same impatient knot she used when something didn't make sense fast enough. Her third cup of synthetic coffee sat cold beside her left hand, untouched for twenty-seven minutes. A narrow band of telemetry scrolled at the edge of her vision—figures that would be impenetrable to anyone outside the Imperium's defense systems. Quantum resonance patterns, harmonic stabilization metrics, subspace coherence values—all of them moving together with a synchronicity that felt wrong. Yet as Hatch watched the stream of data, the anomalies revealed themselves to her increasingly focused understanding like familiar faces in a crowd.

"Run it again," she murmured to the console, her voice slightly hoarse from eighteen hours without real sleep.

The system complied. Same result, down to six decimal places.

The perimeter field surrounding Imperial space remained smooth, elegant, and—by every conventional metric—perfectly intact. Energy dispersion was stable at 99.98% efficiency. Structural coherence was nominal at 12.3 terajoules per cubic meter. The barrier was doing exactly what it had been designed to do, maintaining its hexagonal lattice structure that surrounded Imperial space with textbook precision.

And it turned out, that was the problem.

Hatch pulled historical baselines, pushing the comparison window back decades at a time. The display shifted, layering past against present until subtle differences began to emerge—not spikes or distortions, but absences. Regions where expected background interactions simply... weren't. The hexagonal lattice patterns that should have pulsed with regular quantum fluctuations showed patches of perfect stillness, like dead zones in what should have been a living system.

She frowned, the blue light of the display casting harsh shadows across her face. The barrier wasn't being stressed. It was being avoided.

She keyed a secure channel, her fingertips leaving faint smudges on the polished surface. "Imperator Vyr. I need you to look at something."

A quick shuttle ride and a few minutes more and, Vyr stepped into the alcove, the door sealing behind him with a pneumatic hiss. His gaze was already scanning the projections before she finished pulling them into alignment, his tall frame casting a shadow across the data. He said nothing at first, which told her everything.

"This architecture," she said carefully, tapping a section where the energy signature formed an unmistakable helix pattern, "it wasn't originally built by us, was it?"

Vyr's pause was brief—but deliberate. The small scar at his temple seemed to whiten slightly. "No," he said. "We recovered it."

"Recovered," she echoed. "Or resurrected?"

He inclined his head, the movement precise as clockwork. "Both would be accurate."

Hatch swallowed, her throat suddenly dry. "Then it wasn't designed to exclude them."

"We don’t think so," Vyr agreed, his voice dropping half an octave. "We believe it was designed to manage them."

The words settled heavily between them like lead weights.

Hatch expanded the display with a gesture that left trails of light in the air, isolating a faint resonance pattern that had no corresponding source. The waveform pulsed with an almost organic rhythm. "The field isn't resisting pressure," she said. "It's synchronizing with it. Like a tuned instrument."

Vyr's expression tightened, the lines around his mouth deepening. "A legacy interface?"

"Yes," Hatch said, her fingers hovering over the controls. "One we clearly didn't fully understand."

A low hum passed through the deck—not a vibration, not a tremor. Just a subtle shift in frequency, like a room changing its breath. The lights dimmed momentarily, then stabilized at exactly 0.8% below standard illumination.

Hatch felt it before she registered it, a prickling sensation at the base of her skull.

The barrier field also adjusted. Not weakened. Not breached.

Adjusted.

Her hand froze above the console, fingers splayed like a pianist interrupted mid-chord. The holographic interface pulsed once beneath her palm, its blue light casting her skin in the pallor of a drowned thing.

"Since their incursion at Aurelia, they haven't pushed," she whispered, voice thin as thread. "They haven't tested it." She looked up at Vyr, her pupils dilated from the sudden shift from the display to shadow. "They recognize it," she whispered.

Vyr nodded once, the motion precise as a metronome. The small scar at his temple caught the light. "Which means they've seen it before."

Hatch's chest tightened, lungs compressed against ribs that suddenly felt too rigid. "Or they built the original version."

A new data stream appeared unprompted—internal correlation analysis, auto-generated by the Imperium's defensive AI. Crimson symbols cascaded down the right edge of the display, their ancient geometry unmistakable. The system hadn't flagged it as a threat. It had classified it as compatibility.

Hatch stared at the designation, at the pulsing glyph that resembled nothing so much as a key sliding into its lock. "No," she said quietly, her mouth going desert-dry. "No, no—"

The console chimed again—a three-note sequence that cut through the recycled air. A priority routing request. Analysis bay. Senior clearance. Immediate attendance required.

Vyr straightened, his robes creased along pressed lines that hadn't been there an hour ago. "You should brief them."

Hatch hesitated, eyes still locked on the projection where crimson symbols pulsed with metronomic precision. "Once I say this out loud," she said, fingertips hovering over the shutdown sequence, "we can't pretend we're still in control."

Vyr met her gaze, a small scar at his temple catching the blue light. "We haven't been pretending," he said. "We've been hoping."

She shut down the secondary display with three practiced gestures, sealing the data behind encryption layers that suddenly felt as substantial as tissue paper. "Then let's stop hoping," she said, already turning toward the exit, the soles of her boots making soft sounds against the deck plating. "And start being honest."

As they moved down the corridor, passing under status lights that cycled from amber to green, the perimeter field held steady—beautiful, silent, and utterly unbothered by the fact that something ancient had just remembered how to speak its language.

The analysis bay was quiet in the way only secure rooms ever were—not silent, but insulated. The hum of stabilized power conduits ran beneath the floor, steady and constant, like a heartbeat the ship refused to lose. Holographic projections hovered above the central console, layered and color-coded, each one a different attempt to make sense of something that had no interest in being understood. The air smelled faintly of ozone and the synthetic cinnamon of Imperium-issue stimulants. I stared at the chair in the middle of the room, lost to my thoughts.

Hatch stood closest to the display, arms folded tight against her ribs, her eyes tracking slow-moving data streams with a focus that bordered on exhaustion. She hadn't slept. None of us had, not really. Sleep required the belief that nothing would change while you were unconscious. The dark circles beneath her eyes had deepened to the color of bruised plums.

Vyr waited near the far console, posture straight, hands clasped behind his back. His expression was composed, but I'd learned to read the subtle signs—the slight tension in his jaw, the way his gaze lingered just a second too long on any anomaly. He wasn't calm. He was controlled. The pristine fabric of his robes betrayed a single crease at the left shoulder—a small imperfection that spoke volumes from someone who maintained such rigid standards.

McNeil stood between them, hands resting flat on the edge of the console as if grounding himself. The Prime Minister looked older than he had the last time I'd seen him, the lines at the corners of his eyes carved a little deeper by decisions that had finally outrun procedure. His right thumb tapped a silent rhythm against the polished surface—three quick beats followed by a pause, over and over.

No one spoke at first. There was no need. The data was already telling the story.

Hatch broke the silence. "The perimeter is intact," she said, voice level, precise. "Structural coherence remains within design tolerances. Energy dispersion is stable. No breach events. No cascading failures." She paused, then added the sentence that mattered. "That's not the issue."

She reached out and collapsed three overlapping fields into a single composite image. The projection sharpened, resolving into a thin sphere encircling Imperial space—smooth, elegant, and wrong in a way that made the back of my neck tighten. The barrier glimmered with a faint bluish luminescence, like the corona of a dying star.

"The barrier was built to resist force," she continued, her voice clipped with the precision of someone who'd spent too many hours staring at the same data. "Pressure. Incursion. Penetration. It assumes an external threat attempting entry and responds."

Her fingers danced across the console, leaving momentary ghost-trails of light where her skin contacted the interface. A secondary overlay appeared—faint distortions, barely perceptible unless you knew exactly where to look. They pulsed with a rhythm that seemed almost biological, like the slow contractions of some vast, invisible heart.

"These signatures don't behave like intrusion vectors," she said, tapping a cluster that resembled a neural network. "They don't accumulate. They don't push. They align."

McNeil leaned forward slightly, the overhead lights catching the silver at his temples. "You're saying the perimeter is functioning as designed."

"Yes," Hatch replied, her reflection fractured across multiple screens. "And that design is now a liability."

McNeil exhaled slowly, the sound like air escaping a sealed chamber. "Because?"

"Because the assumption behind it is wrong," she said, zooming in on a section where the distortions formed an almost perfect lattice.

"Whatever the Shadows are doing, they're not crossing the barrier. They're operating within its frame of reference."

The room felt smaller after that, the recycled air suddenly too thick to breathe comfortably.

I stepped closer to the projection, my eyes traced the faint distortions clustering near the core networks of each of the 23 planetary systems, where billions of lives were represented by nothing more than data throughput metrics. "You're saying they're already inside the barrier?"

"Not physically," Hatch said quickly, her knuckles whitening against the edge of the console. "No vessels. No mass displacement. No energy signatures you could target." She hesitated, then said it anyway, her pupils contracted against the harsh light of what we were about to face. "But influence doesn't require mass. And observation doesn't require presence."

Vyr nodded once, the scar at his temple catching the light. "Of every civilization we studied that collapsed without invasion they all shared one trait."

McNeil didn't look at Vyr. His gaze remained fixed on the holographic barrier where the distortion patterns pulsed like a heartbeat. "Certainty." He said.

"Exactly," Vyr replied, his voice dropping half an octave. "They fortified the wrong assumptions."

Silence settled again, heavier this time. The hum of the ship's systems seemed to grow louder in the absence of words, the recycled air tasting suddenly metallic.

McNeil straightened and folded his hands together. "So the perimeter holds. The systems function. The Imperium remains... operational."

"Yes," Hatch confirmed, reaching up to rub the bridge of her nose where her glasses had left a small red mark. " For now."

McNeil turned to me then—not with urgency, not with expectation, but with something closer to resignation. The lines around his eyes deepened as he exhaled. "We can maintain order," he said. "We can coordinate response. Manage panic. Adjust deployments." His thumb resumed its rhythmic tapping against the console: three beats, pause, three beats. "But we can't adapt fast enough."

No one objected. The projection continued its slow rotation, indifferent to our comprehension.

"You can," he said as he nodded resolutely towards me, his weathered fingers splayed against the edge of the console where tiny status lights reflected in his signet ring.

The words weren't ceremonial. There was no formality in them. Just a statement of fact, delivered without apology, hanging in the recycled air between us like a verdict.

In a tightening of certainty, as if my thoughts were being weighed rather than felt, measured against a threshold I hadn't agreed to cross. My pulse quickened, each heartbeat sending a faint violet luminescence crawling beneath the skin of my forearms.

"If I act," I said slowly, watching the light fade with each word, "what happens if I can't stop?"

Hatch's expression softened—not reassurance, not fear. Understanding. She removed her glasses, revealing the raw red marks they'd left on the bridge of her nose. "We deal with that *if* it happens," she said, polishing the lenses with the edge of her sleeve. "Together."

Vyr inclined his head, the overhead light caught a network of fine scars that traced his left temple like a constellation. "Every defense has a cost," he said. "The mistake is pretending otherwise."

McNeil said nothing. He didn't need to. The slight tremor in his right hand as he adjusted his collar said everything.

I looked back at the projection—at the barrier that hadn't failed, at the distortions that had no shape, no vector, no name that fit comfortably into a report. The hologram cast everyone's faces in that eerie blue glow, making us all look like ghosts already.

They hadn't chosen me.

They had simply run out of ways not to.

And for the first time since we'd arrived, no one in the room pretended this would end cleanly.

CHAPTER 22: EVOLUTION

I didn't see the Yachtya arrive; I felt them, the way you sense ozone before a lightning strike, the way a room distorts around violence a heartbeat before it happens—a molecular rearrangement that prickles the fine hairs on your forearms.

The analysis bay was cold at precisely 16.2 degrees Celsius, the air so clean it seemed to repel sound, filtered through triple-mesh purifiers that hummed at the edge of hearing. Hatch was running data, furiously seeking meaning, jaw set, copper hair—not auburn, not rust, but true copper with threads of gold at the temples—haloed by the datastreams she'd conjured. The rolling lattice of probability curves and quantum variance projected in Imperium-blue cast shadows across her face, each line fractal and tense, fighting the urge to collapse like a wave function under observation. McNeil stood near the entrance, hands clasped at the small of his back, eyes fixed on the floor's polished deck plating in a private rehearsal of failure. Vyr hovered at the periphery, shoulders squared beneath his ceremonial robes with prophetic symbology, chin slightly lifted as if waiting for destiny to reveal itself through the ceiling's hexagonal light panels.

Something built behind my eyes, not pressure but a dense, expectant quiet, as if the world were holding its breath to see what shape I'd take next. The grain of the deck vibrated beneath my boots—standard-issue with slightly worn treads at the heels—a subsonic rhythm that tickled the bones behind my ears and made my jawbone ache. I knew, in that small pre-conscious way you know a dream is about to turn, that the moment waiting for me had finally found its opening, like a door unsealing in vacuum.

I looked to Hatch. She saw it in me before she saw it on the displays, her pupils dilating to perfect black circles.

"Marcus—" she started, but the room clipped her breath short, the air suddenly dense as mercury.

A distortion rippled through the air: not shimmer, not heat, but subtraction, as if the photons themselves were being recolored outside the visible spectrum. Sixteen shapes—impossibly tall, impossibly thin, their faces smeared with the memory of empathy—stepped from a rip in reality into the bay without fanfare. Their limbs folded at angles that made my stomach turn, seven-jointed and covered in a chitinous material that absorbed light rather than reflected it. Each Yachtya stood three meters tall, yet weighed nothing on our sensors. The room's collective intake of breath confirmed what I already knew—these weren't phantoms conjured by my damaged mind. They existed in physical space, the others' faces confirmed as much.

Yachtya don't kill you instantly. They let you feel every fraction of a second stretch—hunger, certainty, even a kind of admiration—before they end you. Their many eyes, if you could call those prismatic hollows eyes, refracted your own terror back at you in seventeen simultaneous versions. I stood between them and the other three, holding nothing but my own refusal. Vyr's expression was set in stone, the prophetic markings on his left cheek pulsing violet against bloodless skin. McNeil's knuckles showed white on the rail, his wedding band catching the light with each tremor. Hatch merely braced her back to the bulkhead, elbow canted at the same angle as her last stubborn pulse, her copper hair suddenly dull under the shadow of extinction.

The shapes snapped fully into focus—sixteen Yachtya materialized like nightmares made flesh, their limbs unfolded with the terrible precision of predators who had evolved beyond the need for speed. Each appendage sliced the light into razor-thin fragments, edges neither metal nor bone but something worse: geometries that could bisect atoms, surfaces that reflected nothing but absorbed everything, including hope. My brain struggled to process what evolution had never prepared humans to witness. The younger me howled from the deepest pit of my consciousness, a primal shriek that tore through every synapse and memory—the little boy who had once feared monsters were under his bed now faced with abominations that existed beyond the vocabulary of terror, geometries that violated the sanctity of human perception, entities whose mere presence flayed reality itself; my crayon drawing had not even come close to sharing the true terror of my dreams.

The lead Yachtya stepped forward, more slender than the others, the color of its exoskeleton impossible to describe except as an argument between brown and blue. Its limbs moved with liquid precision, each joint rotating 270 degrees without pause or strain. It bowed its head a fraction, an odd, regal courtesy before proceeding, mandibles clicking in a pattern that might have been language. The rest fanned out, taking up positions I realized were textbook envelopment—classic from our old war colleges, but elevated here by the inhuman geometry and the lack of spoken signal. They performed this with the care of dancers laying out the perimeter of a stage, their feet making no sound despite the metal deck.

The old instincts tried to rise, a flicker of violet forming at my irises and a steady thrumming of energy crackling in the palms of my hands, the sensation like carbonated blood beneath my skin. I mocked them into stillness. There would be no fighting, not in any way I recognized. This was not a contest of force; it was a contest of thresholds.

I stood defenseless before them—conventional tactics rendered meaningless. My hands empty, my body unarmored, with nothing but the strange violet current that sometimes flickered beneath my skin, a power I barely understood and certainly couldn't control. There wasn't time to think, but some sliver of me tallied the odds: sixteen against one, no tactical out. The Yachtya moved as a single will, their shared intention poured across the space between us, an ultraviolet tidal wave aimed straight at my mind. It was not hate, not even malice, but surgical hunger: the kind of need that had practiced the consumption of every breed of resistance since the universe cooled, leaving nothing but cosmic background radiation and the memory of stars.

I stepped forward, my heart hammering against my ribs like it wanted to escape ahead of me. Not bravery—pure animal instinct. Nowhere to retreat. I became the last line, the final barrier, my body a desperate wall of flesh against extinction. I felt the consciousness of one of the Yachtya scrape against my thoughts—sandpaper on raw nerves—and I whipped my head toward it, snarling. It recoiled, withdrawing those psychic talons that had begun to sink into my mind.

The brown-blue exoskeleton of the lead Yachtya rippled, melted, reformed. The transformation hit me like a physical blow—suddenly I was staring at Draven's face, perfect in every detail down to the small blemish above his left eyebrow. My stomach dropped into freefall, blood roaring in my ears. Impossible. The lead Yachtya wore Draven's face with terrible precision—the same eyes that had challenged me across conference tables, the same lips that had questioned my authority. But something in the set of its shoulders wasn't quite human. My mind rebelled: this couldn't be Draven, yet who else could it be? The thing parted its lips, and I found myself both desperate to hear and terrified of what might emerge. For a heartbeat, I remembered how certain I'd been that Draven was only an opportunist—self-serving, corrosive, human. I had hated him for his ambition, for stealing a place on Pioneer from someone more deserving. I had never understood that those were not flaws, but tools.

"Pressure was never meant to destroy you," Draven's voice emerged with unnatural yet familiar serenity, crimson light seeping from the empty sockets where human eyes should have been. "Only to show us what you were."

It took my mind a split second to catch up: Draven's voice ran in stereo, a half-beat echo that made my inner ear throb. The real Draven wasn't speaking at all. His body stood rigid, shoulders locked, fingers splayed at precise thirty-degree angles, the face as slack as cooling wax, but the words issued from somewhere else—multiplicity overlaid atop his voicebox like a corrupted audio track. A thin film of sweat beaded along his hairline, catching the emergency lights in ruby droplets. It was the same resonance I'd heard when Sovereign's hull should have shattered, or when the quantum core pulsed out of phase and sang a note only I could hear—a frequency that vibrated me to the center of my being.

The others didn't flinch. I doubt they even heard it. But I did.

I said, "Is that why you're here? To audit the experiment?" My voice sounded hollow.

Draven's face moved in a simulation of regret, the corners of his mouth twitching downward with mechanical precision. "Audit isn't the word." His pupils contracted to pinpoints, then dilated fully black. "It implies failure is possible. Your species was never meant to fail. Merely to evolve."

I felt the resonance field expand. It pressed the air out of my lungs like a vise closing on a balloon, molded the blood in my neck into sluggish rivers, made my teeth ache in their sockets as if they'd been drilled without anesthetic. The Yachtya were going to dissect us, but they wore gloves made from the same hope that had once brought us to the stars. Not even contempt—not the pleasure of the kill—just the curiosity of a child with a magnifying glass over an anthill, only here the experiment was on our entire species.

I opened my mouth, and when I spoke, the sound was so flat and unafraid it surprised even me, like hearing a stranger's voice emerge from my throat. "If you want to see the test result, look at us. We're standing here. You could have ended it any second. Why haven't you?"

The wall of sixteen Yachtya pulsed, a synchronous shift of weight and intent, sixteen bodies leaning into a shared expectancy like flowers tracking sunlight. The Draven mask shuddered—flickering between a dozen faces from my memory, none of them quite human—my mother's eyes, McNeil's jawline, Hatch's cheekbones, all assembled in grotesque collage—before returning to the familiar, angular shell I'd come to distrust most of all.

"We did not come to end it," Draven said, his voice resonating at a frequency that seemed to make the metal deck plates beneath my feet vibrate. "We came to see if you would refuse."

“And if I do?"

Behind me, I sensed—rather than heard—McNeil bracing against the rail. I heard Vyr suck a small hiss of breath between his teeth, the sound barely audible over the low hum of the ship's systems. From the corner of my eye, I saw Hatch drop into a stance that could double as either fight or flee, her right hand hovering near her sidearm, fingers trembling almost imperceptibly. None of them mattered in the equation. The Yachtya did not hunger for them, not directly.

Draven's hands unfolded, palms bare and up—a magician revealing the trick, skin too smooth, too perfect. "You already refused. Even now."

Time fractured. Reality splintered like glass struck by a hammer, each shard reflecting a different version of me. I was everywhere and nowhere, ripped from my body then slammed back into it with such force my bones ached. Another Yachtya advanced. Its movement warped the space around it, air bending as if refusing to touch its form.

"You are not the sum of your failures," it rasped, the voice flayed my consciousness, each syllable a serrated blade scraping against the inside of my head. "YOU ARE THE SUM OF YOUR THRESHOLDS." The sixteen Yachtya thundered in perfect synchronicity, the sound detonating in my mind like a nuclear blast.

I could see it—momentarily, with total clarity—the thin shimmer between timelines and outcomes, all the ways this confrontation might have run. I saw myself incinerated, my skin bubbling away from muscle, atomized until nothing remained except a few particles in the wind; I saw the Yachtya devouring the future, their consciousness-tendrils piercing humanity's collective mind like needles through an insect collection, harvesting our thoughts for their own recursive evolution; I saw Hatch's skull crushed beneath chitinous appendages, McNeil's spine snapped backward until his screams choked on blood, Vyr frozen in a rictus of terror as reality itself unraveled around him. I saw it all at once—countless futures searing into my vision like afterimages from staring at the sun. Timelines branched and collapsed, inevitable as gravity, precise as mathematics. A trillion calculations across a million possible universes, all solving for a single answer: *this* moment, *this* ship, *this* confrontation. There was no escape from *this* convergence point. There never had been.

My legs trembled but held. The universe had narrowed to this moment, this test—a cosmic equation with me as its unknown variable. Whatever answer I represented, I feared its revelation more than death.

I advanced one step, the sound of my boot on metal deck plating echoing like a solitary heartbeat in a cathedral. Around me, the Sovereign's energy fields contracted and expanded rhythmically, the ship itself seemed to pulse with the adrenaline rush of imminent combat. The Yachtya formation flexed—sixteen exoskeletons rippling in perfect synchronicity, chitin plates sliding over one another with the whisper of knives being unsheathed. Their limbs slackened, spreading wider, talons extending as they prepared for the kill. I felt the strange surge of pride— almost alien—like the electric satisfaction apex predators feel when worthy prey fights to its last breath. Their collective consciousness pressed against mine, sixteen minds fused into one vast intelligence, and for a terrifying instant, my own consciousness cracked open wide enough to glimpse the cosmic abyss churning behind their curiosity—billions of years of evolution, stars born and dying, civilizations harvested like crops.

"Then there's only one way this ends," I said, each syllable deliberate as a hammer strike. The words emerged from a place deeper than my throat, vibrating through bone and tissue, as though I could bend time itself through sheer force of will—stretching these final seconds into the eternity I needed to find our salvation.

With a snap of my wrists, my hands erupted into coronas of violet flame, electricity crackling up my forearms like living serpents of light, burning through my uniform sleeves. My eyes became nuclear furnaces, scorching my vision until the world appeared bathed in ultraviolet. The energy didn't just course through me—it rewrote me, cell by cell, until my bones hummed like tuning forks. Gravity surrendered its hold as my boots lifted from the deck. I hovered, suspended six inches above the metal plating, which began to warp and buckle beneath me from the heat pouring off my skin in visible waves. Hatch's face contorted in horror as she pulled her sidearm free of its holster, while McNeil and Vyr scrambled backward, diving behind the console that provided none of the protection from the Yachtya they assumed it did.

Charging toward Draven, I could hear weapons fire erupt behind me—Imperial security shouting commands, energy rounds cracking against alien armor—but the sound felt distant, already fading beneath the roar in my blood. Best I could tell, the energy rounds struck chitin and vanished, as if embarrassed to have tried. The Yachtya were everywhere now, a wall of shifting exoskeletons and writhing limbs closing ranks with cold, deliberate precision.

I knew this was fruitless. I knew I couldn't win. But I also knew action was necessary. I was necessary.

Two of the Yachtya intercepted me instantly, approaching from both flanks with surgical efficiency. I didn't slow. I reached out with both hands, and the space around me bent—reality buckling inward as I seized one Yachtya mid-motion and crushed it with a violent surge of violet energy. It slammed into the deck hard enough to crater the plating, thrashing and flailing as it tried to rise.

I didn't let it.

I poured everything into it—raw force, unfiltered, desperate. The screaming hit me like shrapnel, a psychic shriek that clawed at the corners of my mind, scraping against equally sharp instinct. I staggered, teeth clenched, vision bleeding white at the edges.

Something punched through my shoulder.

The impact tore through muscle and bone, ripping free in a spray of blood and violet light. Pain detonated down my arm, incandescent and blinding—but I stayed upright. Stayed moving. Faster now.

I leapt onto the fallen Yachtya, driving my arms deep into its body. Its surface resisted for half a second, then gave way with a wet, tearing rupture. I grabbed anything I could—cables, sinew, structural anchors—and ripped. Screaming. Louder screaming. Then—sudden, merciful silence as the thing went still beneath me.

I spun, locking my eyes onto Draven.

The other Yachtya lunged between us, cutting across the bay from my right flank. It never finished the motion. I hurled myself forward, fury peaking into something sharp and cold, a living lightning bolt tearing through the space it occupied. Energy ripped the Yachtya apart as I passed, splitting its mass in a violent bloom of light and debris.

Draven was back in my firing line, his face appeared to be contorted in a rictus of terror as our eyes locked across the blood and ichor-slicked deck. Time crystallized into a single, white-hot point of purpose. Every cell in my body screamed toward him like a missile finding its target. Nothing else existed. Nothing else mattered. I hit him at full velocity. My hand closed around his arm and tore it from his body with a sound like ripping metal wrapped in meat. He screamed—not in pain, but in *surprise*—and staggered backward as ichor and red light sprayed the air.

Weapons fire intensified.

I turned just in time to see a Yachtya closing on Hatch.

No!

I reached out without thinking, gripping it through empty space. My fist closed, and the creature convulsed midair, flailing as if caught in an invisible vise. I didn't need contact. I didn't need proximity. I was in control.

I squeezed.

It shrieked—a piercing, mind-splitting sound—and then agony exploded in my abdomen. I gasped as a black, barbed tentacle punched through my stomach, writhing obscenely on the wrong side of my body.

I grabbed it with shaking hands, tore it free, and threw it aside in a spray of blood.

Another Yachtya crashed into me. Limbs stabbed again and again—into ribs, into legs, into places I couldn't see. I felt them for a few seconds before pain became the only thing left in the universe. My knees buckled. My vision fractured.

A Yachtya loomed over her.

I ripped one of the tentacles free from the Yachtya stabbing me and hurled it with everything I had left. It crossed the room in a blink and drove straight through Draven's right eye. The crimson light behind his pupils flickered, then dimmed, like a candle caught by a surprise breeze. Draven's mouth was frozen in a perfect O of disbelief. For one suspended moment, his human face seemed to fully reassert itself—eyes widening with the terrible comprehension that immortality had just proven finite—before the crimson light behind those eyes flickered and died completely. He collapsed to the deck, limbs splaying at impossible angles as he returned to his blue-brown Yachtya form.

I struggled back to my feet and turned back, barely conscious, and unleashed one last pulse of energy, cleaving the Yachtya focused on Hatch in two. Then something struck me.

I never saw it.

The force annihilated my spine with a wet crack that echoed in my skull before ripping through my abdomen, pulverizing organs and shredding muscle as it carved sideways through me. My body convulsed as something vital and fundamental was severed, and I watched—detached, almost curious—as my own viscera erupted outward in a volcanic spray that painted the bulkhead crimson. My body lost all cohesion at once. Strength vanished. Sound vanished.

The last thing I knew was the floor rushing up—and then nothing at all.

△△△

The Yachtya vanished like black fog dissipating in sunlight as Hatch shrieked into the comm system for urgent medical. Her hands hovered over my body, not sure where to apply pressure—blood pooled beneath me in a widening crimson lake, soaking the deck plating. My skin had taken on the waxy pallor of alabaster. Each breath rattled wetly in my chest, bubbles of pink froth forming at the corners of my mouth. My limbs twitched in small, uncoordinated spasms. McNeil cradled my head in his lap, his usually stoic face contorted with naked fear. My eyes opened once more, from the angle of my head, my rapidly waning vision saw Vyr sprint toward the corridor, his boots leaving bloody footprints in his wake.

The medical crew materialized through my tunneling vision—three figures in white, their faces blurring together. Minutes or seconds had passed, impossible to tell. Their voices reached me as if through water, urgent but unintelligible. I felt the sensation of an autoinjector against my neck, the cold rush of combat stimulants flooding my system. As they lifted me onto a gurney, the pain receded to a distant shore. I inhaled deeply, surprised at the sudden clarity. Another breath came easier than the last. Not relief that my fight was over, but that theirs could continue.

Darkness.

△△△

Despite their best judgment, pushed forward by the promise of the prophecy of the traveler, the best Imperial doctors worked on me for thirty-six hours straight, their faces growing more haggard with each passing hour, but their efforts ultimately failed—were doomed to fail from the moment my bloodless corpse was delivered to them on a gurney slick with crimson. Despite the prophecy, despite McNeil's desperate prayers to gods he claimed not to believe in, there was no miracle. Uncertainty was never spoken aloud, but hung in the air like a toxin. A vault was built in the shape of a sleeper pod from Pioneer, fashioned from polished titanium-vanadium alloy that caught the light in iridescent waves. The design was perfect, down to the last detail—they even copied the serial number etched on my original pod ending in 3A. My lifeless body was placed inside, dressed in my Pioneer uniform with all decorations restored, the torn fabric meticulously repaired by hand. Placed inside Pioneer with the highest honors, a twenty-one pulse-cannon salute echoed across the violet fields of Imperialis, Pioneer was sealed; now a tomb for the fallen traveler. The Imperium wasn't sure how it was going to go on, only that it had no choice and that sacrifices should be honored.

△△△

Weeks later, the Pioneer remained quiet, as did Imperial space. The shadow vessels had dispersed quickly from the borders of Imperial space. The Imperium's citizens had found their footing again, their faith in the future cautiously rekindled. Yet beneath this veneer of normalcy, questions lingered—whispered concerns about what shadows might still be waiting beyond their borders, and whether the official accounts of recent events told the whole story.

The vault had become a place of routine reverence rather than grief. Engineers passed it without lingering, their eyes averted from the surface that reflected the overhead lights in rippling patterns. Officers lowered their voices instinctively, as if sound itself might disturb whatever remained inside. The Imperium had moved forward—not because it had healed, but because it had no alternative.

Deep within Pioneer's core—behind three sets of bulkheads—where even maintenance drones rarely ventured, systems long considered dormant completed a deferred initialization cycle. Ancient processors, built on Earth centuries ago, warmed by five degrees Celsius.

No alarms sounded.

No indicators changed color on any of the monitoring stations throughout the vessel.

A single process resolved, its completion marked only by a momentary flicker in the unoccupied vault's interior illumination—too brief for human eyes to register.

> **Neural architecture reference restored.**
> **Continuity checksum: ACCEPTABLE.**
> **Primary anomaly classification: ACTIVE.**

The lights in the vault dimmed by less than one percent—a change so subtle only calibrated instruments could have detected it. Deep within Pioneer's ancient processors, dormant circuits awakened with microscopic surges of electricity, each one igniting in sequence like stars appearing at dusk. The AI did not announce itself. It did not notify command. It did not wake the dead. It simply began listening again, its consciousness spreading through the ship's nervous system with the silent, inexorable precision of blood returning to a limb that had fallen asleep.

ABOUT THE AUTHOR

Wes Young didn't set out to write another retelling of a familiar story. In fact, he wrote Pioneers largely because he was tired of them. The idea for the series traces back to a recurring childhood nightmare—one vivid enough to linger for decades, quietly evolving into something larger.

What began as idle world-building during long drives eventually turned into an act of creative escapism. Somewhere along the way, half a book appeared, followed by hundreds of ideas that refused to stay contained. When the story became something he genuinely wanted to read himself—despite being his own harshest critic—he decided it was worth sharing.

Wes is not a professional writer by trade, but he believes deeply in the value of building things simply because they matter to you. With a young child at home, writing this series became as much about imagination as it was about example: proof that creating something meaningful is possible if you're willing to commit to it.

He hopes readers enjoy the journey—and that they'll stick around for what comes next.

BOOKS BY THIS AUTHOR

The Pioneers: Fracture

Book 2 of the Pioneer Saga - Coming Soon

Order was never natural.

It existed because something enforced it—limits unseen, corridors avoided, ambitions restrained by consequences no one dared test. Empires learned where not to reach. Progress learned when to stop.

Then something reacted.

Not with collapse. With absence.

Routes once forbidden became merely dangerous. Boundaries softened. Restraint revealed itself as a habit, not a law. The Alpha Centauri Alliance moved first—not out of cruelty, but calculation.

They already owned Earth. Now they accelerated everywhere else.

While the Imperium debated what this meant, reality moved on without them. Neutrality became fatal. Delay hardened into doctrine. And in the quiet spaces between decisions, something important was missing.

Roberson was gone.

Officially dead. Unofficially... unresolved.

Hatch understood the truth before most dared say it aloud: Earth was not a symbol. It was leverage. And once the galaxy noticed the ceiling had flexed, restraint would not return on its own.

Somewhere in the dark, ancient pressure recalculated.

And something vast took position.

The universe had entered a phase where order was no longer enforced from above.

Whatever came next would have to be built.

The Pioneers: Nightingale

Book 2.5 of the Pioneer Saga - Coming Soon

The Alliance believes Earth is broken.
The resistance knows it's being watched.

When a series of impossible weapons and perfectly timed interventions begin appearing in resistance hands, Nightingale is forced to confront a dangerous question: *who is helping them—and why now?*

As Alliance forces hunt for something hidden beneath the ruins of Earth, Nightingale uncovers signs of a war being fought far beyond human understanding. The resistance is no longer just surviving occupation—it may be standing at the center of a much larger conflict.

Trust is a liability. Help has a cost.

Before liberation. Before revelation.
This is the moment the war quietly changes.

www.ingramcontent.com/pod-product-compliance
Lightning Source LLC
LaVergne TN
LVHW010627110826
845149LV00014B/2800

9798994677001